SISTERS I

ENTERTAINMENT
DIE
TO
FOR

EDITED BY
GAY TOLTL KINMAN • MEREDITH TAYLOR • SUSAN ROWLAND
INTRODUCTION BY **SARA PARETSKY**

Write
Choice
Ink

Contents

Introduction   VII

1. Possessory Credit   1
   Diana Gould

2. He's No Gary Cooper   22
   Mary Keenan

3. Destination Wedding   35
   Frankie Bow

4. Death Under the Stars   57
   James T. Bartlett

5. Mystery in MB   70
   Laurie Fagen

6. Duet   107
   Cyndra Gernet

7. Unknown Sand Pits!   112
   Laurel Wetzork

8. Careful What You Wish For   136
   Nancy Cole Silverman

9. As Seen on Television   155
   Melinda Loomis

10. Freddi Farr, Behind the Bar   171
Carrie Voorhis

11. All the World's a Stage   183
Kim Keeline

12. Murder in Xanadu   206
Lisa Morton

13. Red Carpet   226
Sherri Leigh James

14. Ordinary to Extraordinary   245
Lynda Palmer

15. Natural Causes   259
Yolanda Reid

16. The Untitled Location Project   277
Anne Louise Bannon

17. The Writers Room   293
L.H. Dillman

18. Transylvania on the Tallahassee   315
Avril Adams

Credits   333

How to reach us   335

Introduction

Sara Paretsky

In 1986, in a small room at a Baltimore hotel, twenty-six women came together over stale sweet rolls to discuss the hurdles we had to jump as we built our careers as crime writers. We were concerned that our own hard work and our talent weren't enough to keep our own voices on the page.

The issues discussed ranged from the isolation that affects all writers to the marginalization of novels by women—they stayed in print about a third as long as those of our male colleagues, they were reviewed (as we later learned) with a seventh the frequency. At crime conferences, we might be told that it was wonderful we had a hobby, so that we didn't make heavy demands on our husbands when they came home from work. Libraries with restricted budgets would buy works by men, because, as one librarian put it, women will read books by men, but men won't read those by women.

Many readers of crime fiction didn't know we were alive, let alone producing wonderful novels. Indeed, from 1960 to 1985, a woman had a better chance of winning the Nobel Prize in Physics than she did of winning the Mystery Writers of America's prize for best novel of the year.

I had been hearing about these issues since that previous March, when I took part in Hunter College's symposium on women in the mystery.

I grew up in a milieu that was a perfect exemplar of a patriarchal system—rural Kansas in the 1950s, with a family where the boys got to drive the family car whenever they wanted while the girl stayed home to look after the house and the babies and all those things.

V.I. Warshawski came out of my urgent need for women to change that model. As a young writer, I was fumbling my way into understanding issues of voice and agency and the fact that my experience was not unique to me, not a sign of my inadequacies, but a signifier of female life.

At Hunter College, I was a newbie; I'd published two novels and didn't know that women writers faced obstacles that women engineers, women welders, women bartenders, women secretaries . . . faced. I did know that I was sick of the depiction of women in the mystery. We were either vamps, trying to get good boys to do bad things ("The woman that thou gavest me made me do it," Adam whines to God), or we were victims, raped and dismembered in horrifying, reifying ways.

At the Hunter conference, I made some provocative remarks about the rape and dismemberment books I'd had to read for an awards committee I was serving on. Those remarks sparked a widespread outcry. All that summer I got letters from women wanting to know what I'd said and if I meant it. Along the way they detailed the walls they were having to climb over to get their books into libraries, bookstores, review outlets.

As I read my mail, I thought of the great Civil Rights lawyer Florynce Kennedy's adjuration: "Don't agonize, organize."

With the support of my editor at Ballantine, Mary Ann Eckels, I convened the Baltimore meeting to see if my sister writers cared enough about these problems to organize and change them. Out of that meeting grew

Sisters in Crime. 2021-22 marks our thirty-fifth anniversary; this collection celebrates that milestone.

In 1987, when about a hundred women were involved, we decided we needed a structure to help keep people in touch with each other, and to make sure the concerns of all the members were heard. We formed a steering committee: Dorothy Salisbury Davis, Charlotte MacLeod, Nancy Pickard, and I were writers; Kate Mattes owned a bookstore; Betty Francis, a corporate executive by day, was a reader with thought-provoking insights into both books and organizations.

That spring, we decided on our first two projects. One was tracking book reviews to see how women fared in the major national publications, and in our own regional papers and magazines; the other, the brochure *Shameless Promotion for Brazen Hussies.* Too many of us had been raised to think that only a brazen hussy tooted her own horn—and we knew that if we wanted people to hear about us, we were going to have to start shouting our names in public. A few years later, Carolyn Hart, Linda Grant, and Sharyn McCrumb did heroic effort in creating Sisters' *Books in Print,* so we'd have a publication to take to bookstores and libraries.

In the last thirty-five years, the organization has grown to around four thousand members worldwide. What's truly wonderful is that readers have grown with us. At first, bookstores or libraries looking at our *Books in Print* would try a few books by our members. These disappeared off the shelves so quickly that they tried a whole shelf, and that grew in turn to an entire wall. Over and over, bookstores told us they heard from women who said, "I hadn't read a mystery since I outgrew *Nancy Drew*, because the characters just didn't speak to me. Now I'm finding dozens of books with characters I can identify with." We in Sisters in Crime feel proud of our role in growing the number of works mystery readers can enjoy.

Entertainment to Die For is the Los Angeles Sisters in Crime chapter's tribute to the many different voices women have. They look at Hollywood in the forties, at the struggles Black filmmakers have always faced, at vampires, at actors dealing with retirement. The stories are all different but they have this in common: women have voices, women have agency. We live in a world where women's voices are at risk, but this collection says, we are on center stage and we aren't leaving.

About the Author

Hailed by P. D. James as "the most remarkable" of modern crime writers, Sara Paretsky is the bestselling author of the renowned V.I. Warshawski series. She has received the Grand Master Award from the Mystery Writers of America and the Cartier Diamond Dagger from the Crime Writers Association. She lives in Chicago.

Possessory Credit

Diana Gould

DAVID MICHAEL MENDELSOHN HAD written many murders, so he didn't think it would be hard to commit one. If it's true that "a coward dies a thousand deaths; a hero dies but one," it was equally true that a writer kills every time he puts himself in the mind-set of a killer. And once he murdered Andrew Lovekin, David Michael Mendelsohn was sure he'd never have to kill again.

The idea came as most of his ideas did: a tug in the gut; embryonic, inchoate. He was having lunch with his agent at Estrusco, a trendy Italian restaurant in Brentwood. At every table. men and women dressed in their best "business casual" schmoozed and networked over delicious expense account meals. The room thrummed with a mixture of adrenaline, bluster, hope, and fear.

Over *insalata carciofi*, his agent told him the good news. *Sins of the Angels*, a movie David had written, would be showcased at Cannes. Not opening night, but still. David was elated. Writing that script was one of the hardest things he'd ever done. He felt it was his best, most personal work yet. Going with it to Cannes would finally be the recognition he'd longed for.

But with the *spaghetti alle vongole* came the rest of the news. The studio was sending the director and the star but would not spend money to send the writer.

"But I wrote the movie! It was completely original! They wouldn't have had anything to work on without me!"

"I know. 'In the beginning was the word.' Believe me, I sympathize," said his agent. "But in the end, it's a director's medium." The director, Andrew Lovekin, would represent the film, and of course, Mariana Winters, its star. Nobody really cares who wrote the movie.

David sat in his car, parked on Sunset, staring at the billboard promoting "Andrew Lovekin's *Sins of the Angels*." The ad featured a close-up of Mariana Winters, staring out to sea, wind whipping the hair around her beautiful face. Her expression was haunted yet radiant, fragile yet fierce. Bold letters bigger than the title proclaimed, "An Andrew Lovekin Film. Starring Mariana Winters." On the bottom, "written by David Michael Mendelsohn" was barely readable in letters squished together to accommodate the names of the other actors, producers, editor, composer, music supervisor, production designer, and director of photography.

David and Andy had gone to film school and made their first film together, written by David, directed by Andy. A horror movie on a film school budget, it became a cult classic, and launched both their careers. Each got an agent, each got jobs. Andy was the studio's bold choice to direct a film that was greenlit and ready to go; David was given a crack at adapting a novel the studio had bought. Andy brought his movie in on time and under budget; it made back its investment, so was considered a success. David's contracted "three drafts and a polish" took almost three years. Not because he was a slow writer, although he was. But by the time he got his notes on each draft from each producing partner and studio executive, there was a lot of down time. His agent suggested he take other work between drafts and got him an uncredited rewrite on another writer's script. After his last contracted polish was complete, the studio gave his script to another writer. Still not happy, they gave it to two more writers before shelving the project, determining that period pieces would not sell overseas.

And so it went. David worked constantly and made a good living. He added his middle name to his credit, thinking it would give him more gravitas, and it did. He became a well-respected screenwriter, to whom producers turned when they couldn't make a script work. It's not unusual for a studio to go through many writers to get a draft that gets the go-ahead. Guild rules allowed credit to be granted only to two. While David was caught in the treadmill of "development hell," working on films that didn't get made, or not receiving credit on ones that did, Andy made one film after another and his reputation grew. Whatever was good in a movie was attributed to him; critics pointed to moments that were "pure Lovekin." Finally, he acquired enough clout to get the prized "possessory credit," a contractual guarantee that any film he directed would be billed as "Andrew Lovekin's . . . [title.]"

The idea that had begun as a tug in the gut twisted into a knot as David remembered the night Andy called, saying he had an idea for a movie. They hadn't worked together since film school.

"It's for Mariana Winters." They were having dinner together at Kaiseki, another expensive restaurant where the elite of show business could go without being bothered by anyone except each other. By this time, Andy had a development deal at the studio, and could pick up the tab.

Mariana Winters had been one of those young actresses whose train-wreck lives provide a running drama unfolding on the covers of tabloid magazines—the twenty-first-century equivalent of the nineteenth-century serial novel. Each weekly installment—falling in love, gaining weight, breaking up, losing weight—bulimic?—car crash, rehab, relapse—had been headline news.

"Is she still alive?"

"And how." His sly smile made David think he must be sleeping with her. "She's got this incredible quality. Sexy, vulnerable, tempestuous, kind of a gutter-tramp sensuality wrapped up in a hungry little girl . . ."

David was sure Andy was sleeping with her. He usually made conquests of the women he directed.

"She had to leave the business for a while to get clean, but she's back. I want to develop a story for her. Something where she can be wild and angry; smart, sexy. . ."

"Like what?"

Andy held up his thumb and index fingers, creating an imaginary frame. "It's the beach at dawn." He moved his hands, simulating a camera panning. "A woman stumbles down to the water's edge. She's in evening dress—plunging neckline, expensive jewels . . . her shoes in her hand . . . she seems haunted, desperate . . . she takes a few steps in . . . foam swirls at her feet . . . she turns to look behind her, we move in close . . . she's terrified . . ."

David could hardly wait to hear what happened next. "Yes . . . ?"

Andy shrugged. "You're the writer." He signaled for the check. "See if you can take it from there."

Andy suggested David get to know Mariana, with the goal of creating a story that captured her essence. He was sure he could get funding if they had the right script.

David met with Mariana a few times, sometimes with Andy, sometimes alone. He did find her all the things that Andy had suggested: vulnerable, sexy, fragile, tempestuous—and insufferable. The years she'd spent on magazine covers had given her a sense of her own importance that David found hard to share. He spent hours listening to operatic arias of self-involvement. She fed on excitement like a vampire on blood; being stuck in traffic was tantamount to being detained at Guantanamo.

Wildly jealous, she found ways to monitor Andy's texts and emails. When she was with David, she badgered him with questions about what Andy did when he was away from her. David often found himself lying to cover for Andy, to avoid the tearful tirades that came with the truth.

Andy felt that being a director required arrogance. He broke dates and told lies with abandon, tantalizing Mariana with his mixture of ardor and indifference. He enraged her, knowing that their reconciliations would be all the more torrid. He was unfaithful every chance he got. A director with a studio deal and possessory credit, he got a lot of chances.

David soon grew weary of their fights. But watching them together did give him a sense of the character he thought she could best play.

He came up with the notion of a gambling addiction, as a metaphor for her insatiable hunger, and decided that the beach Andy had pictured was Monte Carlo, the morning after she'd lost everything and more. He had her character sell her necklace to pay off her debts, becoming entangled with an international crime ring and a jewel thief who was really an Interpol agent. But her gambling addiction caused her to sabotage herself at the worst possible moment, and this layer added depth to what was otherwise a nifty little thriller.

Andy and Mariana loved the idea. David went off to write it.

Responding to an ad in the Writers Guild newsletter, he rented a cabin in Arrowhead, surrounded by woods. The landlady lived down the road and was used to renting to writers. The rent included a daily delivery of supplies, and a guarantee of being left alone.

He began the painstaking work of constructing a story. He wrote detailed biographies of all his characters, until he knew them as a mother knows her child. He wrote ideas for scenes on index cards, and put them up all around the cabin, so he could rearrange and cut them as needed. He spent days coming up with plot points that would turn the action in surprising ways.

Writing had always been hard for David, and this one with its intricate plot lines and intersecting stories was particularly challenging. Sometimes he'd get so stuck, he could only lie in bed, knowing in his heart of hearts that he hadn't the talent to pull it off. His stomach hurt; his head ached. He imagined he had cancer. He hoped he had cancer; it was his only way out.

Then he'd wake up, with a glimmer of an idea, which he knew was stupid, but he'd write it down anyway, and as he did, he could see where it could lead. He'd massage it, nurture it, and then he saw how this idea could be a bridge to the climax, but he'd need a scene to justify it, and that's what he could put in the place he'd been stuck.

He suffered and struggled in solitary battle, working forward and backward, in anguish as intense as labor pains.

Miraculously—no other word would do—what came forth was not only a screenplay that was as well-constructed as the cabin he'd written it in, but a reflection of his truest self, expressing in ways he could only marvel at, his most deeply held views about life. Commercial, yes, but idiosyncratic; nobody could have written it but him.

He delivered it, like giving birth to a child.

Which, as this was Hollywood, was wrenched from his arms, to become "Andrew Lovekin's *Sins of the Angels*, a film by Andrew Lovekin."

He'd need an alibi.

Because, he thought, as the idea to kill Andy took malignant hold of him, among the things he meant to accomplish, not getting caught was first on the list.

He went to work.

He approached the project as he would a screenplay, but this time, instead of being blocked, he was fueled; animated by hatred he found strangely exhilarating. He put notes on index cards, knowing he would destroy them later. He did all his work on computers in public libraries, running searches that could not be traced back to him. He developed a list of possible suspects, writing backstories on each, as he did for the characters in his scripts. He spitballed alternative narratives, determining evidence he could plant that would suggest them. He wasn't planning to frame anyone. He had too much of a conscience to want anyone to go to jail for his crime. He just needed to confuse the police, leading them down wrong paths, away from him.

He contacted a source he'd used for a script about street gangs, and asked how he could get false ID. It was surprisingly easy; for eight hundred dollars, he was able to get a driver's license with his picture and someone else's name. He used that to open a bank account and get a credit card.

With his new identity, he rented a car and drove to Vegas. Stopping in a Western wear store, he shed his screenwriter uniform of jeans, sneakers, and T-shirt, buying instead work boots, tougher jeans, an engraved silver belt buckle, a fringed vest to go over a Jack Daniel's T-shirt and a wool felt Stetson. As he'd hoped, he blended with the crowd at a gun show, where he bought a gun and silencer. He went to a shooting range and took lessons, becoming confident in his ability to use his weapon.

When he returned, he examined his evil plan from every angle, searching out and fixing its flaws. When it worked like a Rubik's cube, he destroyed his notes, called Andy, and suggested lunch.

Over seafood salads at Mersea at the Shore, David pitched an idea for a movie they could do together. A few years back, a beautiful "actress/model/whatever" had been found shot to death, in her Mercedes, on Mulholland Drive. The case had made big headlines. Her name was Jaycee Peyton, but because of a religious icon on her dashboard, she'd been dubbed, "The Mulholland Madonna." The police had pursued various avenues of investigation, but nobody was ever charged. Why not do a film about her?

"What's the angle?" Andy's eyes darted around the room. It was a habit David found exasperating, as if Andy was always looking to see who might have more value to him than the person he was talking to.

"It's *Laura* meets *L.A. Confidential*," said David, knowing those were two of Andy's favorite films. "Good cop, investigating the crime, vs. bad cop—maybe he was sleeping with her, using her to find out dirt about her other johns, and shaking them down for hush money."

Andy's interest was piqued.

"Was there really such a cop?"

David shrugged. "Who knows? There could have been. She's a high-priced call girl, right? The guys she's sleeping with have secrets to protect. Like, let's say there's one who's pulling some financial shenanigans, and she finds out about it."

Andy mulled it over, no longer scanning the room, thoughtful.

"Did they ever find out who killed her?"

"No. Maybe we could actually solve the case. Wouldn't that make a great story. But in any case, there's great material to work with. Wait till you read some of this stuff." He patted his pockets. "Do you have your phone? I must have left mine at home."

Andy handed David his iPhone, and David used it to pull up stories about the case, knowing there'd now be a record of Andy's interest. Andy read and was intrigued.

"It would be great for Mariana," Andy said, clicking on one link after another.

"That's what I thought, too."

This time, David insisted on picking up the check.

David suggested developing the story together, and asked if they could meet at Andy's house, rather than the studio. Andy was surprised; having his own production company with offices and assistants were perks he was proud to have negotiated. But David said the studio made him nervous, and this would be more like their days at film school.

That way, David made sure that all the research on suspects in the unsolved murder was done on Andy's computer, all the calls placed from Andy's phones.

"I called Detective Childs, the lead investigator, but my name means nothing. Maybe if the call came from you?" suggested David. Andy left a message that Andrew Lovekin wanted to speak with Detective Childs and got an immediate callback. But when Andy explained the project, Detective Childs said he could not discuss a case that was still open.

David pretended disappointment, but all that really mattered to him was that there was a record of Andy's interest. He suggested Andy put out word through his publicist that he was researching the case, urging anyone with information to come forward. David said they would fictionalize what they found, but they'd get better material from the true details.

People came forward, and one person led to another. Jaycee Peyton had cut a swath through the upper echelons of Hollywood, as well as its seamy underside. Her clients included businessmen, actors, agents, and executives. She was distributing drugs; had a pimp boyfriend who beat her. Her roommate said Jaycee had found out something incriminating about one of her johns, but she wasn't sure which one. The roommate had told this to the police, but to her knowledge, they hadn't followed up.

"The crooked cop!" said David. "Life imitating art!"

Between them, David and Andy compiled a list of over a dozen people who might have motives to kill her.

"Who do you think really did it?" asked Andy. "The corrupt cop? One of the guys she slept with? The dealer she was fronting for?"

"My money's on the john she got the goods on. The financial shenanigans guy. And the bad cop wouldn't follow up on it, because he was getting a cut. I don't know if that's what happened, but that would make the best story."

All David really cared about was making it appear that one of the people suspected in the old case might have killed Andy for getting too close to the truth.

Once, when they were working together, David ventured, "I wonder . . ." but then changed his mind about saying what he'd been thinking.

"What?" asked Andy.

"Nothing," said David. "Only that . . . never mind."

"Come on."

"Mariana. Do you think she might be too . . ."

Andy waited.

". . . old?"

"She's thirty-three!"

"Exactly. Jaycee Peyton was twenty-four. Our girl should be young and hot."

"Mariana is young and hot."

"Right." And after a pause, "You're the director."

He changed the subject, feigning a desire for a certain kind of cheese that could only be gotten at a specialty cheese shop in Beverly Hills. He borrowed Andy's car and keys to make a run for it—and made a duplicate house key on his way back. He asked Andy for the alarm code, so he could let himself back in.

When he got back, Andy was poring over an online casting directory, checking photos and resumes of younger actresses.

"What about Hilary Wilde?" said David, suggesting an actress he knew from his gym, and showing Andy her headshot online.

Andy wasn't familiar with her work, so David introduced them. They met at a trendy new club. David knew Andy well enough to be pretty sure, when he left them at the end of the evening, where it would go from there.

It did.

The next time David saw Hilary at the gym, she was excited at Andrew Lovekin's interest in her, and the possibility she might be in his new film. David warned her that Andy could be unreliable; he urged her to barrage him with gifts, phone calls, and funny, sexy emails, to keep herself in the forefront of his consciousness.

Then he took Mariana to dinner, and bemoaned Andy's interest in a younger actress to play the part he was writing specifically for her. Mariana wanted to know who the younger woman was. David made a show of regretting that he'd said anything, but in trying to take it back, he let slip Hilary's name.

The next time he saw Hilary, he went back with her to her apartment. While there, he managed to filch a toothbrush, and one of her nightgowns hanging on the bathroom door.

A few days before he planned to commit the murder, David put the last piece of the puzzle in place. He told Andy that a friend was in town from England, selling antique jewelry. Incredible pieces, from estate sales all over the English countryside; he could buy one for Mariana, and it might mollify her about Hilary. Only thing is, he'd have to pay cash. His friend would not accept checks or credit cards.

The meeting with the imaginary friend was postponed. But there was now a record of Andy withdrawing twenty-five thousand dollars from one of his accounts.

Satisfied that he had completed the setup, David went off to Arrowhead, renting the same cabin he'd had before.

He drove out early in the morning, but instead of going straight to the cabin, he drove to a dealership in town for an oil change. From the dealer, he called a rental car company, and asked to be picked up. Wearing his vest and Stetson, he used his false ID to rent a car, drove it back to the dealership, and parked a block away. Then, having taken off the vest and hat, he walked back, picked up his own car, and drove it to the cabin.

He met the landlady to get the keys. He told her he'd be holed up writing; he'd prefer not to be disturbed.

"Oh, I always know, when I see your car there, that you're in there working away. I don't know how you do it."

He took the keys and moved in.

He spent the day putting up index cards and timelines all around the cabin walls, for the bogus project he was pretending to write. He made his dinner, burning his steak, filling the house with the aroma of food, and built a fire in the fireplace. He put on a pot of coffee, and turned on his computer, just as he would to pull an all-nighter. He opened his laptop, and left it on, making an adjustment that the screen would stay lit and not go to sleep.

Shortly after dark, with his computer and work light on and his car parked in the driveway, he went out the back window and walked through the woods back to town. He picked up the rental car and drove two hours back to L.A.

It was a little after one when he got to Andy's house. To his dismay, Andy's car was not in the driveway. He'd hoped to enter by stealth, shoot Andy in his sleep, plant the evidence, and drive back to Arrowhead. But Andy wasn't home.

Quelling his rising panic, he decided to enter anyway. He parked a block away. He was dressed all in black, including his sneakers, gloves, and balaclava ski mask which covered his face completely. He carried a satchel. Instead of going through the front door, where the surveillance cameras would have seen him, he went to the back of the property, breast stroked his way through the protective hedge. Out of range of the camera, he scurried to the side of the house where the pool equipment and electric panels were kept. He tripped the fuse that governed the surveillance cameras and eased his way to the side of the house where outdoor steps led to the lower level. He entered through the back, using his spare key and knowledge of the alarm code.

First, he went upstairs to Andy's office. He put research on The Mulholland Madonna on Andy's desk, with detailed files on each one of the suspects.

And a note, pasted together from cut-out letters, "Twenty-five thousand or I tell—or you die."

Making his way to Andy's bedroom, he took Hilary's toothbrush and nightgown from his satchel. He put the toothbrush in the bathroom, the nightgown under a pillow. He put an assortment of illegal drugs in the nightstand by the bed. He took out the gun and silencer, attached one to the other, and stepped into the closet to wait.

It wasn't long before he heard a car pull into the driveway. He heard the front door open, footsteps come upstairs. He heard someone enter the bedroom, but then—nothing. He was expecting to hear Andy emptying his pockets, or turning on the TV, or going into the bathroom. Taking off his clothes, coming into the closet, where David would be waiting for him. Instead, he heard nothing, except the sound of his own heart pounding, and someone else, breathing.

Whoever else was in the room was opening and closing drawers; it sounded like they were ransacking the room. David held his breath. What if they opened the closet? He was sure it wasn't Andy. Who could it be? He wanted to peer through a crack in the closet door, but he dared not move. The next sound he heard was unmistakable: the safety on a gun being released.

Suddenly, David Michael Mendelsohn realized why he had become a writer. He liked to imagine things, not actually do them. He must have been crazy to think he could go through with this. So Andy had taken credit for the work he had done. So someone else got the glory while he did all the work. Was that really so terrible?

Yes! He conjured the image of the poster for "Andrew Lovekin's *Sins of the Angels*," and felt the familiar knot in his gut, grown large and twisted by his rage. He touched the gun at his waist. He took deep, slow, quiet breaths to bring his blood pressure down.

Finally, there was the sound of a car pulling into the driveway. The front door opened, and this time, the footsteps that sauntered up the stairs toward the bedroom were Andy's.

He heard the sharp intake of breath, as Andy took in whoever else was in the room. There was a long silence.

Andy spoke first, in a voice weary and patronizing.

"Okay. You've made your point. Very dramatic. It's no accident you're a great actress. Now, put it down. Better yet, give it to me."

"Where is she? Isn't she with you?" The voice was vulnerable, sexy, fragile, tempestuous: Mariana.

"Who?"

"The one who left this!"

In the closet, David gulped. He'd meant for the police to find the night-gown and suspect Mariana; not for Mariana to find it and actually shoot Andy.

And yet . . . if the end result was the same, where was the harm?

"Where did you find this?" asked Andy, genuinely puzzled.

"Where were you tonight?" Mariana's voice was trembling.

"With David." Then wearily, "Put that down. Better yet, give it to me."

"Liar! You were with her!"

"Who?"

"You mean there's more than one? Does Hilary know you're cheating on her, too?"

David could hear Andy take a step forward and stop. He imagined that Mariana must have raised the gun and was holding it on him. That's certainly how he would have written the scene.

"Baby, think it through. What is shooting me going to accomplish? Is it worth spending the rest of your life in jail?"

"Yes! It will be worth it to see you suffer. To watch you die, like I've been dying. I'm dying! I'm already dead; you killed me. Lies do that you know, they kill people, just like bullets . . ." Her voice was starting to break, and with it, David imagined, her resolve. "I could shoot you in the heart and it would make no difference; you have no heart!"

He'd bet anything that the hand that held the gun was trembling along with her voice.

"Baby . . ."

"Don't touch me!"

David heard a door slam closed and lock, and then there was silence.

David listened to the sound of his own breathing. He surmised that Mariana had gone into the bathroom, taking the gun with her.

David imagined Mariana locked in the bathroom with a gun. Would she kill herself? Where was Andy? He should be pounding on the door, begging her to come out. David considered coming out of his hiding place and confessing all he had done. He knew he couldn't bear to have Mariana's suicide on his conscience.

He put a hand on the closet door, opening it just the tiniest crack, to allow him a view of the room. Empty. The bathroom door was closed; Andy had walked out onto the balcony, his back to the room.

Cool, detached, arrogant. Typical!

David took the gun from his waist. He had a clean line of sight. He could shoot Andy now, from the closet. And yet, Mariana was in the bathroom. If she heard the shot and discovered him, all his planning would be in vain.

Suddenly, a shot rang out. He looked at his gun. He had only thought to pull the trigger; he hadn't really done it—had he? No. And yet, Andy fell backwards, into the bedroom, blood pouring from his chest. David watched in horror as a man clad in black climbed into the room from the balcony, stood over the bleeding Andy, held a gun to his head at close range, and pulled the trigger; then just as quickly strode back.

The bathroom door opened, and Mariana came out, still holding the gun. She saw Andy and shrieked. The man turned toward her, raising his gun. David heard a shot, much louder than the first two, and the man crumpled.

David stood frozen on the spot. Mariana went to the phone, and quickly dialed 911. Her voice was hysterical as she sobbed into the phone.

"Come quickly! Andrew Lovekin's been shot. A man came in and shot him, I saw him and I . . . I killed him . . ." She broke into sobs. She managed to give the address. "Yes, yes, hurry, please!"

She left the room.

David peered through the crack. Except for the two dead men, the room was empty. As quietly as he could, he came out of the closet, put the gun in the empty satchel, and tip-toed with it back out through the sliding glass doors onto the deck, from which the intruder had come.

He walked quietly down the back stairs to the street and hurried up the block to his rental car. As he drove away, he heard the sirens, and passed the ambulance and police that were arriving at the scene.

He was back in Arrowhead before morning. He parked the rental car and crept through the woods back to his cabin, entering, as he had left, through the window in the rear.

It was late afternoon when the police arrived, interrupting David at his desk. With no phone or internet connection in the cabin, David had not yet heard of the death of Andrew Lovekin. He was shocked, devastated by the news. The police asked him about The Mulholland Madonna project. David said that Andy had done research into the case, but so far as David knew, had never found a way to tell the story. They had discussed it from time to time, but David had been spending his time working on something else. He showed them the index cards around the cabin, describing the musical he was working on.

Had Andy told David that he had been one of the men that The Mulholland Madonna had been sleeping with?

"What?" David did not have to feign his astonishment.

"Did you know he was paying Detective Childs to keep his name out of the files?"

"What??" David was almost too flabbergasted to speak.

"We found twenty-five thousand dollars in cash at his house. When we looked into it, we noticed that every time Andrew Lovekin had withdrawn twenty-five thousand dollars, twenty-five thousand dollars showed up in Detective Childs's account. Starting just after the murder of Jaycee Peyton."

"But Andy didn't kill The Mulholland Madonna." David's mind was reeling. "Did he?"

"No. He was only one of the men paying off Childs to make evidence disappear. He's a real piece of work, Detective Childs. We've suspected for years that he was disposing of evidence in exchange for payoffs, but it took Lovekin's murder to prove it."

"Is that who killed Andy? Detective Childs?"

"No. Turns out, Detective Childs was using Jaycee Peyton to shake down her other johns." The look of astonishment on David's face caused the cop to add, "I know. It's like something out of an Andrew Lovekin film."

David bristled. "But you said he wasn't the one who killed Andy."

"No. The man who shot Lovekin, whom Mariana Winters shot, was Harold Rosenbach."

"Who?" The name was unfamiliar to David.

"Another one of Jaycee Peyton's johns. A business manager. He'd been pulling all sorts of financial shenanigans with his clients' money. Peyton found out and threatened to go public. Rosenbach killed her. But his name never appeared in the files, because Childs had been shaking him down, so they both had something to hide. But Lovekin discovered the truth. Evidently, he was obsessed with finding the killer. We found files of research in his office, and his phone logs show calls to everyone involved. When Childs found out Lovekin was doing the film, he must have tipped off Rosenbach. Rosenbach killed Lovekin, with the gun he'd used on The Mulholland Madonna. If Mariana Winters hadn't been in the bathroom and seen it, he'd have gotten away with it."

David blinked, trying to absorb all that he was being told.

"Good thing you were here the whole time. We went to your apartment, and it was tossed. If you hadn't been here writing, you might have gotten killed too."

"No," David stammered. "I never left . . ."

"We know. Your landlady said your car's been here all night. Well, Lovekin's obsession paid off. He solved the crime and got killed in the process. Amazing story, isn't it? Pure Lovekin."

A short time later, David's agent again took him to lunch at Estrusco. He waited until the *bistecca fiorentina* to broach the delicate subject. The death of Andrew Lovekin would make a sensational movie; he felt sure he could interest at least one studio in the project, if David would agree to write it. He had known Andy the longest and had written two of his films; also, the case was so complex and intricate, it would take a David Michael Mendelsohn to tell the story. David demurred. Andy had been his friend. Writing a film based on his death would feel exploitive.

"Even for two five plus points? I'll bet we could get that."

David shook his head. The material was too close, too personal. Writing it would open wounds that had not yet healed. It would take more than money for it to be worth his while.

"More than money? Like what?"

He smiled, as the knot in his gut finally unraveled.

"Possessory credit."

About the Author

Diana Gould has written features, pilots, episodes, and miniseries, and was writer/producer on *Dynasty* and *Berrenger's*. She served on the board of the Writers Guild, and founded its Women's Committee, the first of its kind. Her novel *Coldwater* (Los Angeles: Rare Bird Books, 2013) won the Independent Book Publishers Association's Ben Franklin silver medal for Best First Book.

He's No Gary Cooper

Mary Keenan

MAVIS HARDCASTLE SAT HALFWAY along a row of girls around her height and around her age, all of them sporting permanent waves, their bright red lips parted as they faced the big screen at the Rialto. The cinema had made its Los Angeles debut the year before in 1936; most of the girls had made theirs not long afterward. But rapture wasn't the unifying reason for those open mouths. A blonde was snoring quietly because the days in the studio typing pool were long. A brunette had a summer cold coming on and her sinuses were congested. A dark-haired beauty was conscious of the gaze of a man nearby, fiddling with the hat on his knee, his long leg stretched into the aisle. That girl slipped the tip of her tongue to the corner of her mouth and adjusted her shoulders slightly.

Only Mavis was enthralled by the movie, riveted as third-tier matinee idol Joe Curtis slammed another actor against the wall of a set painted to look like the back room of a gloomy nightclub.

"Shaddup, ya dumb ox, before I shut ya up myself."

Harriet Orley drove her elbow into Mavis's arm. "You got the line wrong this time."

Mavis felt her face go hot. She'd spent the entire movie parroting along with the actors, thinking she'd been too quiet for anyone to notice. Now the man sitting behind Harriet told them to pipe down already.

Afterward, emerging onto the sidewalk, the girls began to scatter. The one with the admirer accepted his offer to visit a nightclub. The one who'd napped teamed up with two others for the tram. Two more waved good-bye, then linked arms and disappeared into the crowd. That left Harriet, who was giving Mavis a *What am I gonna do with you?* look.

"I don't know what you see in that Joe Curtis. He's not even a good actor."

"Is too. Anyway, what does it matter if he is or he isn't? He's got that that square jaw and those glossy eyebrows with the big soulful eyes under them."

"It matters plenty, believe me."

Harriet liked to know better than other people about things like who's got talent. And she knew a few actors personally, too, so Mavis didn't argue. She owed Harriet for looking out for her, even though Harriet only did it on account of Mavis's older sister having been Harriet's maid of honor at her wedding, before her new husband ran off with somebody else. Harriet put her best face on it, after. She moved to Hollywood to work in the script department at 20th Century Fox. She'd been in Los Angeles longer than any of the girls. She knew the ropes and then some.

"All I know is, there's something about him that makes me want to get out of Hollywood and find a picket fence somewhere with a house behind it."

"Tired of Hollywood after all of one week." Harriet barked a laugh. "You got that line out of a movie."

"Did not." Mavis guessed she probably did, though. She'd seen a lot of movies in her nineteen years, and they'd all kind of merged together by now. "Thanks for inviting me out with the other girls, Harriet."

"Sure. But next time, let somebody else pick the picture. Those gangster movies . . . ugh."

"They're not gangster movies. They're melodramas."

"You can say that again. Dark and dreary and full of desperate people, like a bunch of rats trying to scratch out their next meal. We get enough of that at work."

"I guess so."

"We could see *Easy Living* next time. Anything Jean Arthur does gives me a boost, and after all the fuss the studio made about copyright, I'm interested. Or in a couple of weeks we can see *Topper*. Cary Grant has a lot more going for him than Joe Curtis."

"Maybe."

They went into a diner to cap off the evening. Mavis braced herself for what was coming. She'd noticed already how Harriet liked to linger over a coffee while she went through a list of the flaws she saw in Mavis.

When they'd settled onto their stools at the counter, Harriet got started.

"Listen, Mavis. I have this friend, used to work for Sam Goldwyn himself. She met a guy one day at work. Young kid just coming up. He was hoping for something better than bit parts and boy, she took one look at him and that was it. She talked him up to every big name she came across. Meanwhile, there's him taking her out the whole time so she thought she'd have something to show for the trouble she was taking over him."

"You mean, she didn't?"

"'Course she didn't. An actor, wasting his time on somebody's personal assistant when he's got a career to promote, and two dozen gorgeous girls looking to hang off his arm for the next set of magazine photographs? She didn't stand a chance. And the worst was, she didn't even care. He moved on and she was grateful for the time she had with him. Forgave him everything. Still speaks well of him. Must've been some guy, right? Know who he was?"

Mavis's eyes were the size of the saucer under her coffee cup. She shook her head.

"Gary Cooper." Harriet tapped the counter. "And let me tell you something, Mavis. That Joe Curtis is no Gary Cooper. You find him on the other side of your desk tomorrow morning looking for a leg up, he won't leave you with so much as a good story to show for the work you put in. You had enough trouble back home with your dad gambling away all his money. You're not likely to find many of the good ones out here, but hold out for a guy who's the real thing. Nice and stable. Not an actor."

"I guess."

Harriet lived in one direction, and the rooms Mavis shared with a couple of other girls she'd met at the bus station were in the other, so she walked on her own for a few blocks, pushing through crowds of people going on to the late shows or out for dinner or dancing. She looked at everybody, hoping to recognize somebody famous, getting a little thrill when she did. Then, at the mouth of an alley, she bumped into a big man with his hat pulled low over his face.

"Gosh, mister. I'm sorry."

The man looked Mavis up and down, taking in her dewy looks and the fit of the dress she'd made at home before she came west. She had a good figure, and she knew her way around a sewing machine. Truth be told, she'd have been better off in the costume department than in the typing pool, only Harriet didn't know anybody outside scripts.

"You probably couldn't break a hundred pounds if you were soaking wet, coming out of the ocean." He pointed his thumb at his chest. He had six inches on her. His suit had been cut broad through the shoulders, and he filled them. Even his neck was something. This guy looked strong enough to push a tram uphill. "You don't need to worry about making a dent in me."

He was still shifting his eyes over her, but all she could see was his face. The big jaw. The heavy eyebrows. The soulful eyes.

"Got a light, kid?"

The line from *The Thief at the Side of the Road*, when Joe Curtis's character meets the beautiful girl who breaks his heart.

"My mama'd flip if she thought I ever took up smoking." She felt like a dope as soon as she'd said it, but Joe Curtis didn't seem to mind a bit.

"Boy, you're about as green as they come. How long you been in town?"

"A week and two days."

"You been to the Blue Canoe yet?"

She shook her head. And just like that, he picked up her hand and slipped it onto his arm. The crowds parted for them as he walked her across the street and down the other side toward the Blue Canoe nightclub. He even bought her a steak there. And they danced. Mavis could hardly believe it. His cologne was as wonderful as that beautiful face of his. She couldn't wait to tell Harriet all about it the next morning when she carried the morning's scripts over to her office.

But when she got there, Harriet wasn't interested in scripts. She'd picked up a newspaper and she was waving it at Mavis. "You hear about this murder last night near your place?"

"What murder?"

"Some guy got himself stabbed in an alley, maybe even while we were having coffee. You need to make sure you take the tram home after this, Mavis. No more of this going around with your head in the clouds. You might've walked smack into the murderer."

"I didn't, though. I ran into Joe Curtis."

Harriet didn't believe it any more than Mavis had, until Mavis showed her the slip of paper from the Blue Canoe where he'd written his phone number before escorting her home.

"It's too good to be true, Mavis. You better watch out he doesn't take advantage."

Mavis nodded. Harriet always knew better. "I will. But he couldn't have been nicer."

"Then he's definitely up to something. You're pretty enough, Mavis, but Hollywood's full of pretty women. And you don't exactly have the ear of the head of the studio."

"That's what he says he likes about me. That I'm fresh and new, and not jaded or ambitious like the other girls he's met."

Harriet put a hand on her forehead. "Oh, brother. Do you have a lot to learn."

A few nights later, Joe Curtis took Mavis to see a movie. Another melodrama, but one he didn't star in, the director having decided on somebody else at the last minute. Joe said he thought the guy did a good job. Mavis didn't enjoy it, though. Especially in the scene where the star met the beautiful woman who broke his heart, because Joe had to excuse himself and he was gone for the whole thing. Ten minutes, maybe, but Mavis managed to make the time pass. Afterward he took Mavis to a nightclub, where they danced cheek to cheek till the place closed. The girls she lived with weren't happy she was getting home so late. Mavis was pretty sure Harriet wouldn't be either if she made even more mistakes with her typing than usual.

But if Harriet was annoyed when Mavis was late with the scripts the next day, you'd never know. She was too busy gossiping with the other girls in the office. They were like a little hive in the middle of the room, all the bees buzzing around the queen—Harriet, naturally. When Mavis got to the fringes, Harriet spotted her and filled her in.

"Another murder, Mavis. Hope you were tucked in safe at home and not out at the Metronome watching another one of those depressing movies."

"But I was. That's exactly what I was doing."

Harriet narrowed her eyes. "That Joe Curtis again? I'd watch out for him."

"You said. And I am. But he's the loveliest man, Harriet. I'm sure he's exactly what he seems. Now tell me about this murder."

"Same as before. Guy got stabbed in the alley, right out back of the theater."

"You mean—the same one we were in?" Mavis felt her fingertips resting on the neck of her blouse, and knew she looked even younger. She straightened her shoulders and tried to sound smart, like the others in Harriet's hive. "Maybe somebody's jealous of anybody who talks to his girl."

She should've tried harder.

"You really need to quit with the melodramas, Mavis."

Mavis slumped her shoulders again. "I guess. You want to go see a movie tonight, Harriet? Your choice this time?"

"Sure. If you're not too busy with Joe Curtis."

It was a fact, Mavis being busy with Joe Curtis. He took her out every week at least, for a couple of months. And here and there, now and then, bodies dropped in alleys. Actors, all of them, but that was hardly a distinguishing feature in this town.

Harriet worried Mavis might be next. Mavis thought Harriet worried too much.

"They're all men, Harriet. Nobody's ever going to mistake me for a man."

Harriet looked her up and down, like Joe did that first night. "Maybe not. But there's no telling when the murderer will get tired of the same old same old."

"I'll be fine. I never go anywhere except with you or Joe. You're too smart to get us into trouble, and nobody could beat Joe in a fight."

"Trust me, anybody who tries a fight with me would regret it pretty fast."

A few days later, Joe took Mavis out in his car up Mulholland Drive to see the view, after she asked specially. She thought he might be ready by now to try something, so she was ready with her refusals, but he never did.

"See those lights over there, kid? That's where I started out. Painting billboards."

"Billboards? *Daily Variety* says you were discovered when you were training horses."

He laughed. "That's what I love about you, Mavis. You believe everything. What would a guy my size be doing training horses?"

"I guess you're right. I never thought about it that way." Mavis thought about it some more as a solitary car passed along the road behind them.

Joe checked the parking brake, then made a face. "Listen kid, I gotta see a man about a different kinda horse. You okay sitting here on your own for a few minutes? There's no alleys up here to worry you."

Mavis gave him a sharp look, and he laughed.

"You know, the Alley Cat Murderer."

"Oh, him." Mavis didn't like the name the papers were running with. All the victims died from a single stab wound, perfectly placed, nice and clean, no external bleeding. An alley cat would leave four deep scratches. Mavis liked precision, though she had to work hard to achieve it in her typing. "I'll be fine. I'll scream if I'm not."

"And I'll come running, kid. Don't you worry."

It was October now, and chilly, but one of Mavis's roommates had loaned her a warm coat with conveniently deep pockets and she found the air refreshing. A lot had changed for Mavis since the night she met Joe. She was even moving out of the typing pool next week and getting a raise.

"Miss me?" Joe had been gone a long time, but Mavis had kept herself busy.

"Always." She blushed as soon as the word was out of her mouth, but Joe didn't seem to mind. He didn't seem to mind anything Mavis did. Not like Harriet.

"You know, Joe, Harriet says you're up to no good with me. She'd be awfully suspicious if I told her you'd brought me all the way up here just to see the view."

"You think so?" He looked at Mavis, his big soft eyes shining. "What would she think I'd be doing? Killing a guy?"

"Of course not." With a shy smile she shifted herself on her borrowed coat, where a lump at the seam pressed in and worried at her leg. "She thinks you'll take advantage of me."

"Kid, if I haven't done that by now, I think you're safe."

Mavis took his arm and cuddled into his shoulder. She did feel safe. Safe for the first time since her dad started coming home without any money. She didn't need good-night kisses to know Joe liked her. She didn't even like good-night kisses. What she wanted was Joe's company.

"You're one in a million, Joe."

"Like you, Mavis."

He smiled at her and drove her back home.

The next morning, Harriet didn't wait for Mavis to turn up with the scripts. She came right to Mavis's desk in the typing pool, almost before Mavis could hide her borrowed copy of *Daily Variety*.

"Another body, and this one wasn't in an alley. Please tell me you weren't up on Mulholland Drive last night."

"I was, though."

"For the love of . . . Mavis, you gotta start keeping a closer eye when you go out at night. If you don't think you need to keep yourself safe, you might at least try to figure out who's doing this. Seems like you and Joe are at the scene every time. I don't think much of his brains, but you're a smart girl underneath all that Kansas innocence. You could put one over on the police for sure and tell them who's the alley cat."

Mavis thought this was the nicest thing Harriet had ever said to her.

Maybe the only nice thing.

Then Harriet perched on her desk and showed her how she still knew more than anybody. "I've been thinking it over, Mavis, and doing some digging. It seems to me most of these guys have one thing in common."

"They're actors."

"They're actors who got parts Joe Curtis was up for. I'm worried he might be behind all this. I'm worried he's taking you out as a cover, and he'll hurt you next."

"As a cover? How? I might be out with him, but I can tell the police he leaves me alone for a little while every time. If he wanted a cover, he'd make sure we were never apart."

"He leaves you alone? Mavis, you gotta be *really* careful."

Mavis considered this. "You want to tag along? Make sure I'm okay?"

"Yes. If you're going to keep seeing this guy, I do. Your sister would kill me if anything happened to you. Just bring me along once so I can see for myself how he treats you."

So the next time Mavis went out with Joe, she asked if Harriet could come too, and he said the more the merrier. They went to a little club he knew, and he took turns dancing with them both. Then he excused himself and Harriet watched him go, looking smug.

"Feeling better about me and Joe, Harriet?"

"I'll say. He's definitely using you as a cover."

"I already said—"

"He likes men, Mavis. Didn't you notice how he looks at the waiter, and every other guy in the room? And then making that excuse to slip away—this is the second time tonight, and no man needs twenty minutes for the bathroom when he's on a date, unless the date is in there."

Mavis had never heard of such a thing. She'd never come across it in Kansas. It didn't worry her, that's for sure. If anything, it gave a girl a break.

"As long as he likes me, what difference does it make who else he likes?"

Harriet looked exasperated. "Plenty, believe me. Look, why don't we go out in the alley. This place is too small to attract the Alley Cat. The men's room is at the back, and it's got to have a window. Maybe we can get up on a crate or something and listen."

"Why on earth would we want to do that?"

"Because you've invested a lot of time in Joe Curtis, at the expense of every other man who's tried to take you out. If I can't explain why that's a bad idea, maybe I can show you."

"All right. If it'll make you happy."

"And you'd better bring that awful evening bag with you so it looks like we've gone to the powder room. Honestly, Mavis, you should use your raise to buy something daintier. You might as well be carrying an old boot against your dress."

"I like to have room for my things, that's all."

Harriet made a noise that wasn't very nice and led Mavis to the back of the club.

The alley was about as dirty as you'd expect. There was no shortage of crates to pile up under the window. But as far as Mavis was concerned, they didn't need to use them. They could hear the men inside talking, and Joe's voice was distinctive enough. They were placing bets on horses. A lot of bets. Joe was placing the most, talking as fast as he could. He seemed plenty experienced, too.

"C'mon, Mavis." Harriet's voice came out like a hiss. "Climb up here with me."

Mavis sighed and clambered up beside her friend. Inside, a few men had paired off. One couple was kissing, and another was heading into a cubicle. Joe had his arm around a soft-looking man with tawny hair falling over his narrow forehead. Joe's hand caressed the man's shoulder.

Harriet's eyes went wide, and she crept back down from the crate.

"You recognize that guy, Mavis? That's the son of one of the richest men in Los Angeles. If Joe's got that kind of backing now, he isn't going to be in those third-rate movies much longer. But the guy's dad would shell out a lot of cash to keep it quiet. What do you think? Should we try for a payday?"

The next morning, the papers were full of the latest Alley Cat murder victim. It was a woman this time. The police didn't know what to do with themselves. And when the murders suddenly stopped after Harriet turned up in that alley, they didn't know what angle to pursue. The whole thing faded away, like the print on the pages in the detectives' fat case files.

Mavis missed Harriet's company, in spite of everything. She had time to spare now that she wasn't spending all those evenings with Joe Curtis. She couldn't go on with him once she knew the real reason he kept excusing himself during their dates. She'd had enough of gambling with her dad, and she didn't want a guy who ran through money like that. She valued her peace of mind too much.

She heard he'd picked up another new arrival in town, but Mavis knew that girl couldn't possibly love Joe like she had. She wouldn't lure an actor into the shadows for a little action, then kill the guy so Joe wasn't passed over for the next round of movie parts. And she wouldn't kill a good friend for him either, just to make sure she held her tongue about his interest in men. Mavis might not have a story she could share with other people, like that friend of Harriet's, but at least she had one.

Afterward, though, when Mavis moved on to better movies, with bigger names, she had to admit Harriet knew more than Mavis after all.

When it came to acting, Joe Curtis was no Gary Cooper.

About the Author

Mary Keenan's other short mysteries have appeared in anthologies, and she has been a finalist for both the Daphne du Maurier and Claymore awards. She enjoys art, textiles, historical research, and, of course, classic movies. Her blog, www.hugsforyourhead.com, features dozens of her knit designs, including free patterns for stylish chemo caps.

Destination Wedding

Frankie Bow

EMMA NAKAMURA PLACED HER tiny fists on her ample hips and glared at the squat, wind-blasted building. It was the only structure in sight, other than the utility poles lined up along the two-lane highway.

"This can't be the right place," she declared. "Molly, call the driver back. This is all *ferkakta*." (Emma grew up speaking Hawaiian Creole English, better known as Pidgin, but she did her doctoral work at Cornell, during which time she claims to have picked up Yiddish.)

"I'm not getting a signal," I said. "I think I need to restart my phone. Emma, this is why I suggested renting a car."

"Too humbug. Takes forever." Emma yanked up the handle of her rollaboard. "Guess there's nothing to do now but check into this meth motel and end up in a shallow grave next to a bleached cow skull."

Emma's brother's fiancée had moved their wedding venue at the last minute, from Mahina, Hawaii (where we all lived) to the mountainous wilderness of north central L.A. County. Emma was even grumpier than usual. We had just endured a thirteen-hour flight from Mahina through Honolulu to LAX, followed by a northbound crawl on jampacked freeways, and finally a bone-rattling stretch of potholed Sierra Highway. On the flight, Emma had insisted that Sleepy Valley was where ranch dressing was invented. We bet on it and she ended up having to buy me an airline cocktail.

"Maybe instead of getting buried in the desert," I suggested, "we'll be the secret ingredient in the next batch of Sleepy Valley Ranch Dressing."

"Shut up," Emma pointed out.

"Don't fuss at *me*, Emma. I'm not the one who decided to get hitched in the high desert. Or wherever we are."

"What's wrong with a Hawaiian beach wedding?" Emma grumbled. "The pictures would've been great, and we wouldn't have had to take off work."

Emma was a biology professor at Mahina State University ("Where Your Future Begins Tomorrow") in Mahina, Hawaii. In her early forties and happily childless, Emma loved her research and hated being away from the lab.

I also worked at Mahina State, as chair of the Management Department in the College of Commerce. Unlike Emma, I don't at all mind skipping a few days of work. Also unlike Emma, I have an energetic toddler at home. Although I missed Donnie and baby Francesca, I looked forward to getting a couple nights' uninterrupted sleep.

"Anyway," I said, "this is the right place. Here are Jandie and Jonah now."

Emma's future sister-in-law Jandie Brand came bounding up to us, squealing with apparent delight.

At first glance, Jandie and Emma could be sisters. They were both short and curvy, with round cheeks, dark hair, and a sprinkling of freckles. But Jandie was bubbly, a descriptor no one would dare apply to Emma.

"Emma, I'm *so* happy to see you!" Jandie grasped her in a tight hug, then turned to see what Jonah was doing.

"Baby," Jandie whimpered at Jonah, "you were looking away."

"Huh?" Jonah said. "Oh. Sorry."

Jandie Brand was a social media influencer. Her job, as far as I could tell, was to travel to different places and post photos and videos of herself online. She seemed to be good at it, judging by her large and increasing count of followers and fans. Even Emma was once a "Jandista," although she denied it now.

"Let's try it again." Jandie jogged back to the building's entrance. I noticed the letters stenciled over the double doors: Sleepy Valley Ryokan.

"What's a *ryokan*?" I whispered to Emma.

"A *ryokan* is a traditional Japanese inn. You should know that, Molly."

Jandie was upon us once again before I could ask Emma why, exactly, I should know that. This time Jonah was recording our joyous reunion on his phone as instructed. Jandie hugged Emma again, then she turned to embrace me.

"Oh *Molly*," Jandie squeaked, "I'm *so* happy you're here to share our special day!"

She abruptly dropped her arms and turned to Jonah.

"Did you get that, baby?"

"Yeah," Jonah said.

"Good. I gotta go schedule my posts. Jonah, help them get checked in."

The girl at the front desk was around twenty and frail-looking, with wispy, mouse-colored hair and bulging blue eyes. I was already feeling desiccated by the thin mountain air, and I wondered how a week or two in humid Mahina might affect this young woman. I imagined her standing up straighter and sturdier, like a tomato plant when you water it.

"Welcome to the Sleepy Valley Ryokan," she said. "I'm Keiko."

"Yeah, okay," Emma muttered. Emma, who was half Japanese, was suspicious of people who adopt "exotic" names without any apparent connection to the culture. Or as she called them, "Japanese culture experts 'cause they ate at Benihana's one time."

"Do you do a lot of weddings here?" I asked Keiko.

"No," Keiko replied. "Usually January is our busy time. That's why we were able to accommodate your party on such short notice. Okay, you're in room seven. Have a wonderful stay."

Jonah picked up the handle of each of our bags and started to walk away.

"What about our keys?" I asked Keiko.

"No keys," she said.

Emma and I exchanged a look, then hurried after Jonah.

Our "double" room was smaller than I expected, with two futon mattresses on the floor nearly taking up the entire space. The vinyl floor tiles were printed to look like bamboo. Jonah stood one suitcase at the foot of each of the futon mattresses and moved to leave, but Emma stood in the doorway to block him.

"Jonah, what is this?" Emma flicked the translucent paper on the shoji door. "No keys, no locks, nothing? Anyone could just walk in. What are you smoking? Don't answer that."

I opened my suitcase and set about hanging my clothes on the wall hooks (there was no closet), while Emma hectored her brother.

"I hope you know how inconvenient this was, you guys changing your plans," Emma declared. "The beach wedding woulda been perfect. Know what, Jonah, I think Jandie using your wedding to launch her whatever you call it—"

"Product line," I prompted.

"Yeah. It's, you know, it's *da kine*," Emma said, using the all-purpose Pidgin equivalent of "whatsis" or "whatchamacallit."

"Tacky?" I suggested, then quickly added, "Emma said it, not me."

"Is there anything to do around here?" Emma pulled out her phone. "Jonah, what's the Wi-Fi?"

"There's no Wi-Fi," Jonah said.

"Don't worry, Emma, I have an unlimited data plan." I pulled out my freshly restarted phone to check, but there was no signal.

"You can get signal outside, at night," Jonah said. "And you can text."

"Eh, where's Dad?" Emma asked. "I'd like see him one last time before hillbilly serial killers murder us in our beds while we're calling 911 on our nonworking phones."

"He said he couldn't find a flight at the last minute."

"Smart, him. We should've thought of that." Emma glanced at her watch. "You guys hungry?"

"*Konnichiwa.* Welcome to the Kirei Dining Room at the Sleepy Valley Ryokan. I'm Keiko and I'll be your server tonight." The pale girl from the front desk spoke to Jonah, listing a number of specials then informing him they were out of everything except the poke bowl. Emma took the initiative and ordered three poke bowls.

"Great choice," Keiko said to Jonah, who hadn't said a word the whole time.

"Can we get three waters?" I called after her as she hurried into the kitchen.

Two men in their sixties entered the dining room. I recognized one as Tedd Ladd, the ex-husband of the bride-to-be, and nudged Emma. I wondered who the other man was; they seemed to know each other. Where Tedd Ladd was bald, scrawny, and red like something that had been skinned, the other man was graceful and urbane, with lush salt-and-pepper hair and a neat goatee.

Tedd pulled out a chair and sat down, uninvited. His more tactful companion remained standing.

"Please, join us," I said to the stranger, and not to Tedd. I didn't care for Tedd Ladd. Since his divorce from Jandie, the once-beloved former cartoonist had become something of a social media personality himself. His message to his audience of underachieving young men was that their disappointments could be laid entirely at the feet of overambitious "females" who refused to accept their place in the natural order. Given that Tedd Ladd's much younger ex-wife had surpassed him career-wise, I imagined Ladd himself found considerable comfort in his theory.

The stranger took a seat and introduced himself as Rick Redland.

"Rick and me go way back," Tedd said. "He used to be a decent reporter before he got all woke in his old age."

"I'm an attorney and a climate journalist," Rick explained. "One pays the bills, the other saves my soul."

Keiko reappeared from the kitchen, but Tedd waved her off.

"Tedd," Emma objected, "I was gonna ask for a glass of wine."

"They don't know?" Rick asked.

"We don't know what?" Emma demanded, and I saw Jonah shrink in his seat.

"No alcohol," Tedd said, with relish. "You're not even allowed to bring your own. That's right: no Wi-Fi, no real beds, and no alcohol allowed. Great choice of venue, huh?"

"No alcohol?" Emma glared at Jonah, who looked like he wanted to collapse into another dimension, one where Emma couldn't find him.

"Rick," I blurted out, to distract Emma from murdering her brother, "Hi. Um, are you working on anything interesting right now?"

"I'm doing a series of articles about dropping water levels in reservoirs revealing bodies that have been there for years."

"Did you say bodies, plural?" I asked.

"Yep. In fact, one of the cases I'm looking into is just up the road. When the invitation came for the wedding in Hawaii, I had to turn it down. It worked out great for me that they moved the wedding here."

"At least one person's happy about it," Emma muttered.

"Although I'm not sure how much writing I'm going to get done this weekend. They put me in the room right next to the delivery entrance, so it's noisy, and it's so small there's no desk."

"What's the case up the road?" I asked.

"On May second, a pair of hikers at Bouquet Reservoir spotted something that looked like a skull at the edge of the water, but when they called the sheriff—"

"Geez, Rick, way to bring down the party," Tedd Ladd groused. "No one wants to hear about some dead guy in their drinking water."

"You know something about this one?" Rick asked Tedd. "How did you know this was a male?"

Tedd didn't know anything about the case. Nevertheless, he launched into a lecture about men and death statistics, somehow making it sound like he, Tedd Ladd, lived on the precipice of death, constantly in peril of perishing in some heroic and spectacular way.

Emma disappeared into the kitchen and came back with our two dinners to go. She left her brother Jonah in Tedd Ladd's company as revenge.

Emma and I sat on our rolled-up futons in our tiny room and ate our "poke bowls" out of real ceramic bowls (apparently there was not much call for takeout meals here). The aluminum blinds on the window were hiked up to reveal a nighttime view of the dirt parking lot. Every so often, the headlights of a vehicle on the two-lane road would rake the room.

"This place is a nightmare," Emma said. She was predictably disappointed in the poke bowl. It contained soybeans, chopped kale, and sliced almonds. It was nothing like a real poke bowl, but I was hungry and thought it tasted fine.

"I think this is a rehab center," I said. "Obviously not like the fancy ones my ex's parents used to put him up in. But the non-locking doors, the isolation, January being their high season, what else could it be?"

"*Oy vey*. I think you're right, Molly. Why didn't Jonah tell me—I would've packed my own booze."

"I think that's what Tedd Ladd did," I said. "Brought his own."

"Oh yeah, I could smell him from all the way across the table."

"Notice he didn't offer to share," I said. "He just sat there and gloated. Why would Jandie invite her awful ex-husband to her wedding?"

Emma grimaced. "You know Jandie, she wants everyone to be happy happy friends. Even her *putz* of an ex. Okay, we gotta take action."

Emma and I strolled out through the reception area and stepped outside, avoiding eye contact with the woman at the front desk (not Keiko, but also blond). Outside, our phones were able to connect although the signal was weak. Emma discovered a liquor store a mere ten miles away. Unfortunately, there were no rideshare cars available, and no way to take delivery unobserved. Our room faced the front of the building, and the only two exits were through reception and a door at the far end of the hallway next to the kitchen. We found Rick Redland alone in the dining room, working on a laptop. He seemed not to mind our interrupting him and was willing to go along with our scheme.

Rick's room was serendipitously located at the end of the hallway right next to the delivery door. Emma would go outside once again and call Hi Spirits Liquor to arrange a delivery. At the right time Rick would pop out of his room, travel the two steps to the delivery door, collect the booze, and discreetly bring it back into his room. His payment would be a bottle of Macallan. It was a foolproof plan.

Around one in the morning Emma shook me awake and we rolled our empty suitcases down the hallway to Rick's room. No light shone through the paper panels, and we could hear snoring from inside. Emma slid open the door and we slipped in. Rick's room was half the size of ours. That explained the "1-A" room number painted outside. The management must have sliced off a sliver of the adjoining room to create it.

A snoring, man-sized pile of blankets atop a narrow futon roll took up most of the free floor space. It got cold at night here, and management was being thrifty with the heat.

"Let's make him help." Emma prodded the blanket pile with her toe. It snorted sharply, then resumed snoring.

"Emma, let him sleep," I said. "He already did us a huge favor."

"Yeah, a 'favor' in exchange for a seventy-dollar bottle of scotch," Emma retorted.

I started pulling out the wine bottles one by one and arranging them in my suitcase.

"Emma, why did you buy so much wine? Even we can't drink that much in a weekend."

"They had a buy two cases get ten percent off deal. Molly, I know you appreciate a bargain. Anyway, we can bring it back in our checked bags if there's any left over. I'll text Jonah so he can help us carry some of this stuff."

"I'd rather do this quickly and get out of here, and not wait for anyone." I was starting to imagine what might happen if we were caught, and my enthusiasm for this adventure was waning.

It took just a few minutes to get all the wine bottles packed and wheel our clanking suitcases back down the hallway to our room. I was ready to breathe a sigh of relief when something occurred to me.

"Emma, where *is* that seventy-dollar scotch? I didn't see it."

"The Macallan? He probably drank it all," Emma said as she snuggled into the bedding.

"Then where was the empty bottle?"

"Molly, don't worry about it. You can ask him tomorrow if he's not too hung over."

As Emma snored softly, I tried that trick where you stop yourself from worrying by imagining what's the worst that could happen. After all, what was the worst that could happen? Emma and I would be kicked out of the wedding party of a social media celebrity for smuggling booze into a rehab center, and everyone at Mahina State University would find out and gossip about it for the rest of our lives. My parents would disown me when they heard about it. And what if Rick Redland was a recovering alcoholic and Emma and I had pushed him off the wagon? Now his life and career would be ruined, and it would be our fault.

I was so preoccupied with the "what's the worst that could happen" exercise that I didn't hear the shoji door slide open at first.

Jonah stood there, wearing sweatpants and a navy Mr. Zog's Sex Wax shirt. It may have been the one he wore to Sprezzatura, the fanciest restaurant in Mahina, that one time years ago when Emma had tried to set me up with him.

I slipped out into the hallway and slid the door shut behind me.

"Jonah," I whispered, "what are you doing here?"

He glanced down at the phone in his hand.

"Emma texted me to come help you guys."

"That's very nice of you, but we're fine. Do you think you'll be able to get back into your room without waking Jandie up?"

"She's outside, doing her uploading. Now's when you can get the strongest signal."

I heard clicking to my right. Someone was opening the door of room six, the solid door with the "employees only" placard.

I slid the door back open and motioned Jonah to follow me back into the room, but he just stood there like one of those turkeys who stares up to the sky when it rains and ends up drowning. In his defense, Jonah didn't have anything to hide, unlike me, the booze smuggler. So I pushed the door shut and listened.

"Oh, hi, Jonah. You know, guests are expected to be in bed by ten." It sounded like Keiko.

"It doesn't have to be your *own* bed," she added.

This startled me so much that I lost my balance and tipped over Emma's suitcase full of wine bottles.

"What was that?" Keiko whispered.

"Um, I dunno, but I better go check it out."

Jonah slid the door open and stepped into the room.

"What are you doing?" I whispered, shoving the door back to the closed position.

"I panicked," he whispered back.

"Jonah?" Keiko called from right outside.

"Keiko?" came a woman's voice I didn't recognize. A smoker's voice.

"Mom! What are you doing back?"

"What are you doing out in the hallway?"

"Checking out a noise."

"Oh really. Dressed like that?"

We waited until the door to room six had clicked shut and the bickering voices had faded. I sent Jonah back to his room and lay down on the thin futon. I wasn't going to get much sleep tonight. Rosy light was already glowing through the slats of the blinds.

This wouldn't last much longer, I consoled myself. Rehearsal tomorrow—no, today—and then the ceremony Saturday.

At least we had plenty of wine.

Emma and I were the first ones to show up for the rehearsal, aside from the deeply tanned blond woman I'd seen at the reception desk earlier. Her name was Yoko, we learned, and I immediately recognized her raspy voice from the previous night. Keiko's mom. She was an ordained minister, she told us, and the owner of the Sleepy Valley Ryokan. It was a prime destination for sober events (like this wedding, supposedly) and according to her we were lucky to get a reservation on such short notice.

For the first time, I understood why Jandie Brand might want to stage her combination wedding-product launch here. The setup was simple, a few white folding chairs and a white lattice arch. But beyond that spread an expanse of golden chaparral studded with lavender-edged sage. The horizon blazed magenta, one of those magnificent sunsets you can only get from Southern California's unique blend of particulate air pollution.

Jandie hurried toward us, wearing a flower crown and holding something that looked like a pink teakettle. Her filmy pink dress fluttered behind her. Jonah followed, pointing a phone at her.

"Okay, cut," she called out without turning around, and Jonah slipped the phone into the back pocket of his jeans.

"We're a little late getting started," Yoko said.

"We had to finish the photoshoot for the Magical Mist Intimate Steamer." Jandie brandished the teakettle. "You can't actually show it being used, you just hint at it. Jonah had to go get more dry ice. Hey! Where's Rick and Tedd?"

"We'll get 'em," Emma said, and we started back to the motel before anyone could object.

"If Rick's too hung over to get up, I'm denying everything," Emma whispered to me as we rounded the building.

"Isn't that Rick?" I pointed to a man stepping down from a white pickup truck. The truck sped off, and Rick waved. We ran over to meet him.

"Sorry I'm late for the rehearsal," he said. "It's practically impossible to get an Uber up here. I had to hitchhike back from the reservoir."

"Are you okay?" I asked. "How was the Macallan?"

"Never better, and it was terrific. Thanks!"

"Do you know where Tedd is?" Emma asked.

"Haven't seen him today."

"We'll go find him," I said.

"See you out there," Emma added.

Emma and I checked the dining room first, then the guest rooms, starting with room eight and working our way down. No luck until we got to 1-A, Rick's room.

The room was exactly as it had been earlier this morning. Except the man in the bed was no longer snoring.

The man was Tedd, and he was dead.

It was nearly midnight by the time the sheriffs and the paramedics had finished up.

Emma and I sat on our rolled-up futons, drinking red wine out of Solo cups and trying to make sense of what had happened.

"Racism, that's why," Emma said. "Anybody coulda smothered Tedd Ladd in his sleep, but the sheriff arrests my brother, the one brown guy."

"Who happens to be engaged to the ex-wife of the victim."

"So?" Emma demanded.

"Also, Keiko announcing that Jonah was out after curfew that night didn't help," I said.

"That text from me should've cleared him."

"*Hey dummy get over here and keep your mouth shut*? Emma, we're lucky you weren't arrested as an accomplice."

Emma refilled her cup and then mine.

"Eh, you think whoever it was meant to kill Rick Redland? How many people knew he switched rooms with Tedd Ladd?"

"I was wondering that too," I said. "Doing his friend a favor might have saved his life."

A tapping noise interrupted us, and the shoji door slid open.

"Can I come in?" Jandie Brand asked quietly. Her earlier fits of sobbing seemed to have exhausted her. "Oh, you have wine."

Emma waved her in, and I scooted over to give her room on my futon roll. Emma poured a cup of wine and handed it to her.

"I can't believe it. Teddy's dead, and Jonah's in jail for his murder." Jandie sipped the wine. "Ooh, this is good."

"Did someone let the guests know not to come up tomorrow?" I asked.

"There aren't any other guests," Jandie said. "We can't afford a big event."

"Couldn't your parents help you?" Emma asked.

"My mom died when I was young," Jandie said. "My dad couldn't handle it and he left. So I don't really have parents who can help me."

We sat in awkward silence until Jandie added, "Who would want to kill Teddy?"

"That's a great question," I said. "What do you think, Jandie? Who would be better off with Tedd dead?"

I immediately regretted phrasing it that way, but no one else seemed to notice.

"Well, there's me," she said brightly. "I pay him alimony."

"You supported *him*?" Emma lowered her cup of wine in surprise.

"Wow, if anyone found out, he would—" I stopped myself before I said, "die of embarrassment."

"And Keiko, at the front desk." Jandie sipped her wine. "Teddy screamed at her when he found out about the no alcohol thing. He tried to scream at me too, but I told him if he didn't like it, he could leave, and I'd find someone else to walk me down the aisle."

"Your ex-husband was going to walk you down the aisle?" I asked.

"'Cause everyone should be friends, Molly," Emma said. "No hard feelings."

"That's how it *should* be, Emma," Jandie said earnestly, "but it's not always true."

"What do you mean?" I asked.

"I don't know," she said quietly.

"You do know something," Emma said. "Jandie, what is it?"

"I didn't want to say anything to the sheriff. But Uncle Rick, I call him that 'cause he's like an uncle to me."

"Got it," Emma said. "And then?"

"I think it was right before you guys got here, Uncle Rick and Teddy were having a big argument about something Uncle Rick wrote. Teddy was shouting, 'You think the world would be better off if I died?'" And then Uncle Rick said something about trying on shoes."

"If the shoe fits?" I suggested.

Jandie lit up. "That was it! Molly, I hope I get to be as smart as you when I'm your age."

Emma woke me up the next morning by flinging open the door (to the extent that one can "fling" a shoji screen).

"We got internet," she announced. "And Wi-Fi calling. Rick and me borrowed the truck and got a router at Best Buy. Molly, we should've rented a car."

She handed me one of two large Starbucks cups. I sat up and accepted it gratefully.

"I found out why they really switched rooms," Emma said as she got seated. "Rick told me Tedd Ladd came over with his flask and wanted to talk about old times. Did you know Rick was best man at their wedding? Anyway, Rick says he couldn't get rid of him, so Tedd was there when the booze delivery came. And 'cause Tedd had shared his flask, Rick felt like he had to reciprocate. Tedd drank a bunch of Rick's Macallan and passed out, so Rick went to sleep in Tedd's room. Rick took the scotch with him to Tedd's room, that's how come we didn't see it in Rick's original room."

"I can see why he didn't tell that version in front of everyone," I said. "Do you think Rick killed Tedd on the way out?"

"But Tedd was snoring when we went in—" Her phone rang. "Hey. Jonah? Good. Yeah, I'll—are you sure? Okay, I'm on it. See you soon."

She hung up.

"Everything okay?" I asked.

"Yeah, everything's fine. It's not the first time Dad's had to bail him out."

"So the wedding's still on schedule for this evening?"

"Yeah, and guess what, right before all this *mishigas* went down, Jonah misplaced the wedding ring. He's sure it's somewhere in their room, unless someone stole it."

"Oh no!"

"Yeah, and Jandie doesn't know. He seems more worried about that than about being arrested for murder."

"That's because he's actually guilty of losing the ring," I said. "So what's the plan?"

"I go pick up Jonah, him and me get some takeout on the way back, then Jonah and Jandie go on a nice picnic lunch while you and me search their room and find the ring."

The honeymoon suite was cluttered with clothing, shoes, and product prototypes for the launch of Jandieland, Jandie's new online shop. Spread across the floor were corsets and garter belts, the pink teakettle from the photo shoot, and a number of interestingly shaped devices with spiked, ribbed, or bumpy surfaces. A bulging white garment bag hung from one of the wall hooks. After Emma and I had looked underneath and inside every object in the room, I spotted the corner of a manila envelope sticking out from under the futon. Inside were birth certificates of Jonah Kapaleka-hakai Nakamura and Janelle Suzanne Broniszewski, a reservation made June 2 for rooms at the Sleepy Valley Ryokan from June 15 to 20, and at the bottom of the envelope, the missing ring.

Emma slipped it onto her pinky.

"Leave it to my brother to actually hide the ring somewhere smart," she said, "then forget where he put it. What a waste of time."

"A year ago you would've been thrilled to poke around in your favorite influencer's personal effects," I said.

"Never meet your heroes, Molly. Okay, I'm gonna go find my idiot brother. Wanna come?"

"Now that we have internet, I think I'll go back to our room and Google-stalk Rick Redland."

I sat on my futon with my back against the wall and scrolled through Rick's articles. I should have been searching for whatever it was he and Tedd Ladd were fighting about, but I was drawn in by stories like MORE HUMAN REMAINS FOUND AS RESERVOIR'S WATER LEVEL PLUMMETS and SKELETAL REMAINS LINKED TO MOB HIT.

The most recent article was from June 1, not even three weeks ago: SECRETS UNCOVERED BY CLIMATE CHANGE: BOUQUET RESERVOIR BODY CLOSE TO BEING IDENTIFIED.

I remembered to look for whatever might have started the argument with Tedd Ladd. I searched the page for "better off without," and similar phrases, but didn't find anything.

Then I checked my email, which was more time-consuming than I'd anticipated, and soon enough it was time to shower and dress for the ceremony.

I spotted Rick in one of the folding chairs and sat next to him. Maybe he had killed Tedd Ladd, but he wasn't going to murder me out here with a wedding going on, and I wanted to know whether he'd made any progress on the Bouquet Reservoir story.

"You missed the excitement," he said. "They brought too many Japanese beetles, three blocks of dry ice are missing, and the cake is filled with chocolate ice cream instead of strawberry."

"Japanese beetles?" I repeated.

"That box that looks like a beehive? They're going to release them. The way some people release doves. I guess to stay with the Japanese theme, I don't know."

"Japanese beetles. Emma's going to love that," I said.

"They supposedly don't bite or sting," Rick said.

"Still. We should probably move before the ceremony starts. So I was reading your website. Any updates on the Bouquet Reservoir body?"

"I think we have an ID," he said quietly. "Vernon Broniszewski, fifty-two. Local businessman who went missing around 2010."

"That name sounds familiar." I saw Emma next to the cake, arguing with her brother. I stood up and motioned her over.

"What's up?" She plunked down on the opposite side of Rick.

"Emma, the body in the reservoir is Vernon Broniszewski."

"And?"

"Broniszewski is Jandie Brand's last name. The name on her birth certificate."

"Really?" Rick exclaimed. "That's not a common name."

"Your story about identifying the remains was published June first," I said. "Jandie reserved the Sleepy Valley Ryokan on June second. Rick, I think Jandie's been following your story, and I wonder whether she changed the venue so you could attend and not interrupt your work."

"That was thoughtful of her. But why wouldn't Jandie tell me?"

"Tell you what?"

Jandie stood behind us, looking rather like a wedding cake herself in a voluminous, tiered wedding dress.

Rick stood. "Jandie. You look beautiful."

"Isn't the bride supposed to hide or something until it's time to come down the aisle?" Emma asked.

"Yeah, but I want to make sure everything goes smoothly. What were you talking about?"

Rick cleared his throat.

"The person found in Bouquet Reservoir is most likely Vernon Broniszewski."

Jandie looked at him wide-eyed.

"Who's that?"

"No relation to you?" Rick asked.

"Not that I know about. Okay, I need to go see what I can do about the cake."

Rick had barely sat down again when I saw motion in my peripheral vision. Jandie was walking behind our row of chairs, staring straight ahead. I saw the cake knife flash in her hand.

If I had had time to think it through, I would have grabbed Rick and pulled him to the ground. Or stood up quickly and knocked Jandie off-balance with my chair. What I did instead was yank the lever on the white box.

The beetles swarmed out of the box and spread over the venue like black smoke. It was a great effect, just not for a June wedding.

"No!" Jandie cried as she flailed her arms at the buzzing insects. "The beetles are for AFTER the wedding!"

Rick reached out to calm her, and got his shoulder slashed. Emma climbed over the back of her chair and tackled Jandie. I pulled my sleeve over my hand, reached back, and picked up the knife from the dirt where Jandie had dropped it.

Vernon Broniszewski had not been a strict father. He was a successful insurance salesman who doted on his only daughter, especially after his wife passed. He used his influence in the small community of Agua Dulce, five miles from Sleepy Valley, to get young Janelle out of scrapes and ensure she was never held accountable for her actions. But she wanted to be a professional social media influencer and was enraged when her father failed to support her dream. The breaking point was when he suggested she enroll at College of the Canyons and study something "useful." It was an insult she could not bear.

Jandie (no longer going by the boring old name of Janelle) had kept an eye on stories about Bouquet Reservoir. What a coincidence that it was Uncle Rick who was poking his nose into things! When he turned down the trip to Hawaii, she quickly found an alternate venue right near the reservoir.

The Sleepy Valley Ryokan was better than she could have hoped. Small, well-insulated rooms with bedding on the floor and no locks. Pick a room, push a block of dry ice inside, and shut the door. As it evaporates, the carbon dioxide sinks to the ground and displaces the oxygen.

Only she'd picked the wrong room and Tedd Ladd had died instead.

This unfortunate episode hasn't impeded Jandie's social media career much. She has more followers than ever. On the other hand, she won't be able to launch her online store for another ten to fifteen years.

Emma knows better than to try to set me up with Jonah again. This doesn't stop her from bemoaning the fact that things didn't work out between Jonah and me all those years ago, and speculating how cute (because of Jonah) and smart (my contribution) our children would have been. It's no use reminding her that I already have an adorable toddler, not to mention a husband of whom I am quite fond.

The incident at Sleepy Valley Ryokan made national news, and Rick Redland is under contract to write a book about the Bouquet Reservoir case. He'll be coming to Mahina to get some background, and interview

Emma and me about Jandie Brand and Tedd Ladd, and how we got to know them in the first place.

That could be a whole other book.

About the Author

Like Professor Molly, Frankie Bow works in higher education. Unlike her protagonist, she is blessed with delightful students, sane colleagues, and an adequate office chair. In addition to the Professor Molly mysteries, Frankie writes licensed novellas in Jana DeLeon's Miss Fortune world. Frankie is a lifetime member of Sisters in Crime.

Death Under the Stars

James T. Bartlett

DEATH UNDER THE STARS was the headline in the *Herald & Express*, while the *Examiner* went for DEATH IN THE SPOTLIGHT. My paper, the *Times*, didn't use anything imaginative, but the report began: *Under the curving shell where the great names perform under the moonlit skies . . .*

Very literary. Worthy of a Pulitzer, maybe. What did I know?

But where the hell was my goddamn photo?

I'd thought it was my big break. I got a tip from my (only) contact, jumped in a cab because my car was in the shop (again), and had arrived at the Hollywood Bowl before anyone else.

At the center of the famous stage was the body of a dead man.

He had short black hair and was wearing a suit with a vest but no jacket, and his shirt sleeves were rolled up to the elbow. Looked like he had been singing to the empty seats, and then just laid down and gone to sleep.

"Hey, you! Stay right there!" someone wearing an expensive suit shouted at me. There was a uniformed cop behind him, so I assumed he was a detective.

In the distance I could make out Monty and Bill, but since the detective and the cop were going to intercept them, I only had a minute or two to compose the shot. I stood at the back of the stage and pointed the camera at the rows and rows of wooden benches. They would be in the background, while the body would be in the foreground.

I hesitated, struck for a moment by what I could see through the lens. This was the Hollywood Bowl, after all. I had seen Sinatra here, and lots of classical music concerts too, when I had been trying to impress a girl I met at Schwab's.

I pressed the button: the shot captured the photographers, the cop, and the detective looking at the body like a curious Greek chorus. I chuckled to myself because I knew this was going to make the front page. This was one for my portfolio.

More police arrived, and Monty, Bill, and the other photographers were hustled away before they had taken any shots. They didn't go quietly, as this wasn't the deal: the press and cops were tight in L.A., especially on a juicy callout like this. It had what Monty called "legs," and could run in the paper for a few days. That usually meant everybody got paid. Right down the line.

Not my problem. Without looking back, I ran to Highland and flagged down a cab.

Dusty, the grumpy photo editor at the *Times*, raised a bushy eyebrow when I told him what had happened. I paced up and down while the film was developed—rookies like me don't get to touch the developing equipment—then I heard him shout:

"Go and get a drink, kid. Good job."

I swaggered to the bar like I was the West Coast Weegee, and several beers later someone brought in a copy of that evening's *Times*. Flicking through page after page in disbelief and then anger, I found nothing but a report on the victim, which I didn't even read.

Where the hell was my goddamn photo?

Bill and Monty looked at me sympathetically. "Don't take it to heart, kid. It happens," said Bill, waving to the bartender for another round.

"Yeah. I got page twelve, he was page eleven," Monty added. "You woulda thought it was a given: a dead body at the Hollywood Bowl? Front page, big headline, nice payday."

I stalked to the red telephone hanging outside one of the wooden booths. A clever editor from years ago had it installed here, as he knew freelancers were always nearby, like dogs hanging around a campfire. Not on salary, we were paid by the shot—the published shot.

Maybe it was the beer talking, but the duty news editor told me to come to the office right away. I sobered up real quick as I walked the couple of blocks to the huge *Times* building.

"What's your name?" said the mustachioed news editor, who I had never met.

"I just . . . the photo. The Hollywood Bowl. The dead man."

The mustache reached into a drawer and pulled out a check book. The secretary looked at me and her eyes went wide, like a cartoon owl. Already bored with my existence, mustache flatly said that they "just didn't have the space to run it. It happens."

"Yeah, I've heard that," I said. But mustache was already on the telephone.

"Never seen that before," the secretary whispered to me as I stumbled out of the office with a check in my hand. "You're new, aren't you? What's your name?"

I went back to the bar, because what else was I supposed to do?

"And?" asked Monty.

"It happens," I said, and they nodded in understanding.

"Told you," said Bill.

I didn't mention the check, because two hundred dollars was more money than I'd seen in a long time. My rent was due, and the electricity, and the gas, and the car. Two hundred dollars was a good day, but I was confused. My photo had been spiked, despite the other papers running ones that couldn't have been as good. What the hell?

Bill began reading the report out loud. The dead man's name was Otis Leery; he was thirty-nine, and police had determined it was suicide.

"You woulda thought he was an actor, going out like that," said Monty.

"Close enough," said Bill. "He was an interior decorator. And he wasn't married."

He wolf whistled, and I looked around for a blonde or redhead. Bill wasn't subtle about that kind of thing. But the bar was dark and quiet. Monty rolled his eyes.

"One more for Monty," I shouted to the bartender, putting some coins down on the table. "You can get your own," I hissed at Bill, snatching his newspaper from him as I went.

"What? It was a joke!" he protested.

I didn't laugh. Two hundred dollars in my wallet, but I wasn't in the mood.

I walked a few blocks to clear my head and ended up at one of my favorite places: Angels Flight. On the first day I arrived in L.A., and then every time I came downtown, I took a ride on the silly orange train. Always cheered me up.

"Cheapest ride in town!" I said to a girl I took there one night. She worked for the entertainment section of the paper, and, as I found out, went to lots of swank nightclubs—which is probably why she found my funicular jaunt less than charming. Her face certainly said that, anyhow. It was our only date.

A minute or so of creaking wood, clanging bells, and whining cables later, I realized I still had Bill's newspaper clenched in my fist. I was about to throw it in the trash when I saw his photo that they had published.

It showed Leery's body in a completely different position.

In my photograph, Leery's arms were bent at the elbow, resting on his chest like he had been playing Tarzan, or was ready for his coffin. But in Bill's, his arms were splayed out beside him.

But that was nothing.

In Bill's picture, there was a gun right beside Leery's head. Classic suicide, like the police said.

But I hadn't seen any gun.

That meant that the crime scene must have been tampered with. That Leery might even have been murdered, but it was made to look like a suicide. Was that why they didn't run my photo?

I made straight for the *Times* building, but Dusty wasn't there.

"Vacation. Catalina Island, then Mexico. Lucky bastard," said his grizzled replacement.

"Must be nice," I replied, as I scanned the room to see where Dusty had put my photos. Usually they would be all laid out in sequence, but not this time.

Then I spotted them on a desk that was just too close by, so I made small talk until I could tell I was getting in the way.

With just a splash of coffee in a paper cup—I didn't want to ruin anything—I "accidentally" spilled it. Sure enough I was smartly told to get lost. Which I did, with the photographs now under my arm, wrapped inside Bill's wrinkly newspaper. I walked out apologizing and looking about as confident as I did not feel.

I took the trolley back to my hovel in Hollywood and compared the photos. It suddenly seemed to have gotten quiet everywhere, and even my broken fan stopped clicking.

Should I go to the cops? No. What if they were involved? That detective surely saw my face. And that cop. The *Times*? No. The papers here happily show murder victims cut in half, or add arrows showing where someone jumped from the top floor of a fancy hotel. They'd spiked the photo, simple as that, and still paid me. It would look like sour grapes.

And if I was wrong, it would kill my reputation—such as it wasn't. I'd be a joke. And what about that two hundred dollars? Some might say that was a payoff. I'm new in town, and the L.A. papers are vicious rivals. The freelancers too. Monty and Bill have been kind to me, but they didn't look happy that I got the jump on them at the Bowl.

Maybe I should forget about it. It wouldn't bring Leery back, anyhow.

I sat down and read the report again. The last man to see Leery was a friend of his named Harry Ford, who told police that Leery had seemed depressed, but still insisted nothing was wrong. Leery's sister, Doreena, was mentioned too, but she had no explanation for what had happened either.

Nevertheless, the scandal-hungry anonymous reporter did speculate about what might have been behind the suicide: Leery had won eighty-five hundred dollars on the Irish Sweepstakes a few years ago but had "come up short this year."

That was a chunk of change. Not quit-your-job money, but definitely a first-class cabin on the Queen Mary. Had he spent it all, or did he have a gambling problem? The suicide story certainly made sense if that was true.

But my photo didn't tell that story.

I reached into the fridge, scrabbling for a beer, and banged my head on the chilly door when the telephone rang. It was late, but tips came in at all hours, and I was glad to hear Bill's voice—at least for a couple of seconds.

"The police have been asking about you," he said gruffly, and hung up.

I was chilled, and not just from the beer and the open fridge. Then I remembered I had ragged on Bill in the bar earlier. Maybe he was playing a prank on me.

I looked again at the two photos. If my photo did prove that Leery had been murdered, or even that the body had been moved, it was evidence.

And I had kind of stolen it.

Harry Ford's eastside address had been in the report, and so I drove to his house, even though it was late. His mailbox had a few letters in it, including one from the Irish Sweepstakes, so I took them to the door. As the last person to see Leery alive, the cops would have put him through the wringer—hence the swollen lip and busted nose, which made his Irish brogue even harder to understand.

He worked at Paramount, and said he and Leery met at Santa Anita, but were just "track friends." He seemed sorry that Leery was dead and said that Leery's luck had been "up and down, like 'tis for all us guys," though he "'ad bin on a bit of a bad streak lately. Shame. Can I help yous with anythin' else?"

My final roll of the dice was seeking out Doreena, Leery's sister, but that would have to wait until morning. It was going to be a tough knock. I'm no reporter, no whizz with the ladies either, and she had just lost her brother. How is suicide better than murder?

With nothing but coffee for breakfast, I arrived at her house in Hancock Park as early as I dared.

I introduced myself as Bill Monty from the *Times*, which was only half a lie, and tried to fend off a small dog that wouldn't stop yapping. Judging by the noise there were at least two children in one of the many rooms, and she ordered them to call the dog. Mercifully, it went without a bark.

For a moment she didn't seem convinced by my story about an obituary, but when I tried to distract her by saying she had a beautiful home, tears came to her eyes. It happened so quickly, I thought it was a trick of the light.

"Otis helped me with all of this," she said, gesturing around her. "Please take your shoes off, and come in. Would you like some coffee?"

No, I wouldn't.

"Yes, I would, thank you."

A uniformed maid brought in the coffee, and Doreena talked about her late brother.

They had been close, especially in recent months when—she flushed slightly—she and her husband had been having "difficulties." I had noticed there were no big shoes or boots in the hallway. No men's coats on the hooks, either. I glanced at the pictures on the mantel. City Hall was in a couple of them, and it was clear he was someone "important."

Back in the day Leery had been a promising actor, Doreena said with a smile. He had married an actress, but she left him after just six months—for another actor.

"You know what they're like," she said to me. I smiled as if I did.

"He never went back on stage after that, though I knew he missed it."

Since the report had mentioned the Sweepstakes, I felt I could bring it up.

She said Leery had been generous in his good fortune and had bought the dog for his niece and nephew—a bark nearby seemed to confirm this, and we laughed. "But I think he liked to gamble, sometimes. What man doesn't? But he would never have . . ." she paused, "done that. What they said in the paper."

If I was going to say something, this was the moment.

"And those photographs! There for anybody to stare at like a country bumpkin, or a cheap gawker! Then wrapped round tomorrow's potato scrapings and thrown in the trash!"

I glanced at the doorway, and the children were standing there, the dog at their feet. They looked like they had just found out Santa Claus wasn't real.

"Go and play, please. Mummy's just a little upset. This nice man is a friend of Uncle Otis."

"Yes, Mummy," replied one of them, and disappeared. "When is Uncle Otis coming to visit?" the younger one asked me.

For once I was grateful the dog started yapping.

"The last time I saw him, I asked if he owed money to, well, people who weren't exactly Main Street bankers," Doreena said, dabbing at her eyes and swiping any out-of-place mascara off her cheeks. "He laughed and told me he was about to get a new job. At one of the studios, I think."

I thought of Harry Ford and his job at Paramount. Or maybe it was a job at another big venue in Hollywood?

Instead of driving home, I went back to the Bowl. As I had thought, it would be easy for anyone to get inside. Hop over a fence, or get your hands and knees dirty and scramble up the hillside.

"The box office ain't open until May. Come back then," said an elderly Black man with a bunch of keys on his belt as big as the head of a small child.

"I'm a reporter from the *Times*," I lied again. "My name's Monty Bill. I was told you know all about the secret tunnel under Hollywood Boulevard."

Angels Flight girl had told me about that rumor on our date, and thank god I had just remembered it. But his face was like Buster Keaton. Then he rolled his eyes and laughed.

"Porter Johnson," he said, "but everyone calls me 'Keys.'"

He took me to a small hut that was almost hidden in the bushes and told me several stories.

"I seen raccoons on the stage. A fox too, one night. Came right on stage, dandy as you please, sat behind the pianist. The tuxedo thought the applause was for him!"

He paused for a moment, and on cue, a coyote howled somewhere far away. At least I hoped it was far away.

"A bad business, that poor man who kilt himself," said Keys. "I've chased plenty of kids out of here, some adults up to no good too, but nothing like that."

A three-legged tortoise could have outrun Keys, and while he may have taken a few backhanders to spice up a boring and lonely job, I was sure he wasn't involved in the murder. And I was calling it a murder now, at least in my head. He wasn't on duty that night, anyhow.

After talking to Keys, I called Ford's apartment. The landlord told me he had skipped out on his rent, and probably left town.

Not that I wanted to, but now I'd sort of put it together, and I had no options left.

I had to become a traitor.

In an office off the deserted newsroom, I told the *Examiner*'s managing editor what I thought had happened. His face remained stoic at first, but when he started nodding and shifting in his chair, I knew he was interested. That this really was going to be my front page.

"It wouldn't have been hard to get Leery to agree to meet someone at the Bowl, perhaps on the pretext of a possible job," I began. "Anyhow, for an ex-actor like him, it would have been a thrill stepping out on that stage."

I knew that was true because I had felt it when I was there. Even just in the seats, when I was watching Sinatra.

"Ford and Leery both played the Irish Sweepstakes," I continued.

Used to fund the building of hospitals back in the good old Emerald Isle, it was a straight lottery, which meant your chances of winning were as good as finding me awake before six a.m. I'd heard that the money really went to rebel soldiers fighting the English, something that went way over my head, but the rumor that it was a mob operation rang true.

"Collect the cash from misty-eyed ex-pats who never expect to win, and then fix the draw so that someone like Leery or Ford gets lucky. Not that they win the main prize, that's too obvious. But a few grand, here and there. The lucky 'winners' already owe you of course, so the cash comes straight back."

"Or else," he chipped in.

"Or else. A simple cake and eat it scam, unless someone spends all the money on losing horses."

Or a yapping dog that loves the kids.

"I don't know who met Leery at the Bowl, or what gang he was from. Maybe it was Ford, but I doubt it. That's for the cops to work out anyhow."

Now the managing editor added some details. He told me that the cops and the mob were at each other's throats, more than anyone knew, and that the cops were close to blowing open the Sweepstakes scam. Had promised him the scoop when it happened.

"They found Leery's jacket later," he told me. "It had a Sweepstakes ticket in the pocket. They were keeping that information back."

"Maybe Leery asked to 'win' the Sweepstakes again, and threatened them when they said no. So they decided to make an example of him," I wondered. "And what better place than on the stage at the Hollywood Bowl? That would make all the papers and send a hell of a message. But the cops couldn't allow that to happen, could they?"

"No," said the managing editor. "So they stick a gun beside the poor sap, and it's suicide. Front page to page eleven. It happens all the time."

I thought of Doreena, and her children, and even that damn dog. Otis Leery wasn't a poor sap.

"Where's the picture?" he said, holding out his hand.

I handed it over, and he looked at it for several moments.

"He was actually raising his hands in surrender, or pleading for mercy," I said.

I left the newsroom that night with a five-year contract in the photography department—at the New York office of the *Examiner*. Freelance or not, giving a story to a rival newspaper was always a betrayal. I couldn't go back to the *Times*, ever.

"There's a midnight plane to Idlewild. I'd be on it if I were you," said the managing editor, reaching for the telephone.

I sold my car at a garage near Los Angeles Airport, then waited it out in the echoingly quiet terminal. Just as they were calling my flight, I heard the thump of a bundle of newspapers hitting the floor outside a kiosk. I told the gate attendant to wait and fumbled for ten cents.

Where the hell was my goddamn photo?

About the Author

Journalist James T. Bartlett has written for over 130 publications including the *Los Angeles Times*, BBC, *Westways*, *American Way*, *Hemispheres*, *Crime Reads*, *Real Crime*, *ALTA California*, *Atlas Obscura*, and others.

His latest true crime book, *The Alaskan Blonde: Sex, Secrets, and the Hollywood Story that Shocked America*, is available now.

Mystery in MB

Laurie Fagen

CHAPTER 1

STILL SWEATING FROM THE brutal Zumba class led by a tall, athletic Brazilian woman who gave heavily accented instructions—the "steep left, touch da floor, sving back, keeck right" was especially tough—Katherine dabbed her neck and face with a Manhattan Beach Fitness towel, careful not to scrape herself with the pinned-on key.

She opened her locker, found her cell inside the gym bag, and did a quick scan, checking for text or voice mail messages.

Those two can wait, she thought. She saw an email address she didn't recognize but tossed the mobile back in and closed the door.

As she walked toward the equipment room, she did a double take. *Is that Tom Hanks? Oh my gosh, it is—doing the shoulder press! Maybe I could get my script to him.* Katherine tried not to stare as she put her water bottle and towel near the bicep curl apparatus.

She did a few rounds on the upper-arm machines, where a great-looking guy with wavy blond hair and a killer smile was subtly flirting with her. She smiled pleasantly—until she spotted his wedding ring. She thought of her boyfriend in Phoenix, and immediately felt guilty. She had only been in California three weeks, but she did miss him.

She took a swig of water and looked around for her towel, not finding it. *Eww, did someone else pick up that sweaty thing?* she wondered. *Oh wait, it has my key on it!*

Katherine searched for a moment, then ran back to the women's room. In the middle of the floor, not far from her locker, was a towel—with her key, unpinned, sitting loose on top.

She picked it up and cautiously unlocked her storage compartment. She pulled out her duffel, and touched her phone, wallet, hairbrush, makeup pouch. *Everything's here.* Sighing with relief, she shook her head. *Someone just got the wrong towel*, she mused. *Don't be paranoid.*

She swung her bag over her shoulder and headed out, tossing the damp cloth in the circular bin at the door of the ladies' locker room. She continued into the all-glass lobby with its shiny metal and chartreuse chairs and small round tables scattered appropriately around a juice bar. She paused at the front desk on her way to the exit.

"Hey, when are you guys going to get electronic locks?"

"Uh, we're working on it!" said one of the young attendants. "Hey, anyone ever say you kinda look like Reese Witherspoon?"

"Oh, wow, I'm flattered. See you later."

"Thanks for coming in."

Katherine waved goodbye.

In the parking lot, keys in hand, she clicked open her car door with the key fob. Hearing footsteps, she glanced around behind her—but didn't see anyone.

Great, now I'm imagining things. She was more disgusted than upset. She slid into her blue Toyota sedan with Arizona plates and the engine started with a soft hum. While she knew the doors would lock automatically at about nine miles an hour, she gave the inside latch a tap and the satisfying *click* made her feel more secure.

The young woman threw her leg over the seat of the pink Vespa and turned the key.

As she sped out of the Manhattan Beach Fitness parking lot, her brown, shoulder-length hair whipped behind her, free of a helmet.

CHAPTER 2

Katherine juggled the grocery store sacks, her gym bag, a Salon Star container of hair products, and her keys as she struggled up the short flight of eight wooden stairs to her rental condo.

Her cell phone jingled with Taylor Swift's "Message in a Bottle," and she hurried the last couple of steps, opening the door and relieving her arms of their load onto the bar. She grabbed her pink-colored mobile, looked curiously at the *Unknown* flashing caller ID, but punched the answer button anyway.

"Hello?" she huffed, picking up a bag of groceries to take to the fridge. When only silence greeted her, she said again, "Hello, this is Katherine," and waited. There was a *click* as the phone disconnected.

Hmmm, must've been a wrong number, Katherine thought. *Third one this week . . .*

She pressed the call return code, but nothing came up. Katherine opened the fridge door and put away the salmon, yogurt, and coconut milk.

She glanced in a mirror at her freshly coiffed blond hair, fluffing it out a bit, and placed her Salon Star mousse and hair spray on the bathroom counter. Still panting from the exertion up the stairs, she dug in her purse to find a blue bronchodilator, inhaled a deep puff of her asthma medicine and poured a glass of wine.

Her cell phone rang again with Taylor Swift singing. She smiled when she saw her son's face.

"Hi sweetheart, how are you?" she purred, taking a sip of her drink, her breathing more under control.

"Fine, Mom, how are you feeling?" asked Jason. A freshman at Arizona State University, he was her life since the divorce from his father six years ago.

"I'm good," she replied. "My asthma isn't as bad here. And I'm getting lots of writing done."

They talked a few more minutes, she telling about her latest screenplay scenes, he relating his recent test score. "Congratulations on your good grade!" Katherine said proudly.

They hung up and Katherine lifted the window on the wall opposite the front door to help with the airflow. She sat at the desk and opened the laptop computer lid. She started to tap a few keys.

The noise of the gate opening below caught her attention through the open door. She looked at her watch: 2:30 p.m. Her landlady, a fifty-something woman, should be at work. Katherine got up and peered out the entrance.

If she was coming in, she'd be at the foot of her steps by now. No one. Katherine went to the street side of the porch and looked over.

If she was going out, she'd be . . .

But no one was there, either.

Katherine checked around again, but seeing nothing, went back inside, closing and locking her door.

Putting down the kickstand of her small motorbike, the young woman headed into Salon Star.

She showed a small wad of golden blond hair to the receptionist, who led her back to a stylist's chair.

CHAPTER 3

The great expanse of the beige sand of Manhattan Beach, or "MB" as the locals referred to it, stretched for miles on either side, and ahead, gentle waves lapped at the shore.

It was an overcast Saturday, but several large, bright umbrellas dotted the strand with color. Some kids threw Frisbees, others splashed at the edge of the water and four young men played an intense volleyball game on one of the many nets along the beach.

Katherine loved walking along the sidewalk next to the sea, enjoying the cool, moist air. With her hair pulled back into a ponytail and a cup of hot coffee in her hand, she shared the concrete path with fat-tired bicycles, some with speed gears, some not. A few of the bikes carried tourists, who wheeled slowly along, with no particular agenda, and others transported residents obviously in a hurry to get somewhere. Occasionally, a serious rider went by on a ten-speed, sporting racing shorts and a helmet with a water jug on his back.

Katherine admired the thick vegetation along the walkway. Green agave plants, with dense four-foot arms, edged with yellow and ending in a sharp point, reached to the sky, their thorny sides warning intruders to stay back. Fuchsia flowers popped out among the dark emerald ice plant, and Katherine stopped to feel the silky blooms.

When she stood up, she had the odd feeling that someone was watching her.

Katherine looked around. She was nearly encircled by multi-million-dollar beach houses and windows galore but saw no one other than a mom pushing a baby stroller a block away, going in the opposite direction.

You have been by yourself too long! she scolded, shaking her head. She started walking back to the condo.

A pair of binoculars covered the young woman's face.

She lowered the magnifying lenses, cocked her head to the side, and smiled. Her now blond hair, pulled back into a ponytail, bounced playfully as she stepped away from the green hedge.

CHAPTER 4

". . . I miss you, too. When can you come out?"

Katherine was in her favorite position, propped up on her bed with three fluffy pillows on top of the thick, down spread. A Bluetooth headset in her ear, the pink cell phone rested in sharp contrast against the white covering. She checked email on the computer while talking to her boyfriend, Donald.

"I've got to finish this latest project, then I have a meeting with another client next week," Donald told her. "It's going to be at least another couple of weeks before I can get away."

"Rats," Katherine replied. "My breathing is better here, and I'm finishing Act II in my script. There's something about the energy here in L.A. . . . But I'm going a little crazy out here without you. Just yesterday—"

A beep in her earpiece interrupted Katherine, who felt around the bed to grab the phone.

"Hold on, I've got another call," she told Donald, looking at the glass front of the phone. *Unknown* was flashing. She frowned. "I'll be right back."

Katherine pressed the incoming call button and said "Hello?" But again, no one was on the other end. "Hello? Who is this?" she said more urgently. Still nothing. "Either say something or stop calling!"

The phone clicked as the other person disconnected.

Katherine's breathing grew heavy, her asthma triggered by the stress. She punched the phone to retrieve Donald's call.

"Damn it," she huffed. "It happened . . . again," she said through short breaths.

"What happened? And it sounds like you're having an asthma attack."

"I'm . . . okay," Katherine panted, digging through her purse for her inhaler. "It's . . . another . . . crank call," she told him.

"Stop and take your albuterol," Donald said firmly.

Katherine, getting more frantic, continued to search for the small blue breathing device. "I . . . can't find . . . it . . . anywhere!"

Katherine's breathing was coming in shallow gasps, accompanied by deep coughs.

"Katherine, did you locate it?" Donald asked, alarmed.

"No! It's . . . not in . . . my purse!" she wheezed, her eyes wide with fear.

"Now, try to relax," Donald instructed. "Do you have another by the bed? Or maybe in the bathroom? Go look."

Katherine doubled over with a coughing spell, not able to catch her breath. She quickly rustled through a bedside drawer but came up empty. Still breathing in short inhalations but now with a choking sound, she made her way to the bathroom and opened two more drawers before finally finding an extra inhaler. She put it to her mouth, pressed the container to shoot the medication into her lungs, and took in a deep inhalation. She waited a couple of seconds and took another puff. Her breathing began to slow.

"Oh . . . my god . . . that was . . ." she started to say.

"Honey, are you all right?!" Donald was relieved to hear her voice back on the phone.

"Yes . . . I'm better . . . Just give me . . . a minute." Katherine lay back down on her bed.

"What were you talking about . . . another crank call?" Donald asked.

"Oh, it's probably . . . nothing. Only my imagination," she dismissed, her breaths now coming in slower and deeper. "I . . . wish you were here."

At an internet café, the young woman was seated at a computer, her blond hair falling loose around her shoulders as she typed.

Her favorite actress in the whole wide world was Reese Witherspoon, ever since she played that adorable tomboy in "The Man in the Moon" movie. Katherine looked exactly like her, so she was just as good as the real thing.

The woman stopped, read what was on the screen, grinned, and pressed send. She reached her hand up to the computer monitor and gently stroked the flat surface. Katherine's face, in a photo from her Facebook account, smiled back. To the side of the keyboard sat a blue inhaler.

CHAPTER 5

A knock at Katherine's condo door startled her.

She was deep into her screenplay and wasn't expecting anyone. She got up, peered nervously through the curtain where a floral deliveryman was holding a vase of multicolored flowers.

For goodness' sake, get a grip already, she told herself as she opened the door.

"Katherine Koldare?" the man read from a receipt.

"Yes, that's me." Katherine smiled, taking the beautiful bouquet from the man's arms and sniffing the fragrance. "Probably from my boyfriend." She didn't understand why he had such a puzzled look on his face as he looked back down at the paper. "Wait here a minute," she told him.

Katherine put the vase on the bar inside the door and dug in her purse, turned back and handed the man a five-dollar tip. "Thanks so much!"

"'Preciate it, ma'am," he said as he went down the steps.

Katherine closed the door behind her, and eagerly reached for the small envelope wedged on a plastic stick in the flowers. As she pulled out the card, her broad smile quickly faded into a look of fright. She dropped the note as if it burned her fingers.

"I think someone is stalking me."

Katherine rubbed her hands nervously. She sat in the Manhattan Beach Police Department, across from a weary-looking officer in a cheap suit. Joe Blanken, a balding man in his forties, looked up at her from his computer with indifference.

"Now just what makes ya think that, Miss, er, Koldare?" he asked, glancing at the screen where he had taken her basic information. He looked back at her, squinting his eyes. "Ya know, you kinda look like that actress, ya know . . ."

"Reese Witherspoon? Yeah. Look, it started with . . . I mean I've been getting a few phone calls but no one is there . . ." she started.

"Wrong number?" the officer offered.

"I don't think so. When I ask who it is, the person always waits for a few seconds, then hangs up."

"I see," Blanken said, unimpressed. "What else?"

"Maybe I just misplaced my inhaler, but then I found an email in my junk file from 'MB cutie,'" Katherine explained. "I figured it was spam. But when I opened it, it only had a photo of me from my Facebook account in it. No signature, no message."

"Oh, that online crap," Blanken said, shaking his head. "Biggest invasion of privacy an' the most insecure piece of junk, not to mention a gigantic waste of time. Is that all ya got?" The detective seemed anxious to dismiss Katherine and get on with his coffee break. He eyed a pink-frosted donut sitting on a napkin next to his mug.

"No, there's something else."

Katherine pulled the floral card from her purse and handed it to Blanken.

"Oh, brother." He sighed, turning to his keyboard to input more details.

CHAPTER 6

"So, what we got here is probably a case of 'simple obsession,'" Detective Blanken told a nervous Katherine as he wiped frosting off his chin.

"Happens to a lot of celebrities out here. Usually, it's someone of the opposite sex who is immature, maybe socially incompetent, unable to maintain a regular relationship—some guy with real low self-esteem. Sometimes the perp can be schizophrenic, bipolar, delusional, or have OCD."

"Oh, my gosh," Katherine whispered. "I don't know who that could possibly be. Besides, I'm nobody famous. I live in Phoenix. I'm just here for a few months, to do some writing and get out of the dusty air because of my asthma."

"Huh. I thought Arizona was the best place to be for breathin' problems." He paused. "Thing is, there's not much we can do other than take a report and give you some advice. I s'pose you got a few favorite places you frequent in MB?"

"Well, I go to a yoga studio two times a week, and MB Fitness about every day. I walk to the little coffee shop on the Strand and the market on Fifth Street."

"Yeah, well, you're gonna have to change a few things about what ya do, where ya go. No more posting that you're goin' for a workout or havin' a fancy latte anymore." He took a slurp from his mug. "Most likely it's someone who has seen you at one of those locations and is smitten with you. Maybe he—or she—has mistaken you for that blond actress. But as long as your place hasn't been broken into, or no one's taken a shot at ya . . ."

Katherine's eyed widened in shock.

"What I mean to say, that piece of blond hair taped to the florist's card and *You are my life!* is a doozie, but it ain't a crime. Thing is . . . it looks like a woman's handwriting, not a man's."

CHAPTER 7

Katherine stopped in her tracks when she reached the top of the stairs to her condo.

There, on the welcome mat, was a red rose. But attached to the stem with a satin ribbon was a dead mouse.

Just calm down, and remember what the detective said, Katherine repeated over and over to herself. She gingerly picked up the flower and rodent, then placed the mouse in a plastic baggie. *Document everything in the journal. Write it down. You can do this.*

She got out a small book with a ring binder and flipped a few pages in, skimming over the information already logged.

July 22, 4:30 p.m. she wrote. *Found a long-stemmed red rose on my doorstep after speaking to Manhattan Beach police. A dead mouse was tied to the flower with a pink ribbon. Placed in bag to give to Blanken.*

She checked her email. Nothing from the stalker. She looked at her cell's voice mail. Likewise, nothing. She was putting the phone down when it chirped in her hand, indicating the arrival of a text message. In her alarm, she dropped the mobile on the floor.

"Shoot," she said out loud. She started to reach for the cell, but hesitated. *Is that her?* she thought. *Do not engage, Blanken said, just document.*

She warily picked up her phone, unlocked the home page and flicked her finger down the screen to open the text.

Dear Katherine, did u get my present? Hope u like it!!

It was followed by a happy face with sunglasses on and came from an actual phone number.

"You are so creepy!" she yelled at the phone. *But that number is something concrete I can give to Detective Blanken.* Katherine wrote the information in her book.

CHAPTER 8

"Sorry to break the bad news," the detective said, "but that was a phone with a caller ID spoof.'"

Blanken cracked open a peanut, popped the nuts into his mouth and tossed the shell in the wastebasket. Remnants of other shells scattered the floor where he had obviously missed on previous tries.

"Spoof? What's that?"

"Well, there are dozens of companies out there where you can set up a phony caller ID—both for outgoing and incoming phone calls. You can do it on texts, you can add background noises—like to pretend you're at a bar or a ballgame—and you can even change the sound of your voice," he explained. "It's legit, and supposedly for fun, but the bad guys got ahold of it and are using it for fraud." He cracked open another shell from a sack on his desk.

"What do I do next?!" Katherine exclaimed. "I've changed my cell number, I've changed my passwords, I've changed my whole schedule! This has got to stop! How do I make her quit?"

Katherine's breathing was becoming fast and shallow.

"Hey, you okay?" Detective Blanken said with concern.

Just relax, Katherine told herself, closing her eyes. *Everything will be all right.* Katherine reached into her purse and pulled out an inhaler. She put it to her mouth, pressed, and breathed deeply.

"It's my asthma, but I'll be fine," she told the officer. "You have to tell me what I can do."

"Until we find out who this whack job is, there's nothing much either of us can do—except wait for her to make a mistake so we can catch her. Even if we determine who she is, taking out a restraining order is an option, but most times that just makes the stalker angry. If we ever find and convict her, the court can make her wear a GPS ankle bracelet, so we're able to track the person twenty-four seven."

He tossed more peanut shells toward the trash.

"'Til then," he continued, "keep your eyes open and your wits about you," he said. "Oh, and tell yer landlady to buy a padlock for that yard gate."

The young woman at the internet café computer was becoming agitated.

She would send an email message, but a few seconds later, a *ping* sound noted that the email bounced back. She tried texting, but it, too, was returned unsent. She typed in facebook.com, then Katherine's name, but the search came up empty. She got up in a huff, and in her anger, knocked over the chair as she left. Café patrons glanced her way in disgust.

CHAPTER 9

Katherine threw gym clothes into her bag and thought, *I'm NOT going to let that woman change my whole life!*

It was seven a.m., and while she normally didn't work out until later in the day, Katherine was bound and determined to take an exercise class—especially considering she had missed several over the last week by meeting with police, keeping a journal, and altering all her personal contact information.

Katherine observed all around her porch and stairs, then locked up the condo and ran down through the garage and into her car. She scrutinized everyone she saw on the street—from a landscaping crew to an older man walking his poodle to a young woman jogging. She kept an eye in the rearview mirror in case she was being followed and drove far out of her way to the gym.

Once in the workout facility's parking lot, she got out her cell, punched a speed dial, and waited.

"Hi, Billy, it's Katherine. Would you mind coming out to my car to walk me in?" she asked. She listened for a moment, then added, "Nope, nothing new on the stalker, thanks," and hung up, putting the phone in her bag.

Within seconds, a thin young man with a bad complexion met Katherine. She locked the car and went in with him. He swiped her membership card and handed her a towel. "Hope they find something soon."

"Me, too."

Still with her dark sunglasses on, she continued into the women's dressing room, all the while glancing nervously around her. *I hate looking over my shoulder all the time.* Katherine selected a different locker and stored her belongings. She took a puff of her inhaler, secured the door, pinned the key on her shirt, and headed to Zumba.

Today's class was mostly filled with women who already had amazing bodies, Katherine noted. There was a Lakers' cheerleader, another dancer prepping for a theater audition and a B-list actress along with the other not-so-famous types. A few guys rounded out the attendees, but the estrogen definitely floated around the square, mirrored room.

"Let's do zee salsa!" the Zumba teacher shouted into her headset microphone. "*Uma, duas, tres e quatro* . . . One and two, t'ree and four!"

The class tried to keep up with her as she effortlessly danced to the music.

"That's eet! Keep eet going!"

Katherine, getting a little winded, stopped to rest, her hands on her knees. As she looked down, a reflection in the mirror caught her attention. It was a young blonde, staring angrily at her. Katherine turned to face the woman, but she was gone.

CHAPTER 10

Katherine grabbed her water jug and towel and rushed out the door as the pounding music continued. She looked all around, but didn't spot the woman again.

Was that her? Does she work out here, too? Katherine thought incredulously. *I've got to call the police.*

She ran to her locker, stuck in the key, and reached in the bag for her cell phone. But it was missing. *I know I put it right here,* she thought, puzzled. She dug around wildly, not able to locate it. She suddenly realized that her stalker might actually be employed at MB Fitness.

Katherine took all her belongings and rushed to the front desk.

"Billy, can I use your phone? My cell is missing," she said breathlessly.

"Uh, sure, come on around," Billy said.

Katherine dialed the Manhattan Beach Police Department and asked for Detective Blanken. When he got on the line, her words came fast and were none too coherent.

"Hold on, missy, slow down there," Blanken interrupted. "Are you saying you saw the stalker?"

"Yes, I think so. Well, I don't really know for sure, but she was staring at me and looking furious . . . and I think she might work here at the fitness club, because I went to my locker to get my phone to call you but it was gone and I know I left it in the same spot after I called Billy earlier, and so I had to come to the front desk to call and—"

"But do you see her now?" the detective asked.

Katherine looked cautiously around the lobby, and into the weight room as far as she could.

"Well, no, not at the moment, but if you come down here right away, maybe you can catch her!" Katherine shouted.

"Now, Miss Koldare, we can't arrest anyone for looking at you. If we find out she got access to your locker and stole your cell phone, then that's another story."

"But Detective—I'm scared to death!"

"I know, I know." He sighed. "Okay, I'll send someone down to look around. Meanwhile, you just calm down."

CHAPTER 11

The thirty-something female police officer, who looked like she was a fitness fanatic with her bulging, muscular thighs stretching her uniform's pants, left her partner, a tall Black male, in the lobby.

She accompanied Katherine to the women's area and to the locker she had just used. The name tag on her shirt read Lieutenant Hutchins.

"Hmm, doesn't look like any forced entry," Hutchins remarked, writing in her notebook. She looked around, stopped, and bent down, reaching under the lockers. Her hand came up with Katherine's pink cell phone.

"This it?" Hutchins asked a disbelieving Katherine.

"But it can't be . . . I know I didn't . . ." Her voice trailed off.

"It could've fallen out," Hutchins noted.

"You don't believe me." Katherine looked down at her hands.

"Or our perpetrator might have accessed your locker with a master key, got your cell number, then placed it here to make it look like you dropped it."

Katherine sighed with relief.

"I'll go talk to the manager, get a list of all employees and see what we can find out."

"Thank you," Katherine told her with a weak smile.

Katherine stared at about a dozen photos of the female workers at the club, trying to picture them with blond hair.

"I can't be sure," Katherine told Lieutenant Hutchins. "It was just a second, then she was gone."

Hutchins turned to the manager, a short buff man in his thirties who looked like he once was a wrestler. His name tag read Jeff. "You certain this is all of them?" Hutchins asked. "Any chance a new employee might not be in the records yet?"

"Well, photos are one of the first things we take of all new team members," Jeff replied. He punched a few keys on his computer's keyboard and two more names and photos came on the screen.

"Oh, here are two more who just started with—"

"That's her! That's the one!" Katherine yelled, pointing at a young blond-haired woman smiling sweetly at the camera. Under her picture was the name Pamela M. Sellers.

"You sure, ma'am? I interviewed this girl myself. Very sweet, eager to learn, willing to do anything. We started her as a locker room attendant . . ." His voice got softer, realizing.

"So, it's possible—" Hutchins started.

A shrill scream cut her off, echoing through the facility. "Help! Back here!"

CHAPTER 12

"What the—?" Hutchins ran toward the scream.

A woman in workout gear, who had blood dripping down her cheek, was being helped out of the ladies' area by an MB worker. The woman was holding her head and moaning.

"I found her lying on the locker room floor!" the employee said.

"Someone pushed me from behind . . . hard," the other said. "Then she ran. I caught a glimpse of her. She was blond and wearing a staff shirt."

"Lock the building down, now!" Hutchins shouted, waving to her partner. "Peters, you take the back exit, I'll cover the front. No one goes in or out! Print out that photo!" she directed to the manager.

Hutchins talked into her radio, attached to the top front of her shirt. "Ten-78 at Manhattan Beach Fitness, 80 North Sepulveda, tracking possible 10-66 in stalker case, 10-18."

A number of club members had gathered around the front desk.

"Hey, what's going on?" one said. "How come we can't leave?" asked another. "You can't keep me here without a warrant," still another one shouted.

"Now calm down, everyone," Hutchins said. "We are looking for this woman. Anybody see her today?"

The crowd pressed forward, looking at the photo of Pamela Sellers. "Hey, she's pretty hot," mugged one man, and others laughed with him.

"This is serious business, folks." Hutchins eyed the man sternly.

"Officer, I think I remember her," said an older woman, dressed in a baggy T-shirt and sweatpants. "She was in the locker room earlier, putting towels on the shelves."

"Great, let me get some more information." Hutchins took the woman aside.

Katherine sat down wearily on the nearest chair. Billy came over to her.

"You okay, Katherine?" he asked gently.

"Yes, I'm fine, just . . . stunned that this is happening to me. I mean, I live a quiet and peaceful life. I've never had anything like this happen." Katherine burst into tears, partly from fear and nerves.

Billy cautiously put his arm around her shoulder. "Hey, it's okay, it will be all right. The police will take care of it."

Two squad cars raced up to the entrance, lights flashing and sirens wailing. Four officers ran out, with two heading toward the back of the club, and the other pair coming inside.

"Split up," Hutchins ordered, holding up Pamela's photo. "Our 10-66 is a white female, blond hair, about five foot, two inches. Just started working here five days ago. She was seen here in the past thirty minutes. Find her!"

CHAPTER 13

An hour later and the police officers were calmly conferring with each other, preparing to wrap up their investigation.

The MB Fitness clients detained earlier had been allowed to leave. Others trying to enter for their workout were turned away "for security purposes."

The club was nearly empty except for Hutchins, Katherine, and a few front desk personnel.

"Sorry she managed to evade us," Hutchins said to a dejected Katherine. "But she also knows we're onto her. You have to be even more careful now."

Katherine nodded wearily.

"Look, I think we should put a detail on you, at least for tonight," the officer continued. "Things may escalate."

"What do you mean, 'escalate'?" Katherine asked cautiously.

"Well, she's been playing this little game her way, keeping you at arm's length, running the show," Hutchins explained. "What's the first instinct that kicks in when an animal gets trapped? They lash out. She may realize you've changed the rules and if she's no longer in control, she may become more irate. Who knows what she might do."

Hutchins paused after what was a statement, not a question. She nodded to her partner to take off.

"Come on, I'll follow you home," she told Katherine.

Katherine knew immediately something was wrong.

She and Lieutenant Hutchins were coming around the corner to her stairway when she saw dirt and flowers strewn on the ground. She stopped, as did Hutchins, who also drew her service revolver. With a finger to her lips, she indicated that Katherine should be quiet. Crouched slightly, with arms extended and both hands on her weapon, the officer walked softly around to the stairs. Walking up as noiselessly as possible, there was more dirt, broken pots, and bits of plants scattered on the steps and Katherine's porch. Hutchins reached the top, where a chair and table on the landing had been crushed into many pieces.

But more disturbing were the words spray-painted on the wall, front door, and windows: *U bitch! See what u have done to me!* in angry red.

From the bottom of the stairs, Katherine was shocked at the damage.

"Oh my god," she said in a whisper.

"You're going to a hotel tonight," Hutchins said.

CHAPTER 14

Something was buzzing around Katherine's head.

The sound got louder and louder, like a swarm of killer bees on the move. Katherine waved her hands, as if swatting the insects away, but they kept coming closer and closer. She tried to run, but they chased her, swarming all around, stinging every exposed part of her skin. Katherine screamed. When she opened her eyes, she realized the buzzing noise was from her vibrating cell phone as it danced on the table beside her hotel bed.

Half asleep, she reached for the phone, pressing answer at the same time she saw *Unknown* on the screen. Her eyes widened in fear as she put the cell to her ear.

An electronic voice, which sounded like a robot man, spoke.

"Now you've really done it. You should've kept everything to yourself. They're after me and it's all your fault! I loved you but I don't anymore. I hate you!"

The call disconnected, but Katherine sat there, stunned, still holding the mobile for a few moments more.

Finally, she shook herself out of the daze.

This can't go on. I won't let it continue.

She checked her recent call list and to her surprise, the last number came up on the screen. Katherine pressed call and the phone began dialing. The same electronic male voice answered, "Hello?"

Katherine took a big breath.

"This is Katherine. Don't hang up. I . . . I want to be your friend."

There was silence on the other end. A couple of clicks and a normal female voice replied.

"You . . . you do? Is this some kind of trick?"

"No," Katherine answered quickly. "I'm sorry, but I just didn't know who you were. You sound like a . . . nice person."

Another pause.

"Then you're not mad?"

"Pam, right? No, of course not. I'm actually . . . flattered. I don't know too many people out here. Would you like to go for coffee?"

Again, a long pause.

"Well, I don't know . . . and it's Pamela."

"Oh, sorry, Pamela. I think we could be friends."

"I am a nice person . . . most of the time," Pamela said softly. "All right, I'll call when I'm ready to meet you."

"That will be fine, thanks," Katherine said. "I look forward to hearing from you."

Katherine hung up and let out a big sigh. Her hands trembling, she took a deep inhalation of her asthma meds.

CHAPTER 15

It was a beautiful sunny morning in Southern California as Katherine walked along the Strand, but she felt as if a dark cloud were over her head.

Children swayed back and forth on the old, metal beach swing sets, pushed by their mothers. As their little hands held the chains tight, Katherine heard their laughter, but it didn't help her feel any better about what she was about to do.

She made way on the sidewalk for a guy on a bike, dressed in a surf shirt, baseball cap, and wild Hawaiian print trunks, pulling his surfboard strapped to a wheeled contraption on the end of the carved wood. For a moment, she envied his carefree morning.

She passed the beautiful two- and three-story beach homes, but her mind was not on the architecture. Normally she'd note the stucco or brick, or find her favorite color of robin's egg blue, but today she strode by the patios with elegant furniture, green plants, and flowering blooms as if she didn't even see them.

Katherine approached the Beachside Café with dread. She felt her heart pounding, and questioned whether this was a stupid move. But then she saw Pamela standing by the entrance, an apprehensive look on her face.

Looks like she's as nervous as I am. But Katherine put on a weak smile and waved at her stalker.

"Hi, I'm Katherine, you must be Pam . . . I mean, Pamela." Katherine extended her hand. Pamela didn't take it, instead shrinking back a bit. The woman clutched a purse with both hands, tight against her stomach. Pamela stared at Katherine with a look of adoration mixed with suspicion.

"Two, please," Katherine said brightly to the host, who led them to a table near the patio, just under an open awning from the restaurant. They each took a seat, and Katherine pretended to look at the menu. Pamela continued to grip her bag while scrutinizing Katherine.

"You don't look as much like Reese in person."

"Who, Reese Witherspoon? Oh, I wish . . . Look, I know this may seem awkward, but—" Katherine started.

"Is this a setup?" Pamela interrupted.

"Huh? What? Uh, of course not," Katherine stuttered.

"Are you wearing one of those listening things, you know, a wire?"

Katherine tried to laugh nonchalantly. "Why would you think that?"

"Because I saw you go into the police department the other day. I'm not stupid, you know," Pamela said angrily.

"Of course, I know that, Pamela, you—"

"Take off your jacket," Pamela demanded, one hand now inside her purse.

Katherine attempted to stall. "There's no need to—"

"I said, take it off, now!" Pamela's eyes were dark. Katherine detected a glint of metal as Pamela inched a small handgun part way out of her pocketbook.

"Swordfish, I think I'll have the swordfish," Katherine said loudly.

"That's a code word for the cops! I knew it!" Pamela hissed, looking around wildly. She pulled out the gun and pointed it at Katherine.

CHAPTER 16

There was a huge rumbling in Katherine's ears. She closed her eyes for a moment, expecting the worst.

Keep it together, don't lose it now, they'll be here any minute, she hoped.

But when she opened her eyes, they were drawn to the glasses of water in front of her. The liquid was quivering inside, and the small goblets were sliding their way off the edge of the shaking table. As the roaring noise continued, glass was breaking all around her. Pam's face was a combination of fear and astonishment, similar to the restaurant's patrons around them.

"Earthquake!" someone yelled, as screams and shouts followed, with chairs falling as people attempted to race out of the café.

"What . . . what's happening?" Katherine said, shocked and unable to move. She felt her chair shuddering from side to side, as if someone was jolting it, hard.

Before she could react, a beam from the awning above them came loose and slammed onto Pamela, knocking the gun from her hand. Pamela fell off her seat, blood oozing from her head, and slumped on the floor as people shrieked from inside the eatery.

Katherine, hardly able to stand with the vibrating movement below her feet, made her way to a dazed Pamela. She reached under her stalker's arms and pulled her out from under the long wooden shank.

"We've got to get out of here!" Katherine shouted. She helped Pamela to her feet, and they stumbled toward the sandy beach as sirens wailed around them.

"Katherine? Katherine, where are you?" a voice yelled from over by the restaurant. Katherine looked up and saw Lieutenant Hutchins and her partner.

"Over here! Hurry," she shouted, waving at the blue uniforms. Hutchins and Officer Peters started running toward her, with Detective Blanken not far behind, his chest heaving. Pamela was becoming cognizant of her surroundings and fought to stand up and move away from Katherine.

"No, you don't," said Hutchins, grabbing Pamela's arm and snapping on a pair of handcuffs. "Are you okay?" she asked Katherine, who was staring and turning white.

"I..."

"Peters, catch her, she's dropping!"

Katherine felt a cool breeze come over her and remembered feeling as if time and everything and everyone around her were standing still. Then her world went black.

CHAPTER 17

The gentle sound of the ocean's waves was calming and peaceful, as Katherine sank deeper into her pillow. She breathed in the warm air.

Is that a Coast Guard horn? she wondered, hearing a beeping noise in the distance. *Mmmm, sounds like it's getting closer. Maybe they'll take me for a boat ride,* she thought sleepily. The *beep, beep* came nearer, and the surf now sounded like a steady flow of air near her ears. Katherine's eyes fluttered open.

"Welcome back," said a woman in white.

"What . . . where am I?" Feeling a tickling sensation on her face, Katherine wriggled her nose and tried to scratch it with her hand.

"Hold on," the woman said, gently pushing Katherine's arm to her side. "You are in the hospital, and we're giving you a breathing treatment."

"Hospital? Oh, the earthquake! And Pamela . . ." Suddenly Katherine was awake.

"Oh, your friend, Pamela, is going to be fine. Just a bad bump on the head."

"She's no friend, she's a stalker," said a gruff male voice.

Katherine looked toward the door where the sound came from. Detective Blanken stood with a small vase of flowers and a box of candy in his hand. Lieutenant Hutchins was right behind him.

"Can we come in?" he asked.

"Only for a minute," the nurse replied, taking the plastic mask off Katherine's nose and mouth and shutting off the nebulizer machine.

"Well, like they say, timing is everything." Blanken put the bouquet on the windowsill and the sweets on the bedside table.

"Where were you? What took you so long?" Katherine asked, her throat scratchy and dry.

"We were outside, as planned," said Hutchins.

"But we didn't figure on a 4.8 quake comin' along right in the middle of our sting," Blanken added.

Katherine's eyes widened. "That was my first earthquake," she said.

"Yeah, well, it wasn't mine, but ya never really get used to 'em," Blanken said, shaking his head. He stared at the chocolates.

"And the stalker?"

"Oh, she's here, too. Now, don't worry," he added quickly, seeing Katherine's uneasy look. "We got an officer outside her door. Probably got a concussion and she's gonna have a nasty headache for a few weeks."

Hutchins put her hand on Katherine's. "I'm glad you're okay." She hesitated. "But you didn't have to pull Pamela out of that restaurant, not after she pointed a gun at you." She looked at Katherine curiously.

"I guess you're right." Katherine paused, thinking. "Despite everything, I felt sorry for her. What's going to happen now?"

"We could easily get her for assault, battery, or even attempted murder," Blanken said.

"I don't really want to press charges."

"If you don't, she might come after you again or harass someone else. But if you do, she'll probably go in for a psych eval, maybe receive some treatment."

"I think she just wanted a friend," Katherine said softly. "Let's go with the lowest charge."

There was a moment of silence.

"So, you headin' back to the what, 120-degree temps in Arizona?" Blanken asked, eyeing the candies again.

"Yeah, the moist ocean air is great for my asthma, but I need to be with my family."

"Guess you'd rather bake than shake, huh?" he chuckled.

Lieutenant Hutchins scowled and elbowed him in the side. "You take care of yourself, Katherine," she said, pushing the detective out the door.

"Thanks . . . for everything." Katherine waved.

She could still hear the officers as they headed down the hall.

"You'd rather 'bake than shake'? That's all you could come up with?" Hutchins needled the older man.

"Hey, that reminds me—wanna hit that chicken place on the way back to the station?"

Katherine smiled as she heard Hutchins laugh.

About the Author

Laurie Fagen has penned for radio and television news, corporate video, films, documentaries, magazines, and newspapers. An honorable mention in an *Alfred Hitchcock's Mystery Magazine* contest and love of whodunits led to three published novels in her Behind the Mic mysteries. She is a member of Sisters in Crime Los Angeles, San Diego, and Grand Canyon Writers. www.ReadLaurieFagen.com

Duet

Cyndra Gernet

"WELL, I THINK IT's stupid, singing a concert wearing masks," said my fellow alto Judy, standing next to me in our small performance space. Her hazel eyes, above a mask emblazoned with musical notes, dared me to disagree. We were the first of our choir to arrive.

Serendipity Singers, twenty women of a certain age, was one of many community choirs in the Los Angeles area. We had been singing together for fifteen years, but this would be our first concert since the arrival of COVID.

"And this space." Judy groaned displeasure.

I took in hardwood floors, windows flooding sunlight, brightly cushioned benches, a curved stage. "I think it's charming."

But Judy was looking away, studying the piano to our right, a vintage maple upright. "This must be at least fifty years old," she said rippling her fingers along the keys. "At least it's in tune."

Through the open doors, we heard cars approaching.

"Before the others get here," Judy said, joining me, "I just want to tell you I've enjoyed being your friend all these years. It'll be fun singing our duet."

"I'm really looking forward to it." I met her eyes and we smiled at each other.

"Aaah, my two favorite singers," said Allan as he swept through the entry door draped in an ever-present scarf. Today's choice was one of my favorites, pink pigs and poodles on a blue background.

"You say that to all of us," Judy and I replied.

"And it's true. You're all my favorites." Allan, five feet, two inches of the sweetest man I knew. Gentle and encouraging of even the most challenged singer, he was adored by us all.

"Mask," Judy reminded him.

"Oh, crap," he said, fumbling through his jacket pockets. "Always forget the damn things." Pulling out a garish purple mask, he hooked it over his ears.

Staring at him, I almost missed our piano player, or, as they were now called, collaborative accompanist, slipping silently into place. She was a shy thirty-something and arrived and left rehearsals and performances without speaking. The piano was her voice.

Her warm-up playing greeted the arriving singers, and the room filled with talking females as they found their places on stage. In our black pants and white shirts, we looked like restaurant staff.

"Okay, singers, listen up." Allan tapped the podium with a pencil. "We'll run through the program once. Remember to look at me and at each other. The audience likes to see interaction between you. Create a friendly, welcoming atmosphere."

The assembled altos rolled eyes at each other. We had heard this admonition more than once.

Last to arrive were the first sopranos, the prima donnas of any choir. They most often carried the melody with the workhorse altos supplying the harmony.

Allan continued talking, circling his arms in mock hugs. "Today's concert is about love, so please project *love* as you are singing. Remember, you are *performers*."

After a quick warm-up, we began with "Fly Me to the Moon," moving on to "Walkin' After Midnight" (my favorite) featuring two soprano solos. Seven more love songs, then Judy and I finished the program with our duet in "It Had to Be You."

"Wonderful, you sound absolutely marvelous, ladies. You will wow our audience." He checked his watch. "You have fifteen minutes, so go freshen up."

Early arrivals were kept in the foyer until we left the stage so that we singers could make a dramatic entrance once all were seated.

Twenty of us crowded into a small office, our ad-hoc green room, checking makeup and drinking water from plastic bottles. Checking my face, Judy tried to wipe a smudge from under my right eye. "I'll get it," I said. Pulling away, I moved over to a wall mirror.

After a solid rap, Allan popped his head in the door with a high-wattage smile. "Line up, it's go time."

Walking down the aisle to modest applause, I noted a crowd of about seventy-five people in a space built for a hundred. Not a bad turnout. Once on stage, I scanned the group for familiar faces, smiled and waved at several.

Programs rustled and voices murmured until Allan signaled for quiet. After welcoming the crowd, he turned to face us, an exaggerated smile on his face to remind us to look lively.

A lovely piano introduction started us off on our first selection, "Fly Me to the Moon." As I sang about holding hands and kisses, I visualized lazy days walking the beach at Santa Monica, the sun hot on our skin, the water brisk at our feet. A group hug, including the dogs, after we were soaked by an unseen wave, which left us wet and sandy.

Applause pulled me from my thoughts. I turned to Lucy and smiled.

During our second number, "You'd Be So Nice to Come Home To," as my mouth sang of longing, my mind recalled nights of Hollywood bar hopping, the three of us tumbling into an Uber, too drunk to drive home. The car smelled of spent cigarettes. We kept breaking into giggles as our driver tried to make sense out of the directions we gave him.

Song. Applause. Song. Applause.

So it went until Judy and I began our duet. As we came to the final lines, "It had to be you, wonderful you, it had to be you," and the applause started, I plunged the syringe full of pentobarbital I'd hidden in my pocket into Judy's hip. As she collapsed onto the stage floor, I followed her down, pushing the syringe back into my pants.

"Someone call 911," I shouted. The audience stirred. The other singers clustered around us. "Back up, give her air," I said.

Bringing my face close to Judy's, I looked into her fixed hazel eyes and whispered, "You thought I wouldn't find out? Well, friend, you and my husband have sung your last duet."

About the Author

Cyndra Gernet loves to write short stories but prefers reading novels. "Duet" is her fourth story to appear in Sisters in Crime anthologies.

She is indebted to writing teacher Jerrilyn Farmer and to sister writers Mary Marks and Lori Dillman. Her husband, Michael, and daughter, Harper, provide technical and moral support.

And, yes, she sings alto in a local choir.

Unknown Sand Pits!

Laurel Wetzork

Culver City—The Heart of Screenland

Tuesday, November 7, 1950

about 9 a.m.

"ALL RIGHT. WHICH JOKER buried our number two T-rex upside down?" Earl Carter, assistant director of the soon-to-be-completed movie the *Unknown Sand Pits!* glared at the in-costume cast and crew snickering in front of the dinosaurs' cave entrance. The clawed feet of the fearsome creature stuck out of the set's largest working sand mound.

"It *is not* a T-rex!" Dark-haired, elfin-faced script girl Florence Smith jabbed her pencil on her clipboard and broke the tip. "Only a ceratosaurus or allosaurus have little horns on their snouts *and* tiny arms! No one ever gets this right!"

"I certainly did not bury ol' monster boy," murmured Betty Turner, blond bombshell and leading lady. "How could little ol' me lift such a big ol' heavy thing?"

"Easy," drawled James Hill, leading man and latest B-movie heartthrob. "As simply as you manage to inspire your dreamboats to fulfill your every wish—by slathering on your charm with a shovel. Or by batting those fake eyelashes at handy lapdogs, such as the sound ghouls. Or sitting on a lap, such as the director's."

"Meanie! Sam would stop you talking to me like that." Betty huffed and bounced over to the sound crew, Clarence, and Roy, who patted her back and stared down her specially designed blouse.

The property master, unlit cigarette behind his ear, kicked a small pile of sand back into the pit. "Gonna take forever to clean the sand out of that thing."

At the mention of sand, wiry and gum-chewing cinematographer Ralph Taylor ordered the focus puller to cover the Arriflex and the dolly grips to move the dolly back to its starting mark. They'd attempted a shot rehearsal but then seen the clawed feet.

The property master frowned. "Why bury it upside down?"

"I don't care which way it's buried! Fess up!" Earl used his drill sergeant voice, wishing he was back in the army where orders were followed. Movie people were as alien as butterflies inside bazooka barrels and as cliché as the dialogue in this sequel to the 1948 box office flop, *Unknown Island*. He wondered about the crazy who greenlit this movie. But after the riots of 1945, after the new owner of this studio put productions on hold for six months and fired seven hundred people and still looked for communist sympathizers, Earl was glad to have a job. Any job. "I said 'fess up'!"

The actors and crew avoided his glare and shuffled their feet.

"No takers. Figures." Earl rubbed his hand over his bald head, wishing he still had hair to yank out. "Listen up, ladies and gents, all of you grab brooms and shovels, union rules or not. That means you, Ralph."

Ralph scowled.

Earl ignored him. "One of you grips or sparks start the lift. Men, we'll pull it out after the lift's high enough. Don't want to rip off its legs. It'll cost too much to make another suit. Ladies, you'll sweep, the rest of us'll shovel. Florence, when the mound's reset, check it for continuity while costume and property clean up the T-rex suit."

"Ceratosaurus or allosaurus." Florence pounded her clipboard.

Earl continued. "Mr. Buck'll be furious if we're not ready."

"He's always furious," muttered Clarence, one of the sound ghouls.

The other ghoul, Roy, nodded. "Director's job to be furious."

An older grip trotted behind the cave and the set's rear projection screen and continued across the large stage toward the lift controls. Another grip, young and spotty-faced, trotted to the tool area to scavenge shovels and brooms.

"I refuse to sweep sand." Betty licked a finger and ran it over an errant hair, gluing it back in place.

"Is refusing wise, Betty dear?" James shook his head in mock concern and glanced down at his biceps, cunningly revealed by his torn costume. "Performing physical labor will cause real perspiration and add verisimilitude to an otherwise sloppy makeup application and wooden performance."

"Hey." Doreen, the makeup woman, stomped up to James. "I resent that! It takes time to apply real-looking sweat."

"It must take an hour to ensure her pound of makeup doesn't melt off. Besides," James motioned to his torn and dirtied costume, "we are supposed to die of thirst in the desert whilst attempting to discover these creatures' eggs. Then we destroy them before their alien parents destroy us, remember? Her sweating will add a level of truthfulness."

"Shut your trap, James." Betty crossed her arms under her ample cleavage. Her torn and dirtied blouse, glued in place to keep the censors happy, strained under the pressure. "You're just jealous because the glitterati featured little ol' me with a pic and front-page article in *Variety* and not you! Besides, I don't sweat."

"Everyone sweats." Florence, new pencil in hand, glared at her. Her logical mind refused to believe this was true. "It's a natural process."

"I don't."

Florence chewed the pencil's eraser. "How strange. I've never seen you sweat, even under lights. Is that why Doreen fans you, to cool you off? What happens when you overheat?"

Betty wriggled. "I simply pass out."

James eyed her up and down. "That might prove dangerous in certain, er, positions." The crew sniggered.

Thoughts slow crawled across Betty's face until enlightenment hit. "Oh, no, it's not dangerous. I always keep a carafe of water by the bed. So that Sam, I mean, SAM-one, someone, I mean, if ever I did such a thing, they just pour me a glass."

The sound ghouls swiveled from watching Betty to watching Florence, known for her obsession with Sam. Florence, white-faced, broke her new pencil in half.

"If I point the boom her way," whispered Clarence, the taller of the ghouls, to Roy, "we'd hear her teeth grind."

"Yup." Roy switched the toothpick he was chewing to his pocket and pulled out another.

James sent Betty a mocking look. "And pray tell, how are you revived in these dangerous horizontal positions? Do your attendants pour water upon your head? No, that would disarrange your platinum helmet."

"Silly, I don't wear a helmet. They dip a handkerchief in the water and dab it around my neck, and my—my other parts."

The crew nodded wisely as they pictured Betty's parts.

Florence pulled another pencil from her tool-kit apron.

The stage lift rumbled to life and began its ascent. Sand poured off the mound. The monster's legs stuck straight up.

"Weird," said the property master. "They're not flopping."

The spotty-faced grip sent on the shovel-and-broom hunt, holding a shovel handle with a small white cloth, hurried up to Earl, the assistant director.

"Earl? Lookit on this here shovel's blade." He held it in front of Earl's face. "It ain't fake."

"Shut it, kid." Earl stared at the mound as it disgorged more of the ten-foot creature. The rubber monster—tiny arms stiff, normally floppy body rigid, horned head and angry eyes caked with reddish sand, its large open mouth gaping in a permanent roar—rolled off the lift, down the mound of sand, and knocked over a screaming Florence.

The crew rushed to pull her from under the weight of the creature.

Betty ran up and peered into its jaws. The rubber was slashed open, revealing a pale blob. "Sam? What are you doing in there? Wake up!"

Before Earl could stop her, she reached in and cupped Sam's face. She pulled out her hand. It dripped chunks of bloody sand.

The sound crew ran and caught her as she fainted.

"Holy Jasper," Earl whispered, looking at Sam's face. He knew death when he saw it. He'd seen it too many times during the war. He glanced over at Betty. Florence dumped a carafe of water on her chest.

Betty shot up, gasping and furious. She grabbed Florence's ankle and yanked. Florence slipped in the water and rolled atop Betty. The sound crew wisely stepped aside as the two women yelled and pulled each other's hair. Doreen waded in, took hold of Florence's tool-kit apron, and dragged her away.

"I'm billing you for any damage you've caused to our star and her costume!" Doreen prodded Florence with her foot. "Go on."

Florence crawled over to Betty and apologized.

Earl shook his head. James, deathly pale, appeared at his side. ". . . 'His worries are all over now . . .'"

"What's that?"

"An appropriate line of dialogue from the last movie."

"Earl?" The grip's grip shook as he held the shovel outwards.

Earl stepped around James and held out his hand. "Good thinking, kid, to keep the fingerprints intact. Hand that over and go call the cops."

"At least let me call in another director!" Producer Bert Friddle scurried after the lean figure of Detective Monroe as he strode through the main building's halls.

"No." Monroe, his jaw set and hooded eyes angry, shoved open the double doors and stepped into the foggy mist, pulling his trench coat closer. California wasn't always sunny. Especially this close to the ocean. Things dripped. "Postpone the shoot."

"We can't! The stages are only booked for four more days, plus we're using some set pieces from *King Kong*."

"They burned those sets for *Gone with the Wind*."

"Not the sets—the leftover costumes, props, and some of the jungle greens slated for destruction—so we can't delay."

"Thought your movie was set in the desert."

"Not all of it."

"What's the title?"

"*Unknown Sand Pits!* The sequel to *Unknown Island*."

Monroe snorted. "So Hughes needs a dent in his wallet?"

Bert flushed. "No. Mr. Hughes thought we could recoup some of the losses of *Unknown Island* by reusing the costumes and props, you know. Sam wrote the script with Mr. Hughes's approval. The other was terrible."

"And this one's not?" Monroe thought of Howard Hughes's latest films and his erratic behavior, some said because of opiates, as the mogul had been in pain since he'd crashed his experimental XF-11 plane and destroyed three Beverly Hills mansions. And the man was running multiple businesses and a studio. He shook his head.

Bert pressed prim lips together. "Do you really need to be here? Shouldn't you check his house for suspects? I mean, he was obviously dead. You haven't checked his club, or his—"

"Mistresses. Listen, shorty, no mistress worth her salt would answer the door before noon. She's either rackin' up beauty sleep, or busy and doesn't want to double-book."

Monroe aimed for Stage One. He knew the way. What Culver City detective didn't know the way around this famous studio? The perks of the job included meeting the stars while conducting security checks. And bringing home autographs for the wife. Monroe brought autographs home for his cat, Buster K. There was no wife. Buster liked to shred autographs. Then he'd eat the paper and hack it up. Monroe'd do anything to keep the critter happy. Even seek autographs.

"Mornin', boys."

"Mornin'." The photographer was busy with his camera at the doc's directions while the rest of the team sifted the sand for clues.

Monroe stuck his hands in his pockets and stared down at the sand pile, then at the creature's head, then at Sam Buck's shovel-bashed noggin. The director's remains were still stuck inside the rubber suit. The shovel was properly bagged and set along a growing pile of clues atop a table. The clues didn't inspire: bubblegum paper, a used cigarette, several toothpicks, a half-chewed pencil, and an earring.

"Someone knocked him off in another way, too, boss." Coyote-like Riley, his second-in-command, appeared at his side and handed him a large mug of coffee. Monroe nodded his thanks and took a sip. Black, thick, and strong. "Someone cap him too?"

"Yeah. We had a look under the rubber suit 'til the doc ordered us to stop. They'll ease him out soon. Producer demanded we keep the thing intact."

"He would."

"Anyways, there's a big hole in the vic's chest. But the doc thinks his skull was smashed first."

"What a sweetheart of a killer. Find the gun?"

"They're sifting for it."

Monroe spoke to two of his team and sent them with explicit instructions out into the wild jungles of Los Angeles to the director's house. Another two he sent over to the Culver City Hotel with instructions to check the guest register for cast and crew names, and to check to see if the cast and crew were actually there, then check the tunnel between the hotel and studio.

Monroe joined Riley at the clue table. They examined the newest additions: a spool of thread, a bloodied handkerchief (ladies' model), and a partial Spam sandwich (dried).

"No gun. What else?"

Riley nodded. "Got a flat-foot with the fruits and nuts, over in some tent on Stage Two."

Monroe turned to Bert. "Bedouin?"

"'Bet' or 'win'? No thank you, I'm a religious man." Bert wiped sweat off his brow. "The tent holds them all, the wild animals. Our assistant director, Earl Carter, he's ex-army, is keeping them corralled. And, I do hate to bring it up, Detective, but we really, really need to start shooting in the next four hours. Mr. Hughes will be quite upset at delays."

Monroe drank more of the java and glanced at Riley, who rolled his eyes. They both knew the dance-around-the-ego dance needed for studio types. And Hughes, destroyer of jobs, needed a big dance. Monroe could hear his CO's voice: *Don't anger any studio bigwigs by showing off your smarts, 'cause they'll shuffle their greenbacks elsewhere. Culver City needs that cash and so does our department. So play nice and promise to do all you can.* So, Monroe had to resist telling Bert what a Bedouin was. He put on his serious and kind face. "I'll do all I can. Steer me and Riley here to the wild animals."

Bert brightened at Monroe's implicit promise. "I'll show you myself." They headed across the stage. Bert took three steps to every one of theirs. They passed two miniature brontosauri on a stop-motion table decorated with sand pits and a jungle oasis, then maneuvered around a forty-foot-wide silver UFO in front of another rear projection screen.

Monroe raised his eyebrows. "Dinosaurs *and* aliens?"

Bert shrugged. "We saved money reusing the stop-motion pieces from our first movie, and as I said, using any free props. We drew the line, though, at reusing the giant ground sloth. The costume department couldn't remove all the fake T-rex blood caked in its hair."

Monroe bit back his response—ceratosaurus or allosaurus—and rolled his eyes at Riley. Riley coughed.

"Dinosaurs and aliens will make for a very unique picture, Mr. Friddle." Monroe used his I'm-very-impressed-with-you voice. Bert stood taller and his pace increased. The trio left Stage One and crossed the road. The damp was damper. An officer stood outside Stage Two, yawning. He opened a human-sized entrance. Monroe stepped inside, finished his java, and set the mug on a nearby table.

Two canvas tents set in a faux desert took up most of the stage. The larger tent's beige roof glowed under the working lights. The smaller tent was pale pink. Behind both, plastic palm trees and some incongruous jungle plants were set crookedly around an oasis, with a rear projection screen behind those. The main tent's colorful flags and banners hung limp. A large wind machine stood ready to blow a gentle breeze or gale. Sand was glued to mounds on both tents' sides to make sure nothing changed between shots. Or the actors didn't fall into it and mess up their costumes or hair. Several small mounds of real sand were close to the large tent's entrance.

The smaller tent was probably for the leading lady, thought Monroe, to enact a dramatic scene where she fought off, unsuccessfully, amorous bad guys, only to be rescued by the leading man in a gun battle when the guns would jam and then there'd be a fist fight. Monroe didn't much care for the movies. He strode forward, Bert panting along behind him. Riley trailed them silently.

A harried-looking officer stood outside the main tent's entrance. He saluted and pulled aside the cloth opening. They slipped inside. Another officer, exuding menace, paced along a narrow rug. Hanging brass lamps, loads of wildly embroidered pillows, low couches, divans, rugs, and various braziers with the remains of smoke-making cubes completed the decor. Seated, sprawled, or lying down were the wild animals.

Monroe scanned and matched them to their names.

The spit-polished, obviously ex-military man with the angry scowl must be Earl, assistant director. His bald head reflected various light sources. He looked drill-sergeant ready to shout orders and shift unruly people onto their correct marks.

Blond bombshell, a big furry cat, curled on a cushion. Leading lady, Betty Turner. Recently featured on *Variety's* front page. A dim bulb according to most. She flicked him an intelligent glance with wattage far greater than a usual dim bulb's.

Leading man James Hill, tall and well-muscled, stretched out on one of the divans. Recently been quoted as declaring that the only real acting was to be found on the theatrical stage, thought to be an excuse to cover his flagging popularity. Several divorces, many broken hearts, currently unattached.

A pencil-chewing, elfin-faced, dark-haired young woman sat upright on a small cushion. Script girl as evidenced by her harassed and worried look, the clipboard, and at least a dozen pencils in her tool-kit apron.

From their looks at him, measuring him in foot candles and lighting effects, the three seated on a low couch must be the cinematographer and his camera assistants.

Two sound crew, a makeup woman, a property master or art director, some grips and a gaffer, and various assistants.

Monroe finished his scan in ten seconds and turned to Riley.

"Bring 'em over one at time to the pink tent."

"Right, boss."

Bert cleared his throat. "I must return to my office and search for another director."

Monroe looked at him, then at Earl, who'd turned an angry shade of red, then back at Bert. Monroe smiled. He wondered if smiling over a clenched jaw would appear friendly or not.

Bert stepped back, his face pale.

Okay, not so friendly. Monroe unclenched his jaw. "Bet your assistant director knows the screenplay front and back. Have him step in. Save you time and money. We'll interview him first, then you two can prepare for tomorrow's shoot. We'll clear the other set soon as we can. About any delay, maybe the city'll give you a tax break because of this tragedy." Monroe wasn't sure, but it sounded good. Producers had dollar signs for hearts and calculators for brains.

Bert smiled and puffed out his chest. "That sounds reasonable."

Inside the smaller tent, Monroe sat at a ridiculously flimsy table painted with swirls of neon pinks and greens that matched the interior decor. Riley wandered over to a divan and sat, notebook ready for scribbling. Earl stood at parade rest.

"Earl, who's in cahoots with whom? What's the scuttlebutt? You'll know more than most." This wasn't true. Assistant directors were too busy directing extras, coaxing temperamental actors out of their dressing rooms and trailers onto the set, and making sure the massive amount of paperwork of call sheets, prop lists, and all the machinery that went into making a motion picture, moved along smoothly. They didn't have time for gossip. That would be makeup and hair, and some of the grips and crew. Monroe motioned Earl to sit.

"Incorrect that I know more than most." Earl sat. "For gossip, talk to makeup, hair, grips, sound, and some of the sparks."

"Okay. So start talking."

Earl described the clawed feet, the request for the lift to be raised, the shovel, and the fainting women. He then reddened. "Thanks for putting in a good word that I direct." He rubbed his hand over his bald head. "I'm not sure I'm cut out for show business. Thinking about forestry. A lone outpost, top of a mountain. No one's fainting or backbiting or sleeping around."

"Tell me about the sleeping around."

Earl did and Riley scribbled notes. After Earl left, Monroe shook his head. "Worse than a politicians' convention."

"Boss?" Riley looked up. His hand hurt.

"Sex, politicians. Except the politicians are always lousy actors." Monroe stood. "I'll go help take apart Sam's office in the main building. You continue prying 'em open."

"Right-O, boss."

Sam Buck's office in the main building's corner closest to Stage One proclaimed power and reeked of fear. Monroe turned the last of Sam's desk drawers upside down. "Gotcha." He pulled off a taped manila envelope. People were dumb. The first place where detectives would look. But Sam wasn't thinking of detectives. He was thinking of nosy people without keys.

His team had taken apart everything, including floorboards, and stacked pertinent items atop the gleaming desk. Monroe, after dumping the envelope contents on the pile, looked up. A flat-foot set the hotel register down and pointed at an entry. "The tunnel was used by this person here. And take a gander at page ten, boss."

Riley loped in and set down his notes. "Got their statements here."

Monroe read page ten and the statements, then quickly went through the pile on Sam Buck's desk.

Copies of a diploma, a death certificate, and a tenant agreement. A pleading letter about a stuntman's death along with an eight-by-ten glossy of Wally Anderson featured in *Unknown Island*. A love letter from Earl to Betty. An unsigned letter from Sam Buck on studio stationery to the House Un-American Activities Committee. A signed, ten-year contract. A small pile of photos and negatives from under the floorboards along with some 35 mm film strips. And last, a three-inch pile of C-notes.

Monroe reread the statements. He smiled. They had all lied, every one of them.

ell

Monroe gathered them in the main tent, despite the bleating of Bert Friddle about the shooting schedule. Monroe gently pushed Bert into a seat. Bert stopped bleating. Monroe turned to the weary-looking group. He then told them who could leave. Grips, sparks, and other cast and crew were told to go to Stage One and sign statements.

Monroe told Bert, Betty, Florence, James, Ralph, the two sound ghouls Clarence and Roy, and Earl to stay seated. Doreen he had sit nearby. He grinned; his jaw clenched. "I'll give it to you straight. All of you but Doreen are in it up to your necks."

The crowd gasped and murmured.

He pointed a finger at Bert. "I'll start with you."

Bert inhaled and choked a bit. Riley pounded his back and gave him a cup of water.

Monroe hated that he couldn't risk saying out loud what he'd found, but his own boss would sack him if he messed too much with a producer. He leaned forward and whispered. "Sam was blackmailing you. Seems he had photos of you with a certain lady, who isn't your wife. Plenty of motive. And cash I bet with your fingerprints."

Bert turned deep red.

Monroe finished. "But your alibi checks out. Next time, I'd suggest penning a better name than Mr. and Mrs. Smith in the hotel register and go to another town so your wife doesn't take you to the cleaners. I also found Sam's real accounting book. Now, I didn't follow it all, but I expect if you are innocent, you'll pay these folks their back pay. Or I take those negatives, photos, and the little book to Mr. Hughes. Got it?"

Bert nodded, his face now a pale sweaty pink. Monroe grinned and leaned closer. "Pretend I'm telling you a tidbit about Sam you can't repeat. Tell them about their back pay."

Bert nodded again. Monroe stood back. Bert pitched his voice high. "Thank you, Detective. Of course! Of course, I had no *idea* Sam was cheating, not paying the cast and crew proper rates. I will of course issue back pay. And thank you, for—for telling me this terrible thing about Sam. Of course, it shall remain a secret."

Which in The Heart of Screenland, Monroe knew, would last for five seconds. He turned to Clarence and Roy. "And your alibi, that you were both in the sound booth listening to yesterday's dailies, was a lie; that room was booked by someone else. My team found your little pile of sound reels and had a listen. You caught Sam cheating on his current wife with his latest mistress, didn't you? And you thought blackmail was a good idea?"

Clarence crossed his arms. Roy took out his toothpick and put in another one.

"We're broke," said Clarence. "And Sam owns—owned—the building where we live."

Monroe nodded. "The tenant agreement. Sam overcharged, didn't he?"

"He was a thief." Roy leapt to his feet.

"Sit down. So he was going to kick you out if you didn't sign over your pay."

"Which we did, until we followed him one day—"

"And you crept up and recorded them. What else did you hear?" They glanced everywhere but at one person. Monroe smiled. "I thought so."

Monroe turned suddenly and yanked the cinematographer to his feet.

"Ralph, answer this now or I'll nail your pants to that jail cell door you're about to occupy. You weren't in your hotel room, you were in their bar, halfway to a bender. You went to Sam's office by the tunnel. What'd you do there?"

Ralph gulped loudly. "Okay, okay. Put me down. I wanted to drive over to director Rowland Lee's ranch in Chatsworth—Hitchcock is shooting exteriors of an amusement park for his *Strangers on a Train*—I wanted to see what Robert Burks was up to—"

"Hitchcock's cinematographer?"

"You know that? Sam heard about my jaunt from someone on the set, said I wasn't going to cost the budget any more money with cheap tricks—cheap tricks! Burks is a genius with special effects. And I was going to pick his brain about the difference between Cinecolor and Technicolor, shooting miniatures, that is, but Sam refused to listen to me, even though he couldn't tell an Arriflex from a Fox Cine Simplex. Told me I was a small, petty man. Well, I could have made this picture thousands of times better. Now get your paws off me!"

"That's not where you were. You were in Sam's office, weren't you?" Monroe shook him. "Sam was about to turn your name into the HUAC and tell Mr. Hughes that you're a communist. You'd never work again. So he blackmailed you, made you sign a contract for the next ten moving pictures."

Ralph crumpled in Monroe's grip. "All right! I wanted Sam dead! But I didn't kill him! Don't you understand? I was a noncombatant during the war. I'm not a communist, I'm a Methodist."

"A conscientious objector Methodist. Got it." Monroe released Ralph. "But you lied to me. Don't. Now, think, your dolly wasn't in its usual place, was it?"

Ralph, confused, nodded. "How did you know?"

"Never mind." Monroe turned and grinned at the lead actor. "You."

The sleek and elegant James Hill yawned and examined his fingernails. "Go on."

"You weren't with your tennis partner over at the country club. She was only too happy to let us know who she was really with when she found out this was murder. Your alibi's burnt toast and you've got a stellar motive for murder."

"Oh pray enlighten me, oh Detective from a cheap noir flick."

Monroe took a step forward. Riley pulled him back. "Easy, Monroe."

"This lot makes me sick." He turned on James. "I'll enlighten you, you faded excuse for an actor. Just like the hidey-hole bookmaking operation John Wayne and Bo Roos discovered when renovating the Culver City Hotel, there were plenty of other hidey-holes that were used. Movie cameras hidden behind panels, you know."

James turned pale.

"And you have an interview coming up with John Wayne to play opposite him in a World War Two extravaganza."

"My, the man reads the trades. What does it matter if I am being considered for a co-starring role with Mr. Wayne?"

"You can't deny the 35 mm film reels we found under Sam's office floorboards."

"What?" James staggered to his feet. "You're lying."

"You're a regular visitor at the hotel, it seems, with a certain *young* female."

James's eyes glittered with malice. "I must thank you for your reticence. Uttering that young lady's name and dragging her into this business would be devastating for her career."

"You took advantage."

"Who wouldn't?"

"You disgust me."

"I disgust many people."

Monroe jabbed James in the chest. "Sam's little blackmail plot would seal you to him forever. You'd never play in another movie by another director again. So you took Earl's gun and shot him."

"No." Sweat beaded James's forehead.

"No, that's not true, is it?"

Monroe turned to Betty. "Don't faint. You act like some ditzy broad, but you don't fool me!"

Betty gasped. "I don't understand."

"For one, that blond helmet of hair isn't real." He spun around to Doreen. "Right, Doreen?"

Doreen gulped, shot an anxious look at Betty, then back at Monroe. "Please, Detective, a girl doesn't give away hairstyle secrets."

Monroe shook his head and turned back to Betty. "You got a first-class brain under that shellacked helmet. A diploma in Sam's office proves that. Magna cum laude, right, Miss Turner?"

Betty sat up, her dim-bulb personality fading under the bright wattage of her intelligence. "So what if I did? We all know what type of woman succeeds in this business. And that's what brains are for. Intelligent women in 1950 must hide who they are. I've had to hide. Just ask Florence how it feels to be looked over because some man thinks you're too smart! How else are we to deal with men whose brains reside in their pants?" She panted from the force of her emotions.

Florence flushed and grabbed Betty's hand. "You are wasted in this role. You shine, like a mix of Ingrid Bergman and Rita Hayworth, a smart brunette with curves."

Betty stood and faced Monroe. "I am smart, which is why I didn't kill Sam."

"Then why was your earring found in the sand mound, near Sam's body and the rubber suit?"

"What?" Betty touched her ear. "Oh, no, it's missing?"

"What an act." Monroe sneered. He circled her, hooded eyes flashing, his lean figure looming over her like a hawk. "Tell me, Betty. Why did you plant all these clues in the sand? Florence's pencil, the property master's used cigarette, Ralph's bubblegum wrapper, Roy's toothpick, thread from the costumer, a dried-up Spam sandwich that one of the grips left, and the bloodied handkerchief that's yours."

"I don't know about that."

"Because you knew you'd lost your earring and couldn't spend the time to try and find it, so you covered up your crime by planting more clues. That bruise Doreen so valiantly tried to hide with that plaster of a makeup job?"

Doreen shot to her feet. "Hey! You try hiding what that evil man did to her! And it wasn't the only one."

Monroe practically purred. "Thank you, Doreen, for letting me know Betty's motive."

Doreen's jaw dropped. "No—I didn't mean—she'd never hurt anyone."

Earl stood. "Betty didn't do a damn thing, I did!"

Monroe spun around. "Sit. You're next!"

Earl sat.

Monroe faced Betty. "You didn't fall over the fence in Chatsworth last night, trying to meet Hitchcock and get a part in his latest movie. You were up in Sam's office. Looking for that diploma which he threatened to reveal to the world and begging him for a meeting with Hitchcock, Capra, Cukor, or any other big shot. He not only refused, he threatened you with some photos. Oh yes, I've seen them and so have my boys!"

"I did meet him and he told me—he said—" Betty shook with rage.

"He told you that it didn't matter if the photos were fake, the public wouldn't care and once seen, they'd think you guilty. Sam wanted you all to himself, didn't he? And when you wouldn't play, he wouldn't let you play. Any more parts, that is." Monroe grinned a feral grin. "Florence is right, you're a smart brunette with curves. That's who you really are. You've been playing the ditzy part and playing it badly."

"Arrgh!" She picked up a brazier and flung it. "I didn't kill Sam!" The brass thing missed him.

"Sit down and shut that trap. I know you didn't."

"But, but . . ." Betty sat down, confused.

Monroe stalked over to Earl. "You followed her to Sam's office last night. While Sam wouldn't recommend you for other jobs, and you put up with Sam's brief affair with Betty, you wouldn't put up with him slugging her. So you knocked him cold. Then you and Betty stuck Sam on the camera dolly and moved him here, which is why Ralph's dolly was out of place. Then you stuck Sam in the rubber suit, thinking it'd make a funny headline if you could get Ralph here to photograph Sam on the sand mound. But Ralph wasn't around. You hated Sam so much, Earl, you shot him, beat his face in with the shovel, then activated the lift and buried him headfirst in the sand pit. You were on the set early, you always are. You easily could have done it, and no one would know."

"Prove it." Earl turned a deep red.

The tension in the room grew thick.

Monroe shook his head. "I can't. Because it didn't happen like that, did it?" He was tired and hadn't had breakfast. He glanced at his watch. Almost time for lunch. Better wrap this up.

"You thought Betty shot him, and she thought you shot him. You wiped fingerprints off that shovel with a handkerchief, yet the grip admitted he picked it up without thinking. There should have been more than just your prints on the shovel, Earl. And that handkerchief, you didn't realize it was Betty's, now covered in blood. You stuck it in the sand, hoping to retrieve it later. You two are protecting each other. And you're both wrong."

"Oh for god's sake, man, stop acting like Bogart in *The Maltese Falcon*." James crossed his arms.

Monroe focused his attention on Florence. The room grew still.

"It was you, doll. You and your innocence and little pencil nibblings. All an act to cover up revenge. For you know what Sam did on *Unknown Island*."

"I'm sure I don't know what you're talking about." Florence clutched her clipboard tight to her chest.

Monroe signaled to Riley, who handed him the eight-by-ten glossy of Wally Anderson. Monroe compared Wally's face with Florence's. "This glossy found in Sam's office reminded me of someone, that someone is you. Your brother, isn't it? He wore that rubber ceratosaurus or allosaurus suit in *Unknown Island*, when they shot out in Palmdale. The heat was intense. And Sam wouldn't give them a break or let them take off the suits. Take after take.

"Wally would have sweated buckets. And when he collapsed, Sam kept the cameras rolling. Only when the take was finished was Wally rushed to the hospital. He died of heat stroke. You think he died on the set. But Sam wouldn't allow anything to get in his way, especially some miserable, costume-wearing fool in a rubber suit. And Sam left that shot in the finished product. So anyone and everyone could see your brother die, again and again."

Florence hissed and reached into her tool-kit apron.

"Sam laughed, laughed when I told him who I was." She dropped her clipboard, raised the gun, and smiled. It wasn't a nice smile. "All he had to do, all he had to do was apologize. Just publicly apologize! But no, he told me that he'd ruin me. That he'd leave my name off the credits. He told me I'd never work in this town again."

"And you won't, sweetheart."

"When I saw him, unconscious in that suit he could never call it by its right name, I shot him, worked the lift, and buried him upside down. He deserved to die!"

"A lot of people deserve to die, Florence, but that's not our call." Monroe stepped toward her, holding out his hand. "Give me that pea shooter."

"No. Stay where you are. Betty, you're coming with me."

Betty stood shakily. "Florence, I'm so sorry about your brother."

Florence sniffed and shook her head. "I need you to get out of here and on the road. Any of you interfere, and I'll kill you then Betty." She aimed the gun at Monroe. The other officers had their guns out, but Monroe motioned them down.

"So don't stop me!"

"Riley!"

"I checked that apron, I swear, boss."

Florence snarled. "Stupid, you are all stupid. I hid it in those pillows and sat on it!"

Monroe focused on Florence's shaking gun hand. Florence snapped pencils with regularity. The thought of her tense finger on the trigger wasn't pleasant. He did not want to die on a sand mound in Stage Two in The Heart of Screenland. Who'd feed his cat Buster? Who'd bring Buster autographs to shred?

Betty, moving slowly to Florence's side, shot him an intelligent glance, then one at Earl. Earl stiffened. Great. The bombshell was planning something.

Betty stumbled up to Florence. "Oh, Flo, it's so very hot in here, I really don't think I can—"

Then she fainted, falling forward onto Florence and with one arm, grabbed Florence's waist and with the other, grabbed the shaking gun hand, putting her full bosomy weight onto the thin girl. They crashed to the ground.

Monroe was there before Earl. He wrenched the gun away from a yelling Florence. Earl pulled Betty into his arms and kissed her. She pretended to be dizzy and unaware of the others. An Academy-Award-winning performance. Especially since she glanced at Monroe and gave him a wink.

Riley and the other officers wrestled a maniac Florence out of Stage Two.

"Another day in Culver City," muttered Monroe. He turned to the stunned crew and cast. "Don't lie to the cops, folks, that's the first lesson. The second lesson is don't litter because some murderer might just use your trash against you. And I have a last request. I'd be honored to take home some autographs for my little terror, Buster."

The actors preened and wrote away. He gathered the slips of paper. He fingered Betty's. He might keep this one. She'd kissed his cheek and thanked him. He smiled. She had the makings of a star once she went back to brunette and stopped pretending she was such a dim bulb. She certainly could act. He glanced at his watch. Plenty of time to cruise up to DuPars and grab a late breakfast. Then sleep. For he did work in the land of dreams, The Heart of Screenland.

Author's Note

There is a film entitled *Unknown Island* and a crew member supposedly died wearing the rubber dinosaur suit. The director did leave the shot in the film. Many other story facts are true, but the characters and film *Unknown Sand Pits!* only exist in the author's imagination.

About the Author

Laurel Wetzork's multi-genre work—usually revolving around murder and mysteries—has been described as imaginative, surreal, suspenseful, deeply tragic, funny, and heartfelt. Wetzork received her bachelor of arts and master's degrees from USC. She and her husband enjoy bike touring, sailing, hiking, cooking, and visits with daughter Karina. www.mojewetz orkstudios.com

Careful What You Wish For

Nancy Cole Silverman

BRIDGETTE STREET ARRIVED AT the Hollywood Home for Retired Actors & Artists like she did everything else in her life: with the clothes on her back, a smile on her face, and a hope that, this time, things would work out. She had nowhere else to go. Her career as a young, up-and-coming ingenue had fizzled out years before when she and her leading man, Devon Neilsen, had come to a difference of opinion over method acting: Devon wanted an actual off-stage bedroom experience—Bridgette wanted absolutely nothing to do with him.

Their relationship came to blows after a handsy scene in which Devon had taken advantage of an on-stage embrace and stuck his tongue halfway down her throat. Bridgette marched off the set and demanded the show's producer Sidney Starwaski make a choice—him or her.

Unfortunately for Bridgette, Sidney sided with Devon and hired a fresh-faced and amenable young look-alike to replace her. And to make matters worse, Sidney leaked a few choice words to the trades describing Bridgette as *difficult*. All of which made Bridgette an untouchable, leading to a series of downward spirals and a pile of bills from expenses she had run up while living the high life. Her attempts to rekindle her career faded each passing year until she found herself working as a manager for a cheap movie theater in Van Nuys that made more money selling popcorn than theater tickets.

But when the COVID crisis hit and the theater closed, and Bridgette's meager savings was lower than her rent, she did the only thing she knew to do. She swallowed her pride and went to visit Sidney at the Hollywood Home for Retired Actors & Artists. She had a favor to ask.

The grounds of the HHRAA, affectionately known to those in the business as Hollywood's Last Hurrah, were nestled in the foothills of the San Fernando Valley on what had once been a Western movie set. Thirty acres of landscaped parkways, ideal for slow-moving seniors on their scooters, dotted with small, Spanish-style bungalows, sequestered Zen gardens, an art center, a theater complete with production equipment, a video intranet to each of the resident villas, a bistro, and a large central dining area.

Bridgette still had the size two blue minidress she had worn the day she walked off the show. Despite forty-three years and the dress being a trifle snug, Bridgette was confident she could pull off the same seventies-style sizzle she had when she was twenty-five. A little shimmy as she bypassed security with a wave and a flash of her famous Pepsodent smile, followed by a friendly ask of the groundskeeper to point her in the direction of Sidney's bungalow, was all she would need.

She was fortunate that the security guard, a senior in his own right, was one of the few fans who remembered Bridgette Street. He was happy to oblige. He pointed out Sidney's bungalow on the map. A short jaunt down the yellow brick road, just past the Zen garden.

Bridgette had barely stepped foot onto the campus when a red scooter, going much too fast for the narrow path, beeped from behind.

"Move it or lose it, lady. Don't got all day. Hurry it up."

"Sidney?" Who else would have taken such a tone?

Bridgette stepped off the path. The years hadn't been kind to the old man. He had grown fat and, sitting on his four-wheeled motor scooter, looked like a giant pumpkin melted to the seat. His once thick red hair was now thin and pasted with streaks of gray across his balding scalp.

"Why if it isn't Bridgette Street." Sidney backed his scooter up to get a better look. He hadn't seen her since he'd kicked her off the set. *Ballsy broad.* "How'd you find me?"

Bridgette adjusted the shoulder strap of her bag, threw her shoulders back, and with *the girls* leading the way, sashayed toward her nemesis like she was stepping onto a stage.

"It wasn't hard, Sid. Your name still shows up in the *Hollywood Reporter.*"

"You following me?"

"Maybe." Bridgette took a rolled copy of the magazine from inside her bag and handed it to him. SID STAWARSKI STILL DIRECTING AT 88.

Sidney unrolled the magazine and snorted. The press had always loved him, given him lots of ink, and this month's edition of the *Hollywood Reporter* had included a feature story about his plans to produce a short for the LA Film Festival. A rekindling of *The Ad Agency*, a once top-rated, thirty-minute rom-com with its handsome president, hot young female account exec, and their dysfunctional clients.

"So, what is it you want?"

"Your help. I need a place to live, Sid. Despite not being able to get a job for the last forty-plus years—thank you very much—I was an actress, and I can qualify to live here. But I need a referral, and I figure you owe me."

"I owe you? You walked out on a top-rated show, and—"

"It failed, Sid. Right after I left, it *failed*. The network refused to pick it up again."

"And you think you can come back to me now and ask for my help?"

"You owe me, Sid."

"I don't owe you a damn thing!" Sidney put his scooter in reverse and started to back away, then stopped. "But if you're looking for an audition, leave your card at the front office. You know how it goes. If you're lucky, you'll get a callback."

"Callback my arse!" Bridgette drove back to her apartment, cursing the thought of Sid. What had possessed her to think he might ever help her? The man had lost his mind. Producing a show at his age? What was he thinking?

But when the phone rang the following morning, and Bridgette recognized Sid's tobacco-rusty voice, she couldn't quell the silent prayer that maybe, just maybe, there was hope.

"Birdie?" Sid's voice cracked through the receiver. "I can still call you Birdie, can't I?"

Bridgette took a deep breath. No point in arguing. "You're the only one who ever did."

"Good, 'cause I've decided to bring you back for the reunion show. *The Ad Agency* was a hit then, and it'll be a hit again. People love this stuff. So, wadda ya say? Let's give it one final round for showbiz sake."

Bridgette didn't have to think about it. A chance to get back up on stage and a job that would pay the bills would be a whole lot better than how she had been trying to scrape by.

"On one condition."

"You really think you're in a position to negotiate?"

"I need a place to live, Sid. It's why I came to see you in the first place. You arrange for me to have permanent resident status there, and I'm in."

Sid was quiet.

Bridgette held her breath.

"All right. That's doable. I've given the place millions, and the board will do whatever I say. So here's the deal. There's an empty villa, a single one-bedroom, round the corner from me. Number 109. I'll arrange to have the key put in the mailbox. You move in whenever you like, and we'll see how it goes. You work out, and you can stay. But the role comes with one caveat."

"Devon Neilson?" Bridgette knew before she asked. The two had been household names. One without the other was like bread without butter.

"Take it or leave it, Birdie. Dev's in, and I want you for the role, but," Sid cleared his throat, "Tina was your replacement when you left and will be again if you mess up. What's left of the cast and crew is here at the Last Hurrah. We're all living together like a family, so it's up to you to make nice and fit in."

"I'll take it."

After all these years of struggle, Bridgette couldn't believe she finally had what she wanted. A new beginning. An apartment and a chance to star in a role she had made famous. What she didn't want was to work with Sid again and star opposite Devon. But how bad it could it be? Sid, she could handle. The man was nothing but a voyeur. And Dev ... well ... she hadn't seen her leading man in years. He had to be at least seventy-five, and it was, after all, only one show.

It didn't take Bridgette but half a day to pack up her apartment. Everything she owned—a closet full of clothes, cosmetics, groceries, and a box full of books—she shoved into the back seat of her car, an old, beat-up convertible Mercedes. Then plopping a large sunhat on her head, Bridgette got behind the wheel, raced up the 405, and as the sun was setting, rolled through the wrought iron gates of the Hollywood Home for Retired Actors & Artists.

Maybe it was the time of day—what cameramen call the golden hour—when the air is cooler and softer on the skin, and everyone and everything looks fabulous, or maybe it was that Bridgette felt a sense of belonging, a feeling that she hadn't felt in years, that caused her throat to tighten as she took the key from the mailbox and placed it in the villa's door. Whatever the cause, when she stepped into the small, furnished, one-bedroom unit, her eyes filled with tears. On the coffee table, Sid had arranged for a bouquet of yellow roses—her favorite—with a basket of fresh fruit, nuts, and a welcome card.

It had been a long time. And aside from the nuts, which Bridgette was allergic to, everything was perfect. Back in the day, craft services would have been fired if they had nuts on the set. The joke among them was that they had one too many nuts on the stage already and didn't need another.

Monday morning, Bridgette woke to the sound of birds singing and people greeting each other on the yellow brick road outside her apartment as they walked their dogs. What a contrast the villa was to the endless noise of traffic outside her Van Nuys walk-up, with the stale smell of cigarette smoke in the hallways. Bridgette luxuriated beneath the sheets. In the back of her mind, the spark of an idea began to germinate. While this was only one show, the opportunity might be the relaunch she needed to kickstart her career. And from there . . . who knew? This might only be the beginning. Bridgette tossed off the sheets and dressed quickly, choosing a simple summer shift, blue to match her eyes, and slipping on a pair of spiky heeled sandals, and hurried out the door for the table read in the Zen garden.

"Morning, Birdie. You sleep well?" Sid lifted his coffee, a silent salute to his leading lady, and motored his scooter closer to the picnic table set for the day's table read.

"I did. Thank you." Bridgette took a Styrofoam cup from the table, filled it with coffee, and noticed several cast and crew members huddled at the end of the table. They appeared to be involved in a conversation and, upon seeing her, turned their backs.

Sid snorted. "Hope you weren't expecting a warm welcome there, old gal. When I told the cast and crew I was bringing Bridgette Street back, they weren't exactly wild about it. Some of 'em had a pretty hard time after the show folded and still blame you."

"Well, maybe I can change that."

"That'll be up to you. Anyway, what's left is a skeletal crew. Just one camera, not three like you were used to."

"Is that—?" Bridgette heard a familiar voice behind her and turned to see her favorite cameraman.

"Ben!"

The two embraced, and while they caught up on old times, the cast and crew members finished filling their paper plates with sweet rolls and fresh fruit from the table. Stephen, who played the agency's art director, bumped shoulders with her, and Karen, the bubbly office manager, glanced up from her plate, then turned her back and took a seat at the far end of the table. Matt and Robert, members of the crew, nodded a less than cordial welcome. Bridgette saw everybody was there except for Devon, who was noticeably absent. But not for long. In his stead, Tina approached with her hands full of water bottles.

"Bridgette Street?" Stuffing a bottle beneath her arm, Tina extended her hand. "I'm so pleased to meet you. I hope it's not awkward that I'm here."

Bridgette shook the tips of Tina's fingers, "I'm sorry, I didn't realize—"

"Ugh, don't worry." Tina dropped Bridgette's hand. "I'm not here as an actress. Obviously. I mean, you're here, and Sid's offered you the role. Which is as it should be, being as it's a reunion show and all—who else would he have?" Tina raised her brows as she moved to put the water bottles on the table in front of the actors' chairs. "But I go where Dev goes these days, and Sid asked me to help out, so here I am." Then pausing before placing one final bottle on the table, Tina asked, "Where are you sitting?"

Bridgette pointed to a middle seat at the table and was about to sit down when—

"Well, Miss Street. It is still Miss, isn't it?" Devon appeared from within one of the villas next to the garden and stood on the patio with a bagel in his hand. "She'll sit next to me. We've much to catch up on."

Bridgette locked eyes with Sid. *Keep it cool, Bridgette. You have a lot at stake.*

"Why, I couldn't think of anything I'd like more than to sit next to you, Dev. I've been looking forward to the opportunity." Bridgette flashed him her Pepsodent smile.

Dev wiped his mouth with the back of his hand and, like a much younger man, placed one hand on the short wall separating the patio from the garden and hopped over.

Bridgette sat down at the table, and Dev took the chair next to her. "I see you haven't changed. Always the last to arrive and still a fan of the old sour cream with pickled herring and onions for breakfast routine." Bridgette flicked a small crumb from the side of Dev's face and leaned back to avoid the overwhelming stench of his foul fish breath.

"Children!" Sid shot the two a warning look as he parked his motor scooter at the head of the table. "We're not going to have a problem now, are we?"

"No, not at all." From beneath the table, Bridgette dug the spiky heel of her sandal into Dev's foot.

"Just a friendly exchange," Dev added, his hand firmly on Bridgette's slender wrist, a warning squeeze their past was not forgotten.

"Good." Sidney reached for the script for today's read. "Because I need you to be at your best. We've less than a week to put this together."

~ell~

Table reads are often the first time an actor has a chance to look at a script, and it's not unusual for a writer, who may be hearing their words spoken for the first time, to stop an actor mid-sentence and do a rewrite on the spot. Consequently, a table read for a thirty-minute romantic comedy, which due to commercial breaks, actually clocks in at about twenty-two minutes, is never as quick as expected. But today's table read, despite its commercial-free, twenty-two-minute format, wasn't delayed due to rewrites but because Bridgette couldn't keep her eyes open.

With her elbows on the table and her head in her hands, Bridgette stared down at the script, her eyes heavy. The words floating on the page beneath her.

"Bridgette?" Dev elbowed Bridgette. "Your line."

"What?" Bridgette looked up. The table in front of her was spinning. The last thing she remembered was looking at the water bottle and thinking how thirsty she had been before her elbows collapsed and she fell face-first onto the table.

Dev stood up. "I can't work like this. What is she, drunk?"

Dev stormed back to his villa.

Tina glanced at Sid. "I'll fix it, Sid, don't worry." Then grabbing Bridgette's water bottle in place of Tina's own, Tina chased after Devon.

Day one hadn't ended well. Ben, who had always been a little sweet on Bridgette, helped her back to her bungalow. He didn't think she was drunk, and from the way he had seen Tina switch her water bottle for Bridgette's, he suspected Bridgette had been drugged and suggested she take the rest of the afternoon to sleep it off.

"The cast and crew don't exactly have your best interests at heart, Bridgette."

"Yeah, Sid warned me. But you'd think after all these years, they'd have let it go. After all, Sid didn't cut their careers short."

"True. But a few still have some very bitter memories about how you had left the show, so sudden and all. They blame you for killing the show off. And a lot of people went through some pretty hard times afterward."

"Not harder than me."

Later that evening, after a terse, one-sided conversation with Sidney where he accused Bridgette of being drunk, Bridgette apologized for her actions despite the fact she hadn't touched a drop of alcohol. Easier to admit to a slip-up than to confess that certain cast members—Dev, for instance—were less than enthusiastic about her return. Bridgette wasn't about to risk Sidney's siding with Dev for a second time.

"I promise you, Sid. It won't happen again."

"It better not, Birdie. You've got one shot at this. This film gets picked up for a show, it could be your come back. But you screw this up, every-thing—the villa, the job, your future—it all goes away."

Day two was a continuation of day one, but with a revised script for the table read. New pages were delivered, and the rehearsal was completed on schedule. All of which allowed Bridgette time for a wardrobe fitting she had missed the day before and another unexpected face-to-face with Tina, who Sid had asked to help with costumes. Bridgette promised herself she wouldn't fall victim to Dev or Tina's dirty tricks to get her kicked off the show and was braced for the unexpected.

"Ouch!" Bridgette pulled a straight pin from beneath the sleeve of her costume. "Don't you check for pins?"

"Sorry. I must have missed it." Tina removed the pin and stuck it in a pincushion on the floor next to her.

"Look," Bridgette turned away from the fitting mirror and glared at Tina. "I know what you're up to. And it's not going to work. I'm not leaving the production. And you're not taking my role."

Tina stood up. "I don't know what you're talking about. I think you're being paranoid. Sid asked for my help, and I'm with Dev now. Dev always said you were difficult."

"Difficult? Believe me, you don't know difficult. I've lived difficult the past forty years, and I'm not about to roll over now. So whatever fantasy you have about stepping in for me, like you did last time, it's not going to happen."

Bridgette ripped the dress off and tossed it on the floor. "Finish it up and deliver it to my bungalow. I'll let you know how it fits."

On the way out the door, Bridgette was nearly run off the yellow brick road. Sidney waved for Bridgette to move as he sped past her toward the theater with his hand above his head and a cigar clenched between his teeth. If the Last Hurrah had ever posted a speed limit, the old man exceeded it. Any faster, and he would have toppled his cart off the path.

By Wednesday, Sidney had arranged for the entire cast and crew to take over the Last Hurrah's fifty-seat theater for an off-book rehearsal. Actors were all expected to know their lines and be ready to begin blocking for each scene. Blocking can be a slow process, and Bridgette thought the cast was a bit punch drunk, slyly passing water bottles among themselves, which she avoided, while Sid ran through the show scene by scene, letting each actor know where they needed to be on stage, and when.

"Dev, I need you upstage center for the next scene. Bridgette, you're downstage right, seated on the desk, legs crossed, looking at the phone. When the phone rings, pick it up. Dev, once you hear the phone ring, you cross downstage, take the receiver from her hand, and slam it down on the desk."

"Got it." Both actors nodded and took their places.

Bridgette positioned herself on the desk and crossed her legs, her foot wiggling impatiently while Dev took his time to find his place upstage. When the phone rang, Dev did exactly as instructed and crossed the stage just as Bridgette was about to place the receiver to her ear. But rather than grabbing the phone and slamming it down, Dev stumbled. His shoulder crashed into Bridgette, shoving her onto the floor like a rag doll.

"Oh, sorry. I must have slipped." Dev regained his balance and held out a hand. "Need some help?"

"No, thank you." Bridgette looked at Sidney with his head buried in his notes. Wasn't he going to say anything? Then realizing there was no point, she brushed herself off and stood up. "I'll be just fine."

Sid raised his pencil and pointed to Dev. "Let's take it from the top, people. And this time, Dev, try not to crush Bridgette."

Try not to crush Bridgette? Was that all Sid had to say about Dev's blatant personal attack on her? Anyone who had spent time in the theater could see Dev's stumble had been choreographed. A fake fall designed to injure Bridgette so that Sid would need to replace her with Tina.

With a little more force, Dev's fall might have resulted in Bridgette being carted off stage and unable to finish the show. And not one member of the cast or crew seemed to be concerned about it. They all just kind of ignored it and laughed it off. What was Bridgette supposed to do, just buck up? Pretend Dev wasn't out to get her? Bridgette had been down this path before with both Dev and Sid, but this time she wasn't about to leave.

On day four, the final draft for the script was presented to the actors, the camera positions were locked, and the actors appeared in costume on the set. And Bridgette was ready, prepared for the unexpected. She knew her lines and had spent the night before chatting with Ben regarding her concerns about Dev and Tina. If Dev didn't do something on the set today, tomorrow would be too late.

"I'm concerned about what might happen on stage. You said some of the crew members were still angry at me for leaving when I did. If Dev convinced Matt maybe to loosen one of the lamps from the grid above the stage, it could fall and kill me."

"Let me worry about that, Bridgette. I've always looked out for you. You know that."

"And what about the stage's trap door? Is it bolted shut?"

"Probably, we've no plans to use it for this production. But there's a scene switch in the second act. If Dev wanted to, he might be able to get down beneath the stage and unbolt the door. I'll check."

"Thanks, Ben. At least I know you're in my corner."

Ben winked when Bridgette came back on stage for the second act and stood center stage directly about the trap door. With Ben there to watch over her, Bridgette knew she had nothing to worry about.

Bridgette glanced at Dev. He stood just feet from her—center stage right. Waiting. Anticipating. Hoping. But when the floor didn't fall beneath Bridgette's feet, Dev's face did. And for the first time in the actor's life, he went up on his line.

Dev blanked and screamed, "Line!"

Day five: Bridgette called Sidney first thing in the morning and told him she planned to do her own makeup. She wouldn't risk a final encounter with Tina and arrived on set a few minutes late, looking flawless and wearing the same tightfitting little blue dress she had worn the day she had walked off the show.

Sidney looked up from his scooter as Bridgette took her place on stage. "You changed your dress, Birdie. That's not the costume I wanted."

Bridgette shrugged, her hands in the air. "Wardrobe malfunction, what can I say?"

Sidney didn't like surprises. Bridgette knew they would have words later, just like old times, but it was too late now.

Sidney yelled, "Quiet on the set. Action."

Once the camera began to roll, Bridgette and Dev fell into their roles exactly as they had many years before. Their timing and delivery were spontaneous. Their chemistry on stage was undeniable. Bridgette even ad-libbed a few lines adding to the hilarity of the script, which drew a few unexpected chuckles from the crew. What Bridgette had dreaded would be twenty-two minutes of hell turned out to be a delight. She was back in the spotlight again, and she loved it.

"Cut! That's a wrap, folks." Sidney raised his hands above his head, waited until he knew he had Bridgette's eye, then clapped slowly before the cast and crew joined in enthusiastically.

While the cast and crew retreated to their private bungalows to get ready for the wrap party, Sidney loaded the video file onto the center's private intranet so they could all watch the show from their rooms. What they all saw were old friends, some with a few more gray hairs, others a few extra pounds, all together again on the small screen. Sidney's direction had been excellent. And Ben's camerawork—he always shot Bridgette's best angle—was even better. In Bridgette's mind, the show was everything she wanted it to be and, despite her age, would prove to the critics that she could still hold her own. Other actresses had returned to the stage late in life. Why couldn't she?

Bridgette picked up the phone to call Sidney. She wanted to congratulate him and thank him for asking her back for the reunion show. She knew he wanted to talk to her. Not so much about how successful the show had been but about the ad-libs, her dress, and arriving late on set.

Sidney was stubborn that way. He took everything personally and never let anything go. No one dared to change anything and not pay for it. It had to be his way, all the time. Bridgette knew it wouldn't be easy to convince him to let it go, but she figured she could cajole him into forgiving her.

But Sidney wasn't about to be charmed.

"I've half a mind to fire you and start over! How dare you?"

"What? But, Sid—" Had the man lost his mind? There wasn't time to shoot another short film. And what would he do if he did? Use Tina?

"Pack your bags, Birdie. You're out of here."

"No! I'm not leaving. Meet me in the edit bay. We can talk this out, Sid. Give me fifteen minutes."

Bridgette panicked. She didn't trust that Sidney wouldn't do exactly as he had threatened to do and destroy the video file. The old man had always been headstrong and a bit crazy. Allowing her to walk off the set years ago was only one of his famous hard-nosed tactics. Sidney Stawarski had the power to destroy careers. And he used it. Every actor in town knew that it was a make-or-break deal when they worked for Sidney. They either got in line with his thinking, or they would be booted off the show, and good luck trying to resurrect a career after Sidney had finished with them. That wasn't going to happen to Bridgette. Not again.

Bridgette grabbed her keys, took the dress Tina had altered from the back of the bathroom door, folded the costume in its plastic sheeting over her arm, and marched out of her apartment toward the edit bay. Sidney was mad. Not just angry, but crazy. Destroying a film over a couple of ad-libs and a dress? Who did that? The man had lost his mind, and his threats to kill the show would not only cost her a place to live but her chances of any return to Hollywood. She had to make Sid see reason. Either that or eliminate the problem.

Bridgette took the yellow brick road to the theater and stopped where the path split. Directly ahead was the theater, but to her left was a smaller, seldom used path leading to an outside entrance to the edit bay. Bridgette paused and hung the dress on a branch of a Palo Verde tree just past the fork in the road. When Sidney saw the dress, he would know she had taken the back way to the edit bay. All Bridgette needed to do was unlock the back door and wait.

When Bridgette heard Sidney's scooter speeding down the narrow path, she counted until she knew he was close. "Ten . . . nine . . . eight . . . seven

. . ." Then, just as she thought Sid was about to approach the door, she opened it exactly as she had planned.

BAM!

Sidney swerved to avoid hitting the door, and what followed looked like a scene from a horror movie. The red scooter careened off the narrow road. Sidney was thrown from the scooter's seat and fell headfirst into the cactus garden, splitting his head, with the scooter landing directly on top of him.

Bridgette stared down at Sidney's motionless body. Whoever would find him would think he had driven his scooter too fast one too many times and had met with an unfortunate accident. His death would come as no surprise. Bridgette dusted her hands. She wouldn't have to worry about Sidney destroying the film, ruining her reputation, or her chance for a comeback. Bridgette grabbed the dress from the tree and returned it to her apartment. She had a wrap party to attend.

Nobody was surprised when Sidney didn't show up at the wrap party. No one thought that the reason for Bridgette's late arrival had anything to do with Sidney's absence. Most figured the old director had gone back to the edit bay to tweak the video while the cast and crew were busy congratulating each other on a job well done.

"Hey! Look who's finally arrived." Ben stood behind the bar inside the bistro and welcomed Bridgette as she entered with his hands in the air. Behind Ben was a colorful balloon bouquet and in front of him on the bar, a sheet cake with a picture of Bridgette in the blue dress.

Dev and Tina stood with the rest of the cast and crew at the end of the bar. Dev teased Bridgette about her late entrance, then put his arm around Tina.

"All kidding aside, Bridgette, congratulations are in order. Despite your ad-libs, I have to say, things turned out better than I expected."

"It was a good show, Dev. And Tina, I know you wanted the role—"

"Don't even think about it." Tina air-kissed Bridgette on the cheek. "Sid was right. It was better with you. And just to show you how much we all care, we got together and had this cake made in your honor."

Bridgette glanced at Ben. He crossed his arms and nodded to the cake. "It's fine, Bridgette. Chocolate caramel. Your favorite. Go ahead."

"I hope you like it." Tina took the knife, cut a small piece, and offered it to Bridgette.

Bridgette took a dainty bite and wiped her lips. "Delicious."

Dev took her hand. "Hey, eat the whole thing. You know you love it, and you don't have to squeeze into the blue dress again. The show's over."

"You're right." Bridgette took another healthy bite of the cake, and Ben handed her a glass of champagne.

"Hey, how about a toast?" Dev lifted his glass. "To our leading lady."

"Hear." Ben saluted Dev with his glass. "We've all been waiting a long time for this moment."

"Thank you. It's good to be back." Bridgette clicked her glass to Dev, Tina, and the rest of the cast and crew, and took a sip. But rather than the cool chill of bubbles in her mouth, she felt her throat start to close. She put her hand to her neck, and when she did, she knew she had made a mistake. A deadly mistake. She pointed to the cake.

"Was that?"

"Made with peanuts?" Dev answered.

Bridgette dropped her drink, and the glass fell to the ground. Even a tiny amount of peanut dust was enough to kill her.

"Why?" Bridgette slumped, and Dev grabbed her as her eyes rolled back in her head.

Ben leaned in close and whispered in her ear. "I tried to warn you, Bridgette. We all suffered after you stormed off the show. Careful what you wish for."

About the Author

After twenty-five years in news/talk radio, Nancy Cole Silverman retired to write fiction. Her crime-focused novels have attracted readers throughout America, and her short stories have appeared in numerous anthologies. Silverman writes the Carol Childs and Misty Dawn Mysteries (Henery Press), and *The Navigator's Daughter*, a Kat Lawson Mystery (Level Best Books).

As Seen on Television

Melinda Loomis

MY PHONE BUZZED AND I took a big gulp of coffee. It was early and I hadn't had my caffeine yet, and me without caffeine is like a car without gas.

I wasn't surprised to see Carmen's name pop up on the screen, even at the crack of dawn. She and I had been friends since meeting at the police academy. I had gone the detective route, but Carmen preferred community policing, and since she worked out of Hollywood Station her community meant never a dull moment.

"Laura, guess who they just hauled in here!"

"Could you give me a hint?" I asked wearily. "Narrow it down from everyone in the greater Los Angeles area."

She tsked me over the phone. "Fine. You're gonna get him soon enough. Joey Lombardi from the TV murder you and your hot partner are investigating."

That woke me up. Hot partner Detective Eddie Faith and I had been working a high-profile case involving sitcom stars—one presumed dead, the other with motive—and brass wanted results yesterday. I couldn't blame them. We were getting hounded twenty-four seven by the media. Everyone wanted to be the first to break the news of an arrest, plus social media was going bonkers with conspiracy theories—crazy and otherwise. Meanwhile, TMZ was being its usual unhelpful self.

We weren't ready to arrest Lombardi yet, so I was surprised and annoyed that he'd been brought in without my knowledge. "You're kidding. For what?"

"Drunk and disorderly. Emphasis on drunk, from what I heard. Like totally hammered. Some tourists found him an hour ago in an alley off Sunset, semiconscious and blubbering about a dead guy. They recognized him too, and I'm not sure we got their cameras before they shared their Hollywood moment with the world."

I was awake now. After holding his own during hours of interrogation, had Joey gotten loaded and confessed? Could we get that lucky? Had the conscience we'd become convinced he didn't have ratted him out?

"Does the media know?"

"I don't think so," Carmen answered. "But if they don't, they will soon enough. Arresting officers are trying to sober him up before they ship him downtown. Oh, and did you hear what else happened this morning? A guy jumped off the Hollywood Sign."

"What?"

"Yeah," she said. "No ID yet, but I'd bet good money he's a failed actor. *Was* a failed actor. I don't know how he accessed it—it's supposed to be fenced off."

"As long as it wasn't Nick Tran," I answered. "And yes, it's *very* fenced off."

"Not Nick. Blond guy." The missing Nick, of Vietnamese descent, was dark-haired. "Formerly very good-looking blond guy from what I'm hearing," Carmen continued. "I think that's why everyone thinks he's an actor. Or was."

My phone buzzed again. I looked at the screen: Captain Keegan. Official notification time.

"Carmen, it's Keegan. I gotta go."

"Try to act surprised when he gives you the big news. It won't take a detective for people to find out how you knew."

I hung up on Carmen and answered the captain's call. He didn't tell me anything I didn't already know, but for Carmen's sake, I pretended to be shocked at the news of Joey Lombardi's alcohol-fueled meltdown and hoped-for confession.

I bypassed what would no doubt be a media circus at Hollywood Station and headed directly to headquarters in downtown. Eddie was waiting in the lobby, along with Captain Keegan, who nodded curtly and greeted me with, "Detective Mercer." That was the closest to "Good morning" I would get from him. Keegan's the old school strong, silent type.

"Looks like we had the right guy all along," Eddie observed as the elevator doors opened.

We stepped in. Keegan shook his head. "Not so fast. DA's not gonna go to trial on a drunken admission. Plus, there's no way to confirm what he may or may not have actually said in front of the tourists. Any halfway decent lawyer will rip that apart in court, and he's going to have the best money can buy."

Eddie smirked. "He'll probably claim he was researching a role."

I laughed. "He's a sitcom actor, Eddie, not method."

Eddie nodded. "Great. Now prove it in court."

Exactly.

Our big, high-profile case was the sudden disappearance and presumed death of one of Joey Lombardi's cast mates. Joey had become a celebrity on some inane reality show, then parlayed that into the lead on an equally inane sitcom called *Life with Newbie*. Joey starred as a big-city guy newly arrived at a small-town college, and in each episode helped enlighten his hick peers, professors, and anyone else who crossed his path, dispersing meaningful lessons about diversity, inclusion, tolerance, and other socially relevant issues.

These were all delivered with the condescending subtlety of a sledge-hammer on steroids, accompanied by a laugh track that was way over the top. I hate laugh tracks and I hate sitcoms. It's not funny if they have to cue you when to guffaw. However, eight million people a week—no doubt mostly teens and twenty-somethings, who swooned over Joey's pouty, pretty-boy looks—disagreed with me. Both the show and Joey were big hits.

After two seasons of *Newbie*, having established himself as not-particularly talented—but a star nonetheless—Joey had scored the leading role in a parody teen vampire movie. He decided it was time to leave lowly sitcoms behind. He was so sure of his impending film stardom that he'd advised the show's producers to prepare for life without Joey. Since he wasn't the shiny new toy anymore, they dealt with it and brought in an unknown actor named Nick Tran. They eased him in while Joey was still on the show to make the replacement less jarring for viewers. Luckily, fans loved the new newbie. In fact, the show's ratings had risen and so had Nick's stardom. Bonus for Nick—unlike Joey, he could actually act. He was eclipsing Joey on his own show.

But before Joey could escape the clutches of half-hour television, *Sucks to Be You* hit the big screen and did the one thing Joey never anticipated: it bombed. Not only was the movie savaged by critics, it died a quick death at the box office. To stay in the public eye, Joey had to stick with *Newbie*. The show kept him, but now he had to share the spotlight with Nick. All in all, not a happy situation for Newbie Number One, and he wasn't shy about expressing his displeasure.

Then a week ago, Nick Tran vanished. He'd finished filming on a Friday evening, wasn't seen over the weekend, then never reported for work the following Monday. His lost weekend was still a mystery, his body out there somewhere. Although we hadn't found him, we quickly moved from treating the case as a missing person to a homicide. A guy like that doesn't just walk away from a life like that on his own volition. A guy recognizable from a hit show can't stay hidden for long in Los Angeles.

We had two suspects that we considered to be co-conspirators. There was Joey Lombardi, of course, a slimy jerk who stood to benefit the most from a Nick-less show, and Tracy Warren, the *Newbie* writers' assistant who had a starry-eyed case of the hots for Joey. This had been brought to our attention thanks to Gina Cullen, a *Newbie* producer who had been extremely helpful. The rest of the production and network types had gone into damage control overdrive and proven less than useful to our investigation.

After quickly eliminating a couple of obsessive fans—they had rock-solid alibis—we'd gone back to Joey and Tracy. The besotted Tracy would, in Gina's opinion, do anything for Joey. She let us know that behind the scenes, the *Life with Newbie* brain trust had been working on a plan to dump the increasingly difficult Joey and his decreasing popularity and go forward with just Nick. Gina was sure Tracy blabbed the news to him despite being told to keep it to herself. Which gave him motive to get rid of his more popular replacement.

But no matter how much we leaned on Joey, he doggedly stuck to his non-story. He claimed that he last saw Nick that Friday evening while leaving the lot. They said good night and that was that. He also claimed that he and Nick got along fine, asserting that he was the bigger star, so Nick was no threat. Tracy also played dumb. Neither of them knew anything. Yeah, right.

There was one other problem. So far, we had little forensic evidence. We were waiting on phone records and traffic cameras were being scrutinized, but there was little else to go on besides instinct. Captain Keegan, already sick to death of being hounded by the media, had even dropped a couple hints that maybe Eddie and I were barking up the wrong tree. It had crossed my mind in a moment of weakness. But neither Eddie nor I could get past the feeling there was something hinky with those two.

"Those tourists," I asked the captain. "American? Fluent in English?"

"Japanese, with very broken English. And very star-struck, according to our translator."

Great. So Joey was big in Japan. That wasn't going to hold up in court at all. If they had trouble with sober English, there was no way we could persuade a jury they had clearly understood what Joey said while wasted.

As we stepped into the Robbery-Homicide bullpen, Eddie observed, "You know what the problem is? He's not the least bit intimidated by us and she feels protected by proxy. It's like his stardom is protecting them from on high and they know it."

"Goes with the territory," was all Keegan had to say before heading off to his office. And he was right. It's hard to convict celebrities, especially at the height of their stardom. Juries just can't wrap their heads around the idea of someone who has it all—fame, money, adoration—just throwing it away like that, like a common criminal. If Joey was just some average Joe, I wouldn't be as concerned about nailing him. But he wasn't, and the longer our investigation went on without being able to build a case, the weaker we were going to look when we finally arrested him. That was true in the eyes of the media, not to mention in the hands of a high-powered Hollywood defense attorney.

A few hours later we had Joey in Interview 1, and although he was a little worse for wear, he'd sucked down a few buckets of coffee and had sobered up enough to be his usual condescending, uncooperative self. He was also still refusing to call in a lawyer. He explained to us that only guilty people needed lawyers. I think he got that idea from watching television. Spoiler alert, and I say this as a cop: always get a lawyer. It doesn't make you look guilty; it makes you look smart. Luckily for us, Joey wasn't too bright.

We went to work on him again. Eddie and I kept hammering that we knew he was withholding information, but he just shrugged us off time and time again. It went something like this:

Me: Joey, we know you know more about Nick's disappearance than you've told us so far.

Joey: No, I don't.

Eddie: You can't account for where you were that weekend.

Joey: I was home all weekend. I was wasted.

Me: How convenient.

Eddie: Either you or Tracy will crack eventually and whoever talks first gets the better deal. So take your pick—you or her.

Joey: If you're so sure, why don't you arrest me?

Rinse and repeat.

And that was the problem. We couldn't arrest him, not yet. Not based on what we had. Hence the need for one of them to fess up.

After a couple hours of the three of us having that conversation over and over, Eddie and I took a break. We were frustrated and I wasn't sure how Joey was still hanging in there.

I was pissed off and gulping down bad coffee. Eddie slammed a Diet Coke. Then we glanced into Interview 2, where Tracy had been deposited.

She looked exhausted, pale with teary, dark-ringed eyes. She'd also had the sense to call her lawyer, who was in the room with her, trying to calm her down without being obvious about it. Unlike Tracy, he noticed they were sitting in front of a big, fat pane of two-way glass. We could see them from outside the room, but they couldn't see us. When you're in that hot seat and you try to look out to see what's waiting for you, all you see is your own mirrored reflection. Some people I've hauled in here, the terrible things they've done, I'm surprised they could look at themselves. Looking at Tracy, I was convinced more than ever that she and Joey had done something terrible to Nick Tran. Joey might have been conscience-free, but Tracy seemed haunted. Unfortunately for us, so far her infatuation with Joey overrode whatever guilt she might be feeling about Nick.

"Wanna try her next?" Eddie asked. "She looks like she's ready to crack, the lawyer notwithstanding."

I'd had a feeling from the beginning that Tracy was the weak link, but there was another thought percolating in my head, especially since unlike Joey, she had an attorney at her side.

While researching Joey's brief career, among the things we'd learned about him was that he was notoriously bad at improv. He hated studying any aspect of his craft; he just wanted to be famous. Eddie and I held a Joey Lombardi film festival a few days after he became a suspect. His *Saturday Night Live* appearance had been an epic train wreck with his inability to think on his feet. He bobbled lines, and when he did get them right, it was obvious he was reading them off cue cards. It was painful to behold, because he was so crappy and didn't know how to recover.

He was used to trying to make fiction convincing, but he needed a script, rehearsal, and the opportunity for a redo when he screwed up. Not a one-take guy, nor was he a particularly bright guy off camera. I had an idea that I thought could work that to our advantage.

"He can't think on his feet and he's not as smart as he thinks," I told Eddie. He nodded. No argument there.

"We've been playing to his strength: sticking to the script. Asking him questions he's heard a million times on cop shows. He's prepared for that," I explained.

Eddie smiled. "Somehow I have a feeling this isn't the usual good cop/bad cop thing," he said. "He's also seen that on television."

"I have an idea, and if it works, I'm a creative genius. On the other hand . . ." My plan was not without risks. But we didn't have much of a hand to play, and Joey felt bulletproof. I had to hope he still wouldn't be able to improv.

"Tracy will probably crack eventually," I said. "But she wants to protect him. She probably won't fall apart until and unless she thinks Joey is throwing her to the wolves to cover his own ass."

Eddie nodded in agreement.

"We can wait and see what forensics comes up with, but I'd rather get a confession now than hope for something later," I reasoned.

"Captain Keegan would appreciate it too," Eddie pointed out. "He's getting beaten up in the press and online."

So we went back into Interview 1 and started up the same old conversation with Joey, over and over again. He was fatigued, but stayed smug and simply shrugged when we pressed him for details about Nick's fate. Joey held his own while Eddie and I got more and more frustrated, until finally Eddie got so caught up in his righteous indignation that he almost stormed out of the room, catching himself as he was yanking the door open. He glanced back nervously at me, eyes wide as saucers, as though he feared he'd just blown the interview.

That's when Joey broke up laughing and I blew a gasket.

"You think that's funny?" I bellowed at him. "Tell me what happened to Nick Tran!"

He gave me yet another theatrical shrug. "Detective Mercer, for the last time, I've told you *everything* I know, which is nothing. The last time I saw Nick he was alive and well. I didn't kill him, and I don't know who did. Fade to black. The End."

I glared at him, but he wouldn't give. We weren't going to get anything more from Joey. That's when I caved.

"Fine," I snapped. "Here . . ." There was a pad of paper and a pen on the table, brought in earlier for Joey to eventually scrawl his confession, and I tossed them at him, a little harder than necessary. His Hollywood sleazebag lawyer would probably upgrade it to police brutality in court. I repeated the words he'd just said that I wanted in writing, and he scribbled obligingly. "Now sign it and date it," I ordered. He did.

"You know, Detective," he smirked, as he handed the pad back to me, "there was no need for so much drama. If you wanted an autograph, all you had to do was ask." He nodded at his handwritten statement, complete with his ridiculously fancy signature. "You should keep that after I'm released. It'll be worth a fortune on eBay."

I didn't respond, just grabbed the pad and stomped out of the room, Eddie trailing nervously in my wake.

"So I get to go now, right?" Joey yelled.

"Sit tight, we'll get to that," Eddie called back.

When the door clicked shut, I stopped and observed Joey and his triumphant smile mocking us through the two-way glass. He actually turned his head a couple different ways, varying his expression from a small, smug grin to a sparkling, movie star smile, admiring his famous reflection. No doubt planning for his departure from custody into flashing cameras and shouts from the media. I wasn't worried. There was a uniform posted outside the door. Joey Lombardi wasn't going anywhere.

Eddie and I took a few calming breaths, then burst into Interview 2, beaming. Tracy's lawyer had helped her get herself together and she glared at us defiantly. I don't know what she thought the payoff would be for devotion to scum like Joey, but unfortunately for her, she was about to find out.

Her lawyer stood up, but I waved him off before he could get a word out. "Your Prince Charming just threw you under the bus," I announced triumphantly.

Her lawyer sneered at me. "Nice try. Is that all you've got?"

I clicked record on my digital recorder and set it down on the table, then tossed the pad in front of Tracy and told her, "Read it." She did.

I have told Detectives Mercer and Faith everything I know about the death of Nick Tran. Joey Lombardi 5/20/22.

Tracy's mouth fell open, her face showing genuine shock. She kept rereading the statement, as if it would morph into something less incriminating if she went over it enough. Finally, she burst into tears. "That idiot!" she wailed.

Her lawyer barked out her name, but the floodgates had swung open. Tracy Warren was now a woman scorned by a man she'd worshipped and adored. Well, that's what she was supposed to think, anyway.

"He gets the better deal," I told her. "It's all damage control now. He's going to heap as much of this on you as he and some high-powered lawyer can manage. And it's a lot easier to get a jury to convict a non-celebrity than someone famous."

Now it was Eddie's turn to shine. He sat across from Tracy and gently said, "We've heard his version. Why don't you tell us yours?"

It took a couple minutes of internal wrestling, but eventually Tracy looked into Eddie's mesmerizing blue eyes and made her decision. After a brief exchange with her lawyer, we began to learn what happened to Nick Tran, Eddie solicitously pushing Kleenex at Tracy while I tried to stay out of the way.

Gina had been right about Tracy blabbing plans to get Joey off the show. Joey had been livid, but once he'd calmed down, he'd started plotting.

"He actually said he was going to miss me when they kicked him off the show." Tracy sniffled. "That made me feel so good, but now I don't think he meant it. I think he was using me."

I resisted the urge to blurt out, "No shit," while Eddie gave her a sad, *guys are such jerks* smile and nodded sympathetically. "Then he said that if Nick was gone, they'd have to keep him on."

Looking back on it, I think Joey's belief that he would have remained on the show was one of the saddest things about this case. I knew that even if Joey got away with killing Nick, they still wouldn't have kept him on. Gina had told us he'd become so difficult that the network agreed to eat the rest of his contract. He was literally more trouble than he was worth. As far as the show was concerned, he was a goner, period.

Tracy hung her head in embarrassment. "He totally played me."

"I need you to walk us through it," I said. She looked at Eddie for validation, and he nodded and told her, "Begin at the beginning."

"It was all Joey's idea. I had to be the one to approach Nick about going out for drinks after he'd wrapped for the day, because it would have seemed weird if it was Joey. Things were so bad between them . . ."

She'd gotten Nick to a prearranged meeting place in a dark, seedy part of downtown L.A. on the pretense that some friends were trying out a hip new place. But "they" were just her and Joey. There was no hip new place, just Newbie Number One lying in wait in his SUV. Once Nick got out of Tracy's car, he was a dead man.

"How did he get Nick into his car?" I asked.

Prompted again by Eddie, she said, "I think he hit him over the head with something." She didn't want to examine it too closely. She wasn't sure what happened to Nick after that, but the following Monday morning Joey, in passing, had winked at her and whispered, "Problem solved."

By then she already knew that, because Nick had missed his call time and no one could get ahold of him. Gina was already on her way to his house, where she would find nothing. That's when he was reported missing.

We headed down the hall back to Interview 1. The uniform on the door looked annoyed. "He's been making a racket," she complained. "He wants out."

I smiled smugly at her. "That's too bad." She grinned back.

We burst through the door and before Joey could start, I announced loudly, "Joseph Lombardi, you are under arrest for the murder of Nick Tran."

I waved my cuffs at him, and Eddie told him to turn around and put his hands behind his back.

That set him off. "You guys are so full of shit!" he yelled at us. "You are both going to be sorry! I'm going to have both your badges!"

Eddie winced. "You're going to have our badges? Dear god, that's so cliché."

"Yeah," I agreed. "We should have had Tracy write something more original for you."

The mention of Tracy's name brought his histrionics to a screeching halt. "That's right," I told him. "She ratted you out. Told us everything."

"She wouldn't do that," he insisted, but his bravado was evaporating.

I put his written statement on the table where he could see it, but not get at it. "Well, she did. And would you like to know why? Because she thought you'd already thrown her under the bus. So she sang like a canary." I looked at Eddie, daring him. He bit.

"Again," he sighed, "so cliché."

"But so true," I added. Then I nodded at the paper and Joey looked over at it.

I have told Detectives Mercer and Faith everything I know about the death of Nick Tran . . .

For someone as dumb as Joey, he twigged right away to what had just occurred. "You showed her that?" he wailed. "You can't do that! That's private!"

"No, it's not," I told him. "And yes, I can."

Underhanded? Maybe. But the important thing was that it worked, which it wouldn't have if Joey and Tracy weren't guilty in the first place. Joey must have missed that episode. That's the thing about criminals—they always think they're smarter than cops, and we're not above using that to our advantage. Although I will admit I did heave a deep sigh of relief that we were right and that it worked out. There may be no such thing as bad publicity in Hollywood, but for the LAPD it's an ongoing curse we'll probably never completely escape from. Botching this case would have been a nightmare.

By the time we got back to my place, it was close to sunset. I uncorked a bottle of wine, and Eddie and I headed out back to toast our victory, although it was a muted celebration. We'd brought his killers to justice, but Nick Tran was still dead, his promising future snuffed out because Joey Lombardi treasured fame more than the life of someone he felt was a threat to it.

We'd spent the rest of the day running the media gamut, but Captain Keegan took the brunt of it. Joey's lawyer finally appeared and kicked up a fuss that he hadn't been brought in earlier, but that wasn't our problem—that had been Joey's call from the moment we'd first approached him. We did advise him that it would be in his client's best interest to let us know where he'd left Nick's body so the guy could get a proper burial. Even after I snapped cuffs on him, Joey kept insisting he knew nothing, but we knew better. If he thought not telling us where he stashed his victim was going to help his cause, I was pretty confident his lawyer would soon disabuse him of that idea.

Eventually Eddie and I began discussing Carmen's Hollywood Sign jumper. If he'd been trying to make a very public statement, he'd picked the wrong day for it. Poor guy leapt into oblivion on the same day sitcom darling Joey Lombardi was arrested for killing his co-star. His death wasn't going to make headlines, not even in L.A.

We wondered why he decided to end it all, and why so dramatically? He was definitely sending a message doing it the way he did, and we figured when he was ID'd, there was a good chance he'd turn out to be a failed actor.

Had he come to L.A. to be a star? Had he envied the Joey Lombardis of the world their success? He should have held out a little longer. Due to the publicity surrounding Nick Tran's death, more people than ever would be interested in *Life with Newbie*. Within hours of Joey's arrest, the network had announced that the show would return with yet another newbie. The publicity machine would crank up and the search would on for the next big thing. I couldn't help wondering if Nick and Joey's loss could have been Mr. Jumper's big break. Stranger things have happened in this town.

About the Author

Melinda Loomis was born and raised in Southern California. Her short stories have appeared in anthologies from various chapters of Sisters in Crime. Melinda lives in the Los Angeles area with her extremely photogenic cat, Sophie. Visit her online at www.melindaloomis.com.

Freddi Farr, Behind the Bar

Carrie Voorhis

APRIL 8, 1963

The detective pulled a limp, soiled handkerchief out of his breast pocket and handed it to me to wipe the blood off my face. I pushed it away and grabbed a stack of cocktail napkins from under the bar. Blood smeared across the "Mai Tai Tuesdays $2.10" printed on the front. Mai Tais are $2.10 and they'd been $2.10 since 1961. I made them big and I made them strong. They should probably be $2.50 by now. I shook my head. My ears were still ringing from the gunshots ten minutes ago and there was a dead guy right on the other side of the bar. Bookkeeping would have to wait.

I scrubbed at the steep neckline of my gold lamé halter dress until the napkin disintegrated into little red pills of slimy paper. Club soda would get that stuff out.

"You not married?" I said to the detective.

"I am, according to my lawyer," he said. He stuffed the handkerchief back into his pocket. "So nobody saw anything?"

"Right," I said, focused on my neckline.

"'Cause the lights were out?"

"It's called a scorpion bowl. One giant drink in a giant bowl with six straws. Lots of rum, lots of gin, lots of vodka, lots more rum. We fill the little cup in the middle of the bowl with some of the really high-octane stuff, turn off the lights, and *voila*, sexy flaming drink. People love it."

"Sounds lethal," said the detective.

His eyes scanned the bottles and pictures and movie posters on the wall behind my back while he waited for me to talk too much. His eyes landed on the one poster everyone's eyes land on eventually. On it, a slinky brunette gazed over a bare shoulder at you, her scarlet satin dress pressed against her chest by an unseen man's hand. *Mortal Sin* yelled the title. The film that ended my career. Seventeen-year-old me was a little too hot for 1935 and the good folks at the Hays Commission. My dead husband had loved that picture of me, and I left it there for him. We were such a great team.

"That's you," the detective said, like they always do. "You're Freddi Hale."

"A long time ago," I said, like I always do. "Now I'm Freddi Farr, behind the bar, babies." I flicked a rocks glass with a long, red fingernail. The shrill *ping* made the other detective look up from the body on the floor and frown.

"So you knew him pretty well. The vic." The detective nodded toward the body.

The "vic" was that director you've heard of, Alistair Stevens. *Mortal Sin* may have tanked my career all those years back, but it had been great for Ali. He'd gone on to direct "quality films" that became big award getters. He always had his awards show after-parties here at my place—Taboo Room on Ventura Boulevard. The movie folks came here because I make a mean Rumrunner and I can keep a secret.

I looked around. The bamboo chairs and the red leather booths were draped with maybe a dozen or so exhausted partiers in evening gowns and tuxes. Gold statues crowded the tables beside the brown-and-green tiki mugs. A blonde whose agent had named her Sheila Grand (Mary Sue Higginbottom when she worked for me a couple years back) slumped in the lap of the wooden tiki idol that towered over my bar.

That idol looked like my dead husband. Not just because it was big and wooden and silent, like my Sam. The legendary set builder Raymond "Marty" Martinez made that for us back in the good days before Marty's tragic fall on set years ago. Marty had to be put in the Motion Picture Retirement Home for full-time care. I didn't have Sam anymore either. He died last year fighting a lion on the set of *The Fall of Man*. One of the golden statues on one of the tables in front of me was the award Alistair Stevens got a few hours ago for directing *The Fall of Man*.

I scanned the room until my eyes found Camila and I felt my shoulders relax. I didn't have Sam or Marty anymore, but I had Camila. She was Marty's daughter who had come to live with us after Marty's fall. She'd been eight. I didn't know who her mother was and, as far as I was concerned, it was me. She called me her Tia, her aunt. She'd worked with Sam and me at the bar since she was sixteen and now, at twenty-four, she was my right hand. And my heart.

I rolled one of the hand-carved wooden straws that we used in the scorpion bowls along the edge of the bar. Camila had inherited her father's woodworking talent and made them for us as well as most of the other small wooden idols and candleholders scattered around the place. These straws, though, they were special. Sought after by people like Alistair Stevens and Sheila Grand. That straw meant you had been to some exclusive event here at the Taboo Room. That you had the money for over-the-top expensive drinks like scorpion bowls or, even better, knew the sort of people who did.

The straws had four tiny holes along the side. Put your fingers over the holes to drink, take your fingers off to play a little tune. Camila had made tonight's straws with a snarling idol baring its teeth on the front and the date—April 8, 1963—on the back. They were gorgeous. Just like her.

Camila was standing next to another detective who was taking way too much care wrapping brown paper around the massive scorpion bowl. The bowl, also made by Camila, was covered with intricate carvings. I watched her talk to him, her glossy black hair coiled up around the crown of her head and the sleek dark blue satin dress that fit like she was born in it. The detective next to her was clearly appreciative even though on the floor at their feet was Alistair Stevens, his pristine white shirtfront covered in bright red blood. He had taken two shots to the chest from a gun that had disappeared. Even with the lights turned up full, never a great thing to do in a bar, that gun was nowhere to be seen. I'd had my guy Ricardo pull the shades on the front window an hour ago. Word would get out fast now that it was almost five a.m.

"You might want to . . ." The detective talking to me gestured at my face. I could feel the blood sliding down my cheek, right under my eye. I swiped at it with a napkin, and the liquid hit my lips. The detective looked away, pretty green for someone who looked at blood for a living. I scrubbed at it. Sweet. It tasted sweet. I sniffed the red stain on my napkin. Did I smell chocolate?

I ran my fingertip through the blood on my chest and stuck it in my mouth. The detective stared at me, his jaw hanging open.

"Kensington gore," I said. Kensington gore was what we called it back in my contract days. Karo syrup, red food coloring, and cocoa powder. I had all three ingredients right here in my back kitchen. The detective shook his head, still staring at my pinkish fingertip.

"The blood's fake," I said. I hiked my dress up and hopped over the bar. The detective who'd been wrapping the bowl dropped it with a crash and grabbed my shoulders, pulling me back. I shoved him away and ripped open Stevens's shirt. Camila gasped.

I saw what I knew I'd see. The shredded remains of two plastic squares taped to his chest. The strings that had torn the plastic open ran from his chest, down his shirt sleeves and into his hands.

"It's all fake," I said. The detectives looked on while I pointed out a rather nice bit of movie magic I'd learned from Sam. "You fold these plastic squares into a bundle, syringe the blood in until the bundle is about to burst. Then you tape the bundle to wherever you're going to be shot, tape the strings on the bundle, run the strings to a hand or a leg, depending on the scene. The actor pulls the string and, bang, it looks like he's been shot. It's a stuntman's trick."

Sam Farr, before the lion, had been the stunt coordinator everyone wanted on their sets. I had helped Sam set up this particular stunt a thousand times. I could mix up a batch of that blood in my sleep.

"You know the vic, you know how to do this stunt. Any idea what he was trying to accomplish with all this?" He waved a hand at the body.

I shrugged. "Ali was a showman. Remember the plane?"

Three years ago, Alistair was promoting a film called *Sky's the Limit* and hired a pilot to fly a plane through the Os in the Hollywood sign. The pilot had to tip the plane sideways, three times, to make it. It was death-defying and dumb and the newspapers ate it up. *Sky's the Limit* was a massive hit.

"*The Fall of Man* was taking home the hardware." I nodded to the tables crammed with trophies. "But the *Hollywood Reporter* says no one's going to see it. Stupid stunts have worked for him before, maybe he tried it again."

The shorter detective stood up from the body and came over to us.

"The lady's right, Mac," he said. "No bullet holes."

"So why's he dead if none of this is real?"

"Heart attack? Stroke? Ali is in his sixties, probably older between you and me. Drank like a fish, smoked like it was his job, and had just had a pretty big night. And when those blood packs pop, it's a quite a wallop right on the ticker."

"I think you need to come with me so we can talk this out more," the detective said.

"And I think you'll need to wait for my lawyer before I go anywhere," I said. "Can I get you something while we wait?" I held up a bottle of Myer's rum—one of my best—and wiggled it at him.

"It's five a.m.," he said.

"So I'll put in some juice," I said. The detective loosened his tie and plunked himself down on a stool.

"I'm officially on duty," he said with a little smile.

"I can keep a secret," I said. I gave him a stiff pour, added some orange juice, a squeeze of lime, and a dash of pearly red grenadine.

"This is terrific," he said. I nodded over my shoulder as I headed back to the kitchen to find my handbag and the card with my lawyer's number. Camila grabbed my arm as I was reaching for the kitchen door.

"Everything okay, Tia?" she said.

I patted her hand. "Everything is fine, baby. I'm used to handling Alistair's messes."

The small kitchen was quiet and empty. The heavy steel door swung shut behind me with the familiar *squeak-grind-squeak* dampening the noise of the people in the bar and the rhythmic thrum of the happy island music that I really needed to turn off.

I didn't have an office, I had two hooks over a stack of supplies in the corner away from the stove and sink on the other wall. One hook for my handbag, one for a sweater. I grabbed my bag and pulled a case of whisky away from the wall so I could sit on it while I rifled for that card. I leaned an elbow on another stack of cardboard boxes. The stack was shorter than it had been when I sat here yesterday. A box was missing. I looked down at the stack. Cleaning supplies—toilet bowl cleaner, dishwashing liquid, fly papers, vinegar. Maybe Ricardo had made up more of the vinegar solution we used to clean the sticky film that was left on the bar every night.

The kitchen door squeaked again and Ricardo walked in. He pushed his sweaty hair back from his forehead and headed toward me, his eyes on the floor. I felt a confession coming on.

"Ms. Farr," he said. "I think I'm in trouble. It's about Mr. Stevens. I did it."

"You did what?" I said.

Ricardo pulled a knife out of his apron pocket and slit open the tape on a box of glassware next to my feet. He reached in and pulled something out. Something black with a dark sheen. The gun.

"I was supposed to drop it on the sidewalk outside after the police left," he said. "So the photographers would see it when they got here."

"You helped Ali set this up?" I said.

"I still owe those people—you know which people I mean."

I nodded.

"I still owe them money from that . . . the stuff I stole."

I nodded again.

"Mr. Stevens said he'd pay me if I could help him play a little joke. He said he had friends on the police force, at the hospital, all these people who were in on it. It would be a great recovery. A miracle. He said the newspapers would talk about who tried to kill him—but couldn't—for years."

That certainly sounded like the Ali I knew. Take advantage of some poor kid to get more for himself.

"What should I do?" Ricardo said.

"Nothing," I said. "Tape the gun back into the box. I'll figure something out. He died of a heart attack. You didn't kill anyone."

Ricardo slumped with relief. "Thank you, Ms. Farr, I owe you," he said.

"Stop owing people, Ricardo," I said. "Go away, I have to make a phone call."

Ricardo disappeared back through the swinging door.

The heavy black phone was on the small set of shelves near the door where we kept our stock of the evening's setups—napkins in a basket, old produce cans full of silverware, swizzle sticks, and paper straws. Three of Camila's wood straws from tonight's party were still on the shelf. I picked one up and twirled it around my fingers while the phone rang. I'd leave a message with my lawyer's answering service; he'd get his messages and call me back in less than twenty minutes. I fumbled the phone and dropped the straw on the floor where it snapped in two at the growling teeth. I muttered a few curse words at myself as I bent my back, stiff from the long day, to pick up the pieces. I held the sharp bits in my hands and peeked out the kitchen door window into the dining room. Both detectives' backs were to the door, and me.

Two minutes later, I was through the back door of the restaurant and into the alley behind, striding the four blocks to my house in the early morning light.

—*ell*—

We'd moved all of Marty's tools and gear into our detached garage when he went into the home. By the time Camila was ten years old, she and Sam were out here for hours every day, building models, making toys. I got good with splinters and tweezers.

Sam, Marty, Camila, they were all perfectionists. Trying, testing, adjusting, trying again. Then, later in the evening, standing together around the brick fire pit in the backyard, having a cocktail while we burned the day's leftover wood scraps and first attempts.

The fire pit. The knot in my stomach twisted. I put one foot in front of the other through the back door of the garage and into the yard. My roses had started to bloom, sharp reds against the dawn sky. Like Alistair's shirt. I picked up a stick and walked to the pit.

Something had been burned in here within the last few days. I could smell the familiar scent of the wood—like honey when it was fresh, like roasted pork when it burned. I poked the stick through the ashes.

"Please don't do that," said Camila. She was standing behind me, her arms wrapped around her bare shoulders in the chilly evening air. I slipped off my cardigan and draped it around her. She was eight again, having nightmares and wanting me to read her one more story. I turned back to the fire pit and rummaged around in the ashes until I found a partially burnt piece of a wooden straw. I held it up on the end of the stick. I could see where she'd snapped the straw in half to correct the angle of the hole inside of the straw.

"You hollowed out the tooth in the statue," I said. Camila nodded.

"Then you put arsenic in the hole," I said. Camila's mouth dropped open. "The fly papers I use in the kitchen. There should have been three boxes and there were only two. Soak fly paper in water and *voila*, arsenic. A pea-sized drop held into the tooth with . . . what?"

"Sugar glass," Camila said. "I used to help Sam make the glass for the stunts with bottles or windows breaking, remember?"

"I do," I said. Oh, I remembered. I felt tears sting my eyes. I hadn't cried since the lion.

"Clever," I said. Camila only nodded.

"But what does killing him help?" I said.

"No one was going to stop him," she said. "Alistair Stevens was a horror. He let people die. He got people injured on his sets and then the studio heads blame them for their injuries, and they have to live on donations and charity. He wanted me . . ." She stopped.

The heat rose in my cheeks. "Go on."

"Alistair was at the retirement home a couple of weeks ago when I was spending some time with Dad. He told me he liked what he saw of my woodwork at the bar. He wanted me to come by the next day, to talk about an apprenticeship in the props department. I went to his office and . . ."

"There was no apprenticeship," I said.

Camila shook her head.

"He said he had endowed the wing of the home Dad was in. He's on the board. He said he could get my dad kicked out if I didn't do what he wanted. He said he'd expect me in his hotel suite after the party tonight." A tear slid down her cheek and I wiped it away with the sleeve of my cardigan. She took a breath and went on.

"A few days ago, I started carving the straws for the party and thinking about how wonderful it would be if Alistair would just die. I plotted it out, like I learned from Dad and Tio Sam."

I rubbed my fingers on my forehead and she grabbed my hand.

"But I couldn't do that to you, Tia," she said. "In your bar? What if the police blamed you?" She squeezed my hand so tight my knuckles cracked.

"Then, on Friday, I was in the bathroom at the bar and the transom window was open. I heard Ricardo and Alastair outside in the alley planning their prank with the gun and the blood. Tonight was my chance. Alistair would die and it would look like one of his dumb stunts finally failed."

I pulled her close and she sobbed against my shoulder while I rubbed her back.

"You and I know people die doing stunts all the time," she said into my neck.

"I know," I said. Yes, I knew.

"Bring me some newspaper," I said. Camila went silent and walked into the garage. She came back with shredded pages that she started twisting into neat bundles. I pulled my cigarettes out of the deep pocket of my skirt and tapped the lighter out of the pack. When the newspapers were lined into the fire pit, I dropped the wooden straw fragment on top and lit the newspapers. The flames flared, then settled, then began to eat away the edges of the straw.

"I can keep a secret," I said. Camila took my hand again and we watched the flames glow orange in the dark.

About the Author

Carrie Voorhis, a copywriter turned writer-writer, is at work on the second novel of a humor mystery series, the first of which was nominated for a Claymore. Her short story set in 1890s San Francisco is in the 2020 Bouchercon anthology.

She also cooks, eats, and reads about cooking, eating, and people killing each other.

All the World's a Stage

Kim Keeline

"Melissa, another disaster." Josh stormed into my office, his face screwed up into the unpleasant scowl he now wore so often.

"What now?" I wasn't bothering to hide my impatience anymore.

The lead actor waved some papers in front of me. "This production's cursed."

It wasn't like we were performing Shakespeare's Scottish play. "Stop fussing and explain."

"No van for tomorrow. Plus, Craig's girlfriend can't get us the chairs and sunshade."

That *was* a disaster. For *As You Like It*'s Forest of Arden, otherwise known as the abandoned Los Angeles Zoo in Griffith Park, we needed the van to haul in seating, shade tents, and props each day.

I could rent a new van, but the day before opening was short notice to replace the rest. I'd used most of our grant money already.

Ah, the life of community theater.

Josh strummed his fingers on my desk, staring at me, so I grabbed the papers from him. "I thought 'Nique was in charge of the folding chairs."

"Leave Monique out of it."

I forced myself to take a deep breath. I was a professional. I needed to act like it. "I'll get to the bottom of it."

"You'd better." He turned on his heel and left my office.

It wasn't just our past—I had to admit our disastrous dating life was as much my fault as his—but his constant anger that was getting to me.

Well, that and 'Nique, as she liked to be called. "Because I'm so unique, you see?" Then that inane giggle and flick of long hair. Josh and her being together—it only made the whole situation more difficult.

Could I stick it out another two weeks without Josh and me killing each other?

Robbie was waiting in Griffith Park's Spring Canyon parking lot. I immediately recognized his *bad news* face.

As I got out of the car, I grimaced at him. "Spill. What now?"

He leaned against my Toyota as I got my chair and bag out of the trunk. "'Nique is telling everyone you screwed up the chairs."

I tossed my bag on the ground and looked at Robbie in amazement. "That was her job. She's friends with Craig's girlfriend."

Robbie spread his hands helplessly. "I know that. You know that."

"I spent two hours fixing it this afternoon."

"So it *is* fixed?"

"With no help from her."

Robbie looked amused. "She was getting a manicure to be ready for her big role."

'Nique was a bit player at best. She showed up the first day of rehearsals and volunteered to help. I'd been glad for the assistance then. I gave her a few odd jobs and eventually a minor role because someone I'd cast flaked on us.

As the goddess of marriage, 'Nique escorted the audience throughout the park while playing tambourine and singing with other bit players. The only one not in modern dress, she swanned around in an ethereal white gown with flowers in her hair and led the marriage ceremony at the end of the play. Her few lines were probably all she could manage.

I snorted. "I can hardly wait for her nails to act." I handed my folding chair to Robbie. "Come on. I can handle this."

We headed down the slope toward the old zoo picnic area where our performance began and ended. Most of the cast was already adding the last details to their costumes or digging out a prop from one of the boxes Sharon had lugged in with the help of her teenage sons.

All the world may be a stage, but the abandoned Los Angeles Zoo was an inspired setting for a "moving" production of Shakespeare. The audience followed the actors to different backdrops used as sets. As artistic director, I had more than just the actors' lines and their entrances and exits to deal with. I was beginning to wish I'd never written that grant. Site-specific immersive promenade theater—fancy words for nothing but headaches, was what it was.

I clapped my hands. "Gather 'round." With Robbie's help, I stepped up on the picnic table nearby and waved everyone over. "I have arranged for a new van, chairs, and shade tents." There was a collective sigh of relief and some murmurs from the crowd.

I looked around the upturned faces. 'Nique stood to the side of the group looking a bit disappointed. I threw her a meaningful look. "The show will go on."

Smiles and claps all around. Nothing like that comforting adage to get actors pulling together.

I continued, feeling a little calmer myself. "Ten minutes to costume inspection and then a full run through. No stops. I'll do notes at the end."

The energy in the park was increasing. This was the magic of theater. "Go on. You'll be marvelous."

'Nique shot me a look and then trailed after Josh, locking her arms around his waist. There had been other mysterious issues during rehearsal: missing props, cast told the wrong time to show up, and now this. Maybe I was paranoid, but were those two up to something?

Robbie helped me down off the table with a grin. "Taking the high road suits you, *honey*," he drawled.

I rolled my eyes. He was the only person in the world I'd allow to call me honey. He'd been doing it ever since we met performing in a college play a dozen years ago or so, where it was in the script for his Southern gentleman character.

I gave him a good-natured punch on the shoulder and made a scoffing noise. "I'm all about the high road, mister."

He raised an eyebrow. "Then will I be in Scotland 'afore you'?"

I didn't want him bursting into song, so I gave him a fake stern glance. "I'll be in the Forest of Arden. Go get ready to be Orlando's nasty older brother. I've got things to do."

With a jaunty salute and a grin, Robbie took off.

I was soon too busy to think about 'Nique and Josh. The actress playing Celia forgot her costume shoes. The curtain hung from a tree for the women's changing area kept collapsing on one side. Several bit players had questions or grievances, including the actress playing Rosalind complaining about her wig.

Actors. Part of my job was stroking egos and soothing troubles.

We started the rehearsal on time despite these few hiccups. The first few scenes went well with only minimal chaos with the promenade to the wrestling area. I settled down in my chair as the musical interlude came to an end and the actors began.

Rosalind, itchy in her black wig but suitably feminine to help sell her transformation into a "boy" later, called to Orlando, "Young man, have you challenged Charles the wrestler?"

When Josh was playing Orlando, it was easier to remember what I had seen in him. Josh's sandy brown hair shone as he deferentially bowed to the two young women before him.

"No, fair princess; he is the general challenger: I come but in, as others do, to try with him the strength of my youth."

Janine, the actress playing Celia, was slow on her cue again, so I made a note. I had to hope that one more reminder could help cure her of it.

At least she sounded worried about Orlando's safety. Considering how muscular the actor playing Charles was, her concern was reasonable. A very handsome, large man, several years younger than Josh, Brian had been cast mostly because of his experience in college wrestling, but, luckily, he was coming along on his acting, too.

Soon enough, the two men were grappling each other. We'd blocked this scene thoroughly to make sure they'd be safe. The rest of the cast gathered to the sides, cheering on the performed competition.

Brian grabbed Josh and tossed him gently to the side, and Josh propelled himself into a nearby tree, panting. It looked realistic but was more like a complicated dance. The fight continued as choreographed, with Orlando winning, much to the delight of Rosalind and the others.

We shifted to the lower zoo trail for the next few scenes, using the backdrop of empty cages and graffiti-covered buildings, and then to more wooded areas for the Forest of Arden.

Sharon had tied paper poems to several trees along the trail. It was our first time for this set decoration, and I made a note to add another dozen or so. We had to sell the idea that Orlando was papering the woods with love poetry for Rosalind, not realizing she was in exile disguised as a boy in the same forest. Only Shakespeare could make such a ridiculous premise both funny and romantic.

A shout offstage made everyone pause, then Brian dashed off. I stood up, alarmed. "What's going on?"

The actress playing Celia emerged from the bushes with clothing and a towel in her hand. "Bedlam Tom."

I hated that the crew named the homeless guy hanging around the park after *King Lear*'s lunatic. He was harmless. Well, he *was*, usually. "What did he do?"

Janine clutched the towel to her chest, her shirt partially unbuttoned. "I saw him creeping around while I was changing."

Brian came back out. "It's that guy again. I ran him off."

I nodded. "Janine, you okay to go on?"

She bit her lip but shrugged. "He just startled me."

Everything went smoothly as we continued, leading back to the first stage. During the wedding scene, 'Nique waved her hands to show off her impressively long painted nails. It went in the notes.

Afterward, we all gathered 'round the picnic tables where we started. Many of the cast and crew lounged in the grass, leaning on each other. Theater often forged bonds like family amongst cast and crew.

Of course, we all know that family isn't always pleasant. Case in point, when I gave the notes. Some actors took direction well. Others, not so much.

"Janine, you are still a bit slow on your cues. Get someone to run lines with you."

Janine was young but I knew she was trying to improve her craft. She looked embarrassed but nodded.

I braced myself. "Josh, in the wrestling scene—"

"That was Brian's fault." Josh was flushed. 'Nique stroked his arm reassuringly.

Brian stood up. "What's my fault?"

Now Josh stood up. "For that scene dragging."

Those two had been rubbing each other the wrong way since their first rehearsal. "Settle down." I raised an eyebrow at Brian, and he sank back down.

Josh was still on his feet, quivering with outrage. I pointed at him. "I was just going to remind you I don't want to see any improvisation tomorrow. I know you think it helps make the performance more 'real' but I won't have it—especially not with a choreographed fight scene."

For a second, I thought Josh was going to argue, but 'Nique whispered something to him, and he gave a crooked smile, settling down beside her in the grass. I'd have to settle for that.

"Does this look okay?" I tucked the last of the brochures advertising our next season onto the display on the promo table and turned toward board members Anna and Gilberto.

"I think so." Gilberto scanned the area. "Hopefully, this free production will help our bottom line through donations and promotion." Gilberto's role as treasurer often made him focus on the financial side.

The performance was what I lived for—there was nothing like live theater. The energy in the park this afternoon was amazing. Last-minute details were coming together. The first stage and audience area were set. Just to the left I could see the rope outline for the wrestling scene where the audience would stand to cheer on the fight.

Anna pulled the donation box out of a bag. "I'm sure it'll help. Melissa, you can check on the scene setup down the trail, if you like. We'll finish up here."

I nodded my thanks and headed down the path. I was pleased to find we were almost ready. For the most part, I had a good team.

No time to rest though. A few minutes later, I gathered everyone for a short pep talk and then we took our stations. As people arrived, actors mingled in character. I talked to arriving guests and watched the process.

Rosalind and Celia were sitting on the front of the stage leading a group of actors in song. Touchstone and a few others were doing stand-up routines or juggling near the parking lot path. Brian, as the wrestler Charles, was showing off his physique near the promo table.

No sign of Josh and 'Nique. Were they goofing off while the audience was arriving? I scanned the growing crowd for them.

A disturbance near the front left of the stage caught my eye. There was Josh arguing with Robbie. I couldn't tell what they were saying, but it was in character for the two squabbling brothers Orlando and Oliver, so I left it alone. 'Nique would show up eventually.

The homeless guy was standing near the bushes on the edge of the picnic area, but as long as he didn't cause problems, he was welcome.

Maybe ten minutes later, when the seating area was almost full, Robbie came by, leaning in to whisper, "Heads up. Josh is schmoozing with board members."

I glanced in the direction of the promo table and sure enough, Josh was talking to Anna and Gilberto with a charming smile on his face. I headed that way to see what was up. I was relatively secure in my job, but admittedly all theater companies had been hit hard the last two years. No need to take chances if Josh was trying to cause trouble.

When I got closer, Josh broke off and headed in a different direction. I shrugged and went on another circuit of the audience. Soon Rosalind rang the bell for people to take their seats and I went up to welcome everyone.

The opening scenes unfolded smoothly. The first promenade came, and the singing actors escorted everyone to the wrestling arena. It started fine. Orlando challenged Charles and refused to back down when the young ladies warned him of the wrestler's abilities. The two men sized each other up, grasped arms, and struggled.

When they reached Charles's dramatic throw of Orlando, instead of following the script, Josh ducked, twisted, and threw Brian off balance by this sudden, unscripted move.

The startled look on Brian's face as he stumbled was real enough. He paused about a foot from the largest tree at the back of the wrestling arena.

Before Brian could recover, Josh lunged at the younger man, knocking him back into the tree with some force. Brian's cry of pain was a shock not just to me and the rest of those watching, but to Josh. Josh backed up rapidly and glanced around the crowd.

Brian was standing propped against the tree. His left hand went up to his right shoulder and came back wet with blood.

Some of the audience may have thought it was part of the show, but I knew otherwise. I rushed forward, followed by a surge of cast members from both sides. The audience, now realizing this wasn't part of the play, began talking and moving forward.

I reached Brian's side and waved back everyone else. "Stand back." Brian was still resting against the tree, his left hand to a bloody right shoulder. "Brian, what's wrong?"

His face was pinched and sweating. "My shoulder." He moved his hand away. There was something metal sticking through his shirt high on his right shoulder. Whatever it was, it was surrounded by an increasing circle of blood. Brian shifted as if to pull himself forward.

I put my hand out to stop him. "Whoa, don't move yet." I looked around. Robbie was nearby with the rest of the actors. "Robbie, call for paramedics." He nodded and moved off, looking pale.

Gilberto was pushing his way through the crowd gathered steps away. What help could an accountant with a love of theater be? I was about to yell for everyone to stay clear when Brian called out. "Gil—oh god, it hurts."

Gilberto was immediately by his side, clutching his hand, saying it would be okay. This was a development I hadn't known about. They were clearly a couple.

I nodded grimly to Gilberto, and while he comforted Brian, I peered at the area between Brian's shoulder and the tree.

A dark metal spike about the thickness of a finger seemed to be hammered into the trunk. A section of it had pierced Brian's right shoulder. The point of it must be what I could see poking out of the front of his shirt, which meant it had gone straight through. Who knows how much damage that could cause? There was a lot of blood seeping out of the back wound and spreading on the front of his shirt.

I called out to Janine standing on the edge of the crowd, "Get something to stop the bleeding."

She sprinted off and soon came back with several towels. Brian was looking like he might pass out, so Gilberto and I held him steady and placed the towels where we could. If we pulled him off the tree, we might hurt him worse. As long as he could stand, it seemed safer to keep him still.

The ambulance arrived quickly, although it felt like forever. A few minutes later they were loading Brian into the back of the ambulance and Gilberto was going with him.

Some of the audience was already leaving. After conferring with Anna, I announced to the rest that the play was over for the night.

That's when the police car pulled up.

"Oh god." I sat down in the nearest seat and realized that there was a bloody towel still in my hand.

Time passed in a blur. The police asked everyone to remain and called for more officers. I was asked what had happened, what was supposed to happen, whether we always used the same tree, who had been around, and so on. A seemingly never-ending circle of questions.

The members of the audience were released after giving brief statements and contact info, so they trickled out of the park. The cast was made to wait at the picnic tables and then questioned one by one. Eventually they began to leave.

My police questioning was finally over, but I had been told to wait. I sat on a picnic bench and watched two grim-looking officers question Josh over by the stage. Surely, they couldn't blame him? It had to be an accident.

I was positive the spike hadn't been there during rehearsal yesterday. You'd think it would have been noticed during setup today. I should've checked the area better. What a disaster.

Anna appearing with an empty donation box, which didn't make the night any better. "We had about a hundred dollars," she said quietly.

"What about the cash box for the ticket sales?"

"Gone entirely." Anna looked embarrassed. "Gil left the table to watch Brian. He said they've been together a few months and he was the one who encouraged Brian to try out for the role. They were keeping their relationship quiet, so it wouldn't look like Brian got the role because of Gilberto's position on the board." She ran her fingers through her hair. "When Brian was injured, I forgot all about the cash."

The police were not pleased when I told them this latest news.

Eventually we were all allowed to leave, but the police roped the area off and didn't let us take anything but personal items. I was told to call the next morning and we'd find out when we were allowed back.

As I was leaving, I had a sudden thought. I paused at the nearest officer. "Just FYI, there's a homeless man hanging around. He's bothered my crew a few times and was chased off."

The cop told me not to worry but I begged him to keep an eye on our stuff. After all, the chairs and tents were rented. Then there were our props.

I hated to leave things there, but what could I do?

I went home with a huge headache from all the questions bouncing around in my head. I called Gilberto who told me that Brian was in surgery but expected to recover. That, at least, was a relief.

My phone woke me up. I rolled over and, as I picked it up off my nightstand, I looked at the time. Are you kidding me? An unknown number too.

I almost threw the phone back down, but I was awake, might as well find out what was happening.

"Melissa?" That voice made me sorry I had answered. 'Nique was not the way to start a morning.

"You know it's not even six a.m.?" I lay back down, phone pressed to my ear.

"The police took Josh in."

I sat up straight in bed. "They did what?" I felt a lot more awake.

"The police took Josh in for questioning," she repeated slowly, like I was a child. "I think he needs a lawyer."

"They didn't say anything about an arrest, did they?"

"I don't know. And I don't know how to get a lawyer."

My mind was racing. "I'll see what I can learn. And I know a lawyer."

"Okay. Are we performing tonight?"

I paused. "I'm beginning to think not."

Before I could deal with anything, I needed coffee and a shower.

Dressed and on my third cup of coffee, I began making calls. Brian had made it through surgery and was in recovery. Relieved, I made a note to send flowers.

While I was talking to the hospital, Robbie left a message asking about Brian's condition and if I had known the actor was dating Gilberto. I called him back and told him about Josh being taken in by the police.

After a brief pause, he said, "Honey, I told you never to fall for actors. They will break your heart every time."

I chuckled. "Weren't you dating that guy who played the lead in the play when we met?"

Robbie at least sounded abashed. "And I should've learned then. You should too."

Before I could reply, the phone beeped, so I excused myself.

Anna was on the other line. We quickly agreed to have the communications team put the word out that we'd canceled this afternoon's performance. We'd play it by ear afterwards.

One of the bit players could take on the role of Charles—it wasn't that big of a part. Josh had an understudy, if it came to that. Would the police let us back in the park? Plus, it was sure to end up on the news. *Was* there truly no such thing as bad publicity?

In my next call I learned that the police apparently had already "released the scene." I called around for volunteers to load our things into the van in the parking lot for now. Then I called the park rangers and made sure the van could stay there at least another day. I didn't want anything to happen to our props or rented equipment.

I emailed the cast and crew explaining our cancellation for the day and promising more info.

Everyone would have a lot of questions. I certainly did. Was this an accident or sabotage? And if it was planned, was Josh the target? Because it was *his* back that was supposed to end up against that tree.

Cassie, the lawyer I'd contacted earlier, called back as I was finally driving into work.

"Are they really arresting Josh?" I still couldn't wrap my mind around it.

"He's been charged but I'm working on getting him released." Her voice echoed a bit through my Bluetooth speaker. "I don't think they have a strong case."

"Josh was supposed to hit the tree." There was a lot of traffic. I put on my blinker and waited until someone let me in the next lane. It was hard to concentrate on driving when so much was going on.

"Exactly why they think he changed the choreography to injure Brian. Several witnesses said they'd argued."

Finally made the lane change. "Josh's a prima donna, sometimes." I sighed and tried to be fair. "Brian was new to Shakespeare and Josh didn't think he was a good actor." I gave a short laugh. "I wondered if Josh disliked him because Brian's better looking. Josh's quite vain." I might not have succeeded in avoiding sounding like a bitter ex. Ah, well. It was true.

"The spike was garden railing from nearby. Someone sharpened the spike. Perhaps more spontaneous or random? All I know right now is Josh says he didn't do it. Gotta go. I'll keep you informed." She hung up.

The question of whether Josh improvised the scene to hurt Brian went round in my mind for the rest of my commute.

"'Nique, calm down." She wasn't following directions, but what else was new?

"This is your fault." She was pacing my tiny office, making me feel like a spectator in tennis keeping up with her movements.

"I told the police Josh didn't do this."

"Of course, he didn't do it. *He* was supposed to be against the tree." Her voice scaled up to truly dazzling heights. "Someone tried to *kill* him."

She was either truly upset or it was the finest acting she had ever done.

"Who knew he was going to change the choreography?"

She threw up her hands in the air. "No one."

"Did *you* know?" I asked. Her eyes shifted. "I think he told you."

She heaved a melodramatic sigh. "Only a little before the play started, as he went to mingle with the audience. Nobody else heard us." She began pacing again. "This was meant for him."

If only *she* knew about the change, maybe 'Nique had tried to kill Brian? But why? No, it was more likely she was right. The spike had been meant for Josh. "So who would try to kill Josh?"

"Besides you?"

Apparently, I wasn't the only one with a suspicious mind.

"You've got to be kidding me."

Her hands were on her hips. "You've been jealous of us."

Sure, it stung that I'd been cheated on and then dumped—and the entire cast knew. But jealous? She sat down in the chair opposite me and we stared at each other for a few seconds. I said slowly, "Are you sure you weren't jealous of *me* because I dated Josh before you?"

She looked me up and down scornfully. That hurt too. "You were afraid he'd take your job."

Robbie had been right about their plotting. "Believe me, my job is not in danger because of anything Josh could do or say." Even more so, now. Gilberto would never be on Josh's side so long as he thought there was a chance that Josh had hurt Brian.

"That's not what the police will believe." She smiled and flounced out of my office.

Eventually, I sighed and got back to the work I'd been doing when she interrupted me.

Everyone in the cast and crew checked in throughout the day. Nothing they said shed any light on the events of last night.

Josh's understudy, Nathan, called twice and texted three times to assure me that he was ready to step into the role. He was so desperate, I briefly wondered if he could be responsible for the spike but then felt bad. Surely nobody would do something so awful just to get a role in a community theater production.

I edited the press release and sent it to the board for approval and distribution. It wasn't quite normal quitting time, but I told the staff to go home and rest. There was nothing else we could do there today.

I pounded the last cancellation sign into place at the park. I wish I knew when we'd restart. I hated uncertainty like this.

Caution tape still roped off the tree where Brian had been injured. The police had removed the spike, leaving a gaping hole that reminded me too much of his wound. A dark stain down the trunk might be blood.

I shivered, despite the heat of the late afternoon sun beating down on my shoulders.

A rustling in the bushes made me draw back a little. "Is someone there?" I couldn't see anyone. "Come out of there."

The man the crew called Bedlam Tom peered from behind a bush. "I wasn't responsible for what happened here."

"I believe you. Did you see what happened?"

He stepped further out into the light. "Big guy got hurt during your show when Orlando wrestles Charles."

I could see the man clearly for the first time. He was younger than I'd realized. His gray sweatpants were dirty from rough sleeping, and there were leaves on his T-shirt and hoodie. Behind him sat a wheeled wire cart full of blankets, bags of chips, crushed soda cans, and a duffel bag.

"Do you live here?"

He gave me a nervous look. "It's a public park. I have a right to be here during the day."

I tried a different tack. "Have you been watching our performances?"

His face was hard. "It's a public park."

"I'm sorry we ran you off the other day. You startled one of our actresses."

He frowned. "I didn't mean to."

"What's your name?"

"I'm not causing any trouble."

He must get run out of places a lot. "What's your name? Can I give you some cash for food?"

Here he looked more interested, but still cautious. "Kyle. I could use some food."

Kyle. Better than thinking of him as Bedlam Tom. "Come over to this picnic table, Kyle, and tell me what you saw that night, and I'll give you enough for dinner."

Kyle eyed me nervously but followed to a nearby picnic table and sat on the opposite end from me.

I might as well ask directly. "Did you see anything last night?"

He stared off into the distance, his face expressionless.

This was a waste of time. He was nervous and might have alcohol or drug problems, if not mental problems. I should just give him a few bucks and get going.

Suddenly he leaned forward. "Both of those guys from the wrestling scene ran me off a couple of times. The one playing Orlando even threw a rock and cursed me." His hands balled up but then he flushed and looked down. "This area's quiet and I've got a spot away from some of the dangers of the street."

I could only imagine how difficult it must be. "You've watched our rehearsals."

He smiled at me slightly. "It's been interesting, but I'm not a peeping Tom. I came around a corner and that girl started shouting at me. Didn't even know she was changing clothes in the bushes until she yelled."

"Okay. And what about yesterday?"

"I saw the two men arguing during your setup. Then the smaller one, Orlando, went off with that girl with the long hair. He was miming some wrestling moves. I heard someone walking nearby. I didn't want to be seen, so I went to other side of the field for a bit. Next time I saw Orlando, the other man was arguing with him."

"The wrestler? The one who got hurt?"

"Nah, I told you, I saw them argue when they first arrived. Mostly bragging from the smaller guy. About how he could beat him in a real fight, not just in a staged one. Guy thinks a lot of himself."

"You don't know the half of it."

"This second argument was with the brother."

Orlando's brother, Oliver—so Josh arguing with Robbie. "Where was this?"

"They were down by the back of the stage."

This must have been the start of the argument I saw the end of. Was this for the play or a real argument? Not that Robbie would do anything awful, but it was weird he hadn't told me about it. "Did you hear what it was about?"

"You going to pay me?"

"After you tell me everything."

He squinted at me suspiciously. "They were talking about you, I think."

Me? "What did they say?"

"The older one said to leave you alone. Orlando just laughed and said not everyone thought you walked on water. Made some threats. Bragging mostly." He paused. "Is he really that good an actor?"

"He's no Laurence Olivier." I tried not to smirk. "Some actors have an exaggerated sense of their abilities."

He nodded. "Thought so. They switched to stuff about being brothers when people approached them."

"Did you see anything about the tree?"

"Nah, what do I care about a tree? There are hundreds here."

True enough. Another thought. "When Brian was hurt, some people guarding our back table got distracted. Money was taken from a donation box. Plus, a cash box disappeared. Know anything about that?"

He stood up. "I'm homeless. Don't mean I'm a thief."

"I wasn't saying that. Did you see who took it?"

He shook his head. "No cash. I saw the box, though."

"Where?"

"The woman with the long hair threw it in the bushes. Just before the police arrived." He shrugged. "If I had stolen it, I'd have found a cheap place to hole up for the night, not been here today."

'Nique? Perhaps part of their attempt to discredit me. Or Kyle could be covering for himself.

I got out what little cash I had. "Forty dollars is all I have on me. If you're still around when we return, I'll see how else I can help."

He plucked the bills from my hand. "You're all right." He started to walk away then turned back. "Wait here." He trotted off, leaving his cart behind. A minute later, he returned with the broken cash box and placed it on the table. "Police didn't see it. Not that it helps, but it's all I can do."

I thanked him and watched him drag his cart across the picnic area back into the bushes. If he did steal our money, I hoped he got good use out of it.

But I suspected he had told the truth. 'Nique was trouble and I'd have to deal with her soon.

I sat there for a few seconds and then texted Robbie, asking him to come over to my place later for some drinks. We could use them.

—*ell*—

"Maybe we could do a fundraiser for a homeless nonprofit or something." Robbie took a gulp of beer and leaned back in his chair. When he had arrived, it looked like he had already had a few. He was certainly pounding them back now, which was unusual for him. Then again, we were all under a lot of stress. Still, it was bothering me.

"Could work," I said slowly, watching him drink. "Kyle said you argued with Josh about me. Please tell me now that you didn't try to hurt him."

Robbie shifted in his chair, scowling. "I'm not a method actor taking my character's hatred for Orlando offstage." He laughed but didn't look at me. "He's a twit. I hate seeing you unhappy but that's it."

"A twit trying to sabotage me with the board."

"He'll never succeed. Especially now." Robbie grimaced. "If that spike had been any lower, it might have killed Brian." Another swig of beer.

That was true. It was a terrible thing to do to someone, whether meant to injure or kill. On Josh, that spike was probably head height.

Was that the intention? If so, it was unlikely to have worked. Josh's head never got close to the tree in rehearsals. He always tucked and hit the tree with his lower back. It looked good but was soft and all for show. But only Josh, and whoever overheard his plan, knew that Brian would be in his place.

I watched Robbie carefully. "Now I've got two actors to replace. Brian needs to recover and with this charge against Josh . . ."

"Yep," Robbie said cheerfully, raising his beer bottle before drinking it down. He got up and crossed my small living room to the kitchen where he grabbed himself another bottle. "Silver lining for you." He threw himself heavily back into his armchair.

Kyle hadn't said it was Robbie who was watching Josh's wrestling plan, but it seemed likely from his description of events. I had to be sure. If Robbie was the only one who knew the plan besides 'Nique and Josh, it would help clear Josh because the spike would've been meant for him.

"Kyle said you overheard Josh's plan and knew Brian would be thrown against the tree. Please tell me you didn't do this to frame Josh."

Robbie froze. After a few seconds of silence, he sipped his beer again and then looked at me. "That was just a side benefit. I didn't mean for Brian to get hurt so badly. I didn't think Josh could push him that hard."

This unexpected answer hit me like an avalanche. We sat in silence and I tried to breathe. Finally, I sat my beer down and leaned over to clasp Robbie's hand and said the only thing I could think of, "Why?"

He squeezed my hand. There were tears in his eyes. "I didn't know Brian was dating Gilberto. Not till earlier that night."

I tried to put the pieces together. "You'd been seeing Brian?" Was I so distracted with my own problems that I hadn't noticed something like that? While Robbie was always there for me, I'd ignored what was going on with him.

He pulled his hand away. "We'd had a couple of nights together the past few weeks. I guess I never learned not to fall for another actor. I fell hard." He buried his head in his hands. "I didn't realize I was just a fling. That he already had a boyfriend."

The image of the spike in Brian's shoulder came back to me. "But this?"

"I lost my head." He looked up, pleading. "A scratch, honey, that's all I wanted. Just enough to make him want to quit the production. So I wouldn't have to see him every day for two weeks."

It had ended up so much worse than a scratch, whatever his intent. "Robbie, you'll have to tell the police."

He looked so broken, slumped in my armchair. "I've been chickening out. Tomorrow morning, I promise." He grabbed his beer bottle and gulped down some more.

He'd screwed up really badly, but he was my best friend. I stared at him for a few seconds and then went to the kitchen and got us both another beer.

We spent the night toasting to lost loves and the theater. He'd face whatever consequences there were tomorrow when I'd call the lawyer.

Robbie and I both might be happier if we could learn to keep the drama onstage.

About the Author

Kim Keeline, when not running a 1907 steam locomotive or lecturing on Shakespeare, is active in the mystery community. She is organizing Bouchercon 2023: San Diego. Her first published story was a 2021 Derringer finalist. She is revising her novel while freelancing for authors in marketing and web designing. www.kimkeeline.com

Murder in Xanadu

Lisa Morton

WHEN I WAS MURDERED, it didn't hurt at all.

I'd like to think the same was true for my friend, but . . . well, I know how much his murder hurt *me*.

My murder went like this: One minute I was dancing with my BFF a hundred feet above Xanadu, and the next there was a deafening blast of amplified feedback and an explosion of red light so intense I reached up and ripped my VR headset away.

I sat there for a few seconds, staring out the window of my bedroom into the disappointing reality of everyday life, then I grabbed my phone and texted Zendrix: *What just happened?*

His response came fast: *Don't know—you just vanished. Checking now—think Xanadu mighta been hacked.*

I sighed and set the headset aside. I found myself gazing at the framed photo on my dresser, the one of me and Zendrix dressed up for a Halloween party at the Biltmore Hotel downtown, him looking gorgeous (of course) in a shimmery suit made of iridescent fabric that caught light and broke it up into fantastic colors, and me looking predictably silly in an outfit that was supposed to suggest a Greek goddess but somehow just made me look like a high school girl who'd had a terrible accident at her prom.

I wondered again: why did someone as amazing as Zenny even hang out with me? He was everything I wasn't: a computer genius, artistic, and OMG beautiful, with flawless dark skin and eyes like smoky green amber. I even thought his name was incredible, given to him by a single mom who was both into old music and Buddhism. We'd known each other for most of our lives, so maybe he thought of me as sort of his little sister, or his sidekick. I knew he didn't feel about me the same way I felt about him because he was gay, and that was fine, because I loved just hanging out with him and being part of his world.

Or *worlds*, I guess I should say, because he'd decided a few years ago that nobody else had yet done a virtual world right, so it was up to him.

"See, Chloe, all the other virtual worlds," he'd say while still typing code, "are mundane, flat, like being stuck inside the world's worst cartoon. If it's called virtual *reality*, then it should look real even while it takes you to unreal places, right?"

It took him a year, working after his courses at UCLA. He let me sit nearby as he spent hours at his computer typing and testing, sometimes staying up all night. I contributed a few designs for characters and buildings (Zenny told me I really should be majoring in art, not English), but it was really his baby. In Zendrix's world, there wouldn't be any clunky polygons or jerky movement; he'd figured out new algorithms that made even the most detailed graphics load instantly. When he finished, he really had made a whole world, and it really was better than everyone else's.

Xanadu.

That's what he called it; he said the name was partly inspired by a famous poem and partly by a campy old movie from half a century ago. He kept

Xanadu on his desktop computer, and gave access to five of us: me, him, and our friends Brytni, Jason, and Carmen.

I'll never forget the first time I put on the headset and logged in to Xanadu: what Zenny had created wasn't just a virtual world, it was *art*, a masterpiece. Xanadu was a place of pink skies and emerald forests inhabited by tiny fairies. There were buildings in turquoise and gold, so perfect that you could study the chisel marks in sculpted friezes. You could hover above the surface, chatting with friendly dragons, or dive beneath a lake and have tea with starfish.

Zenny had worked with Carmen, who was obsessed with AI, to create characters that remembered you and were really fun to talk to (and sometimes looked very much like the designs I'd given him). Best of all: in Xanadu, I wasn't this twentysomething with body dysmorphic disorder and a bad haircut that I'd somehow thought would look hip. I looked like that Greek goddess I'd wanted to be on Halloween.

Zendrix, on the other hand, looked like himself. Of course, how could he look any better?

All five of us instantly fell in love with Xanadu.

Jason—whose Xanadu avatar wore a black cape and a little half-mask—looked around that first time and said, "Dude, put some guns in here and this could make you famous. *Seriously.*"

Zenny snorted. "It's not a shooter. And I don't want to be famous."

Brytni, who was a golden-winged demigoddess in Xanadu, flitted up to Zendrix. "He's right, Zen. It *could* make you famous—and *rich*. With or without guns."

After that we'd flown and explored and danced.

Now I look back and wonder if I missed clues, considering what a nightmare our shared dream soon turned out to be.

Xanadu almost instantly became the best part of my life.

Not that the rest of my life was terrible; I had it pretty good. I loved my family, even my two stupid little brothers; I was still living at home in the Valley while I went to college, but I didn't mind. My parents made just enough money that we all had our own bedrooms and every other year we took vacations to interesting places.

None of them were as interesting as Xanadu.

Zenny kept adding to it, so there were always new things to see. I'd log in, put on the headset, and nothing else mattered. Sometimes all five of us would be plugged in, and we'd listen to music, usually something new Brytni had discovered; other times it might be just two or three of us. Even being there alone, chatting with Arfer, a talking dog, or walking through a forest of laughing trees, was better than anything in real life.

One day Zenny and I were there alone, just talking about college and stuff, when he said, "You wanna hear something strange? Brytni asked me if I'd sell Xanadu to her."

"Brytni? Why?"

He shrugged. "You know, she likes making deals. She thinks she could resell it to some game company or something."

Brytni was the poorest of our little group. She shared a dumpy apartment in Sun Valley with four other kids, and it was still better than living at home. "Where would she even get the money to buy it?"

"She thought Jason would loan it to her. He'd be like the investor, I guess."

"Well, he could afford it," I answered. Jason's family had money—*lots* of money. They lived in Brentwood, and I used to joke that his bedroom was the size of our whole house. But I wouldn't have traded with him; Jason's dad was really hard on him. He'd made his fortune as a financial manager, and he expected Jason to do the same thing. Jason was pretty good with numbers and had always accepted that he'd wind up following in Dad's footsteps, but I'd often wondered how happy he was with that idea. I loved him as a good friend, but he wasn't always the most cheerful guy.

"Brytni thinks," Zenny said, as we strolled through a field of multicolored flowers that sang softly around us, "that it could be huge."

"She's right. It's *amazing*, Zenny. Everyone would love it."

Zenny shook his head, and I pictured him IRL, sitting in his bedroom with his VR set on, shaking his head. "You know what Jason said? He thinks it would be the biggest shooter game ever. But I didn't build it for people who want to shoot stuff; I built it for people who want *magic*. I built it for the five of us, you know? So we could have a place to hang that wasn't real life."

This was a discussion Zenny and I had had before: he was the artist, creating just for the sake of the work, sharing it only with friends. But the rest of us knew he could make money doing this. Of course, they also said I could make money with my art, but I knew I was nowhere near Zenny's level. He was a genius; I was a college junior who'd changed my major three times already.

"You know, you could skip the rest of college, go right to millionaire with stuff like Xanadu."

He shrugged. "I guess." Just then the golden goddess that was Brytni materialized before us, so we broke off. She had more new music for us to listen to. She wanted to manage bands, and I knew she'd be good at it.

Everybody seemed to have a path but me.

Two days later I was murdered. In Xanadu.

Zendrix dug into the logs and said we'd been hacked, although he couldn't figure out exactly who had done it or how. He thought they'd accidentally wiped out my file while trying to steal code. Fortunately, he was obsessed with backups—he had one entire backup drive sitting on his desk that was only for Xanadu—so he was able to restore me. He also thought that, given a few more days and running some traces, he could figure out who'd tried to hack us.

"Who even knows about Xanadu?" I'd asked. "Have you told other people about it?"

"No," he said. "It could be some weird random hack . . . or it could be something that one of us let slip."

I thought furiously: had I mentioned Xanadu to anyone else yet? I was pretty sure I hadn't. My mom had asked me why I was spending so much time with the VR set on lately, but I'd answered that it was a new game, and she'd just shrugged. That left (maybe) Brytni, Jason, and Carmen.

"Brytni talks a lot," I said, "and she's got all those roomies."

Zenny laughed. "I thought about that, too. Well, I'll just make sure the security protocols are solid and hope for the best."

We had that conversation at exactly 10:34 p.m. on a Friday, in Xanadu.

At 2:43 p.m. the next day, the police showed up at my door to tell me that Zendrix was dead, and I was the last person he'd talked to.

Hearing that my best friend was dead wasn't anything like it is on television or in a movie. I didn't laugh nervously and say, "Is this a joke?" I didn't immediately start wailing. Instead, I managed to back up to the living room couch just before my legs gave way.

I knew it was true. Because they were police. Because Zenny and I always texted on Saturday mornings, and I hadn't heard from him today. Because . . . well, my gut just *knew*.

Dad had taken the boys to Little League, but fortunately Mom was there to ask the questions I couldn't. I could only try to breathe and believe this was really happening. This wasn't Xanadu.

But it *had* happened, in this world.

I barely heard as they answered Mom's questions: yes, Zendrix Henson was dead; yes, it was murder—it looked like an intruder had broken into his Santa Monica house at about midnight, entered his room, and clubbed him over the head with Zenny's old wooden baseball bat; they didn't think robbery was the motive, although they couldn't tell if anything was missing; no, his mother wasn't doing well, and they'd waited with her until her sister had arrived; no, there were no suspects yet.

But then they started to ask me questions: was Zendrix my best friend? Did I know if he had any enemies? Could I think of anyone who might have had a grudge against him? And then: Where was I last night about midnight?

Was I a suspect?

When Mom asked them exactly that, they assured her I wasn't . . . but I saw the way one of the detectives, a haggard-looking middle-aged woman in a rumpled pantsuit, squinted at me.

Yes, I was a suspect.

When they finally left, that detective—whose name was Marisa Gomez—wasn't squinting quite so hard at me, at least.

As soon as they were gone, I told Mom I had to go to my room. "Of course, honey," she said, kissing me on the head. She was a pretty great mom, I have to say; she treated me as an adult and trusted me enough to give me space when she knew I needed it. "I'll be here if you need anything."

I walked to my room on legs made of rubber, closed the door, and immediately sat down at my desktop. I put on the VR headset and logged into Xanadu. I half-expected it to be gone, but no—that was just Zenny. The rest of Xanadu was still there.

But it was empty. For the first time it seemed lifeless, even slightly silly to me. "Hey, girlfriend," I heard a voice say. I turned, my heart thumping—but it wasn't Zenny. It was Arfer, the talking dog. "What's going on?" he asked.

"You're not even real," I said.

"That's true," Arfer said, looking surprisingly thoughtful for a terrier, "but I can still be your friend, can't I?"

"My real friend is dead," I said, just before the tears came hard and heavy.

I had to take off the headset after a few seconds, but the last thing I heard was Arfer saying, "I want to help."

"There's nothing you can do," I said between sobs, even though I'd already tossed the headset aside. "Nothing at all."

The next day Mom and I went to see Zendrix's mother. She looked terrible; her face was puffy, her speech slightly slurred from some pills her doctor had prescribed to help her get through this. Zendrix, after all, had been her only child, and they'd been close.

While my mom sat with Ms. Henson, I went back to see Zenny's room. It looked pretty much the way it always did, with Zenny's computer station in one corner, his bed (forever unmade), dresser, and bookcase all the same. He'd always loved toys and knickknacks, and the room was full of them; he especially adored crazy little figures like Japanese anime characters and robots and all. I found my eyes scanning the shelves, remembering how he'd gotten each one.

One was missing. It was a little three-inch-tall figure of a cat-like creature holding an umbrella. I looked around but couldn't find it anywhere, and the figures next to it had been rearranged so there was no giveaway gap.

In the middle of the floor was a place where a towel had been spread out. I didn't want to think why, or what was under that towel. Instead, I went to Zenny's desk and examined it.

It took me a few minutes to figure out what was missing there: his backup drive. He'd been obsessed with backing up his work since he'd had a hard-drive failure two years ago and lost a bunch of files. That backup drive was *always* there, right on top of the main computer.

But it wasn't there now.

I noticed one other thing: the light on his printer was blinking. Zenny sometimes printed things out on paper; he said it was easier for him to find missing links in his code. He'd been printing something when he'd run out of paper.

I found some under his desk, loaded the printer, and hit the OK button. In a few seconds, it was spitting out pages.

They were logs related to Xanadu. Most of it was techie stuff I couldn't figure out. But there was one section I *did* understand: a list of log-ins the night I'd been murdered.

There were five. I recognized the usernames: Zenny, me, Brytni, Jason, and Carmen.

So whoever had hacked into Xanadu that night had been good enough to fool the servers. Who was that good aside from Zenny? And had my "murder" had anything to do with Zenny's? It seemed too coincidental to not be related.

After we checked one last time on Ms. Henson and told her we were always there for her, we left. When we got home, I dug out Detective Marisa Gomez's card and called her. I told her that I'd just been in Zendrix Henson's room, and that there were two items missing. The action figure wasn't a big deal to her, but the missing backup drive was.

By the end of the day, the police had taken Zenny's computer in for evidence.

Xanadu was gone for good.

The regular world no longer seemed quite real without him in it. It wasn't colorful and fun like Xanadu, though; it was like Earth had slid off its axis into an alternate dimension where everything was gray and sad.

It was hard not to see him around campus. Hard not to see him at the all the places online we'd hung out together. Hard not to see him in his room, bent over his computer. Hard not to hear his laugh, feel his hugs.

It was all the hardest thing ever.

Three days after he'd died, I had lunch with Carmen at a falafel place near campus. We sat down quietly together a table, neither of us saying anything, neither of us smiling. I wondered if either of us would ever smile again.

"You haven't heard anything more from the police, have you?" I asked her. I was guessing they hadn't caught anyone yet or we would have known.

Carmen shook her head. "Nothing."

She put her backpack on the table, digging for something, pulling stuff out—and my blood froze at what I saw.

Zenny's missing figure was there, mixed in with lipstick and coins. For a moment I couldn't even speak. Carmen must have seen a look on my face because she asked, "You okay?"

"Yeah, I just . . . I didn't expect to see one of Zenny's little toys in your backpack."

She glanced down, saw the figure, picked it up. "Oh, yeah. He gave it to me the day before he died. Said it was a gift for all the programming I did for Xanadu. I knew how much he liked this little guy, so I thought that was a pretty badass thing for him to do, but Zenny was like that, you know?"

I just nodded, my throat so dry it was hard to speak. Zenny *had* loved that figure. I knew he'd spent a lot for it; it was an artist-signed limited edition. Would he really have given it to Carmen?

And was I really suspecting somebody who'd been a friend for years of committing *murder*?

Then: what if the printout from Zenny's computer didn't mean that the murderer was a great hacker who could hide their tracks, but that one of *us*—the friends who'd logged in to Xanadu that night—had clubbed Zenny over the head?

I felt sick.

Should I tell Detective Gomez? She'd show up at Carmen's home again (I knew we'd all been questioned) and just freak out her family. It was probably nothing, and Zenny really had just given her the figure.

I decided not to say anything . . . but I'd be keeping a closer eye on *all* of my friends.

Zenny was cremated a few days later. His mom didn't want any services; she said she didn't think she could get through them.

I felt the same way.

But those of us who knew Zenny wanted to celebrate him in some way, so Jason offered to hold a party in Zenny's honor. It would be at his house on Saturday night. We should all bring something that reminded us of our late friend and share it with everyone else.

What I most wanted to bring, of course, was what I no longer had: Xanadu. I wanted to have everyone put on a headset and enter Zenny's magnificent creation. I wondered if the police had visited it. Did Detective Gomez even appreciate what an amazing thing it was?

I had talked to her about it, after they'd taken his computer. Detective Gomez told me they were quite sure the killer had known Zenny. They didn't have much to go on: none of the neighbors had seen anything; Zendrix's mom had already been in bed and hadn't heard anything; they had the murder weapon but no fingerprints; there hadn't been a struggle, and they didn't have any of the murderer's DNA . . . but the missing backup drive holding Xanadu was certainly a strong motive.

She'd asked me for a list of everyone who knew about it, who'd visited it, who'd worked on it. I told her it had just been the five of us . . . or so we thought.

Then she asked me something that was like a punch to the gut. "Could Zendrix have had other friends you didn't know about, maybe that he kept secret?"

"No," I blurted out without even thinking. "We shared everything. I knew all of his friends, and he knew all of mine."

"You're sure about that?"

"Yes."

She had one last question. "Chloe, why did Zendrix make Xanadu?"

I wasn't prepared for that, and it kind of perplexed me at first. "What do you mean?"

"Had he planned on selling it? Maybe to a tech company, a gaming company, anything like that?"

"No, he said it was just . . ." I broke off then as realization hit me. Zenny hadn't been interested in selling Xanadu . . . but I knew somebody who'd been interested in buying.

"Chloe?"

"Sorry, Detective Gomez. Zendrix made Xanadu just for us, his friends. He really didn't want to sell it."

I didn't tell her about Brytni, just as I hadn't told her about Carmen.

But after that conversation, I started to wonder: were there parts of Zenny's life I didn't know about? Could it be possible?

Nothing felt real anymore.

In the end, I decided to take the Halloween photo of Zenny and me to the party. I could share the photo and tell everyone about the conversation we'd had when Zenny had first shown me the suit he planned to wear on Halloween, when we went to the big party at the old DTLA hotel. "What's that from?" I'd asked, eyeing the shiny fabric.

"It's from *me*," he answered, smiling.

"Well, it's chill, but . . . is it a costume?"

"Isn't being chill enough?"

I'd admitted at the time it was. Now I wondered if it had been a costume, if maybe everything about Zenny was an elaborate costume. Somebody I knew and loved had lied: either Zenny really *had* been planning to sell Xanadu to people I didn't know who had killed him for it, or one of our friends had committed the murder.

Saturday night came, and I headed to Brentwood for Jason's party, feeling more anxious than I should. Would I be able to look Brytni in the eye, believe anything Carmen said? Would I hear great stories about Zenny and want to cry . . . or doubt?

Like I said before, Jason's family had money, so their house was huge, with a brick wall surrounding the property and a massive, water-sucking green lawn—and I think every square inch of it was packed when I got there. It looked more like a frat party than a wake: people I didn't know were staggering around with cans and glasses, music was blasting, voices were shouting.

What *was* this?

I pushed through into the main house, looking for Jason, looking for *anyone*. In the living room I spotted Carmen, who waved at me. I was so glad to see her that I immediately felt guilty about suspecting her. She came up and hugged me, and I shouted over the hip hop, "hey, what's going on?"

She glanced around and frowned. "I know, right? I thought it'd be you, me, Jason, Brytni, maybe a few others, but . . . I doubt that many of these people ever even heard of Zendrix."

"Have you seen Jason?"

Carmen shook her head. "Not in a while."

"I'm going to go find him." Carmen nodded as I walked away.

The truth was, I was *mad*. This was no way to honor our friend. Zenny was about as far from a party boy as you could get. He would've stayed five minutes at this and gone home. I *hated* that this was how we were supposed to remember him, and I was going to tell Jason exactly that before I left.

I made my way out onto the back patio, where the crowd seemed especially dense. Somebody was barbecuing at a grill, but it wasn't Jason. I walked around the huge pool, already full of splashing, shrieking, half-dressed assholes, and then I spotted something that made me freeze:

In a little circular seating area around a fire pit, four people—none of whom I knew—were wearing VR headsets.

I felt numb, but I forced myself to walk up to them. When I got nearer, I saw they weren't really wearing full VR sets, but cardboard holders for their phones that converted them into VR headsets. They were all gaping and exclaiming at what they saw, obviously impressed.

"What are you guys looking at?" I asked, already feeling the answer in my gut.

A pretty girl about my age said, without taking off the headset, "It's a beta test for a new game."

A dude with a spiky, half-shaved haircut that told me he was desperate to be considered cool glanced at me over his headset before handing it to me. "Check it out. It's really sick."

I put it on.

I was in Xanadu.

I gasped and fell onto the stone bench beside the others. "See?" I heard the guy who'd given me the headset say. "What'd I tell you?"

I couldn't even answer. I tilted my head, looking around, and spotted my old friend Arfer not far away. I called out happily, "Arfer!"

The dog saw me and ran up, wagging his tail. "Chloe! I've missed you!"

I heard one of the kids nearby mutter, "Whoa, the talking dog knows her!" I ignored it and focused on Arfer, wishing I could really touch him, hug him. "I've missed you, too!"

Arfer suddenly turned serious. "I think something terrible has happened, though."

"It has. Zendrix—the one who created you, who created all this—is dead."

Arfer's expression fell. "I knew it. I'm so sorry, Chloe. I know you were close."

It occurred to me just then to wonder: just how smart *were* these AI characters in Xanadu? Could they provide any clues? How much about what had happened might they know, if they were tied into Zenny's computers?

"Arfer, you don't know who killed Zendrix, do you?"

"I'm sorry, Chloe, I don't." Well, that was disappointing. But then Arfer added, "But I know who killed you in Xanadu that one time."

I took a deep breath before asking, "Who was it, Arfer?"

"Whoever has the log-in blackcape1."

Blackcape1 . . . *Jason.*

I heard one of the others (I'd forgotten they were plugged into Xanadu, too) say, "Hey, you already died in Xanadu? So are the guns hidden?"

I tore off the headset and tossed it back to the guy who'd given it to me, then headed off. Behind me, I heard him say, "Uhh . . . you're welcome?"

I was too upset to deal with anything else.

What was my next step? Find Jason and confront him? Tell Carmen? Call Detective Gomez?

No, wait: If Jason really was the one who had killed Zenny, then he'd have Zenny's backup drive. Knowing that he had Xanadu wasn't enough; I wanted to see the backup drive for myself.

I made my way through the backyard, into the house, and up the stairs. The second floor of the house was a lot quieter, and it was easy to get to Jason's bedroom. The door was closed. If it was locked—

It wasn't. I opened it and went in.

Jason's room was cleaner than any of my other friends', partly because his family had maids and partly because his father bugged him about it all the time. He had a stylish black desk in one corner under a window overlooking the backyard. His expensive tablet was on the desk.

Zenny's backup drive was plugged into it. I'd helped Zenny buy that drive; I knew that was it, that the drive was how the kids downstairs were enjoying Xanadu.

For a moment I thought I might cry. But I held on long enough to pull my phone, call Detective Gomez, and tell her what I'd found.

She told me to go home right now, to not tell anyone else. She was already outside the house, watching the party. I was nearly done with the call when a voice behind me said, "What's up, Chloe?"

I spun and saw Jason standing there in the doorway. I hadn't thought to close the door behind me when I'd entered. *Stupid.* I almost hung up the call, but decided I wasn't going to be stupid twice. I heard Detective Gomez calling my name, and knew I needed her to hear whatever came next. I pretended to disconnect and put the phone in my pocket.

"This party isn't for Zendrix, is it, Jason? It's a celebration for *you.*"

Jason smiled and asked, "What are you talking about?"

I nodded down at the desk. "That's Zenny's backup drive, the one with Xanadu on it."

Without missing a beat, he said, "Sure. He sold it to me."

"What?"

"I was going to tell you all, but then . . . well, you know, that awful thing happened, and . . ." Jason walked past me, and I almost shuddered as he came near. He reached down to his desk and picked up some printouts. "Here's the contract."

I scanned the pages, less interested in the legalese than the signature at the end. It was a good forgery of Zenny's autograph, I had to admit, but not good enough. "It's fake."

Jason barked a disbelieving laugh. "So, what, you really think I killed him? Really, Chloe?"

I forced myself to look him in the eye as I said, "Really, Jason. Because I know you were the one who accidentally killed me in Xanadu when you tried to steal it the first time. Arfer told me."

He tried to come back with a response, but his mouth moved as if it had just tripped over its own lies.

"I don't get it, Jason. Why? You've already got plenty of money."

"No, I don't," he said, his voice almost choked with hatred. "My *father* does. He thinks I'm an idiot who'll wind up flipping burgers and couch-surfing with friends."

It all made sense, then: Jason saw how valuable Xanadu was, and saw it as his way of proving dear old Dad wrong, of making his own fortune. "Why'd you have to kill him, though?"

"He was never going to sell it. The rest of it . . . that was an *accident*. I was just going to break into his room at night and steal the backup drive, but he was still awake and . . ."

I wiped at my eyes before saying, "So what now, Jason? Am I next, so you can defy Daddy?"

I saw emotion flit across his face before it settled into cold calculation. "I could make you a partner in Xanadu, Chloe. We'd both be rich."

"Did you really think you could get away with this, Jason?"

"Yeah, I did." His eyes moved around his room before settling on a big sports trophy on a bookcase. I remembered when he'd won it a year ago for being on our school's winning wrestling team. We all knew he was a terrible wrestler, that the rest of the team really deserved that trophy. He picked it up and ran his fingers along it as he said, "I *did* get away with it, and I will continue to get away with it." He hefted the trophy, feeling its weight, and I knew what he planned to do with it.

I tried to run to the door, but he was faster than me. He pushed it shut, locked it, and started walking toward me. "Right here, Chloe—I'll bet I can kill you *right here* in my bedroom and get away with it. There are around two hundred other people here tonight I can blame it on. Or I can say that you went crazy, and I had to defend myself."

He raised the trophy over his head. I backed up against a wall, nowhere left to go. I put up my hands, waiting for the blow, waiting for Jason to bash in my head just as he'd bashed in Zenny's.

The door burst open, and a figure rushed into the room, shouting, "Freeze! Drop it!"

It was Detective Gomez.

I saw a second of indecision on Jason's face, and then he smiled and casually lowered the trophy. "Oh, c'mon, chill, we're just playing—"

Detective Gomez wasn't. She had her gun drawn and aimed at Jason. Two minutes later he was in handcuffs and being led to a waiting squad car.

The detective turned to me before going out to read Jason his rights. "Are you okay?"

"Yeah. The backup drive is right there." I nodded at Jason's desk. "He thinks he'll get away with it because he's got money."

She laughed and said, "There's not that much money in the world."

She was right . . . sort of. Jason managed to get a sweet plea deal, and he could be out of prison before he's thirty. Everybody thinks his dad managed to help that along with a few deals of his own.

They're still holding Zenny's computer and the backup drive as evidence, but Detective Gomez has been really great and let me make a copy, so we've got Xanadu, at least. Brytni's already set up a deal with a big game company who's going to buy it. The money will at least mean that Zenny's mom will never have to work.

Of course, she also won't have her son.

Neither will I. I miss him every day. At first the idea of going back into Xanadu was too much, but I finally tried it one day and it was a bittersweet comfort.

Yesterday Carmen texted me, said she'd been working on something and had a surprise. I should log into Xanadu right away.

So I put on my headset and logged in.

At first, I didn't see anything new—the same beautiful place. Then I heard a voice behind me call, "Chloe!"

I nearly fainted. I knew that voice.

I turned, and there was Zenny, walking up to me, looking incredible in that crazy Halloween suit. I started to cry so hard I had to take off the headset. After a few minutes, I texted Carmen. She told me she had enough recordings of Zenny and the programming for his avatar, so she'd recreated him. He was an AI, so he'd change and learn.

I know he's not the real thing, but he is a little *piece* of the real Zendrix. I'll take it. Earlier today I told him that I've decided to get serious about my own art, that I was changing my major. His laugh sounded so right.

It's almost enough to make you believe in magic after all.

About the Author

Lisa Morton is a screenwriter, author of non-fiction books, and novelist. She has published over 150 short stories, with recent appearances in *Best American Mystery Stories 2020, Scream and Scream Again, Literally Dead,* and *Classic Monsters Unleashed.* Lisa lives in Los Angeles and online at www.lisamorton.com.

Red Carpet

Sherri Leigh James

"SALLY, I'M MORE THAN happy to attend the premiere of your new film, but I'm not, not, *not* going to walk down the red carpet into the Dolby Theater."

"Well, Cissy, I thought you would effing like it."

That's my Sally: a glamorous actress, and my best interior design client. She's also become my good friend. She tends to use the F-word at least once in every sentence, which can be awkward as she also uses her stage voice in public. Like now as we sat on the patio of The Ivy.

We'd been shopping in the Pacific Design Center when Sally insisted she had to have a lunch break. I would've been concerned that we didn't have reservations for lunch at this exclusive restaurant, but from experience hanging with Sally, I knew that would not be a problem. Her famous face gave us immediate entry, and no one seemed to mind her colorful vocabulary.

"I'm not a movie star. Or any kind of celebrity," I murmured, uncomfortably aware of how close we sat to so many recognizable faces. "It would just be embarrassing. And no way do I want to end up on camera."

"Why the f*** not?"

"Please, Sally! Can we discuss this later?"

"Here's the thing, Cissy. The producer I want you to go with won't attract a lot of media attention, but he wants to be seen with a classy woman. Not an effing starlet. Not someone way too effing young for him. He's not one of those assholes; he doesn't wanta look like one of those a-holes if he happens to get photographed by effing paparazzi."

She glanced over to the shop entrance across the street from The Ivy. "Speak of the effing devils."

I saw a man with a giant microphone on a pole and another guy with a huge camera, both instruments aimed in our direction.

"Sally, please. Let's eat and get back to shopping."

Sally nodded and ate a few bites of her salad before standing up and waving goodbye to the waiter.

I picked up my purse and looked for my wallet.

"Leave it, Cissy."

"We haven't gotten the check."

"Oh, for f*** sake! They'll put it on my tab."

I couldn't help but wonder if that was true. Or if we had just paid for our lunch by displaying Sally's famous face on their patio.

We went back to our design work. I was relieved the paparazzi did not follow us into the Pacific Design Center. We picked up fabric samples from the Kravet and Schumacher showrooms and selected a beautiful crimson carpet from Carl Marias Co.

I hoped Sally was going to drop the subject of the premiere completely, but on our drive back to Los Feliz, she brought up the producer again.

"Look, here's the thing: This film went way over budget, and Paul had to come up with significantly more bucks. I kinda feel like I effing owe him."

I sighed. How could I say no? My friend needed my help.

"What would I wear? I can't afford those expensive clothes. And you know I'm not famous enough to get designers throwing clothes at me."

"You can wear one of my gowns."

"Have you noticed how my body compares to yours?" Sally was slender but voluptuous in all the right places. I was definitely not voluptuous.

"Here's what you maybe don't know about designers and the clothes they offer us: In the weeks leading up to the premiere, every really big effing megastar––including the men––will be bombarded with deliveries of gowns and tuxedos from designers begging us to wear their clothes on the red carpet. And they often have to be altered to fit properly. So, we'll just pick out one you like."

What were the odds that anything sent to Sally would be appropriate for me? But I did still have a few gowns left from the days when I attended balls as a rich man's wife. Besides, nobody would be paying attention to me. Who cares if my dress is last season?

Sally kept after me for the hour in traffic that it took to get to Los Feliz. I finally said, "Okay, okay, I'll do it. If your producer friend agrees."

Sally laughed. "Oh, he definitely will. He already has. He asked me to persuade you."

"Sally, that car behind us? Do you know who that is? That car has made every turn we have for the last several miles."

A whole lot of F-words followed. "It's them again."

"Paparazzi?"

"Who else." Sally swore repeatedly. "Don't bother trying to lose them. They already know where I live."

"Really?"

"Yeah. I recognize those two. Joe and Mack. They're not too bad. Not like the ones who use drones to catch me swimming naked in my backyard. I especially hate that when I'm not in good shape. That f***er, the drone guy. If I'd had a gun . . . A girl should have a right to swim nude in her own yard."

For the hell of it I pulled over to the curb to wait a moment not far from Sally's house. Sure enough, when we arrived at her drive, their car was waiting at the curb outside her gates. She pushed a button on her phone, and I quickly drove into her grounds as she waved to Joe and Mack.

⸺ℓℓℓ⸺

Paul Hamill, my date for the premiere, picked me up exactly on time and was complimentary, even though I wore my own clothes. I had, however, gone up to Sally's house to have my makeup and hair done.

Sally's best friend and co-star, Nikki, plus Sally and I had spent hours in the two weeks before the premiere trying on all the gowns they both had been sent. Nikki decided she would wear pale blue that matched her stunning eyes. Sally wore her signature jade color done in ombrè silk with a plunging neckline emphasizing her beautiful décolletage. Sally said the mocha gown with a Venetian lace overlay I planned to wear looked like baby shit brown. Nikki said it was lovely and set off my blond hair.

"I'm so glad you agreed to join me for this occasion. Thank you." Paul smiled as the driver opened the limo door.

Sally had warned me that everyone attending the premiere would be hiring limos so they could be dropped off and *make an entrance*. I dreaded we were going to *make an entrance*.

"Sally said you were not enthusiastic about walking a red carpet. You needn't worry. I don't attract much attention." Paul smiled as if to reassure me that I would not be embarrassed. "To be honest, I had to borrow a lot of money to handle cost overruns. Lots of it from people I don't know well. I think it might reassure them to see me mingling with the stars. And the lovely interior designer to the stars."

Our limo pulled to a stop in front of the Dolby. He stepped out and offered his arm. I looked up at him and forced a smile.

Megastars Nikki and her husband, Jack Trevor, exited their limo just in front of us. It was fun to watch the flurry of excitement that greeted the two major personalities. TV cameras, microphones, and flashing lights covered Jack offering his hand to his beautiful wife, who gracefully slid from the limo and flashed her famous smile.

With perfect timing, Paul and I trailed after the famous couple and watched the enthusiastic greetings as Nikki twirled her frock for the cameras and repeatedly named the designer she wore.

Paul and I must have looked like their entourage. A few people said hello to me. The stars as well as the director and scriptwriters greeted Paul with respect and even invited him to pose with them for a group photo. I stood back and watched from the edge of the carpet.

Sally had yet to make an appearance. As the group gathered in the lobby for cocktails, I pulled my phone from my evening bag and tried to call her. The call went straight to voice mail. I hoped she was on the phone coordinating their arrival with Nate. Or maybe she hadn't brought her phone.

She and Nikki had both explained to me that rather than carry a bag or clutch, they left their grooming accoutrements in the limo and stashed a lipstick in their escort's pocket, but Sally had decided not to arrive with a date. She would walk the carpet with her fellow star, Nate, and knowing Nate, he would not carry a lipstick that might ruin the line of his tuxedo. Besides, they were coming from two different directions—Sally from Los Feliz and Nate from Beverly Hills. It would have been too complicated to use the same limo.

Paul shrugged his apology to me as he answered his phone. Nate was yelling loud enough that I could hear him.

"Where is that stupid bitch? I've been sitting here on Highland waiting for her call. She's not answering her phone. What the f***?"

My phone buzzed. I saw it was Manny Rodriquez, Beverly Hills Homicide detective. He had acted as a consultant on the film, so I expected to see him at the premiere. "Hi, Manny. Are you arriving soon?"

"Cissy, is Sally there?"

"Not yet. Why do you ask?"

"Do you know what limo service she was using?"

"No. I imagine her production office booked it. Why are you asking?"

"Text me that number."

"The office might not be open. Sending you her personal assistant's number."

I scrolled through my numbers and sent the info to Manny, then turned to Paul. "Paul, I'm going out to the runway to look for Sally."

"Coming with you."

The media was still on the carpet waiting for the two stars. A few of the photographers with competing print media were talking quietly with one of the reporters. A couple of the red-carpet interviewers headed toward the media group hoping to find out how soon to expect Sally and Nate to arrive.

Paul put his phone to his ear again. "Nate, calm down. Give her five minutes."

The reporter walked over to us. "Is it true?"

"Is what true?" Paul asked.

"That Sally Abby has been abducted," the reporter answered.

"What?" Paul and I gasped in unison.

I felt the blood drain from my face.

Paul called Nate. "Come on over here. She may not be on her way."

Paul put his phone on speaker. I heard Nate say, "It's all over the internet. Her driver was found dead at Los Feliz and Western."

Panicked, I stumbled to one side of the red carpet and called Manny. "What's happening? Nate says her driver is dead."

"That appears to be true."

My heart raced. "What about the two guys who follow her everywhere? Can you find out how to get in touch with them?"

"What two guys?"

"Paparazzi."

"Who do they work for?"

"I don't know. If you'll come get me, I'll show you who they are."

I hid my trembling hands behind my back and joined the group of media. "Who do the guys that follow Sally around work for? I think their names are Joe and Mack?"

"They're freelance."

"Who do they sell to?"

"Magazines like *People*, pulp like the *Enquirer*. Sometimes video to on-line sites. Sometimes YouTube."

Paul pulled me aside. "Cissy, I'm going around the corner to get Nate. Will you join me? Or hang with Nikki and Jack?"

"I'll be fine. Go ahead."

"See you soon." Paul hurried to Highland near Hollywood Boulevard.

I called Manny back.

"Are you on your way over here?"

"I'm in the parking structure. What did you find out?"

"Pick me up. I'm headed to the parking entrance."

"What did you find out?"

"They're freelance."

"Shit."

"Pick me up."

I climbed up and into Manny's Jeep. "I've seen these guys, Joe and Mack. They follow her from her house all the time."

"Is it them posting all the stuff on the internet?" Manny pulled out of the parking lot and headed north to Franklin Avenue.

I grabbed my phone out of my tiny purse and hit the icon for news, then scrolled down video footage of a sandy-blond-haired body in a black suit sprawled on the sidewalk next to a bus bench on Los Felix Boulevard. A lot of cursing by excited male voices could be heard. Video shots of a white limo that continued down Western, then turned right on Franklin. The sound had been blocked since shortly after the body was shown. The chase continued to La Brea, then went right on Sunset Boulevard.

Manny followed the same route, passing LAPD vehicles and then Beverly Hills police cars.

"We're getting close to Nate's house."

"Why would they go there? They've gotta know he's not there."

"His sisters might be, but––no, we've just passed the turn to his house."

"What does the paparazzi car look like?"

"Dark, very dirty, small black SUV. Might be a Ford."

"A Ford Escape?"

"I don't know. When I saw it, I was intent on getting away from them, but Sally said not to bother trying to lose 'em. They hang in her block waiting to get a shot."

Manny picked up a microphone attached to his dash. "Attention all units, watch for a small black SUV following a white limo. Locate. Do not apprehend or approach either vehicle."

"Detective, two vehicles headed west on Mulholland Drive," said a voice over the radio.

"Stay back. May be active kidnap in limo." He replaced the microphone, picked up his phone, tapped buttons, and hit the speaker. "Get me the captain."

"Detective, what can we do?"

"Shut down those clowns that are broadcasting. We don't need 'em now that we've got the limo in sight. Can that be done without them knowing?"

"Gotcha, will take care of it."

"And tell the FBI we've got this and to please stay back until we ask for their help."

"You know by law we have to notify them of a kidnapping, but I'll let them know we've got this."

Manny turned right in front of the Beverly Hills Hotel, onto North Beverly Drive to Coldwater, headed up to Mulholland. Traffic was heavy on the twisting, two-lane road, and even with a siren blaring, we couldn't safely pass any traffic.

Manny called the police vehicle following the two cars. "Do you still have both cars in sight?"

"Yes, sir. Limo pulled into Stone Canyon Overlook parking. The dark Ford followed, and cameraman walked up the path, camera trained on limo. We're past overlook, parked at next turnout. Got a view of exit."

"Good. Stay back." Manny ordered.

"I know Stone Canyon Overlook," I said. "It's the one with views of a lake and reservoir on one side. The path leads up to signs about local animal life and views of the Valley. There's a street leading to a residential area just before the entrance to the overlook. We aren't far away. A few minutes, if we could get out of this traffic."

"They might hear a siren blaring up the canyon," Manny said, "so I'm not using it. We're almost to Mulholland, and it won't be as busy. This traffic will continue into the Valley."

"What are we going to do when we get there?"

"I don't know. Are those guys still filming?"

I checked my internet connection. "They might be filming, but they aren't posting. You have a knife or anything in this vehicle?"

Manny gave me a look. "I've got a gun locked in the back." He sighed. "We'd be a bit conspicuous in these clothes don't you think?"

"That's why I want a knife."

He pointed at the console compartment where I found a Swiss Army knife with a handy little pair of scissors. I picked up the hem of my gown and chopped a couple feet of Venetian lace off the bottom. It was slow going, but maybe by the time we arrived at the lookout, I wouldn't be wearing a ball gown.

"You take off that jacket and tie and you'll be okay."

"What do you have in mind?"

"A drunk couple stumbling around the parking lot of a romantic overlook."

Manny smiled and shook his head. "Won't they recognize you? After all, these paps will have seen you with Sally." He sighed. "Better to wait for the SWAT team. They're trained to handle hostage situations."

"What do you think will happen to Sally in the meantime?"

Manny shook his head again. "We don't know what they're up to. No one's called us about a ransom demand. We don't know why they stopped or where they're headed."

"I'm worried that they've stopped. Maybe they're meeting someone to switch cars to a less conspicuous vehicle. And what happens then? What if the people they're meeting know about the paparazzi? What if they decide to get rid of her like they did the driver?"

I suddenly realized what a traumatic scene that was for Sally. Not only did she really like the driver she always booked, it must have scared the hell out of her to see him murdered like that.

"I don't know the answer to any of that," Manny said.

I smeared my lipstick and rearranged my hair so it messily covered my face. I'd had a cocktail before leaving the theater. That might have impaired my judgment. I hoped it had just made me smell like a drunk. I took off my high heels and slung the velvet strap of my evening bag across my chest.

"There's the outlook just ahead. I see the limo. Turn left here onto Nicada Drive."

Manny made the turn and parked just past the red curb, where we had a sight line to the parking area. The limo had parked facing the San Fernando Valley. Unlikely that they would notice us behind them and through the trees and bushes. The small black SUV was parked on the opposite end of the lot in a space surrounded by vegetation. Mustard flowers on bushes four feet tall surrounded the lot and flanked the railed path leading up to the overlook.

Manny turned off the engine and took off his jacket and tie. "So, now what?"

"I don't see Sally in the back seat. What if they've already moved her? Or hurt her?" My voice shook.

"What if she's lying down? Who's in the front seats?"

"Two big men."

"I'm letting SWAT know where we are," Manny said. "What the hell are you doing?"

"I'm just gonna take a drunken stroll up to the overlook." I opened the door and climbed down to the sidewalk.

I squeezed between the bushy trees along Nicada Drive and into the parking lot. The dirty black vehicle was empty. I pushed past another planting area with a small tree, then hurried through mustard plants to the path. I didn't see Sally. I tucked under the railing along the path, climbed between manzanita bushes, stumbled behind a sycamore and a pine tree, and nearly fell onto the two paparazzi.

"What the hell? Who the f*** are you?" the camera man hissed.

The other one looked me over. "You're her friend, aren't cha?"

"Yes. Where is she?" I whispered.

"On the floor in the back seat."

"Is she okay?"

"Don't think they hurt her. I think it was just a drug."

"Did you see them kill the driver?"

"Shot through the window, pulled 'im out, dumped 'im on the effing sidewalk."

"Did you get that on film?"

"Only the last part," he whispered. "We were planning to follow her to the premiere, see if we could get a few shots and sound bites of her and Nate swearing at each other. I think we just got the body being dumped."

We both looked at the driver's compartment of the limo. The man in the driver's seat was on a cell phone. The other man had the radio on and was frantically changing channels. They may have just learned they had been followed by the paparazzi.

"Can your microphone pick up voices inside the limo since there's no window on the driver's side?"

"Probably. Yeah. That'd be the money! But with that radio on . . ."

I thought about ways to get him to turn the radio off. What would happen if I walked over there? Luckily, the radio went silent.

"Are you Joe or Mack?"

"You know our names? Does Sally?"

I nodded. "She actually likes you guys."

"No shit." He grinned. "I'm Joe."

"Joe, please, can I use those?" I pointed to his headphones. He frowned but handed them to me. I listened while Joe dialed adjustments. I gave him a thumbs up when I could hear the conversations.

The driver who had been on the cell spoke. "That was the asshole who hired us. We are so f***ed. Some paparazzi were following us until we hit Bev Hills. They posted everything on the internet. They might've seen me shoot the driver. The asshole was really pissed about that. He asked, 'Why do you think I gave you a gun without bullets?'"

The man in the passenger seat muttered under his breath. "Why'd you have to do that? You just needed to knock 'im out and get 'im outa the car."

The driver looked at the ringing cell. "Asshole again," he grumbled to his accomplice. He picked up and listened before he answered, "No, there's no cops here." He paused and then said, "No lady. Haven't seen anyone like that. Just some drunk homeless bitch climbing around in the bushes." He tapped off the phone.

"What're we supposed ta do now?"

"Drive down Benedict Canyon. Head for the back of the hotel."

"She might wake up soon. Don't think I've enough to knock her out again. And she got a good look at us."

"We're already gonna fry for killin' the driver."

"You thinkin' ta kill her, too?"

"Not yet. When we don't need her anymore. Ya know: for proof of life."

Panicked, I pulled out my phone and texted Manny with shaking hands. *She's drugged on back seat floor; they plan to kill her. WHERE is SWAT?*

He responded, *Stay put. Coming to you.*

Peeking through the chaparral, I saw Manny get out of the Jeep and open the back. He had untucked his white shirt and rolled up his sleeves. He looked a little overdressed for a hike or picnic, but I doubted these two would notice.

Manny walked past where we had the mike set up and continued up the path to the picnic area. He sat down and motioned for me to join him. "What did you find out?" he asked quietly.

"They're supposed to drive down Benedict Canyon to the back of the hotel. That must be the Beverly Hills Hotel," I whispered. "They're supposed to meet him there."

"It'd be good to get him, but if they make a move toward Sally . . . I'll have to stop 'em.

"Those guys––Joe and Mack, the paparazzi––have almost everything recorded."

"Good."

"Uh-oh, one's getting out!"

Both front doors of the white limo opened.

Manny headed down the path to the limo. I ran after him.

One man pulled Sally out of the back. His partner picked up her feet.

Manny pulled out his gun. "Stop! Put her on the seat."

The larger man tried to hold Sally with one hand and find his gun with the other. He dropped the gun, and I kicked it away toward Manny.

As the two men released her, I rushed to Sally before she could fall and got her slouched on the seat.

Manny beckoned to me. "Cissy, check for another gun!"

I patted pockets on both of them.

"Pat them . . . never mind. Come hold the gun."

Manny handed me the gun. "You know how to use this, right?"

"Sure," I lied. "And I'd love it if you two dirt bags would give me an excuse to shoot you."

Manny patted them down thoroughly from head to toe while carefully staying out of my line of fire. He called the SWAT team. "We've got two suspects in custody."

A SWAT vehicle and a red ambulance pulled into the parking lot immediately. I hurried back to Sally while Manny spoke to the policeman. "They were supposed to meet their boss in the back parking lot of the Beverly Hills Hotel," he explained. "Get a couple cars over there to see any possibles."

I sat next to Sally and could see she was breathing, but she was pale beneath her smeared makeup and still asleep. I sighed with relief when I saw medical people headed our way. They loaded her onto a gurney, and I followed them as they rolled her into the back of the ambulance.

"Is she going to be okay?" I asked when I could breathe again.

The paramedics checking her nodded and told me they were headed for Cedars on Beverly Boulevard.

The SWAT team had handcuffed the two kidnappers. Manny handed the team the thug's gun, and I called Nikki to tell her we had found Sally and what the paramedics said.

"Okay." Nikki's voice shook. "We'll meet you at Cedars-Sinai."

I wiped away tears. "Manny, can you take me to Cedars?"

"Sure, but I'll probably have to put in an appearance at my office at some point. Hope you understand. I'll drop you off." He looked me over. "On second thought, I better walk you in. You don't look much like their usual visitors at the moment."

We climbed back in his Jeep and went down through Coldwater Canyon, headed to the hospital complex.

"Manny, do you think Sally will be okay?"

"They always have to be careful what they say. She's healthy, in good shape. She should pull through." He patted my hand.

I shivered.

"Put on my jacket."

"It's just nerves." But I reached for the jacket.

So, I walked into the posh suite Sally would be admitted to later with a jagged-hemmed gown sawn off and ripped at the knee, and a black tux jacket with sleeves dangling six inches off each arm. My hair was hanging in my face, which was covered with lipstick smears and runny mascara.

Nikki ran to hug me, but the shaking of her body was not reassuring. "She's down in the trauma center. They haven't told us much other than where she is, and that we can't go in there."

Jack handed me a hot cup of coffee.

Manny explained he needed to check in at his office. "I'll be back."

I finished the coffee and stopped shivering. "Do you think I can use that bathroom? Should I ask the nurse?"

Jack chuckled.

Nikki smiled. "Between Sally, Jack, and Nate, they probably cover the annual budget for this complex. You can use any damn bathroom you want. Not to mention, this suite has two," she said as she looked me up and down. "I'm amazed what you will do for a friend. Sally owes you a gown."

I was grateful for the chance to wash up, neaten my hair, and wipe off the smear of lipstick.

When I came out of the washroom, Jack was on the phone looking very serious. "I'll let you know if he shows up."

"What's happening?" I nearly shrieked.

"It's okay. He's talking to Manny I think," Nikki said as she led me over to a very plush sofa, sat me down, and covered my legs with a warm blanket. "Are you hungry?"

I shook my head just as Nate opened the door. I was surprised to see my date, Paul, right behind him.

Jack said, "He's here," and hung up.

Nate, true to form, immediately complained. "Is this the best suite they have? I think I've seen better." He sighed. "My god, what an effing nightmare! They caught the guys, though, right?"

"Cissy and Manny caught 'em," Jack said.

"With lots of help from Joe and Mack, the two paparazzi who follow Sally around," I said. "And the SWAT team."

No one spoke for a few minutes.

Nikki paced the length of the room.

Jack asked the hospital kitchen for a bottle of brandy and, predictably, Nate didn't approve of the brand when it arrived. Jack poured us each a snifter anyway.

After a few sips, I asked how the premiere went.

A chorus of Sally's favorite swear words answered my stupid question.

Paul said, "Neither of the two leading stars showed up. And the other two stars," he nodded at Nikki and Jack, "apparently left partway through the screening. Should make for a tremendous amount of free publicity though."

Jack looked at Nate. "Where the hell did you go?"

"Paul had a hunch and had us looking for Sally and her white limo behind the Beverly Hills Hotel. You know how many limos there are in those two parking lots?"

"Just think of the publicity if Nate had rescued Sally," Paul whined.

"What?" Jack, Nikki, and I said in unison.

Nate groaned, "What the hell, Paul? Is that why we went up to the hotel?"

Manny entered the room. "Well, we have had some developments. How's Sally?" he asked as he patted down Paul, evidently checking for a weapon.

We all listened, stunned, as Manny read Paul his rights and escorted him to the hallway. As he went out the door, we heard him say, "Guess I borrowed money from the wrong people. They made me do this. And the gun didn't have bullets in it."

Two officers handcuffed him and led him, whining loudly, down the hall.

"The two we arrested claim all their instructions, except the killing the driver part, came from Paul. But they didn't actually know him by his real name so that wouldn't have been enough, except the gun recovered from the kidnappers is registered to Paul Hamill. And the cell number on the kidnapper's phone is Paul's." Manny smiled. "And apparently, he's talking."

No one even swore.

The room was dead silent.

Until we heard the sound of Sally's voice and her colorful vocabulary coming down the hall. The gurney carrying our dear friend was pushed into the room. "Well, WHAT THE F*** are all you doing here? And WHAT THE HELL do you have on, Cissy?"

About the Author

Sherri Leigh James created Cissy Huntington, interior designer, based on her own international interior design career that revealed the private world of the rich and famous. One Amazon reviewer described her writing as a "witty Hollywood dish served with masterful plotting." Murder mysteries *Blood Red* and *Iced Blue* begin the series. www.sherrileighjames.com

Ordinary to Extraordinary

Lynda Palmer

I, CHARLIE, HAVE DREAMED of being extraordinary, but my entire life has been ordinary. I live for the day when Charlie Winston is on the lips of a grateful nation. I would say the world, but I'm not that egocentric.

I'm an accounting clerk in a local Los Angeles bank. We're a small neighborhood bank. So, I know everything financially about our clients. I'll admit the bank is the best gossip source in town. My co-workers think I'm too proper for gossip, but I'll concede it interests me as much as the next person. Of course, I would never reveal rumors or financial information about our clients. Los Angeles is the heart of the entertainment world. Some of our customers are moderately famous. Did I realistically think I might end up more famous than they are? No, but I dreamed of it.

The bank serves the neighborhood of Angelino Heights. One of the loveliest areas in L.A. My family and I have lived here for years. It's our home, and we are very comfortable here. We know and socialize with our neighbors.

I live in a modest two-story house that is cozy for our family of four. It's a mansion by the standards of the working class in L.A. But small compared to the large Victorian homes in the neighborhood. I married my college sweetheart, Janice. We have been married over twenty years. Sadly, I think sometimes about how long and wasted those years have been. They have not been extraordinary.

We have two good kids, Adam, fifteen, and Judy, twelve. Adam participates in sports. He's a good team player. Judy is a budding filmmaker. She loves to tinker with videos. She's never been an internet super star. No trophy cases or awards cover the walls, but they are happy, well-adjusted kids. I'm thankful they are, and most of the time, I'm grateful. But I've dreamed of being extraordinary like my friend Bobby.

Bobby is my best friend from grade school. We went off to college together. He lives in a twenty-room mansion with a swimming pool, a tennis court, a stable, and a butler. Bobby married his college sweetheart, Betty Sue. She's a former Miss California and heir to the largest pharmaceutical company in the world. I always said Bobby majored in fun in college. He didn't have to worry about a job, money, or anything when he graduated. Instead, he walked into it once they got married.

I don't mean that to sound like sour grapes. I may envy Bobby, but I'm proud of him, too. He has worked hard and long hours for his father-in-law.

Bobby and Betty Sue have two kids, Rob, sixteen, and Mary Ellen, twelve. They are academically gifted, superior athletes, talented musicians, charity stars, and good kids. Betty Sue heads several charity organizations and is a neighborhood leader. We're invited to most of their social events. Bobby teases that I'm his token geek. Our wives and kids get along well.

I don't want you to think we're perfect. There have been a few episodes. Our sons got hauled in for vandalism. They ended up doing community service, cleaning up our trashy streets. The mere thought of roadkill gives them shudders.

So why all the background? I need you to understand the setting of my adventure. This is the tale of my extraordinary day.

The event that turned my life upside down began on a typical Monday. I got a call to come to the front of the bank to talk to a customer. Accountants never talk to customers in person. We live behind locked doors, never to be seen by the customers as we toil. So, being called to the front of the bank set my heart racing and sent the little hairs on the back of my neck into a panic. I put down the phone and turned to walk to the front of the bank. George gave me a look. I shrugged my shoulders and kept walking. In the cubicle environment, there are no private conversations.

I was escorted into Dale Earnest's office, one of the vice presidents. Across from Dale, I was shocked to see one of my favorite actors, even though he hasn't been in anything recently.

"Charlie, meet Mr. and Mrs. Stewart. They're here because they feel there's been an error in their account. As of this morning, they were overdrawn by several thousands. Can you explain this?"

I remembered this account. I had checked it over twice, and it was correct. The charge was from our local pharmacy for a monthly electronic prescription. I told the Stewarts and Mr. Earnest it was a legitimate charge and where it came from.

Mrs. Stewart started to cry, and Mr. Stewart murmured, "How can that be correct? How could the price go up that much in a month? I'm on the verge of bankruptcy as it is, paying for these drugs."

Then I got a good look at Mrs. Stewart, seeing the gaunt gray face with the sunken eyes and thin hair.

"The medication is the only thing keeping her alive."

"Thanks, Charlie. I'll take it from here."

I walked back to my cubicle feeling angry, sad, and miserable. Why hadn't the Stewarts' insurance helped? How can a pharmaceutical company raise the price by over seven hundred percent in one month?

I spent the rest of the day stewing over the problem. By the time I got home, I was in full-blown outrage. Unfortunately, I ended up being short with my wife and kids. So, I spent the rest of the evening alone, huffing into my newspaper.

I began to formulate a plan by bedtime. First, I needed to determine who was at fault. Not the family, not Clark's drugstore, and not the bank. I even gave a rare break to the insurance company. The pharmaceutical company was at fault for this crisis.

Second, I needed to determine which company caused the financial problems for our customers. Finally, I needed to do something to help the Stewarts.

I had a restless night with little sleep. I was being chased by pills, greedily swallowing me up like the old Pac-Man game. By morning, I was nowhere near a solution.

In the morning, I found ten more customer families facing ruin over skyrocketing drug costs. These overcharges were not for the same drug but all from the same drug company, Bobby's firm.

I'm usually a creature of habit and eat a sandwich at my desk. But today, I needed a drink. While sitting at a local bar nursing my beer, I overheard a news report about a hacking crisis. They warned opening a phishing email would make you a victim. Victims would find their computers kidnapped, forcing them to pay a fee.

Could I hack the pharmaceutical company's computers and take charge of their pricing? Then, I could lower the prices on the rampant drug increases. I needed a malware that wouldn't allow them to raise the prices immediately after they noticed my changes. I wanted the company's executives to think about what they were doing and be fair. I wasn't out to bankrupt them. I hoped the shock of lost profits would get them to take responsibility and get the prices back to a reasonable level.

But I'm not a hacker. I would need help. How does one find a hacker and ask them to perform an illegal act for no monetary reward? Heck, if they're a hacker, I suspect they're already doing unlawful deeds. Asking them to do it for no compensation could be complicated.

What if I solicited the affected families? I could get lucky and find the perfect partner. I knew what the families would want.

Get us out of debt, bankrupt the drug companies, jail the CEOs, go after the insurance companies.

These might make them feel good in the short-term but provide no long-term solution. The families needed these drugs for themselves or their loved ones. I spent the afternoon searching the records of the affected families, hoping to find my perfect candidate. My search provided two possible candidates. One was Jeff Brady, a recent computer science graduate. I called him right away.

"Mr. Brady, this is Charlie Winston at the bank."

"Look, Mr. Winston, we're doing everything we can to take care of that balance."

"Mr. Brady, I'm calling for a different reason. I have an idea about something that may help you. Can we meet for coffee?"

We set up a meeting in an hour. Jeff was anxious to hear any idea I had to help him. So, as we sat sipping our coffee, I explained my idea and need of a computer expert or, precisely, a hacker.

"I appreciate your offer to help, but you're looking at the wrong man. You need someone with skills far better than me. Sorry." With that, he walked away.

I crossed him off my list and moved on to candidate number two. Sara Edwards held a master's degree in library science. I knew from experience that librarians were wizards on computers. I called her and set up a meeting. She sounded very positive on the phone. I was looking forward to meeting her.

We ordered our coffee, and I explained my idea and need to her. I saw tears forming in her eyes.

"Oh, Mr. Winston, I thought you were going to get me out of this mess. I'm in debt over ten thousand dollars for one week of pills." With that, she began to cry in earnest.

"Sara, I'm so sorry. Unfortunately, I have no quick cure for your debt. But I have a plan I feel will help."

"I'm sorry, I'm not your hacker," she said, running out the door.

I watched her and felt worse than ever. I hoped there was no reward for turning in a person who offered to help someone in an illegal way.

Thursday morning, reception called me about a visitor. Walking to the front, I had the feeling of hope and fear. Was my visitor a hacker or a cop? Now was the time to take a leap of faith. These families needed my help. As I came through the door, I recognized Jeff Brady.

"Mr. Brady, how can I help you?"

"Can we talk somewhere private?"

I escorted him to a private office and closed the door.

"Did you mean it about helping us?"

"Absolutely, I want to help everyone in your predicament. I have a plan but need help."

"My nephew, Carl, is what you call a hacker. I'm not proud of it, but maybe he can do some good with his skills. I told him I expected him to help you."

"Jeff, that's great. When can I meet him?"

"How about Saturday at midnight? I know it's an odd time, but he operates at strange hours. Here's his address. He wrote it on paper. He doesn't want any phone calls, emails, or text records of this meeting. Written word only."

"See you then."

"Oh, I won't be there, only you."

I had no intention of sharing my deeds with my wife. She needed plausible deniability. I told her it was a new bank program we could only test at night. I wouldn't be gone long.

During the drive over I wondered if I needed a secret knock or password. GPS brought me to a neighborhood and an ordinary, two-story home. I was thinking more of a dark alley or basement lair. Oddly, there were no visible lights, no car in the driveway, and no doorbell, so I knocked.

"What's the password?"

"Oh, shit, I knew it."

"Gotcha," a boy, appearing not old enough to be in high school, said as he opened the door. "I can't help myself."

As he led me inside, he explained he lived with his grandma who was sleeping in the back room.

He knew a lot of the story from his uncle. He interrupted me once as I told him what I thought I needed to accomplish my goal. Who was I to tell him what I needed? I knew nothing about hacking.

"We're going to need a trojan horse. Pharmaceutical companies are more difficult to hack than the government. Phishing won't work as companies have strict rules about opening non-work emails. Employees fear losing their jobs. I'll contact you when I've got something."

With that, I was dismissed, and our meeting was over. Filled with fear, dread, and anticipation, I drove home. What was I doing? I got no answer from Carl. Those families had little time left.

Sunday evening, at the dinner table, there was a rap at the door.

"That's odd. Are you expecting anyone? I'll check it out." I excused myself and headed to the door.

An envelope was on the mat with a note inside. It told me to come to Carl's house at midnight.

"What was it?" asked my wife.

"Just a coupon from a pizza place," I said and tossed the note away.

This time, I escaped without my wife noticing. I drove to Carl's house and parked. I walked up to the porch and found a box instructing me to take it. I looked to see if anyone was watching and grabbed the box. I felt like a porch pirate. I left the neighborhood, parked my car in the garage, and tore open the box. Inside was a sheet of handwritten instructions, a laptop, and several thumb drives.

So, I would hand these to employees as they arrived at work. Then what? Ask them to download the malware onto their computers? Thank you very much. It seemed like a stupid plan. This was not what I had imagined.

Reading on, he wanted me to scatter the thumb drives in the garage and parking lots of the drug company. He predicted that sixty percent of the employees would take the thumb drive. At least one would load it onto their computer out of curiosity. Of course, when they did, the malware would download. Ready for me to attack their pricing sheets.

I brought them into the house and hid them in the hall closet, still not convinced such a plan would work. But, then again, I felt I had no option for these families. They faced bankruptcy, foreclosure, and possible homelessness. Let alone a family member's death.

Executing the plan seemed too easy. The next night I drove to the drug company parking areas late. I chose to park in a back alley. I figured there would be no cameras there. Unfortunately, it also had no lights. Excellent planning, I thought, as I tripped over a curb, falling flat. I picked myself up and proceeded to plant the thumb drives. I wore a hat, a mask, and gloves. I had seen enough cop shows to make me an expert on disguise and getting rid of the evidence. Truthfully, I felt this was getting too complicated. I was certain my days of freedom were numbered.

Deed done, I anxiously waited to see if it was successful. Carl had given me instructions to use only the provided laptop.

Monday was an ordinary day, but I had a chance to make it extraordinary. I opened the laptop finding my nerves were getting to me. What was taking so long? I was ready to give up when it worked. Holy crap! I found their pricing spreadsheets and changed over a hundred prices, making sure to include the specific ones affecting the bank families. As I hit enter, I wondered if it would work, how long it would help these families, and when I would get caught.

My phone was ringing when I arrived at my cubicle. It was Mr. Earnest.

"I don't know how this happened, Charlie, but I got a call from the Stewarts this morning telling me the charges were gone. Their account was back to normal."

"Wonderful, Mr. Earnest. Thanks for letting me know."

"I want you to check into other accounts that may have had a similar issue. It's extraordinary. Lucky families."

I knew which accounts to investigate. Refunds had posted to each family's account. I called the families to give them the good news. I was darn proud of myself and Carl.

A month later, we were spending time with Bobby and his family. As CEO of the drug company I hacked, Bobby couldn't help spilling the story. More importantly, he related they had no clue about the source of the malware or how to get rid of it. Bobby reported his father-in-law was looking into their pricing policies. He asked Bobby to oversee the investigation. Bobby was happy looking into what he considered to be a longtime problem at his company.

I only smiled in relief. I wanted to call Carl and congratulate him. But I couldn't do it as I remembered his words: Never contact him again for any reason. I wanted to spill the beans to Bobby, but all seemed to be working out well for him.

Six months later, I opened my door to two policemen. I could tell by their demeanor that I was in trouble. But at least they hadn't arrived sirens blaring and guns drawn.

"Mr. Winston, we need you to come down to the station with us. We've got a few questions for you."

"Give me a minute. I'll get my coat and tell my wife I'm going with you."

From the knock on my door to my incarceration, I must have set a Guinness World Record for speed.

"Charlie, can you explain this?" asked Bill, the older policeman, showing me a video off a thumb drive.

"Honestly, I can't."

They told me an employee of the drug company turned the drive over to them last week.

"She had strong reservations about doing it as she was your ally. She hated what the company was doing. She knew it was hurting people. Fortunately for us, her guilty conscience got the better of her, and she turned it over to us. She found it the same time the malware got loaded onto their computers."

Funny story, my daughter, our family videographer, had made a video. She loaded it on a thumb drive and added to the others she found in the closet. She thought I was working on some family surprise and wanted to help. It was clearly images of my family. When they asked me to explain it,

I saw no reason to refuse. It was my family. The video was impressive for her first attempt.

I confessed to my crime, seeing no reason to deny it. I started this sitting in a holding cell, waiting for my sentencing hearing. So, I figured it was as good a time as any to get my story out.

I think of this as a victimless crime. You can make a case for the drug company, but it would be weak. The publicity against them has been overwhelming. The drug company agreed to reevaluate its pricing policy, or greed, as I label it. Due to public opinion, they didn't go after the families. Instead, they ended up helping those families with their financial woes. The result is better than I hoped for. I've become kind of a folk hero.

"Was it worth it? You could end up with twenty-plus years in jail. How did you get caught? How's your family doing with all this?"

I was in jail, and a local news reporter, Jennifer, got permission to interview me.

"I'll answer all your questions. I've got plenty of time and nothing to do as I can't afford to post bail."

I felt I could trust her with my story. Nothing wrong with admitting your guilt to a beautiful, intelligent woman.

At first, my wife and kids were angry, upset, and disbelieving. But, after I explained my motives, they became my greatest allies. They mounted a social media blitz to get my story out and painted the drug company as the bad guy. They hoped it would influence my jail time. Swaying public opinion never hurts. It certainly affected the drug company.

The cops convinced me giving up Carl would only help me. So, I told them all about him. It turns out Carl didn't exist, according to the police. There was no record of him, the house we met at was foreclosed on nine months ago, and there was no grandma. On the other hand, Jeff Brady, his uncle, had plausible deniability. He was contacted by some distant relative who knew about Jeff's problem and put him onto Carl. That relative? He denied making the phone call. So, at present, Carl is a dead end.

I was escorted into the courtroom. My lawyer was seated at the table. The opposing attorneys were there to ensure I got proper punishment for my crimes. Seated behind me were my family, friends from the bank, neighbors, and the families I helped.

"All rise for the honorable Judge Anderson."

"Be seated."

Judge Anderson had complete control of my life. The judge looked ordinary, and I hoped she was a kindred spirit. At least I prayed she was as I needed all the help I could muster.

I didn't hear the judge going over the details of my charges or summarizing the damage my crimes had caused. Instead, all I could hear was the beating of my heart. Then, suddenly, I was aware of my lawyer pulling me up to hear the judge proclaim her sentence. The sentence which would end my life as I knew it for me and my family.

"While I understand your desire to help these families, Mr. Winston, desire does not make it legal."

I felt my knees go weak and I shook as she continued.

"You've cost the drug company millions of dollars. You did, however, end up helping those families. You also got the drug company to review its pricing policy."

I began to feel slightly better. After all, Judge Anderson gave me a compliment.

"Unfortunately, good deeds do not change the law, and I am bound by the law."

I looked for a place to land when I fainted from her sentence.

Judge Anderson took a deep breath and looked straight at me as if she could read my mind. I was white, shaking, and sweating for what seemed like forever. All I wanted to do was run.

"You, Mr. Winston, have pled guilty to all charges. Accordingly, I sentence you to time served and five years' supervised probation. Don't let me see you in my courtroom again."

"Yes, your honor," I whispered, not believing what happened.

The courtroom erupted in applause, and I looked for my family. I caught the judge's eye as my family ran forward for a group hug. For a moment, I swear I saw a small smile on the judge's face.

Now, I'm living a semi-retired life. I find myself writing books, lecturing, and appearing on TV. People say I'm a media darling. Often, I can't believe it.

There's talk of a movie deal. I also run a small nonprofit helping people in a similar fix. It turns out that you can help people legally, and I'm pretty good at it.

Supervised probation means I don't go anywhere or do anything my parole officer doesn't know about. My ankle monitor keeps him informed. He has me on a short leash, at the drug company's request.

I got an unsigned card with no postmark or return address at Christmas this year. Inside, I found a handwritten note giving instructions on bypassing my monitor. Those instructions have given me a little freedom back.

Thanks, Carl!

About the Author

Lynda Palmer is a retired medical professional who has written several medical articles, lectures, and patient instructions. Post retirement, she branched out to fiction writing and has several short stories published in anthologies along with articles in magazines. She has been a member of several chapters of Sisters in Crime.

Natural Causes

Yolanda Reid

DASH MCDONALD WAS HANDSOME. In 1958, when he won his first Oscar. When he was awarded his second Oscar, in the mid-1970s, his visage had morphed into the polite and respectful "classic" category. Macbeth, but not yet King Lear. By the time he was admitted to the "Actors' Playhouse" in Hollywood, at the age of ninety-eight, he would best be cast as Gollum, and, like most of his peers, had yielded to the temptation and ensured his online presence displayed no photos taken after 1994. And none that weren't photoshopped to meet 2022 standards of beauty—and heat. After all, even in the twenty-first century, plastic surgery can only do so much, right?

As a new nurse at the renowned nursing home for industry veterans, I still wasn't used to seeing half of Hollywood's Golden Age in the dining room every suppertime struggling to eat the airline food we charge airline prices for. We do try to provide multicolored bibs to help brighten dulled appetites for the very elderly. I can't help but crack a smile watching so many anorexic actresses finally give in to the calories they eschewed in their working years. Those 1994 pictures are enough to keep up the illusion of rich and thin, when both left the building decades ago.

Didn't take me long to identify many of our residents, even though they were typically admitted under their unfamiliar real names. Not everyone was recognizable to this old movie buff; a few of our residents looked familiar, but their health records didn't reveal a history of fame. They must have been production staff or crew, and not talent. On a slow night covering memory care, I googled our newest resident, Tatyana Smirnoff, and only got a weird urge to hit the closed bar. I found out nothing about her online, even in the IMDB or NNDB. And she didn't seem to be a secretary, script supervisor, or a first wife. Intelius People Search had her at age eighty-five, but, according to her medical chart, dementia had arrived a decade before. At least she could walk with a cane and eat by herself, even though she would forget each bite after she swallowed. Her brief conversations were launched with a "Hey, you" and were limited to the day's events. Our name tags and Post-it reminders seemed to help. The only name she never forgot was Babushka, her miserable, superannuated cat. That ball of evil would scratch me anytime I got within a foot—or near a paw. I had to wear personal protective equipment to safely do my job, but it had never before included bite protection sleeves.

Fortunately, nursing homes are nothing like prisons. You can sleep in till seven a.m., get three squares a day that don't taste like yesterday's gruel, watch the staff do arts and crafts for you, and be led on occasional supervised field trips around the block. Better than rehab. But seeing the same old, same old every day, even with carpeted floors, is soul-crushing. And it's worse when the weakest souls disappear week by week; it helps to remind those left behind that though we are all meek before death, the meek shall inherit heaven, right?

Every once in a while, some film school grad student working for their hometown news catches a freelance gig to interview one of the "movie stars" waiting for Godot in our facility. We set them up with a younger family member still in the will or a public relations pro who provides text beyond the actor's one well-rehearsed and pithy quote. But hundredth birthdays are special and have our phones ringing all day. Not just gossip rags and social media, but actual broadcast TV. Well, syndicated, but still. We act on those calls ASAP, as the publicity helps us get more donors to keep our services afloat. Not every one of our resident "stars" has a robust fortune to fully support our care facility after multiple marriages and a dearth of work after age forty.

So, when the calls started coming in for Daniel Dewar's—I mean, Dash McDonald's—century celebration, we were grateful for the publicity, and even promised to call in our makeup mavens to prepare Dash for a softly lit, lens-filtered, three-picture photo shoot. Hundredth birthdays aren't just for the adoring public and their expensive fanzines, but a chance for a party at our Playhouse for the other residents as well. We gather everyone in stir into our dining room and have several birthday cakes prepared to allow for a slice for every resident and seconds for those with a sweet tooth or functioning implants. Considering his memory issues, Dash's party went better than expected, and he ended up not needing his cue cards for his brief "live" greeting and thanks. Way to go, Dash!

Rocio and I had helped Wolfgang and the kitchen staff set up the buffet and played gaffers to keep the lights from melting the icing on the cakes until everyone had put their glasses on and read the *Happy 100th, Dash!* scripted in blue in twenty-point font on top of the frosting. Of course, we didn't have Dash blow out the candles; we're still under those damned pandemic precautions and didn't want aerosols sprinkled all over the desserts. We just lit some sparklers in camera view and handed a mic to the visiting Dash son who wasn't yawning, asking him to introduce his father.

Slash turned toward the Entertainment Tonight camera and mumbled some platitudes about his father before pitching his own upcoming techno album. A suddenly alert Cash quickly grabbed the microphone from his brother and took over the spotlight, thanking Dad Dash for his guidance and support that allowed Cash to win the Culver City Film Festival's "Best Indie Film from a Connected Industry Hack" Award, or something like that. Didn't catch the end, because Dash's publicist had seized the mic back and waved the ET crew over to Dash, nudging him awake and cueing him to deliver his memorized line. "Thank you to all my fans, thank you," Dash mumbled before asking, "Gimme some cake?"

"Coming right up," I answered. I handed him one of the slices we'd already readied for the eager residents to enjoy and pulling out a new bib with my clean gloved hand.

"Hold it!" said the PR flack. "He's not eating till we get all the video. Take that thing away." He nodded at the clothing protector as he tugged the plate out of Dash's hands and handed it back to me. "Media first, then you can serve him." Shaking his head, he said, "Ten minutes."

I put the cake piece back on the table with the other slices and tried to console several hungry residents whose faces registered disappointment at having to wait even longer for the treat. Ten minutes became an hour as getting acceptable video and photos of Dash was understandably challenging during his regular naptime. But, what price beauty?

The residents weren't the only ones tired after the long day's events. I was off duty at seven p.m. that week, so I stayed 'til 6:59 and left with a quick sign-out, "It's been a good day. They're all alive. I'm outta here." I took Eleanor out for her evening walk, and, with the new leash, I could keep her from racing off and causing hobbling ole me to face-plant in the poop-seasoned grass on the curb. Had to thank my vet's wife at Eleanor's next checkup for the lead on a better lead. We hit the sack at nine, and I set the alarm for six so I could make it back to the Playhouse in the 101 traffic before seven a.m. and find a parking space.

Except today I couldn't—find a parking space, that is. The facility lot was full. Not just the coroner's van, but a couple of police cars and three

TV satellite trucks, one again from ET. None of them parking between the lines in the small lot. Thanks loads. Why don't you all park on the curb grass?

"Guess they're not all alive," I muttered to a colleague as I entered the building. "Who isn't this morning?"

Rocio shook her head. "Dash. I can hardly believe it."

"Come on. At least he made it to a hundred. We should all be so lucky." I looked back out at the crowded parking lot. "Why the cops?"

"Coroner called them. Apparently, two of his kids were overheard fighting about their inheritance, and he wondered if—"

"Rocio!" Santiago, the day manager strode toward us. "*La poli* are done, get your crew in his room and start cleanup."

Rocio muttered something X-rated and sped off, leaving me standing a few feet away from the CSU van that was being loaded up with just-collected materials from Dash's suite. Mostly his pills and a few of the snacks he had stashed away in his mini-fridge next to the water bottles which held his vodka. One bag had blue slime lining the plastic. It took me a minute to recognize that it had once been frosting from his slice of birthday cake. I don't blame Dash for not finishing the dessert. I'd tried a piece myself in the kitchen and could only savor a few bites of the cardboard taste Chef "Wolfgang" Gemelli had perfected during his army years.

"So," I asked one of the techs, "any theories about what happened to Dash?"

"Another *CSI* viewer," the tech muttered to his colleague. To me: "Yeah. He died. Cut to commercial."

The second tech's tone was a bit gentler. "We won't know for a few days or more. They're fantastically fast on TV. 'Fantasy' being the keyword. Wouldn't be surprised, though, if they do the autopsy in a day or two seeing it's Dash, but it'll be at least a week for the labs. Press the fast forward," he added, winking at me.

I nodded. "Got it. Still, Dash McDonald. A hundred. Damned shame."

"That's what I've heard," said the first tech as he stepped into his van. "The cool cat really hit the wall on his ninth life."

Fast forward. You saw the news reports. Famous movie star and romantic rogue found dead in his bed by a night shift nurse. No breathing, no pulse. Vomit on his pajamas. Diaper soiled. Photos only in the *Enquirer*. The other rags had to make do with tidbits from whistleblowers who snuck a peek into his medical records. History of mild heart failure. Dash had high blood pressure and was being treated for atrial fibrillation, an irregular heartbeat. But no pacemaker. Nobody mentioned the smoking, the drinking, and the rest of his contributing sins. In the end, nothing out of the ordinary, especially for someone one hundred or more, said the rumor mill. Time to deify one of the last living "stars" of the Golden Age. His Oscar should have been mine.

The cops interviewed every one of us—no one had seen anything suspicious. Dash wasn't exactly the most popular resident. Even at ninety-nine, he was a bit too handsy with the help—of both genders. But nothing bubbled up that would result in his "cancellation" in this #MeToo era, taking his age, condition, and cognitive status into account.

We'd been waiting for a week for the lab to test anything that Dash might have put in his mouth. Hey, I'm not going there. I'm talking about the stuff the CSU collected: food, pens, the mics, the remotes, the john . . . as I said, I'm not going there. Dash's pills were all in order as prescribed, and his legendary water bottle actually had water in it for once. Maybe Dash had gotten too old to notice someone had made off with his vodka. The only persons of interest still of interest after the initial investigation were the kitchen team and the dueling duo Slash and Cash, who'd hovered by the dessert table while waiting to speak about their beloved father. If the food came back clear, so would the Playhouse. The odds were, it'd be death by natural causes.

Mystery fans like me might ask if the Playhouse had security cameras. Of course. Outside. Our residents deserved confidentiality—HIPAA Privacy Rule and all. We'd already cleared and tested the media crews for COVID-19 before they arrived—and, with HIPAA in mind, we made sure they'd been supervised during the entire event so they didn't go digging for paydirt.

The cops did "borrow" everyone's phones for days to see if anybody had a video that might provide a clue to a cause of death other than an act of God. *Nada*. Those residents that could shoot with their smartphones couldn't shoot straight. They sure captured a lot of blurry footage of muddy shoes and the peeling ceiling. And we staff were too busy throwing the party to record it. Video from the media folks was also reviewed, but the only possible lead there came from the animated "discussion" Slash and Cash were having behind Dash, off-mic. Santiago relayed that they couldn't make out much of the conversation, though he did hear them growl "bastard" and "son of a bitch" a couple of times. Referring to each other? Dash?

Dash's autopsy report a few days later held no surprises. He had an enlarged heart with atrophied muscle. Stenosis—stiffening—of the heart valves, cirrhosis of the liver, colonic polyps, esophageal varices. Par for the course after a lifetime of cigarettes and booze. Nothing seen on the standard drug screen. Looked like natural causes to me; why look further? Lay the bastard to rest already.

ell

Babushka bit me again when I was taking Tatyana's vital signs this morning. Broke the skin on my arm, bleeding and bruising. Damn, another trek downtown to HMO workers' comp. Which I hated almost as much as that cat. Santiago and HR finally agreed that the little fiend had to go, but Tatyana would not let us take her guard cat out of her sight.

After a dramatic sigh, Santiago texted Joseph, our shuttle van driver, to escort Babushka and Tatyana to the vet. I offered to ride along and help, hoping I could get an antibiotic for free and advocate for feline euthanasia for the repeat offender. No sutures would be needed; a closed bite wound is ripe for infection. And the workers' comp tent updated my tetanus shot last time. Good to know I won't get tetanus, diphtheria, or whooping cough. Whoopee.

The vet and his wife Nancy greeted me warmly when we arrived. He wrapped Babushka in his burly arms and carried her into an open exam room. Tatyana followed slowly, lugging her oversize bag, and stumbling forward with her cane, fighting back tears. Joseph took her by her free arm and guided her into the room with her fur demon.

Spying my oozing wound, Nancy waved an assistant over to cover their front desk, led me into a different room, and asked me to take a seat. My Pilates-trained arms lifted me onto the exam table.

"That looks awful. Let me clean it for you," she soothed. "Have you had a—"

"Tetanus shot? Many, many. Last one, last summer, after Eleanor knocked me down. But I wouldn't mind some antibiotic coverage today," I added as she started with the Betadine wipes. "And three shots of whiskey and something to bite on, all right?" Yeow! Dang it! Even the gauze bandage hurt!

A few minutes that felt like an hour later, the vet stuck his head in our room and said, "Nancy, get me the propofol and the phenobarb. We'd been hoping the ketamine would make her calmer, but . . ."

"Maybe she accidentally got dogamine," I jumped in. Seeing the pained smiles, I added, "So you're going to put her down? The cat, I mean. Tatyana must be devastated."

The vet nodded and left the room. Nancy shuffled over to a digi-locked cabinet above the nearby sink and punched in her four numbers. She pulled out a couple of syringes, the meds, and an IV setup, then closed and relocked the cabinet before turning back to me. "You can go ahead and wait here. I'll be back in a bit. I've got some free drug company samples in the back, and I think some are antibiotics. I don't think hubby will mind; we can spare a few."

Sparing me a visit to the HMO is the best gift. I pulled my phone out of my pocket, turned it on, and gave her a smile. "Thanks. I'll just catch up on *Better Call Saul*."

Two episodes later, Nancy came in with a plastic bag filled with the requisite number of augmentin pill samples. Re-donning my mask, I thanked her with another hug, and headed out toward the foyer. Tatyana stumbled out, sobbing, and leaning on Joseph. "My baby . . ."

"Cat heaven, dear. Lots of things she can scratch and bite." I patted her arm. "You'll be fine in a day." *Or an hour, after you forget.*

It must have been the wound pain, but I thought I saw Tatyana's eyes flash for a moment before she dived into another sob. Nah. It's the ache in my arm, that's all. Rolling my eyes, I buckled up my fanny pack and led the way back to our van. *Do svidaniya, Babushka. You will not be missed.*

We had barely gotten Tatyana settled in her room before Santiago paged us to the conference room. Most of the staff were eagerly waiting for news, but I noted that Wolfgang and the kitchen staff were absent.

"They found something?" I asked.

Santiago nodded. "But I still think it was one of those two *fracadasos*, not Wolfgang."

"What'd they find?" interrupted Rocio.

"Poison," he said. "In the body, and in the cake. Ketamine."

A cough from the staff gallery.

"No, *m'hijo*, you were in rehab when Dash died," Santiago continued. "The police are interrogating the kitchen team again, but they'll be coming back to talk to health services, too."

I frowned. "Where would Dash get ketamine?"

"We keep some in our dispensary," Santiago admitted.

"Bet you wish you knew *that*," said Stevie, poking Santiago's son in the ribs with an elbow.

Miguel shook his head. "I don't shit where I eat, dude."

"I've asked Luzon to check for unauthorized entry. She's printing out a list of everyone who used their access code."

I shook my head. "Might not help. Special K is easy to get on the street. If you want to get high." I glanced at Miguel.

"Why do *we* have it?" Santiago pressed.

"Dr. Subramanian's clinical trial. Depression and pain treatment," I reminded him. "Low dose therapy. Our folks don't need to get the anxiety and amnesia side effects from SNRIs. Or chemical dependency." A thought. "But the kitchen staff wouldn't have dispensary access either.

Besides, it's a powder. It needs to be liquefied to inject. Someone would have seen something. Any needle marks on the autopsy? Or stuff in Dash's nose?"

"Nope. His last blood draw was a month ago. Nothing recent."

"And we don't carry the nasal," Luzon said entering the room. "Here's the report you texted me about. All access this month was authorized, just Dr. Subramanian's nurse, Xochitl, and me for prep." She shrugged.

"Well, Xochitl doesn't work memory care," I said as we stood up. "And neither does Dr. S., far as I can tell."

Trudging back to our worksites, I overheard Luzon talking to Santiago. "Wolf's got a record, you know."

No, I didn't.

The detectives started a floor-to-floor search of our building, hitting all the rooms once again. They also ordered an analysis for ketamine of collected waste from every floor of the Playhouse. If someone was using, the drug might show up in the collections and identify a floor where the user might be . . . using the toilet.

We workers got called to the conference room one at a time to talk with the two investigators about our activities on the fateful day of dear Dash's death. They didn't waste any time with me. Right to the point.

"We had you on video. You served him cake," said the bad cop. With that tone, I hoped she wasn't the good one.

"Whoa." I raised a bare hand. "Our chef's the one with the record. And the opportunity. I just picked up a slice from the table and took it over to him. You should have that on your TV tape."

"It's digital," said the other bad cop. "And, yes, we saw that."

"Then you saw me put it back, right? And then someone else grabbed it when they opened the gates." I looked them each in the eyes. "I just picked one plate off the table for him at random. Besides, nobody else got sick. Maybe Dash got the ketamine on his own. Or from his kids."

"We're looking at everything," said the female investigator. "Everything."

"Well, good. There's no way I could've gotten ketamine into him at the party. Or after," I intoned. "I left right after the cameras did. I've got a hyperactive dog with a weak bladder. Maybe you guys should try to find out why his kids think Dash was a bastard instead."

"Where'd you hear that?" said the male cop.

"Uh, a little bird?" Should've kept my mouth shut. Didn't want to out Santiago and his mole. "TMZ? Look, none of us had anything to gain by helping Dash climb the stairway to heaven. No opportunity, no motive."

I expected more questions, but lady cop stared at me for a long minute, then dropped her gaze, mumbling, "What's past is present." She stood up and walked to the door, opened it, waved me out, and announced "Next."

I took my cue and exited her stage.

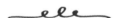

TMZ did run a story almost every night about the lawsuits Slash and Cash were filing against each other, no surprise. Keeps the hot story alive. What *did* knock me for a loop was "the bastard." It was well-known that Dash had been a real player back in the day and had apparently left many women brokenhearted—and at least one of them pregnant. One who wasn't one of his four official wives. The swinging sixties in Hollywood were one big party and Dash was a popular guest. And condoms weren't required for admission.

Apparently, Dash had a child out of wedlock, who'd now be a fifty-something woman, and was—natch—seeking a share of the McDonald pie. The "bastard" daughter (who I called Lady B) had only identified herself through her lawyer and was aiming to get a third of Dash's fortune, as well as damages for pain and distress. Good luck with that.

Lady B had her legal team file suit to get DNA samples from Dash's body, or from one of his two "legitimate" sons, to confirm her biological relationship. The attorney was a good negotiator, because he offered both of the men sixty percent of Lady B's cut if they provided the DNA sample. Suddenly, thirty-three percent plus nineteen percent seemed more appealing than just fifty percent. Cash, living up to his accounting skills, was the first to accept the deal, and offered his DNA sample to get that fifty-two percent of the pot of gold.

You know there's always a *but*, right? Well, TMZ reported this evening that Lady B's and Cash's DNA were (gasp!) NOT a match at all. Yup. You guessed it. Dash's third wife had cheated on him before their split, and delivered the Cash cow—or bull—while she and Dash were divorcing. Cash is now arguing that he deserves to inherit because Dash was still married to his mother when he was born and acted like his father when he was growing up. That strategy might work, but maybe not. Looks like a lot of the McDonald inheritance is going to end up with the high-priced lawyers who figure all this out. Nobody deserved it more.

I hadn't been assigned to Tatyana for a couple of weeks after the "passing" of Babushka. The cops had given up on penning a "Poirot ending" to their investigation. Ketamine was not found in any of the residents' rooms, or among any of the belongings of the residents or the staff. A trace of ketamine was identified in the waste collection samples from the memory care floor, but there was no way to determine which toilet it had come from. Perhaps Dr. Subramanian did treat a patient or two in memory care after all.

What *was* discovered at the Playhouse was a host of health code and ICE violations, which cost Santiago and Miguel their jobs, along with a good number of the staff. Most of our residents were going to have to be moved to another facility until the Playhouse could be restaffed and get up to code. Tatyana would be leaving tomorrow for her new venue at the Woodland Hills Actors' Home.

The lab had identified a high dose of ketamine in Dash's body and tissues, but not at a level that was automatically lethal. Perhaps the combination of the hallucinogen and Dash's lifetime of debauchery were synergistic in causing his death. "Natural causes" was not off the table. If Dash's death had been murder, its investigation was speeding toward the cold case pile.

After donning my required PPE, sans bite protectors, thank the vet, I entered room 265 and found Tatyana watching cable news. There were lots of other true crimes for the media to focus on, and Dash's death had taken a back seat this week to the mutual defamation trial two erstwhile movie stars were using to destroy or advance their careers. I sighed and flipped the channel to black-and-white reruns of *Perry Mason*, where nuance was not yet allowed in the courtroom.

"Turn it off completely," I heard Tatyana rasp in an unusually directive tone. "It's all an illusion."

That was a big word for my patient. "Really?" I said, waiting for a nonsensical response.

A scoff. "So many people buy into the image. Hollywood, bright lights, and shining stars."

"That's pretty poetic, Tatyana," I returned. "Speaking from experience?"

"Unfortunately." She waved at a chair next to hers for me to sit down. "But I wasn't drawn to the glamour, not enough to make the sacrifices needed for stardom."

Whoa. "You were an actress?"

"Aren't we all?" She smiled, a little longer than was comfortable. "But it was my mother who really wanted me to make it. Stage mother from the time I was a child." Her voice broke. "You know, I wasn't much older than a child when I met Dash."

I took her hand and squeezed it. Memories, real or not, could be disturbing for patients with dementia.

"Fifteen or sixteen years old, no more, back in the mid-fifties," Tatyana continued. "Mother had arranged the meeting at the Beverly Hills Hotel. I was supposed to go up to his room, turn on the charm, and convince him to cast me in his next movie. That blockbuster."

I didn't ask which one. Patients with dementia sometimes have these moments of clarity, but with that clarity can come pain and agitation. "Are you sure you want to talk about this?"

"It helps. I'm not going to be around forever. Or for much longer. Now that my dear little Babushka is gone . . ." She sipped some water, handed me her empty glass, and cleared her throat. "The word is rape. I got out of there as soon as I could, and I raced back down to the car where my mother was waiting, only to have her scream and start slapping me when I told her I hadn't gotten a part."

"How awful. I am so sorry. I can only imagine . . ."

Tatyana looked directly at me. "I think you can probably do more than that." A pause. "You played Lady Macduff in that remake of *MacBeth* Dash directed thirty years ago on TV, yes?"

"Um," I started, and looked around by instinct. How—? Oh, what's the use. "Not bad at facial rec, are you, Tatyana?"

"Did he slip you drugs?"

"Um, I was a little older. Twenty-two. I could have said no, but I didn't think I had another option. Not back then. It was the sixties. Everybody was getting high. Everybody was saying 'yes.'"

"Me, too, eh?" Tatyana said. "You know, I just froze. I couldn't move when he took me. Couldn't."

I strove for my empathetic look. A sudden thought. "You aren't related to Lady B, are you? I mean the Lady suing the McDonald estate for paternity. Did you get pregnant?"

Tatyana's eyes welled up with tears. "Sometimes I wish I had. No, I got something else. Chlamydia. Didn't know anything about it, and, by the time I was diagnosed, the damage was done. I could never have children . . . and back then, there was no IVF. Dash McDonald took my future away from me, and . . ." She didn't finish her sentence. She didn't need to.

I met her clear damp eyes and took the chance. "You don't have dementia, do you?"

She smiled. "Oh, once in a while. But I *am* a very good actress." A chuckle. "Dash never went anywhere without a pair of goons protecting him. Until he got old and sick. When I found out where he was housed, and how easy it would be to outwit nursing home security as a client, I started to 'need' access to memory care as well."

"You sure fooled me. Brava." I hesitated, but I had to pose the question. "You can tell me, Tatyana, just between us, did you kill Dash McDonald?"

She took a moment. "I wanted to. I've spent much of my life thinking about retribution and revenge."

It all made sense. "So you got some ketamine, the cat anesthetic, from the vet's office, yes?" Finger quotes. "'For your cat.'"

A nod. "Vet staff should be more careful with their cabinet codes," she muttered. "But I flushed it down the toilet the night Dash died."

"What? You changed your mind?"

"No, *you* changed my mind." A wan smile. "Ketamine is also a dog anesthetic. I'd seen you and your lively dog at our vet's last year—before I moved into the Playhouse. You had that distinctive gait, like my father after the war. But I didn't say anything. I had my own goal in mind for my stay here. And then, at Dash's birthday party, I saw you turn your back to the cameras and take the second plate of cake off the table. You'd hidden the ketamine solution in your glove, didn't you?"

I didn't move a muscle.

"All it took was to stretch open the base of the glove a bit and the clear liquid would pour down the inside of your wrist onto the cake. Only a little push over the edge was needed in light of his other medical problems. If his appetite had been a little better and he'd eaten more of that slice, he might've gotten his comeuppance on national television right away, instead of in his bed later that night." Another chuckle. "Not good to eat leftover snacks after eight p.m."

The chuckle morphed into a cough. I reached for the pitcher on her end table and began pouring fresh water into her glass. Shouldn't I add a "little helper" to her *aqua pura*? I'd brought it with me, just in case.

Tatyana's hoarse voice grew louder. "Either way, on behalf of all the women he screwed, I wanted to cover for you. You lost your leg in that accident because Dash drove drunk; you shouldn't have to lose your freedom. So, before I handed my phone off to the Keystone cops, I deleted my video of the party and said nothing. The curtain falls. Fade out."

Fade out? Still holding the pristine drink, I turned to face her. To my surprise, her expression radiated compassion. For me. For *me*. I sighed. No,

Tatyana, take your curtain call; you deserve my applause. I rested the glass on the end table and reached over to hug her. "Thank you."

"I should thank *you*."

Her twinkling eyes met mine, and, for a moment, I glimpsed a young, beautiful woman behind the wrinkled face. I gasped. "Why you, you're, you're—"

She put a gentle finger on my lips. "Shhh . . ."

"But I thought you were dead!" I exclaimed.

A warm smile. "Dash McDonald is dead. And I, my dear, for the short time I have left, am finally alive."

About the Author

Yolanda Reid (Chassiakos) is a physician and author of fiction and non-fiction. She is a member of the WGAW. As Linda Reid, she co-authored the award-winning Sammy Greene thrillers with Dr. Deborah Shlian, and, as YS Pascal, wrote the award-winning Zygan Emprise trilogy. Her essays have been published in the *L.A. Times, HuffPost,* and the *Washington Post.*

The Untitled Location Project

Anne Louise Bannon

WHEN I SAW THE yellow crime scene tape staked around the Demke place, I was not alarmed. After all, we were shooting a film about a (sort of) true crime there. I was, however, annoyed.

"What's with the crime scene tape?" I asked Todd Pedrano, the set decorator. "The contract says we're not supposed to be shooting an exterior."

"That's the real thing," Todd said grimly. Tall and burly, with black hair shaved short and gray temples, his face was pale. Todd would know about police tape. He's got barrels full of the prop stuff.

The flashing blue-and-red lights finally registered in my brain. Cut me some slack. All the way up in the shuttle from the crew parking I'd been focused on an intense series of text messages with a local city film permit office and the owner of the place where we expected to be shooting the next week.

The iconic yellow tape encircled the entire front yard and wrapped around wooden stakes that had been jammed into the ground at intervals. The house behind it had the Old Colonial thing going on, with a white exterior, columns, and a white railing along the roof.

Bo Demke, the owner, was going to have a conniption when he saw those stakes. He wasn't there—he'd gone out of town for the movie shoot—but he was a large, imposing man in his early sixties, with gray hair and a broken nose. He was notoriously picky about what happened to his property.

Tracey Stevens, who was not only my immediate boss as the location manager but one of my good friends, wandered up to Todd and me. She's shorter than average, with coffee-colored skin and black hair in short, tight braids.

"What the hell is going on?" I asked, adjusting my messenger bag.

The three of us stood near the edge of the driveway. Other crew members shuffled in place along the sides of two white semis parked in front of Demke's house and along the street. We were in a part of Pasadena shaded by huge old-growth trees. Police cars—real police cars—with lights flashing were parked across the street and at both ends of the line of trucks. Again, crew members shuffling is not unusual, but this time there was an awkward, frightened pall over everyone.

"Someone killed Tom Fortnam last night and left him in the house." Todd shuddered.

I felt the breath leaving my body in a whoosh. "What?"

"Mr. Big-Shot Asshat Director was murdered on the set," Todd said.

"And they're going to be looking at me," Tracey moaned. "They have to. I found him. Oh, god, it was awful. He was just lying there, and there was blood and the back of his head . . ." Tracey gagged.

My gut twisted at the image. "I'm sorry, Tracey." A location manager would be in first. Of course she found him.

She grabbed my arm. "Bridget, you and I were the last two in the house last night, right? You know how much I've been whining about him. But you'll tell them we were together the whole time, right? You'll tell the cops?"

"Well, we were," I said, then tried to gulp back my own upset. "This wasn't supposed to happen."

Todd snorted. "Sugar, the only surprise is that someone didn't kill him sooner."

Todd had a point. Fortnam was possibly the most unpopular man in Hollywood except for the studio executives and producers who kept giving him projects. They loved Fortnam because his films made lots and lots of money. Which meant the executives were willing to ignore complaints about him feeling up cute extras and engaging in smuggling, theft, and possibly drugs. Fortnam was emphatic that people were not to bring drugs onto the set. I wondered if some "special" crew member was dealing and Fortnam got a cut.

Another shuttle pulled up, this time dropping off two of our stars, Lynn Farber and DelRoy Turner, along with makeup and costume crew. Neither Farber, who was playing the female lead, nor DelRoy Turner, who was the third lead, were camera ready. In fact, Farber's full blond hair was still pulled back into a messy ponytail and her face was makeup free. DelRoy wore an Egyptian cotton starched white shirt over his tight jeans, instead of the T-shirt that was his costume. Even the dark chocolate of his skin looked gray.

The script supervisor wandered up.

"What's DelRoy doing here?" Todd asked her. "I thought they finished his scenes last week."

Our script maven, Karen Ibsen, rolled her eyes. "Another rewrite. I swear we've gone through every color they make."

That, I believed. Film and TV projects are frequently rewritten during shooting, and the easiest way to keep track of which page in the script is still current is to print out the changed pages on a different color of paper with each change. Lots of colors mean lots of rewrites and massive headaches for just about everyone involved. Karen, in particular, had the worst of it since her job was to make sure that everything on the set was consistent with the script and with each take. That way the gun the actor picked up in the scene was put back onto the table in the same place before they shot the next take.

"But why is everyone coming up from the parking lot?" Todd asked.

"The cops want to talk to everyone," Karen said, and nervously flicked her dark braid over her shoulder. "Even the caterers are coming up."

"Where's Bonnie, damn it?" Carl Krasno, the transportation chief, came up to us and hollered into his walkie-talkie. He rolled his eyes at the answer.

I thought I'd seen Bonnie Wing, one of the shuttle drivers who reported to Carl, running for her car as I'd gotten on the other shuttle earlier.

"They're not going to care about the caterers," Tracey moaned. "They'll be looking at me. Everyone knows Fortnam was out to get me. I'll never get another job."

The whole "you'll never work in this town again" routine almost never happens. Unless you worked for Thomas Fortnam, although the problem was not Fortnam throwing his weight around. You didn't get another job because you'd be known for hiding all sorts of fun things in the prop barrels, like Cuban cigars, absinthe, art from the houses where they'd been shooting, guns waiting to be sold. It was even rumored that a couple underage girls had been hidden in a cord crate, but that could have been an exaggeration.

Of course, that begs the question why I was working for the man. Tracey had taken the job because she really needed it and the money was better than usual. I followed Tracey, a first-rate location manager, because in working for Fortnam, I spotted an opportunity. I was beginning to wish I hadn't.

"Tracey, you've got a solid rep," I said, patting her arm. I shifted my bag again. "And everyone knows Fortnam always hires a few nice folks."

This was done to appease the studio execs so that they could point to the nice folks and pretend they didn't know anything about any other shenanigans. My gut twisted again.

"I've gotten other jobs," Todd said. His eyes flitted back toward the house and the police officers milling around out front and he grimaced. "It's the grips who have to worry."

He looked right at McGill and Neil Tripley, two huge guys with long, dark beards, who were hanging near the open back door of the semi closest to us. The two kept looking at the cops, then muttering between themselves. Mac and Neil were regulars on Fortnam's crew even though they didn't really seem to do much. Yeah, I know. When you're on a set, it seems like the grips mostly stand around, but they set up most, if not all, of the equipment, then take it down. It's actually pretty arduous work.

That morning, Mac and Neil were sweating as if they'd laid out a mile of dolly tracks, and I was fairly sure all they'd done was tape some cardboard pieces together and laid them on the house's living room floor two days before. This was done to protect the flooring.

"You think they're going to question all of us?" Todd asked, fidgeting with his wedding band. "That would be seriously scary."

I shrugged. "It depends on how fast they decide who killed Fortnam." I looked at Todd. "They can tell who's acting guilty and who isn't."

Todd went even more pale. "Nice to know."

Tracey sniffed and shuddered.

Okay. I don't know a lot about police work, but I do know more than most. My surrogate son is a cop in Pasadena. He'd just made the detective squad a few months before. Oh. And I'm not that kind of surrogate. I just helped raise him is all.

My name is Bridget Arnold. It was Bridget O'Shaughnessy, but I took advantage of my eight-month marriage to change it, back when I was a freshman in college. Nobody could pronounce O'Shaughnessy, let alone spell it.

So I got married at age eighteen. I know it was not one of my smarter moves, but it could have been worse. We got the marriage annulled with minimal pain. My dear friend Celia Vila came and got me from school, talked me into transferring to a college local to L.A. rather than just dropping out, and took me in to live at her great-aunt's house, where we've been ever since. Celia is only about three years older than me, and was pregnant with Gabriel at the time, thanks to a one-night stand with a total loser. Getting pregnant is not the best way to straighten your head out, but it worked for Celia. She was also lucky to be working as a nurse's aide at a women's shelter at the time, and the women who were her bosses saw that she was ready and helped her get her stuff together. Then Celia turned around and helped me get my stuff together, and we both raised Gabriel as platonic life partners. He's a really great kid, too.

Celia and I met as foster kids in the same home. Celia had been in the system most of her life. I was put into it at age eleven when the cops finally realized a nice-looking white guy could be a drug dealer. Seriously. My dad got away with dealing dope for years simply because everyone thinks drug dealers are scary Mexican or Black guys, not white boys from the 'burbs. My mom was long gone. Not dead, or at least, I don't think she is. But thanks to my dad and the drugs he gave her, she's been in jail, in rehab, or on the streets for as long as I can remember. Dad's in prison. I think.

Anyway, Celia aged out before I did, did nurse's aide training, then inherited her great-aunt's house. Celia's mom died when Celia was a baby, thanks to a drug habit. We're not sure who her father is. Celia bounced back and forth between foster homes and her great-aunt, who was probably manic-depressive. But they didn't really think of that when Celia was a kid, which made things really hard. But Celia survived. We both did.

I saw two guys in plainclothes and a woman come out of Bo Demke's house. One of the guys was our Gabriel Vila. I couldn't help smiling. He's a little over average height, with full black hair and deep brown eyes that twinkle when he's happy. He got a full four-year degree before going to the police academy and made detective surprisingly fast. I mean, the kid is brilliant, and I am not biased. Okay, maybe a little biased.

Todd touched my arm, then pulled me aside and away from Tracey.

"Bridget, what's the odds they're going to think I'm acting guilty?" he asked, nodding at the detectives, who were talking to several uniforms and pointing out different places in the yard.

Demke was going to have two conniptions about all the people on his lawn, which was bright green, water restrictions be damned. He was not known for forgiving film companies when they messed up his place, never mind how much he liked their money. And Demke was not someone you wanted to piss off. I had been really surprised he'd agreed to let Fortnam and company on the property. Glad at the time that he had, but still surprised. I was not so glad anymore.

"Are you guilty?" I asked Todd, swallowing. Why would our production designer have a motive?

He gasped. "No. Well, not of killing Fortnam. I went home with everyone else last night. I think Fortnam was still there. I heard him talking on the phone. Another rewrite."

"You think one of the writers or Karen did it?" I shuddered. My bag's strap dug into my shoulder, and I shifted it.

"No. Bridget, I gotta tell you so you'll believe me and tell the cops." Todd looked like he was going to cry. "I signed on for this film because I wanted to get Fortnam. The guy totally messed me up. I stopped working for him and couldn't get any jobs for three years. Jeff Washington finally gave me a chance and here I am. But I almost had to go back to Texas and work for my dad on the oil rigs. If those toughs had found out what I do, they'd have killed me."

"So, what does this mean besides a reason to kill Fortnam?" I asked.

"It's why I signed on." Todd looked around. "You know what a crook Fortnam is. I figured I could find the evidence, then turn it in. I'm finally close enough to retirement that I won't be in too much trouble if I can't get any more work now. But, damn, Bridget, I wasn't going to kill him."

"Know that feeling." I winced and sighed.

"You know who could have, though." Todd glanced over at Mac and Neil.

"They're grips," I said.

"They've got the concession on drugs on the set," Todd said. "I found a whole bag full of pills, syringes, you name it, in one of their bags."

"Fortnam didn't want anybody bringing drugs in."

"Yeah. He didn't want any competition. I heard Mac complaining the other day that Fortnam wanted an even bigger cut of their business." Todd looked back at another of the trucks. "Heaven only knows what those cops are going to find in those prop barrels."

"It won't be anything from the house."

"And how sure are you of that?"

"Because that's why Tracey and I are the last people out every night. We take pictures of all the rooms just to be sure someone hasn't gotten light-fingered."

"But if you two were the last people out of the house, how is it that Fortnam was still there?"

I frowned. "He came back?" I closed my eyes. "He could have avoided us, though. When we were in one room, he went to another, maybe. Now that I think about it, I thought I saw his car parked across the street when we got on the shuttle."

"That's very interesting," said a female voice behind me.

I turned. The woman detective stood next to Todd and me, her arms folded across her chest. She looked to be in her mid-forties, wore a nice gray suit and had dark brown hair, pulled back and alert brown eyes.

"Sergeant Lorena Salcido," she said, flipping out her ID case. She looked at me. "You're Ms. Arnold, right?"

"Yes, ma'am."

"Come with me, please." It was not a request.

Salcido pulled me several feet down the sidewalk to the edge of the yard.

"Can you repeat what you just said about Fortnam still being in the house?"

"I don't know that he was," I said, then repeated what I'd told Todd. "But we did check the house, and it certainly looked empty."

Salcido glanced over at Gabriel, and I sighed. She, apparently, knew how I was related to him.

"Okay. What's your job here?" she asked.

"I'm the location scout and assistant location manager. I found the place and everywhere else we're shooting."

Salcido nodded. "So, what's your beef with the deceased?"

"He was a complete jerk and made my life insanely difficult. One of the reasons Tracey wanted me to help was that Fortnam kept changing things and I'd have to scout out a new location every few days."

"When did you get this one set up?"

"Actually, pretty early on. I was holding my breath most of the other day when they were moving in. But we finally started shooting."

"Where's the owner?"

"Mr. Demke went out of town, which was odd. Tracey told me that she'd heard he could be a real pain in the backside about sticking around during shoots."

"Yeah. Bo Demke, right?" Salcido looked even more grim. Grimmer.

I couldn't help eyeing her. "You know him?"

"Possibly. What do you know about him?"

"Not much, personally. I've been told that he's not a very nice person."

Salcido glanced back at Gabriel. "No, he's not."

She walked away. I let my breath out. Salcido talked to Todd. Tracey wandered up.

"They want to see our pictures," she told me, fidgeting with her walkie-talkie.

"Why didn't the sergeant say so?"

She shrugged. "Did you hear what happened to our driver, Bonnie?"

"No. What?"

"The cops got her before she could leave the crew lot. Turned out she had a bunch of pills on her. She said Fortnam had hidden them in her shuttle sometime yesterday. She found them this morning and was terrified that the cops would blame her. You think she could have done it?"

"How?" I asked. "She took us down to the crew lot and was outside the whole time. If she'd killed Fortnam, we would have seen him."

"Oh. Right."

"Ladies," said one of the uniforms. "Can you join us in the house?"

It, too, was not a request. We met another uniform in the doorway. She explained that we were supposed to look around the house to see if anything was missing.

"Wonder why they're asking about that," Tracey muttered as we looked around the living room.

All was as we had left it. Or it looked like it was. It was an elegant room, with light blue satin upholstery on the couch. A marble fireplace had a tall pewter statuette shaped sort of like a long, thin flame on the mantle. The Baroque coffee table and several of the vases and other statuettes had been moved to another room. It was kind of a weird sort of decor, with eighteenth-century-style furniture and very modern art. Todd had taken down several of the paintings and replaced them with stuff closer to the furniture's style.

Cardboard sheets covered the floors well into the front hall, and a large camera rig had been pushed next to the open archway into the hallway. Light standards were scattered about the room. None of it had been moved.

We'd only been shooting in the living room, and the rest of the house hadn't been touched, except for the study upstairs, where we'd piled all the stuff we'd taken out of the living room. There was a lock on the door, which is why we left the stuff there. After checking the other rooms, we landed in the study. Cardboard covered the floor with a chunk missing.

"That's where he was," Tracey whispered to me with a small sob.

Gabriel appeared in the doorway. "Well?"

"Everything seems to be here," I said. "We should probably check the photos we took." I looked at Gabriel. "Is there anything we should be looking for?"

He sighed. "Can't say."

I reached for my messenger bag. "I've got my laptop. We can look at the pics from last night on here. It'll be easier."

I booted up and put the laptop on the desk. I opened the photo in the viewer. Tracey spotted it first. She pointed at the screen, then looked at the pile of art objects next to the wall.

"There. That brushed silver flame thingy. It's gone."

"It's pewter," I said, then looked at the photo. That's when I got it. I scrolled through the photos, then opened another one in a second window.

"Tracey, you locked this door when we left last night, right?"

"Of course," she said.

"Was it locked this morning?" I asked.

"Uh, yeah."

I pointed to the screen. "Look at this."

"What, Mamacita?" Gabriel calls me that because he calls Celia Mamí.

"Here's the photo I took of the living room when I was scouting the house." I got the two windows with the pics side by side on my laptop screen. "Look what's on the fireplace mantle."

"That flame thingy," said Tracey. "So?"

"It was in here last night, but now it's back on the mantle." I suddenly grinned at Gabriel. "Where it belongs."

"I don't get it," said Tracey.

"Who else would put it there? And who else would be able to relock the door to this room?" I watched as Gabriel nodded. "We've got him."

He hissed, "Mamacita, you said you weren't going to do that."

"I never said that." I put my hand on his shoulder. "You've got your first big collar, kid."

"Not yet. But you're right. It's enough to look more closely at him."

"At who?" Tracey asked.

I signaled her to stay quiet. "Later."

She and I headed downstairs, and Gabriel said something into a walkie-talkie that he had. Bo Demke himself paced around the front yard, having the conniption I'd expected.

"You'd better not have touched anything!" he screamed at a couple of the uniforms. "This is my house. You don't have a warrant. You can't go in there! And what are you doing on my grass? Get off! Now!"

It seemed almost too convenient that Demke had arrived home from San Francisco just then. The uniforms were keeping him contained, so I simply kept my distance. It would be safer for me that way.

It took a couple more hours before we were dismissed, then Tracey and I had to supervise getting the set struck and the equipment moved out because production had been officially shut down. The sun was setting as Tracey and I finally got to the crew parking. Tracey insisted on us going to a bar.

"That detective, he's your kid, right?" she asked as we settled in with some wine.

"Yeah. So?"

"What's with the collar thing?"

I closed my eyes and sighed. "Look, I don't want you to think that I was trying to get Fortnam. And I didn't want him to die."

"But you were so excited about that dumb statue."

"Think about it, Tracey. The office had been unlocked, then locked back up after Fortnam was killed. Only you had the key and one other person. The house's owner."

"Well, duh."

"And while it is possible somebody on the crew would have remembered where that statue belongs, why would they put it there when we'd moved it to the office? Why even move it in the first place?" I watched as Tracey frowned, then shook her head. "The statue was probably the murder weapon. That's why it got moved. Demke probably washed it off, then had to get out of there quickly, so he did the most natural thing in the world. He put it back where it belonged."

"Demke?" Tracey blinked. "He was in San Francisco."

"I'll bet, but you can get to San Francisco and back here within twelve hours if you drive. He probably didn't fly back because you need ID to get on a plane, which means there's a record."

"But why would Demke kill Thomas Fortnam?"

"I don't know." I scrunched my face up. "There was probably some skanky deal going on. Maybe something with drugs. It's why I was so surprised when we signed Demke's house for the shoot. With Fortnam's lousy rep for trashing places, and Demke's rep for fussing about his place, I didn't think it would fly. But I had to give it a shot."

"Why?"

I looked away and almost groaned. "I wanted Demke's ass in a sling. He and Fortnam were made for each other, and I figured something illegal would happen." I suddenly blinked my eyes. "I didn't think it would be murder, but . . . At the very least, I'd have a reason to search Demke's house and maybe find something that would get him sent away for a very long time."

Tracey looked at me funny. "Why would you care?"

"Demke is the guy who turned my father into a drug dealer. I mean, Dad went along with it. But it was Demke who recruited him." I swallowed and blinked again. "I can't get revenge on my father. But maybe taking down the guy who started it would help me feel better. Plus, if I set it up so my kid would get the credit for it, so much the better. Gabe could use a really good collar right now."

Tracey shuddered and got a long drink of wine as my mobile phone rang. It was Gabriel.

"We've got Demke. Turns out a bell hop saw him leave his hotel yesterday around three p.m. and get into a car that was later reported stolen. And Fortnam's mobile was found unlocked in one of the trash cans at the house, with several phone calls to Demke. According to those two grips,

Demke was supplying Fortnam with his drugs, and Fortnam was cutting Demke out of the deal." Gabriel chuckled. "Fortnam also got a text from Demke saying that Demke would be there around ten that night."

"Who leaves their phone unlocked?"

"Fortnam, apparently." Gabriel laughed full out. "And I've got the credit for it. Thanks, Mamacita."

"You're welcome, sweetie. Your mamí will be so proud."

And Celia was very proud, as she should have been. Me? I was proud of Gabriel for picking up what I had, but I still felt like crap about how everything had fallen out. I hadn't wanted anyone to die, for crying out loud. Fortnam's family decided to keep his memorial service very private. I managed to find out where and when it was and showed up. It was really depressing how few people were there.

Demke's house had become a crime scene, and Gabriel gave the district attorneys probable cause for a full search. Gabriel and his colleagues found plenty of evidence they wouldn't have otherwise. Which meant that even Demke's high-priced lawyers couldn't get him off on the murder or the drug charges. Demke ended up pleading out to second-degree murder and some trafficking charges. Given his age, he will probably be in prison for the rest of his life. That should have made me feel a lot better than it did. Apparently, revenge isn't as sweet as it's supposed to be.

We did get some days down on the film, but the execs had us back to shooting someplace else with a new director just after Fortnam's memorial service. The movie came out last week and was roundly panned. It did have a good opening weekend, thanks to Fortnam's murder. Demke had to sell his house, and I just signed with the new owners to shoot there again. The good news is that the crime scene tape was a set decoration.

About the Author

Author Anne Louise Bannon's husband says that his wife kills people for a living. Bannon does mostly write mysteries, including the Old Los Angeles series. Her short stories have appeared in *Jacked* and *Mystery Most Theatrical*. Visit her website at www.AnneLouiseBann.com or follow her on Facebook www.facebook.com/RobinGoodfellowEnt and Twitter: https://twitter.com/albannon.

The Writers Room

L.H. Dillman

THE MOST IMPORTANT INGREDIENT in the making of a successful TV show isn't the cast or the director or the cameramen; it's the writer. Make that writer*s*, plural, because it takes a team, as my boss, the legendary Billy Bannon, likes to say. Openings in a TV writers room are rare, and winning a spot is a real coup. Smarts aren't enough. You need to be a natural storyteller, a good collaborator, and a clever wordsmith with an ear for dialogue. Once you're in the writers room, you need thick skin and a strong stomach to survive—plus eyes in the back of your head to see the bastard with a knife in his fist.

I served time as a lowly writer's assistant and a harried script coordinator before Billy Bannon promoted me to staff writer on his hit HBO drama, *Mayberry Mayhem*. In the unlikely event you haven't watched our show, *Mayberry Mayhem* is homespun horror for the eighteen-to-twenty-five crowd. *Stranger Things* meets *Saw*. Yes, I have a dark side. When I first came to L.A., starry-eyed and naive, I held out for a job penning high-quality *disturbia*, a la *Ozark* or *Breaking Bad*, but after two years of part-time waitressing and a diet of Rice Crispies, I was ready to sign on as gopher for *The Walking Dead*. Fortunately, *Mayberry* happened to be going through its fourth season shake-up, and I landed an entry-level spot.

It turns out that, despite the show's pedestrian themes and Gen Z appeal, its writers are mainly Ivy League white dudes with thinning hair. I'm the only one who went to a state school, the only woman, and the only one under forty. Color me lucky.

One of the great things about having a seat in the writers room is that my whacky ideas are valued. Another major plus is the money: I make more than most thirty-year-olds outside of Silicon Valley. Last, but not least, they gave me a parking spot next to the building. Now that the role is mine, I, Jennifer Dixon, have no intention of letting some *douche* take it from me—which is why I'm constantly looking over my shoulder whenever Alejandro Smith, the new personal assistant, is in the writers room.

Like he is right now.

"Yo, anyone up for a sandwich or salad?" asks Alejandro. He's just interrupted six writers wrestling with the last act of a pivotal episode, but he seems not to notice. "Speak now or forever hold your hunger," he adds, deadpan, as if he's a very clever young man rather than Billy Bannon's stepson who's just earned a degree in "semiotics" from Brown University—otherwise known as a BS in BS—but can't craft a grammatically correct sentence.

We go around the table placing our orders, starting with the most senior person. Today being Wednesday, Billy is out (they say he flies to Vegas each Tuesday night, loses at the tables, and spends the entire next day in a gamblers' anonymous program), so the top dog is Zach Franklin, our co-executive producer. As usual, Alejandro taps our requests into his mobile phone, which, as usual, takes way longer than it should.

"Get that guy a pencil and paper already," says Peter Ogilvie, our co-producer. I think Peter has come to the same conclusion I have: Alejandro is prolonging his presence in the writers room so he can insert himself into the conversation. Otherwise, as a personal assistant, his role is basically to run errands—to be seen and not heard, like children back in the Victorian era, or today on a fundamentalist Mormon farm. (Which gives me an idea for a story line for *Mayhem*: offspring of cult members finally break free only to be captured by their lunatic parents who cut out their tongues. It's about the right level of gross for our target audience.)

When at last Alejandro gets to me, I ask for a grilled chicken salad, hold the dressing.

"Wise choice," he says.

Like I'm smart to skip the fattening ingredients! This guy is definitely trying to get under my skin. Two weeks ago, he "accidentally" spilled coffee on a spec script I'd left on my desk. Last Friday, he "forgot" to send my credit for episode five to the Writers Guild.

How to respond? I don't want my colleagues to think I'm overly sensitive, but ignoring Alejandro will make me look weak. I come up with this:

"Sounds like you found your calling as a menu consultant, A-ho."

Eyebrows shoot up as if I've insulted the crown prince.

"Did you just call him an asshole?" asks Zach.

"A-ho, short for Al-e-han-dro," I clarify, pronouncing each syllable. "It's a nickname, not an epithet." Do I need to remind them that he was "Alexander" until he applied to college, that his father is English, and that his only Latin connection is his mother, Billy's third wife, Marguerite, who's one-eighth Puerto Rican and an heiress to a sugar cane fortune? No, I don't. The guys are grinning and chuckling. Emboldened, I look at the punk and say, "I'll bet you get called A-ho a lot."

This earns "Oooohs" and "Whooooos" from the boys, advancing my admittance to their wiseass club. But the kid is red in the face.

"Yeah," he says. "I've been called that, but never more than once from the same person 'cause they know—"

"Okay, okay," says Peter. "Go place those orders so we can eat. Thanks, Alejandro."

A-ho takes off. We writers return to our whiteboards, trying to nail the last few beats of what we hope will be an awesome climax. But today is not our day. It's a relief, forty minutes later, when we get word that lunch is waiting. As we head to the door, Zach catches my eye. "Can I talk to you for a minute?"

"Absolutely." A one-on-one with the second-in-command is usually a good thing. Zach knows the business inside and out, he's a brilliant writer, and he's always been fair with me.

When the room is clear, Zach says, "Listen, take it easy on Alejandro; he's just a kid."

"It was a joke. What, we can't have fun anymore?"

"Good-natured fun is fine, but we can't be mean. This is supposed to be a safe space."

"Fine, but shouldn't it be a two-way street? He's shot some snark in my direction, if you haven't noticed. And why do we let him hang around the writers room so much? We've never had an assistant push the boundaries the way he does."

"Yeah, I know, but we need to be tolerant," Zach says apologetically.

"Because he's Billy's stepson?" I'm thinking of the Hollywood maxim: It's not how talented you are, it's how connected you are.

"Billy told me Alejandro's going through a tough time. The twenties aren't easy. You should recall that, Jen, since it wasn't so long ago you were there yourself."

"Okay, but it's hard to work up sympathy for a twenty-three-year-old white Ivy-Leaguer who drives a Tesla and lives in a house Mommy bought."

"I get it," Zach says, shaking his head. "I went to school with guys like him. Irritates the hell outta me, too. But let's be patient. He won't be around forever; he's his own worst enemy. In the meantime, Billy asked me to show him 'generosity of spirit,' so I am, and I'd appreciate your cooperation."

I follow Zach out, chin dragging like a scolded puppy.

In the next room, sandwiches and salads are arrayed on a counter, each package bearing a name. Mine is misspelled: *Genifur*. I glance at Alejandro over by the door. I think I see a smirk and a middle finger, but both disappear too quickly to be sure. Should I be worried that he spat in my salad? Or is that paranoid? I grab my food and go back to the writers room.

The rule is we can't talk shop at lunch. Instead, on Wednesdays, we try our hands at humor. Andy describes his travails in house training his new St.-Bernard-a-Doodle, no scatological detail left out. Josh updates us on the drama unfolding in the home next to his where, by the sounds of it, there's going to be a murder-suicide any night now. (There's a reason Josh isn't writing for a sitcom.) Peter entertains us with impressions of effete New Englanders at his Harvard class reunion, amateur comedy that, if you ask me, is an excuse to drop the H-bomb (for the zillionth time). Now it's my turn. Suddenly I'm feeling a little light-headed and nauseous, bad enough to make me put down my salad fork.

Zach turns to me. "What've you got for us, Jen?"

What I've got is a looming gastrointestinal calamity. I raise my index finger and dash to the ladies' room, where I leave a double offering at the great white porcelain altar. It was the salad, for sure, but I can't go making accusations like a crazy person. I clean up and return to the writers room, playing it chill.

"You okay?" Peter asks.

I nod. "Never better."

"Good," Zach says. "'Cause you're up."

I did have an anecdote, but it's flown out of my head. *Shit.* The QB has thrown the ball, and my brain has fumbled. A tortuous four seconds tick by. Finally, an idea pops up:

"Why are there so many unsolved cold case murders in Arkansas?"

"I dunno, why?" ask Zach, Peter, Josh, Wayne, and Andy in unison.

"Because there are no dental records, and all the DNA matches."

Laughter breaks out. I smile at the boys, grateful to have remembered the joke I heard from my brother, the one who is stationed in Arkansas and is therefore permitted to poke fun at the place.

Then I hear, "Not cool, not funny at all." Alejandro is standing at the door with his arms folded across his chest, looking highly offended. "I'm from Little Rock originally, and we don't appreciate the way you coastal elites stereotype us."

The mirth evaporates. Everyone is suddenly mortified.

"Sorry, man," Zach says. "She meant no harm. Right, Jen?"

"Of course not." I shrink into my seat.

"No hard feelings, right, Alejandro?" says Peter.

"Well . . ." The kid narrows his eyes at me.

"I'm really sorry," I tell him.

"Hah, just messin' with ya!" he says. "I'm from Newport Beach!"

Uproarious laughter from all but Zach.

"Good one," says Peter.

"You got her," says Josh.

"Burn," says Andy.

"Hilarious," I say, seething. That little shit. He's definitely gunning for my spot. The only questions are: how low will he go to get it, and how can I stop him?

The afternoon is a bust. Ideas get floated and make an orbit or two, but nothing lands. I'm half tempted to share a draft of an episode I intend to pitch for next season, once I work out the kinks.

"That's a wrap, folks," Zach announces at seven. "Tomorrow's going to be intense. Billy's going to be here, and he'll want this episode broken by the end of the day."

The writers begin to pack up. I'm about to close my laptop when my cell phone buzzes. It's my therapist wanting to reschedule our next appointment, so I step into the hall to discuss calendar issues while my colleagues stream out. By the time my session's rebooked, they've all exited the building. I go back in for my computer and come face-to-chest with A-ho. He's a big guy. Six feet, at least, and close to two bucks. I shift to the left to get around him. He shifts to block my way.

"What the hell?!" I blurt.

"You think you're *all that*, bitch, but you're nothing—*nothing*."

I scoff, but in truth I'm a little shaken.

"Do not speak to me from here on," he hisses. "Do not look at me. And you best get out my way when you see me comin'."

"Or else what?" I wish Zach were here to witness this. I wish I knew how to activate the record feature of the phone in my pocket. I wish I were five inches taller and fifty pounds heavier.

"Or else you're done. I can get you tossed, like *that*." A-ho snaps his fingers.

"You're delusional."

"Try me." He smirks, turns, and walks out.

The only sound I hear is the pounding of my heart. *Shake it off*. A talentless hack in diapers can't get a guild-member staff writer fired even if he *is* the showrunner's stepson. I mean, there's got to be some integrity in show business, right?

At nine the next morning, we're all seated at the table in the writers room: Billy, Zach, Peter, Josh, Andy, Wayne, and me. Other than the collection of Starbucks lattes and cappuccinos in the center of the table, there's no sign of Alejandro. Maybe he's decided to lie low. I took Zach aside a few minutes ago to tell him what happened last night. He agreed that Alejandro was way out of line and said he'd handle it. But can he, given Alejandro's protected status? I have my doubts.

"Ah, it's great to be here," Billy says, sweeping his gaze around the table like a lord surveying his serfs. He looks the part, too: a mountainous belly, a neatly trimmed gray beard, and a nose made purple by too much booze. His toe is so swollen with gout that he needs a cane to walk and has to prop his foot up whenever he sits. The massive gold Rolex I'm used to seeing on his wrist is gone. *Odd.* I wonder if he's had to hock it; I wonder if the rumors about gambling debts are true.

"I'm so fortunate," he continues, "to be able to spend my days with such brilliant guys, creating amazing stories that change people's lives." He talks as if we're scientists on the cusp of curing cancer, when, really, we're a bunch of awkward intellectuals who get paid a shit ton of money to dream up entertainment that on its best day qualifies as lowbrow. Billy knows lowbrow: before he took HBO's bait, he was the King of Grindhouse.

"Speaking of which," he says, "let's get started. By the end of the day, I'm going to assign one of you the first draft of the script."

I've worked as hard as anyone on this episode, probably harder, so I figure I have a shot.

The morning moves in fits and starts. We can't decide whether the biology teacher / alien seductress gets the high school football star / telepathic savant into bed. And we can't agree on how the stay-at-home mom / undercover CIA agent kills the pharmacist / zombie—whether it's with stake through the heart (cliché) or with a chain saw (derivative) or by means of a fentanyl capsule disguised as Xanax (common). Paula, the intern, takes our lunch orders, explaining that Alejandro is tied up. Sounds mildly suspicious, but I'm focusing on the story. Unfortunately, the afternoon is as frustrating as the morning.

"What the hell's wrong today?" Billy muses at five. "It shouldn't be this hard—"

"Excuse me?" It's Alejandro. "Sorry to interrupt," he says, stepping into the room. "I have an idea, Billy, and I've written kind of a treatment, and it might be total shit, but I thought, well, what the hell?"

Billy cocks his head. "An idea for this episode?"

"Yeah," Alejandro says, waving a stack of pages. "I mean, I'm a total amateur, but it sounds like a fresh voice might be helpful, you know, since the pros are sort of struggling."

All eyes turn to our showrunner.

"Well, well, well," Billy says. "C'mon in, show us what you've got."

Zach and I exchange *Can-you-believe-it?* looks. There's a long and heretofore unbroken tradition in this writers room—in every writers room, from what I've heard—that personal assistants do not speak, much less pitch.

Alejandro rounds the table passing out two-page treatments. I can't help thinking Billy is off his rocker, or he's somehow beholden to this punk. I'm the last one to be handed the document. Reading the first line, I get a weird feeling. The second line rings a bell. By the middle of the third line, I know why: I wrote it.

A-ho stole my story!

He's changed the names, a few adjectives, and a verb or two, but there's no question this is the draft I had on my computer. Everyone's got his nose in the print. I don't need to read the whole thing because I know how it ends. I open my MacBook. My draft has vanished. There's no sign that A-ho emailed it to himself. He must have copied it onto a flash drive, then deleted the file from my laptop. I'm about to whisper to Zach that this is my script when Billy smacks his palm on the tabletop.

"Damn, kid, this is pretty good!"

"Hold on!" I spring to my feet, but it dawns on me that I'm going to accuse the boss's stepson of theft in public, and A-ho must have anticipated my reaction, and maybe this is a trap. "Can I talk to you, Billy? It can't wait. Sorry, everyone."

"What's this about?"

"I'd rather explain in private. Please. Two minutes."

Billy relents. We walk down the hall, him swaying elephant-like, his heavy cane thumping on the floorboards. Once in his office with the door closed, I tell him, rapid fire, that Alejandro didn't write the "treatment," that it's essentially a draft I've been working on for weeks, that it's a draft I left open on my laptop last night while he was alone in the room. "Alejandro must've been snooping, found it, changed a few details—"

"You sure?" Billy props his cane against the wall alongside several others. "There're only so many plots in the world, Jen. Maybe it's a coincidence—"

Alejandro barges in. "It's not true, Billy. She's got something against me. Been trying to sabotage me since day one."

"You're out of your mind," I tell him.

"Ask Zach," Alejandro says. "She called me 'asshole' in front of everyone yesterday. I can handle profanity, but there was, like, a racial tint to it—"

"Bullshit!" I say.

Billy turns to me. "*Did* you call him 'asshole'?"

"I called him *A-ho*. It was a play on words, or a play on sounds; nothing racial. The point is, he stole a document from my computer—"

"It's the company's computer," Billy says.

"He's trying to pass off my work as his, and that's totally not okay."

"Who're you gonna believe?" Alejandro says. "She's fuckin' nuts, Billy. Disturbed. Can't get through work without a therapy session. Takes calls from her shrink in the writers room."

"That happened once, at the end of the day," I protest. "Anyway, that's not the point—"

"I don't wanna hear this," our showrunner says. "This is not how we operate. A writers room is supposed to be collaborative, okay? A place where we can trust each other."

The great Billy Bannon, creative champion and veteran screenwriter, is brushing off the theft of intellectual property. Unreal.

"There's right and there's wrong," I say. "He shouldn't get a pass just because he's related to you."

"There's more to it than that," Alejandro says.

"Enough! Zip it, both of you." Billy rubs his temples like he's battling a migraine. "Okay, here's what we're gonna do. We're gonna deal with who-wrote-what some other time. Today, we're gonna do what's best for the show, and that's finish the episode. The boys upstairs are champing at the bit for a completed season, and we gotta deliver so we can all keep earning the big bucks. Which means, you, Jennifer, are not going to say one word. If the treatment works, and we use it, we'll figure out who gets the credit then. We clear? Now let's get back to business."

I glare at A-ho. "You won't get away with it."

He glares back. "Is that a threat?"

"Jennifer," Billy says, choosing a cane from his collection, "you need to calm down."

Somehow, I doubt that a man who stands his ground would be told to "calm down." We leave the office—me, followed by A-ho and Billy. I can practically feel the blade between my shoulders.

Back in the writers room, A-ho joins us at the table. I'm so mad, I can't concentrate. We finish breaking the episode at nine. Sometimes, when our team reaches this milestone, Josh, Peter, Zach, and I grab a late dinner at Bestia or Providence or Spago—where we can always show up without a reservation because, hey, we write for Billy Bannon on *Mayberry Mayhem*—but not tonight. They're too shredded, and I'm too bummed. I've lost the assignment: Billy has given the first draft to Andy.

"Better luck next time," Zach says, zipping his canvas briefcase. We're the last ones in the room.

"See you tomorrow," I say glumly.

"Don't let it get to you. Where's the feisty Jen I've come to know and love?"

I raise my eyes to his. "I haven't gone anywhere, Zach. That punk stole my idea. The story line about the chambermaid bludgeoning the prince with a rolling pin? I wrote the treatment. He downloaded it from my laptop."

Zach smacks his forehead. "I thought I recognized your voice in that piece—the gore, the female revenge, the devious humor. Way too good to be Alejandro's."

"Thanks." I wish the praise was coming in a different context.

"The kid's bad news."

"I tried to tell you."

"Yes, you did," Zach says, heaving a sigh. "I take it you told Billy it was yours, and he sided with Alejandro—I mean, with A-ho?"

"Pretty much."

Zach shakes his head in disgust. "That's just wrong. I'll talk to him."

"It won't do any good unless I can prove I wrote the thing. A-ho wiped it off my hard drive."

Zach gives me the contact information for his computer wizard. I thank him but point out that even if the wizard finds the document, there could still be a he-said-she-said fight over who wrote it.

"I'm screwed," I say.

"Hang in there," Zach says with an avuncular squeeze of my shoulder. "I won't let the bastards win."

When Zach's gone, I head down to the assistants' room. One of the cubicles features a bulletin board covered with a half dozen artsy black-and-white photos and a color photo of what look like fraternity bros guzzling Coronas in Cabo. Sparkling smiles, bulging biceps, tanned torsos. Alejandro Smith will be the first staff writer on *Mayberry Mayhem* to boast a six pack. Unless I stop him.

In the bottom drawer of his desk, I discover a handful of flash drives. I slip them into my pocket, turn off the lights, and leave. At home, I make a cup of lavender tea and load the first flash drive onto my laptop. It's got about thirty essays and term papers from Alejandro's college days. The second one has two draft screenplays. Really bad ones, by the way. I'm too tired to finish the project tonight.

The next morning, I sleep through my alarm. There's barely enough time to shower and dress, much less comb through digital documents. I drive to work like a fiend.

"Sorry I'm late—" There are a lot of long faces and downcast eyes in the writers room. Did the guild announce a strike? Did the show get canceled?

Josh says, "Alejandro is dead."

"What?"

"We heard five minutes ago," Zach says.

"Killed late last night or early this morning outside his house in Silver Lake," says Peter. "Apparently, he'd just pulled into his driveway . . ."

"Blunt force trauma to the head," Josh says. "That's all we know."

"Oh my god," I say. "Was it a robbery?"

Peter shrugs. "Twenty-three-year-olds usually don't carry much cash, so I kind of doubt it. Unless the robber killed him in frustration."

"Maybe he was in too deep with his dealer," Josh says.

"Or he owed too much to his bookie," Andy says.

Zach shoots them a frown. "Do you have any basis for that?"

I realize I know very little about Alejandro. Just that his mom had money and lavished him with gifts, that he aimed to make it big in Hollywood and wasn't above cheating to get there, and that what he lacked in talent he made up for in connections. Nothing that would get him killed—except maybe in a screenplay.

"If anyone owes too much to his bookie, it's Billy," Peter says. "I heard he's in for three million."

"I heard four," says Josh.

"Guys, really?" says Zach. Always the adult in the room.

There's a long stretch of silence, then Peter says, "It'll be interesting . . ." He's wondering what we're all wondering: will the show go on? The answer comes later that afternoon.

"We're on hiatus for at least a week," Billy Bannon announces to ten stunned writers and support staff gathered in the writers room. He seems to be trying hard to hold it together. "You'll be paid, but I—I've got to take care of Marguerite. Sorry, folks."

There's a chorus of *No apology necessary, Of course, Don't worry*, and so on. Peter asks if we'll be returning in time to compete the season on schedule. When Billy doesn't answer, Zach steps forward and says, "We'll do what's best for the show."

Billy just nods, looking lost. I notice now that there's a stranger standing in the corner. He's about forty, Black, and wearing a gray suit, which makes him the most formally dressed person in the building. I've watched enough movies to spot a plainclothes detective.

"Okay, everybody, that's all," Zach says. "We'll be in touch."

Billy hobbles off, flanked by his assistant and the detective. As the rest of us gather our things, the room fills with hushed comments and questions: *Someone went to town on him. Did you hear his brains were splattered all over? Who does that? Was it random? Did he have enemies? He's too young to have enemies. He was just a kid.* I keep my head down, contribute nothing to the conversation. Everyone knows Alejandro and I hated each other's guts. I'm sad he was killed, and I feel badly for his family, but to act super grief-stricken would be fake.

There's something else on my mind, something most of my colleagues don't know: the blunt force trauma that killed Alejandro bears a striking resemblance to the mode of murder I dreamed up for the treatment he stole. This is a coincidence, of course—people get clobbered in the head every day, right?—but someone might think otherwise. Someone like the police.

Should I be worried? Or have I been watching too much TV?

I take a last look at the room—the long table piled with neat stacks of notepads and cards; the glass cooler filled with bottles of designer water; the whiteboards covered with handwriting, dotted lines, and arrows outlining a great story. This is where the magic happens. Why do I have the feeling I won't be coming back?

First thing in the morning, after coffee, I go for a run to try to shake off the weirdness of yesterday. It's a typical spring day in L.A.: clear, sunny, and warm. The endorphins are surging, and I'm feeling better. Until I get home. The plainclothes policeman is waiting at my front door. The sweat on my skin turns to ice water.

"Jennifer Dixon? I'm Detective Bob Summers, LAPD."

I nod. "I've been expecting you."

And I have. Last evening, I phoned my brother's girlfriend's father, who's a criminal lawyer, but couldn't reach him. I paced for hours. I nibbled my way through two bags of Red-Hot Cheetos and washed the burn down with four White Claw Hard Seltzers. It wasn't until two-thirty a.m. that I figured out the solution.

The flash drives.

I found my draft script on one of them, but the real prize was on another. It contained photos rather than documents, and the images blew me away.

Billy Bannon, you naughty boy.

"Come in," I say to Detective Summers. "I'm going to pour myself some water, and then we can sit down and talk." I unlock the door and hold it open.

"Sounds like you've got something to tell me."

"I do."

Twenty minutes later, we're sitting across from each other on the matching Italian couches I bought when I thought my job was secure. Summers has a notepad on his knee and a scowl on his face. I've got a towel over my shoulders and a cyclone in my stomach. The conversation has not gone well. I've acknowledged that I have no alibi for Thursday night. I've also admitted what Summers heard from others: that Alejandro was after my job, that I gave him a stupid nickname and got called on it, that he came out on top in the Arkansas debacle, and that he stole my script.

"Sounds like you're better off without him," Detective Summers says.

"We're all better off without him, professionally speaking. He was presumptuous, disruptive, and not a very good writer. I wasn't the only one who wanted him gone."

"Who else?"

"Billy didn't like him. I realize that now, though I didn't at the time. See, with all his faults, Billy's a self-made man, while Alejandro's had everything handed to him. Billy didn't want to bend the rules for Alejandro, but he was forced to. I don't think he had a choice."

"What do you mean?" asks the detective.

"So, on Thursday, the three of us were in Billy's office, and I was angry about Alejandro trying to pass off my work as his—"

"I heard about that argument."

"From Billy, I'll bet."

"Go on," says Summers.

"I said Alejandro shouldn't get away with it just because he's Billy's stepson, and Alejandro said, 'There's more to it.' And there *was* more to it: he was blackmailing Billy."

The detective sits forward. "Blackmailing? With what?"

I turn on my laptop. "This is Alejandro's flash drive." I click the icon. "Somehow, he snagged photos of Billy *in flagrante delicto* with a young redhead. Forty-four shots, to be exact." I turn the screen around.

Summers grimaces. "Jeezus."

The photos show Billy and the woman going at it with gusto in what looks like a swank high-rise apartment. I wouldn't call the pictures titillating, but I'll admit that Billy has ingenuity. Let's just say he earned the title "the King of Grindhouse."

"Where'd you get these?" Summers asks.

I tell him about searching Alejandro's desk and finding flash drives containing not only my draft script but also the explicit images of his stepfather. "Those photos must be the reason Alejandro got away with so much. You see, Billy Bannon is a traditional guy, the kind of showrunner who believes in earning your seat at the table. He'd never tolerate plagiarism or the other bullshit Alejandro was pulling—unless he was being black-mailed. Billy's number-one priority has always been the show."

"No offense," Summers says, "but your show's not that important. I doubt Billy Bannon would kill to save *Mayberry Mayhem*."

"But he might kill to save his marriage. I bet Alejandro was threatening to show those photos to his mom, and Billy was desperate to avoid a divorce because he needs Marguerite's money to cover his gambling debts. The mob can be ruthless when it comes to collecting, from what I've seen on TV."

Summers rolls his eyes. "This isn't TV."

"Billy *is* a heavy gambler, from what I've been told, and he *does* owe millions, so I hear, and his wife *is* loaded, supposedly. And even if that's wrong, the photos prove he was unfaithful. Worth checking out, right?"

The detective makes a note. "I understand the script Alejandro stole, your script, has a plucky heroine bludgeoning an entitled jerk to death with a rolling pin. Interesting. What's that called? Irony? Poetic justice? You writers love that stuff."

"So do readers."

"Meaning?"

"A half dozen people read that script, including Billy Bannon, and he knew his stepson stole it."

Summers arches an eyebrow. "You're saying he chose his method to frame you?"

"It's possible. I mean, it almost worked, didn't it?"

The detective stands. "Thank you for your time, Miss Dixon."

I rise to face him. "Am I cleared?"

"I wouldn't go that far."

"Is Billy a suspect?"

"No comment. But I'm going to need that flash drive. Both of them, actually: the one with the photos and the one with your script."

"Sure thing, Detective." I hand them over. "Except, well, there are limits as to how you can use them."

"I won't try to sell the pictures," he says with a snort.

"It's the script I care about," I tell him as he starts for the door. "It's my intellectual property."

He stops, looks at me, shakes his head. "Writers."

The next few days drag by. I begin another spec script, stream *Better Call Saul*, and go for long runs. The more time passes without news of either the show or the murder, the more anxious I become. I consider a career change. (Momentarily.) I reread *Save the Cat!* (Skim, really.) I go so far as to book a flight to visit my brother in Arkansas. (Refundable.) On the fifth day, I'm about to dial the number for the LAPD's Robbery-Homicide Division, intending to ask Detective Summers for an update, when the phone rings.

"You sitting down?" Zach asks.

I sink onto the couch. "Yes."

"Billy's been charged with first-degree murder."

"No way." Summers seemed so skeptical when I tried to point him in that direction.

"Yes way. My source says someone found his cane in an alley a few blocks from Alejandro's house and turned it in. Thing was covered with blood and tissue. The police must've run tests and identified the DNA as Alejandro's."

"How'd they tie the cane to Billy?"

"I'm guessing it was one of the canes he had his initials engraved onto. Either that or he left a fingerprint on it. Can you believe it? He just threw the thing away, thinking no one would notice."

"What an idiot." I picture the canes arranged neatly along the wall in Billy's office. There were four or five of them, all thick, some with brass handles, and each sturdy enough to support his substantial weight. No doubt his fingerprints were all over every one of them.

"The guy has an ego the size of Manhattan," Zach says. "He thinks he's invincible, and he pretty much is. He hired the best lawyers money can buy."

"Isn't he broke? Doesn't he have huge gambling debts?"

"I don't know how those rumors started. Billy's worth more than you or I can count."

So he didn't need to stay married to Marguerite for her money. There goes half of my blackmail theory. "But why?" I ask. "Why would he kill Alejandro?"

"God knows. The punk was causing a lot of problems in the writers room, but it had to be more than that. The classic stepfather, stepson conflict, probably. Jealousy over Marguerite?"

I walk to the window. "There's something Shakespearean about it, you know? The king dispensing with the young, undeserving challenger."

"Or George R.R. Martinian, to put a Game of Thrones spin on it," Zach says. "Anyway, yes, the challenger to the throne is dead, and the king has been escorted off in handcuffs."

But I realize the analogy is weak. Alejandro wasn't after the throne. He was a meddlesome bit player, and he was using Billy, not challenging him. The people being challenged by Alejandro were the writers—me especially, but all of us because he upset the hierarchy and cheated his way up the ladder.

"Where does that leave us?" I ask. "Not to sound callous, but what's going to happen to our writers room?"

"HBO reached out this afternoon—that's how I heard about the homicide charges; they got a heads-up from Billy's attorney, and they have contacts in the DA's Office—and naturally, they're worried—"

"Are we canceled?"

"No! They asked me to take over as showrunner for the rest of the season, and if all goes well—which it will—*Mayberry Mayhem* will continue next year with me at the helm."

Talk about seizing the throne! But I don't see Zach killing for the showrunner job. His goal has always been to make *Mayberry Mayhem* the best it can be. The show's the thing, to paraphrase old Will.

"Congratulations," I say.

"I'll need a writers room running on all eight cylinders," Zach says. "Smooth and fast, all the parts working together."

I'm thinking of Zach's contempt for Alejandro's entitlement, his anger over the punk's theft of my script, his disgust for Billy's failure to do anything about it. What if Zach could protect the show and make himself the top dog by killing Alejandro and framing Billy for it? Now there's a plot worthy of the Bard.

"Are you with me, Jen?" Zach asks.

I'm thinking of the scene in my script where the obnoxious upstart gets bludgeoned with a piece of turned wood, a script Zach knew Billy was planning to use. I'm thinking of the canes in Billy's office, all lined up for the taking.

"Jen, are you with me?" Zach asks.

I'm thinking I was right about Alejandro extorting his way into our writers room, but I could've been wrong about who killed him. Maybe I should contact Detective Summers.

"Jen?"

On the other hand, I'm known to have an overactive imagination. Things are usually what they appear to be. The police mostly get it right. Life is not like a TV show.

"Oh. Yes. Absolutely."

"Then I'll see you Monday in the writers room."

About the Author

Previously L.H. Dillman practiced law. Currently she lives in Southern California and is working on a novel set in the Central Valley. Her short stories were published in *LAst Exit to Murder*, *LAdies Night*, *LAst Resort*, *Avenging Angelenos*, and *Bould Awards 2021 Short Story* anthologies, and online at KingsRiverLife.com. She's never set foot in a writers room.

Transylvania on the Tallahassee

Avril Adams

HE CAME UP ON us all sneaky-like one day, shiftier than a case of the Spanish flu. We were settin' up for our new single reeler, *The Trials of Miss Maggie*, out in old Tom Jenkins's barn like we always did, that bein' the usual rented stage set for the colored movie-makin' trade. The horses were tied up outside at the hitching rail for the escape scene. My sis, Maggie, costumed in a hoop skirt as the eponymous Miss, was right then affixing her tarty makeup. I was just about to signal the clappers and call "Roll 'em!" when that pockmarked mongrel marched up the steps onto the parlor set with a scrawny, gray-skinned fella in tow. I jumped up from my chair ready to send those troublesome chumps to Ginny Gall when I suddenly grasped that they were White men and decided to keep that hot bit o' cussing to myself for the moment.

"Jake Lowry, film producer, my dear thespians," he said, tipping his hat. He introduced the man beside him as Mr. Mark Russell, financial officer. "You've heard of the Lowrys, of stage and screen, I presume?"

As well we had. The Lowrys were the biggest movie production company in Los Angeles, cranking out more than one hundred one- and two-reelers a year. Their output included Westerns with Tom Mix and romances with Antonia Edmonson. They had the comedy market sewn up, too, with Chaplin, Champ Butler, and Buster Keaton. Next to them, we didn't amount to much. We were like a fancy outhouse next to the grand mansion. But we were a big success in the colored circuit and filled the local movie house late nights and weekends with our more race-affirming, all-colored comedies and dramas which went against the grain of the standard blackface fare. If the White patrons came on the weekdays the managers made the colored scramble up to the balcony, but the show went on later anyway, baby. We all nodded at the obvious but didn't say nothing, thinking we were about to hear the other shoe drop pretty quick anyway.

To break the ice, I said, "Of course we have. What can we do for you?"

"We want to offer you the opportunity to make horror movies, movies with freaks and monsters, don't we, Mark?"

The specter made a noise in his throat which I thought signified agreement.

I was gonna cut that fool right off before he made himself an even bigger fool. "Why us?" I said. "We've got a good thing going."

"You have an untapped market."

"Sorry, can't help you, friend."

"Don't be hasty," he said. "There's a lot of gold in that mine."

"How much?" I said. "What's the paycheck?" All eyes turned to Lowry who turned to Mr. Russell for guidance before he answered.

"You'll be pleased," he said.

He was right.

We had time to finish up two Westerns in the next two weeks because Lowry said the leading man, a fake Polish count from a town called

Rzeszów, named Darkla Ankwicz, (which I was not looking forward to pronouncing a hundred times a day) would need at least that much time to get to the studio. He was taking an ocean liner from Le Havre, France, to New York and from there boarding a transcontinental to Los Angeles and our studio. It was a helluva trek. He didn't arrive on the due date so we killed time until the sheik would be able to make an appearance. It finally happened to much fanfare on a cold Saturday night on the twenty-first of April. I called the crew so they could come down and meet the star of our next attraction. They all grumbled a little due to the late hour, and because most of them had already packed it in.

I thought the star would arrive first and make an introduction, but lo and behold, his gear arrived ahead of him, and on a flat-bed truck, at that, instead of in a taxi. He didn't really have that much: a black leather valise and whatever was in that big, oblong box that looked like a really beat up coffin. I thought, he's for sure a fake count 'cause a real one wouldn't be caught dead traveling around with that splinter machine. He could have packed most of his belongings in a couple of big trunks if he were a practical man. But nooo . . .

Jake Lowry came blowing down the road in his purple bucket and got out before the truck had turned off its engine. He had the truck driver and his helpers park the truck next to the milking shed and carry the box and the valise inside. He and Mr. Russell were sweating when they came back around to the barn door.

"Where's your count, Lowry?" I said. "Where's the star of the show?"

"He's coming. He'll be here presently. Keep your lid on."

I grinned seeing Lowry so agitated. "You know, you didn't have to go all the way to Poland to get a fake count to play a vampire. There's plenty of fellas right here in town who could do a pretty good job. We could have made two or three horror movies in the time it took to get the Count's keister here." Lowry wasn't listening, so I said, "Sometimes White people are too smart for their own good." That got his attention. I waved over our grip, Dewey. I took Dewey's face in my palm and turned it toward Lowry. "If you want pale, he's it. Can't get much paler in a Black man. But if you want a whiter shade of pale, a little pancake makeup would . . ."

"He's coming," breathed Lowry. "Get that grip up there to hang the crepe and turn off the lights."

Dewey ran up the stairs and dimmed the lights. I slipped into my director's chair and cranked my arm at the cameraman. "Roll 'em," I shouted and I heard the steady pulse of film sprockets winding around. The vampire was going to make an entrance and I didn't want to waste a moment, so I screen-rolled the empty doorway. Lowry tried to stop me but it was too late. The Count had made his first appearance and we had caught it all on film. But the look on the Count's face! I had never seen more surprise on a face in my life.

The Count apparently favored black duds, except for a starched white shirt front. He was wrapped in a long black cape that fell to the soles of his black patent leather shoes. I thought the cape made him look like a nincompoop on a mission to get eighty-sixed from a high society party. Not knowing much about vampires except what I'd seen in other people's movies, I wondered who had made the wardrobe choice for that cape. Maybe it was a European thing. He had shiny black hair and black eyes. And talk about pale. I figured Poland must be next to the North Pole 'cause he was the whitest Cracker Jack I ever laid eyes on. Dewey couldn't have pulled that off in a million years. The Count looked like he hadn't had any shut-eye either, not for weeks. He froze. He stared at me.

"Who is this?" he said to Lowry in an angry scream-whisper. "He is black."

I thought with a voice like Darkla's, we might want to film it as a silent.

Lowry shrugged. "Yeah, *capiche*, but we had to get someone out here in the boonies to keep . . ."

"Boonies?" said Darkla.

"You know, Hicktown. The Stix."

"He's black."

"Yes, I know."

"Who is he?"

"Harold, the director of the . . ."

"The other one is also black."

"I know. Relax, Count."

"Why does he have the camera?"

"He's the cameraman."

They went on like that for a while. I knew what that tin plate Nosferatu was saying 'cause I'd heard it all before in better English. So I kept rolling. We could film a cross-cut later of something in the house that would explain the Count's confusion and bafflement.

The Count gaped around with those bloodshot peepers. He turned to Lowry again. "The one on the stairs is white," he said.

"Well, yes and no."

"What do you mean?"

"I'll explain later."

Lowry turned to me. "The Count's ready to go any time you are. He knows the story, so he can ad lib without that script." He winked. "And he don't need much sleep either. In fact, he prefers to work at night." He frowned. "So who you got to play the toady, the first dimwit who blunders into the vampire's castle?"

"It's Jonathan Harker," I said. I picked up the script Lowry had brought and flipped a few pages. It was skimpy on important details, like descriptions and dialogue and everything else. We'd have to make up some of it on the fly. So I said, "At this time of night, I just have Earl Wiggins. He's an orderly at the colored hospital. He's a big jobbie, and he's no Hamlet."

"He'll do. Get him. We can't waste time."

I tipped my head at my sister, Maggie. "You heard the man. Go get him, Mags. Shake a leg." I fished in my pocket and tossed her the keys to the jalopy. "Tell that jimmi it'll be an easy twenty-five clams for a couple of hours' work."

"He's gonna love that," said Maggie. "He's been begging me for a chance . . ."

I rolled my eyes. "Yeah. Just go."

As Mags brushed by him on the way out, the Count drew back and pinched his cape around himself. His catfish-belly-white hand swept to his mouth. I thought he was gonna puke.

"I know, Count, she's Black, too," said Lowry with a sigh. "Don't go crazy. They're everywhere. You'll get used to it."

The Count gasped noisily. "Everywhere?" He blinked about a hundred times.

I got up from my chair and tried to chat him up without jangling him too much more. I asked him a few friendly questions about his folks and his hometown, how he liked the States, but he hissed at me like a tomcat when I got too close. He mostly paced around the room getting a hoot outta picking up the props, turning them over, and thumping them, to see if they were chintzy. I walked over to Lowry who was still in the doorway checking his watch every twenty seconds. I said, "You might not have noticed but this Polish bird you hired doesn't seem to like . . ."

"He's fine. He's from Eastern Europe."

"More like eastern Alabama."

"For Chrissakes, Harold! He just got here. Keep your pants on."

I leaned in closer. "Problem, Jake. Mags is playin' Lucy—and Mina."

"Hmmmm, same woman." Lowry was pensive. He extracted a half-smoked cigar from his pocket. It took some fumbling with matches for him to light it. "Problem?" He puffed. "Maybe." He puffed again.

I glared at him.

"I'm thinkin'," he mumbled. "Keep your shirt on."

"No maybes. This cat's a pickle. Script says he's gotta bite Lucy's neck. How you gonna work that out?"

Lowry took the stogie out of his mouth and pointed the wet end at me. "I'll handle him," he growled.

"Okay, but you sure don't impress me as much of a snake handler," I said.

Just then Mags blew in dragging big Earl Wiggins by the wrist. "Here he is, Hal. He was getting off his shift so I scooped him up."

Earl held his wool cap between his big hands. "I can be here till the crack of dawn if you need me, Mr. Harold." Earl was nothing if not humble. "I can do anything you ask me . . ."

"Go stand over there by the stairs, Earl. In this scene you've just entered the vampire's castle. He's expecting you 'cause there's food on the table and a fire going in the fireplace, but he hasn't arrived yet, got it? He's still coming in the coach. You think the castle is creepy. You call out but the Count doesn't answer. You think you hear the coach's hoof-beats—you're looking around, sorta scared . . ."

"Wait," said Earl, putting up a hand. "Is he gonna beat my ass for breakin' into his castle? Is that it?"

"No, he's not. You're supposed to be working a real estate deal for the guy, okay?"

"If you say so."

I actually thought Earl had asked a pretty good, logical question, being a colored man dressed in, well . . . overalls in a count's castle, but I said,

"Where you been, Earl? Don't you go to the pictures?" Then I said, "Mags, get Earl a suit. He can't wear those overalls." Mags took off to the shed where we kept our wardrobe.

"Just a moment," said Lowry, pushing himself off the wall. His smile could have melted ice. "I think we've got something here."

"What are you talking about, Jake."

"Why didn't we think of this before? It's pure genius. It's solid gold."

"What?" we all said in unison.

"Think of it. Transylvania on the Tallahassee." He held his arms out wide as if to gather us colored folks to his redeeming bosom.

"Says you," I said.

"Keep that boy in overalls, Harold. Put everybody in overalls, hear me? Except the Count, of course. Maybe even him." He chuckled. "Okay, forget it. Not him."

"There's a gal in this picture playing Lucy and Mina, remember? You want her in overalls, too?"

"No, now that you mention it, wise guy. Put her in calico."

"Says you," I said. "Who do you think is going to come to see this picture?" I glanced at the Count, who seemed to be following the conversation with interest.

"You Canadians, of course," said Lowry, "and maybe even some of us. Isn't that so, Mr. Russell?" he said to the specter, who nodded almost imperceptibly.

"Now just a darn minute," I said. "Nobody, *especially* us Canadians, are coming to see your corn-shucker movie about colored clodhoppers and Eastern European bloodsuckers."

But pretty soon we were all outfitted the way Jake Lowry wanted.

The Count began to pick up steam as the night wore on. He was glassy-eyed and energetic, full of enthusiasm. He seemed to enjoy terrifying

Earl, who wasn't putting on an act being scared. The Count chased Earl up the stairs and into the bedroom. When he locked the door behind them, Earl tried to jump out the window and drop two stories to get away. I had to yell "cut" to get them both to stop before something expensive happened. I left Earl out of the scene altogether when it was time for the blood sucking because Earl swore he wouldn't let that "ashy scarecrow" climb on top of him. The Count stamped his foot, flew into the bathroom, and slammed the door. Instead, I filmed the scene with the Count's sneering face filling the screen, a sweep of the cape and voila—fade to black.

I thought it all went pretty smoothly, considering.

After that, things took a turn for the worse. After the bite, it was time for the Count to demand obedience from his victim. The script said Earl, who was playing Harker, was supposed to say, "Yes, Master," after the Count gave an order. But every time the line came up Earl would cross his arms over his chest and proclaim, "I ain't sayin' that," in a surly voice.

"Look," I said. "Earl, I'm not payin' two sawbucks to an actor who won't do what he's told. Script says the Count is your master and you are his slave 'cause he drank your blood."

The Count howled with delight. "You are a man of wisdom, Director," he purred.

"I ain't his slave," said Earl with a pout.

"Yes, you are," said the Count.

"We'll see about that," said Earl.

"Enough," I shouted through my bullhorn. "We have a picture to make and only a couple of days to do it. Count, you have to realize that there are certain sensitivities here. Earl's from Louisiana and has had some experience with the Klan, so he's making a valid point. You, on the other hand, come from . . . " I paused to work out the pronunciation. "Rzeszów, in

Europe, so you don't. It's understandable. Would it be okay if Earl called you just Count, or maybe Mr. Darkla, instead?"

The count stared at me furiously as if I were deliberately speaking Jamaican.

Earl nodded his head vigorously. "Yeah, I can call him that. Count or Mr. Darkla. As long as it's him and not me."

The Count whirled to confront Earl. "Stupid bumpkin," he snarled. "You will pay."

"All right, then," I said. "In this scene, the Count has seen a photograph of Harker's girlfriend, Mina. He lusts to bring her under his dominion. He tells Harker to invite her to dinner." I carefully went over the dialogue for both actors before we were to begin. Earl didn't have a big part, but the Count did, and he ad-libbed like crazy, as Lowry said he would. He was a little overly dramatic but, well, that was just him being him, so I let it go.

We were rolling. After a minute there was a loud whacking of the door knocker. Both men turned to the sound. Cut to Mina (Mags) on the steps wearing a discreet calico dress and carrying a parasol and a basket of fruit. Back to the men.

The Count said to Earl, "Answer the door, dunce man, we have a visitor."

Earl didn't move. I frantically waved my arms in the direction of the door to get his attention and mouthed, *go, go, go.* Finally, Earl stomped to the door and flung it open. "Hey, baby," he said, grinning.

"Cut, cut, cut," I yelled. "Earl, that's not your line." I fed him his line.

"Sorry," he said, "Maggie just looked so good . . ."

"Action," I said again. This time, Earl did it right. Mina stepped in and greeted the Count. He shrank back in horror.

"Cut, cut, cut," I yelled again. "Count," I said, as if speaking to a child, "We all agree Mina is Black. Get over it. When she steps inside, you greet her graciously because your plan is to drink her blood later. Okay?"

Earl took a step toward the Count. He balled his fist. "Don't you dare disrespect my woman."

The count muttered, "Oaf."

Mags said, "I'm not your woman, Earl." She set down her basket but caught her finger on a nail sticking out of one of the props. "Ouch," she cried.

The Count's ears pricked up like a hound dog's at dinnertime. He raced to Mags's side, grasping her fingers tenderly in his own.

"Here, let me help you, my dear," he said. He raised her finger to his lips. His tongue darted out to catch the single bubble of blood that appeared. Mags was too startled to refuse. "We have an ancient saying during summer harvest in Rzeszów," he said. "'The blacker the berry, the sweeter the juice.' I never knew the adage could mean anything more. Do you have that saying in your country?" His eyes shone like a man in love.

"I haven't heard it before," said Mags, withdrawing her hand suspiciously, "but I would tend to agree with the sentiment."

We finished the take, but the Count was jittery. His already lousy acting was now running on fumes.

"What time is it?" he said to Lowry.

Lowry looked at his watch and frowned. "Five," he said. "Sunup's in half an hour."

"Well, I'm exhausted. I must rest," said the Count.

"We're not done," I protested.

"Yes, we are," said Lowry. He shrugged. "It's a wrap. The Count needs his rest."

After Lowry left with the Count, Earl walked up to me. He stood uncomfortably close, and I couldn't avoid the strong, masculine musk he emitted. He poked a large finger in my chest, no longer the shy hospital orderly rube I had hired. "He's got to go," he said.

I raised my eyebrows. "Who's got to go?"

"Don't pretend you don't know."

"Who, the Count?"

"Yeah, Darkla. You saw what he did with Maggie. If he didn't give me the heebie-jeebies, I'd call him an ofay clown to his face."

"Well, he may be unsettling, as you say, giving you the heebie-jeebies, but he stays. I work with lots of people I don't like, including you, but the picture depends on him and without the picture, we may as well go back to farming, or paper-hanging, or doing laundry, like we did before."

"You never did that," said Earl, eying me doubtfully. "Mags says you're a college man."

"A college man with a tan," I said ruefully, "which equals all the professions I named before."

Dewey the grip, his assistant Leon, Mags, Earl, and I sat around the prop table picking at a cold breakfast, feeling pretty burned out. Most of us weren't used to staying up all night. "I'm not a dewdropper," said Leon, "but I sure could stand to turn in right now."

"Me too," said Dewey. "I'm asleep on my feet and the sun is just coming up."

"Funny thing, though," said Leon, "I was out in the milking shed having a smoke a little while ago. Lowry and the Count came in and I didn't want them to see me lollygagging, so I stepped behind a stack of hay bales. Lowry went over to that big box the Count brought with him from Europe and opened it. You won't believe this—I almost didn't myself—but the Count got in and closed the lid on himself. I'll say that jolted me awake."

I smeared a dry roll with cold butter. "Some actors like to stay in character—so much so that they forget who they really are."

"And who is he—really? Didn't they kill off most of the European counts in the last war?" Leon scratched thoughtfully at the stubble sprouting on his unshaved chin. "And something's fishy about the Count's sleeping arrangements."

"Yup," said Dewey. "Sleeping in a coffin is one way to protect a maggot-white complexion."

"He's a fake count, everything's fake." I took a bite of roll.

The next thing I knew Lowry was jabbing me in the ribs with his umbrella and I was staring into his pink, wrinkled face. The sun was going down. I had slept most of the day. He said, "Up an' at 'em. The Count's almost ready to go."

I rolled off the sofa and tried to slap myself awake "All right. Where's the crew?"

"Waiting for you."

Maggie was wearing her calico costume and Earl was still dressed in last night's overalls.

"Back to the drawing board," I said. "Where were we?"

Lowry said, "It's the part where Lucy gets it. It meaning the vampire bites her."

"Right," I said. "I have it marked on the script." I picked up the script and flipped to the correct page. I yawned in Lowry's direction. "Everyone has been ad-libbing so much, sometimes I feel more like a referee than a director." I scowled at all of the crew, and they tried to look sheepish. I said, "Mina's encounter with the vampire takes place outside. She's sleepwalking in the garden in a negligee because . . ."

"She's looking for a man," said Leon. Everybody laughed, except Mags.

I said, "Let's take the camera and the smoke machine over to the milking shed. There are a few tombstones we can use over there."

We piled all our equipment on a truck and deposited it next to the shed's doors. Mags went into the shed to change her costume and makeup and pick out a wig. When she came out she didn't look anything like Mina. She looked like a bearcat. The guys shuffled their feet and looked down, afraid of getting cold-cocked by Earl for taking too long a gander. "Hurry up, it's nippy out here," she said, rubbing her forearms.

"Blow the smoke," I shouted. Leon turned on the machine and within minutes I couldn't see a thing in front of me. "Turn it off, Leon," I shouted again. But the smoke kept coming. "Leon, turn off the smoke," I shouted again. Nothing. "Where'd that boy go?" I said. "Dewey, go check on Leon and get the Count ready."

Dewey traipsed off into the smoke.

Mags came over and stood beside me. "I don't like it out here," she said. "I don't like making movies in a graveyard."

"It's not a graveyard," I said. "There's only a couple of slabs by the shed."

"Don't tell *me* it's not a graveyard. *You* should try standing out here in *your* underwear."

Dewey came back in a twist. "Help, help! Lowry's down—in the shed!"

We all quit what we were doing and raced to the spot. I pulled open the door and there in the dim glow of our lanterns lay Jake Lowry facedown over a hay bale. I called his name, but he didn't stir, and when I turned him over, his head flopped back and his eyes were rolled back in his head.

"Hey, chief," said Dewey. "Under his hat, take a look."

I pulled off Lowry's hat which was only lightly attached to his head. A fist-size dent in his forehead had reshaped his noggin into a loaded baked potato. I checked to see if any part of him was still working. I was disappointed. We all stood around looking at the butter-and-egg man who had put us on the road to the undead, now deceased.

"I don't like this one bit," said Dewey.

"Me neither," said Leon.

"Maybe we should be worried," said Mags. "He didn't bop himself."

"Nope, he didn't," I said.

"Look," shouted Maggie, pointing in Leon's direction. We all followed her finger. "There's a big rock in the hay over there and it has blood on it."

"That big box is still here. Maybe we should look inside it," said Earl.

"Leon said the Count was sleeping in there," said Maggie. "Open it."

Nobody moved.

"Call in the coppers?" said Dewey.

"Unh unh, I ain't walking into *that* frame," said Earl, emphatically. "You *know* who'll be wearin' the bracelets if we do."

For a moment there was silence as we all thought it over.

"I don't know if this means anything, but everybody's here—except the Count," Mags said.

"Open the box," I said.

"Let me help you with that," said Earl. "I'm seriously peeved with that creepy, bloodsuckin' mook. Who's with me?"

"Roll 'em," I whispered to the cameraman. "I've just got a feeling . . ."

Earl and Dewey marched to the coffin, then each grabbed an end of the lid and lifted. They stared for a minute.

"There he is," said Leon.

"In all his glory," said Maggie.

The Count's eyes popped open like two sprung paper window shades.

"*Glupiecs, Dummkopfs*," he roared. "Why are you so-called Canadians," his tone was acid, "such *dummkopfs*?"

Earl grabbed the Count by the lapels, dragged him out of the coffin, and threw him on the ground. The Count hissed and sprang to his feet.

"Who're you callin' dumb?" said Earl. He punched the Count right in the mouth with his big fist, but it had no effect. Darkla didn't even bob.

A spectral figure, lean as a post, stepped inside the shed. It was the money man, Mr. Russell. I think I was the only one who saw him because he stood right beside me. He was so forgettable, the crew hadn't accounted for him.

"You, apparently," he sneered. "Whom do you think you're punching at, maroon? Darkla's the real McCoy. He's a vampire." He held up a finger. "One of the—not the living—not the dead. The undead. None of your fists, your pistols, your fiddle-faddle can keep the Count from his appointed rounds."

I was watching all of this, and suddenly a light went on. "Hey, Mr. Russell," I said. "When did you come out of the woodwork? We've been here for a while, all of us, all together. And we all know where the Count has been for a while too. So where have *you* been lurking? You've been scuttling around here and there, darting among the rocks and trees just waiting—and Mr. Lowry, what was your beef with him?"

"He was an idiot, a carnival barker without imagination; even more of a *dummkopf* than you Canadians, as if that were even *possible*. He was a petty man unable to see the opportunity of a lifetime standing before him in all of its blood-soaked glory."

"What do you mean," I asked. "He was making a picture."

"Yes, that was the problem. He was just making a picture when Darkla could have made him the greatest entertainer in the world. We could have been kings. Hollywood would have been our mistress."

The Count's eyes were blazing. I could see it in the close-up the cameraman was surreptitiously taking. It was cinematic gold.

"Out of my way, simp," he said, and thrust Earl aside like a straw in the wind, possessed by the power of a thousand years of supernatural fury. His arms were outstretched, his fingers crooked into angry claws. He was heading straight for Mr. Russell.

"We could have gone on and on with Darkla. We could have made a million . . ."

Darkla fixed Mr. Russell with yellow eyes that seemed to spiral with hate. "I am not your slave," he said. "You are mine."

Mr. Russell screamed as the Count plunged his fangs into the money man's throat and drew his cape over his head. And *voila*—fade to black.

We had got it all. It was cinematic gold, just like the man said.

Author's Note

A Very Brief History of Hollywood's Black Filmmakers. Black Hollywood begins at the same time as White Hollywood, that is, about 1896. Black Hollywood was subject to segregation, which determined what stories were told, how they were told, and who played in them. The first "Black" Hollywood movies were made by White people and were played by White actors in blackface. Gradually, Black actors began to break out and form their own studios. One of the first all-Black movie production companies was the Lincoln Motion Picture Company, begun in 1921. One of the most important early Black filmmakers was Oscar Micheaux, who was making his films around 1925.

About the Author

Avril Adams lives in the Inland Empire. She writes crime fiction, often in the noir genre. Her work appears in anthologies produced by Sisters in Crime Los Angeles, including *LAst Exit to Murder*, *LAst Resort*, and *Avenging Angelenos*, and several other publications.

Avril also writes science fiction with a humanist twist and children's stories. She is working on a novel starring an African American female PI. Her animals are an inspiration for her fiction.

Credits

About the President

Paula Bernstein is the President of Sisters in Crime Los Angeles. She is also a physician, a scientist, and the author of the Hannah Kline series of medically themed mysteries. She lives in Los Angeles with her husband, and just welcomed their first grandchild.

About the Copy Editor

Chris Rhatigan is a freelance copy editor. He has worked on novels that have gone on to win the Anthony Award, the Independent Publisher Book Award, and the Beverly Hills Book Award. Find out more at his website, chrisrhatiganediting.com.

About the Cover Designer

Scott Montgomery is an award-winning illustrator, animator, and designer based in Studio City. His work for clients like JPMorgan Chase, Delphi, and Microsoft has appeared in Graphis Books, Communication Arts, Adweek, Ad Age's Creativity, and many others. Scott is also a multi-instrumentalist and songwriter in the indie pop project JetBelly.

About the Editors

Gay Toltl Kinman has nine award nominations for her writing including several short stories in magazines and in fifteen anthologies; five children's books; a YA gothic novel; eight adult mysteries; and eight collections of short stories; twenty short plays; professional articles; co-edited two non-fiction books; and two anthologies. Kinman has library and law degrees.

- Meredith Taylor retired from clinical psychology to a life of crime—at least on the page. A series featuring Ali Marchant, therapist and psych professor in the 1980s, will arrive shortly. Meredith published a story in the Sisters in Crime Los Angeles anthology, *Avenging Angelenos*. Editing *Entertainment to Die For* was a pleasure.

- Susan Rowland is a new novelist and longtime Jungian author. Her first novel is *The Sacred Well Murders* (2022), and *The Alchemy Fire Murder: A Mary Wandwalker Mystery* will be out in 2023. See her website: susanrowland-book.com and follow her on Twitter: susanrowland10.

About the Publisher

Award-winning author Sheila Lowe writes the Forensic Handwriting psychological suspense series, Beyond the Veil paranormal suspense series, and non-fiction books about handwriting and personality. Like her fictional character Claudia Rose, Sheila is a real-life forensic handwriting examiner, recognized internationally as an expert in the court system.

How to reach us

www.sistersincrimela.com

Twitter: @SinCLosAngeles

Facebook: Sisters in Crime Los Angeles

Other Sisters in Crime Anthologies

Fatally Haunted

Murder in La-la Land

Avenging Angelenos

A Deadly Dozen

LAndmarked for Murder

LAdies Night

Made in the USA
Las Vegas, NV
13 February 2023

67440866R00193